The HARVEST of GRACE

An Ada's House Novel

CINDY WOODSMALL

New York Times Best-Selling Author of
The Bridge of Peace

Praise for
The Harvest of Grace

"This third entry in the Ada's House series is sure to please fans of the first two novels. Fans of Amy Clipston and Marta Perry will enjoy its engaging characters and homespun feel."

—*Library Journal*

"Oh, blessed insomnia! Cindy Woodsmall is a master at stealing your heart and your sleep with powerful love stories as pure and haunting as the Amish community in which they are set. With crisp prose, flesh-and-blood characters who live and breathe on the page, and a spiritual heritage that nourishes the soul, *The Harvest of Grace* is a rich bounty of unforgettable reading that is just 'plain' perfect."

—JULIE LESSMAN, award-winning author of The Daughters of Boston and Winds of Change series

"You don't have to be a fan of Amish stories to love a Cindy Woodsmall book. *The Harvest of Grace*'s heroine, Sylvia, won me over from the first page, and I cheered her through the story. Woodsmall writes a beautiful page-turner with heart-gripping twists. A worthy read."

—RACHEL HAUCK, award-winning author of *Dining with Joy*

WITHDRAWN
Praise for
Cindy Woodsmall

"A treasure chest, for sure… The wisdom in these stories is time-tested and true—plain and simple."

—KAREN KINGSBURY, *New York Times* best-selling author of *Unlocked* and *Shades of Blue*

"[Cindy Woodsmall] paints a vivid backdrop of Amish and Mennonite cultures with fascinating detail and memorable clarity."

—TAMERA ALEXANDER, best-selling author of *Rekindled*

"Cindy Woodsmall writes real—real people, real conflicts, real emotions. When you open her book, you enter her world and live the story with the characters."

—KIM VOGEL SAWYER, author of *Where Willows Grow* and *Waiting for Summer's Return*

The HARVEST of GRACE

The HARVEST *of* GRACE

AN ADA'S HOUSE NOVEL

CINDY WOODSMALL

New York Times Best-Selling Author of
When the Soul Mends

WATERBROOK
PRESS

THE HARVEST OF GRACE
PUBLISHED BY WATERBROOK PRESS
12265 Oracle Boulevard, Suite 200
Colorado Springs, Colorado 80921

Scripture quotations are taken from the King James Version.

The characters and events in this book are fictional, and any resemblance to actual persons or events is coincidental.

ISBN 978-1-4000-7398-6
ISBN 978-0-307-72962-0 (electronic)

Cover design by Kelly L. Howard

Published in the United States by WaterBrook Multnomah, an imprint of the Crown Publishing Group, a division of Random House Inc., New York.

WATERBROOK and its deer colophon are registered trademarks of Random House Inc.

Library of Congress Cataloging-in-Publication Data
Woodsmall, Cindy.
    The harvest of grace : a novel / Cindy Woodsmall. — 1st ed.
      p. cm.
    ISBN 978-1-4000-7398-6 (alk. paper) — ISBN 978-0-307-72962-0 (electronic)
    1. Amish—Fiction. I. Title.
    PS3623.O678H37 2011
    813'.6—dc22

                              2011016848

Printed in the United States of America
2011—First Edition

10 9 8 7 6 5 4 3 2 1

Books by Cindy Woodsmall

ADA'S HOUSE SERIES
The Hope of Refuge
The Bridge of Peace
The Harvest of Grace

The Sound of Sleigh Bells
The Christmas Singing
(coming in October)

SISTERS OF THE QUILT SERIES
When the Heart Cries
When the Morning Comes
When the Soul Mends

NONFICTION
Plain Wisdom

To Linda Wertz,
a dear woman who values God's creatures
and labors to exhaustion to make a difference.
You touch lives without realizing it.
You offer a different lens to view life through
to all who are blessed to come in contact with you.
And to your husband, Rick,
who believes in you as much as he believes in the One who created you.

And to every farmer,
who understands all too well
the mountain of troubles that you face,
the lack of support from those who need you most,
and the constant effort you put into finding solutions.

The Ada's House Novels

The story so far...

In *The Hope of Refuge,* Cara Atwater Moore is a waitress in New York City. Cara's mother died when Cara was only eight, and she was abandoned by her alcoholic father. Now, at twenty-eight, she is being stalked by a man she knows from growing up in foster care. She escapes New York with her seven-year-old daughter, Lori, whose father died when Lori was just a toddler. Following a diary Cara's mother left her and sketchy memories from a childhood visit to her mother's relatives in Amish country, Cara arrives in Dry Lake, Pennsylvania. Exhausted and fearful of being followed, she and Lori seek shelter in a barn. She is discovered by Ephraim Mast, a thirty-two-year-old, single Amish man who works as a cabinetmaker. To spare Cara from being separated from her daughter by social services, Ephraim takes them in and helps them, even though that creates serious problems for him with the Amish church leaders and community members.

Ephraim's sister, Deborah, is engaged to Mahlon, the only child of Ada Stoltzfus, a forty-three-year-old widow. Mahlon disappears without explanation, leaving his mother and Deborah on their own. Ada takes both Deborah and Cara under her wing, inviting them to live with her in Hope Crossing. After Cara chooses to join the Old Order Amish church, Ephraim and she realize they want to build a life together.

In *The Bridge of Peace,* Lena Kauffman is a twenty-three-year-old Amish schoolteacher in Dry Lake who is sometimes mocked for having a birthmark that covers part of her face and neck. Her longtime friend and confidant, Grey Graber, is struggling in his relationship with his wife, Elsie.

Because they've conceived two children, one who is missing part of an arm and one who was stillborn because of birth defects, Elsie avoids Grey out of fear that they can't have healthy children. Once Grey understands why she's shut him out, he insists they undergo medical tests to determine if there is a genetic reason they should not have more children. They do so, but before the results are revealed, Elsie dies on her parents' farm when a bull mauls her. Grey chooses to burn the envelope containing the test results without looking at them. His relationship with his longtime friend Lena develops, and they fall in love. Lena is a close friend of Deborah Mast and Cara Moore, and she frequently visits them at Ada's House, which has become an Amish tourist attraction because of their home-baked goods and their seasonal activities for families.

**For a list of main characters in *The Harvest of Grace*,
see the end of the book.**

One

From her perch on the milking stool, Sylvia patted the cow's side and cooed to her, enjoying the warm softness of the cow's hide. "You're feeling better now, *ya*?" Puffs of white vapor left her mouth when she spoke, and her fingers ached from the cold.

The cow mooed gently as if answering her.

Sylvia removed the claw milker from the cow's udder and sprayed Udder Care to prevent chaffing and to ward off mastitis. She set the stool and bucket out of the way, moved to the far end of the stalls, and pulled the lever that opened the tie rails, releasing the last round of cows from their milking stalls.

Daed lifted two buckets of milk and headed for the milk house. "What are you humming this morning?"

"Oh. Uh…" She hadn't realized she was humming, so she had to pause for a moment and think. "Moon River."

"Sure does sound nice. This place don't seem the same when you're off. No one else I know hums while working a herd." He disappeared into the milk house to dump the fresh liquid into the milk tank.

Unlike a lot of Daeds, Sylvia's hadn't minded when she bought an iPod during the early years of her *rumschpringe*. The *Englischer* who picked up their milk three times a week had always recharged it for her. But then, five years ago, it fell under a cow during a milking and was trampled to death. Since she still hadn't joined the faith, she could've bought another iPod, but Lilly was seven by then and hanging around the barn more. It would have hurt Lilly to realize that her older sister didn't always keep the Old Ways, so she never replaced it. But she missed some of her favorite songs, like "Moon River." The lyrics about the dream maker always made her think of Elam.

Her pulse quickened as she envisioned Elam next to her in the barn. His good looks seemed more suited to modeling in Englischer ads than managing a dairy herd, and she found his physical presence frustratingly compelling. He frequently mentioned marriage lately, and she could imagine their future together, always being close to him, waking alongside him in the mornings. But she had reservations too. Didn't she want more from true love than heart-pounding attraction? Maybe she just needed to spend more time talking with him about their "rainbow's end," and all her reservations would melt into nothingness.

She patted a few cows on the rump, gently moving them along. The herd desperately wanted in the barn at milking time, each cow hurrying to a stall in the milking parlor, but they weren't eager to leave the building afterward. Their contented lowing and the ease with which they lumbered outdoors toward the bunk feeder and water trough made her smile. The large creatures were the same today as they'd always been—peaceful and productive.

In a side stall a new calf nursed from its mother. Ginger slid her head across the wooden gate, and Sylvia rubbed her long forehead. Sylvia had been up half the night making sure Ginger didn't have any trouble bringing the calf into the world. Fortunately, Sylvia hadn't needed to pull the calf or call a vet. Both were victories she was proud of.

Two years ago after she'd cried over the death of both a cow and her calf, her Daed did the unthinkable. He gave her the right to tend to the breeding of the herd as she saw fit. Her ways took more effort than his, but she'd not lost a cow or a calf yet. Milk production was up, and the overall health of the herd had improved. She had her grandpa's teachings to thank for that.

Her Daed returned from the milk house. "I bet you're thinking about *Daadi* Fisher."

"Ya, I think of him every time a healthy calf is born." As a child she'd been her grandfather's shadow while he tended to the cows, and she'd been young when he began training her in the value of careful breeding and vigilance during every labor and birth. In spite of her being a girl in a patriarchal society, he believed in her. When he'd passed away a couple of years ago, she thought her heart might break.

Daed headed toward the remaining buckets of milk.

Sylvia pushed the wheeled cart that carried all her milking supplies toward the mud sink. "I need the two heaviest of those buckets, Daed."

"Two?" His eyes met hers, reflecting interest. "You making more yogurt already?"

"I am."

"Are we eating that much, or are you selling that much?" He poured the white, frothy liquid into a sterilized milk can for her and securely tamped down the lid.

"The answer to both is yes."

It was rare to see a smile on Daed's face before breakfast, but he grinned broadly. "*Sell iss gut,* ya?"

"Ya, it's a good thing." She pushed the supply cart into the milk house section of the barn and then returned to the parlor. "Daed, do you mind if I go to the house early? A bad dream woke Ruth up last night. I promised her that this morning I'd prove it was just a dream."

He tossed a pitchfork into a wheelbarrow and went into the first stall. "Sure, go on."

Sylvia abandoned her usual routine and climbed the haymow. After finding the mama cat's new hiding place for her kittens, she gently placed

Ruth's favorite tabby into the inside pocket of her coat and then went back down the ladder.

"Hey, Daed."

He turned, and she pulled out the kitten, once again hinting at her ultimate goal: for Ruth to be allowed to keep this one inside the house when the little fur ball was a week or so older.

A lopsided grin caused one side of his face to wrinkle, and she wondered what had him so jovial this morning. "Just don't get me in trouble over it. And make sure Ruthie knows it can't stay inside. Barn cats tend to become mean once they get a little age on them."

Sylvia put the milk cans into a wooden handcart. "They wouldn't if—"

"Go already." He shooed her toward the barn door. "I don't want to hear any more of your newfangled ideas about how I could run this farm differently. They always cost me money and energy."

His tone was playful, but she'd be wise to accept that he meant his words...for now. He'd come a long way in accepting her ideas concerning the farm. She often wondered if he'd give her any say if he had a son. She'd never know, because he had nine daughters, of which she was the eldest and the only one with a heart for farming.

His other daughters were more typical and girlish in every possible way, preferring housework over farm work. The three teenagers—Beckie, Lizzie, and Naomi—hated farming, always had. Lilly, who'd just turned twelve, would never complain about anything, but the smells and hard work made her queasy. The four youngest—Ruth, Barbie Ann, Salome, and Martha—were a hazard in the barn, causing Daed to shoo them away if they set foot inside the milking parlor.

Pushing the milk cart, Sylvia hurried from the barn to the house. Last week's snow glistened under the early morning sunlight. She toted the heavy milk cans inside one by one, being careful not to lean the containers against her body and squish the kitten.

The warmth of the entryway made her cold fingers scream in pain. Delicious aromas of sausage, biscuits, and coffee made her mouth water and her tummy rumble, keen reminders of how long and cold her night had been.

Her *Mamm* was adding wood to the stove, and Lizzie stood at the sink, washing dishes. There was never a shortage of dirty glasses and plates in a house with eleven people.

Sylvia removed her wader boots. "Morning."

Lizzie yawned. "That it is, and it arrives way too early in this house."

"Why, there you are." Mamm closed the door to the stove, smiling and motioning for her. "*Kumm.* Warm yourself. How's that mama cow?"

"Ginger and her newborn are doing great."

"I'm glad, but a girl shouldn't have to work like you do."

"I love it. You know that."

Mamm put her arm around Sylvia's shoulders and squeezed. "Still, we need a solution, and your Daed's found one that is right around the corner."

Sylvia would never get used to Daed making plans about the farm without telling her. "What does that mean?"

Naomi came through the back door, carrying an armload of firewood. She held the door open while Beckie entered with a lighter bundle of wood.

Beckie's blond hair peeked out from under one of Daed's black felt hats, and her blue eyes shone with spunk. "Good grief it's cold out there. Isn't it time for warmer weather?"

Mamm pulled several mugs out of the cabinet. "Your Daed said they're calling for a long winter and a late spring this year."

Clearly her mother had no intention of answering Sylvia's question. She'd find out whenever her Daed was ready for her to know.

Naomi dumped her load of wood into the bin and quickly straightened it. After she finished, Beckie tossed hers in and began warming her hands over the stove. Naomi straightened the mess, piece by piece. Getting the morning firewood used to be Beckie's job, but she wasn't good at doing chores by herself. Not making beds, washing dishes, or getting firewood. She would come back with only a couple of pieces of wood, and later, when Mamm wanted to add fuel to the stove, the bin would be empty. Sylvia and her sisters used to fuss about doing their jobs and then having to help Beckie with hers, but arguing only made everyone's days miserable. In the end, someone still had to help Beckie in order for all the chores to get done.

On washdays when it was time for Beckie to gather the dirty clothes, she seemed half-blind, always forgetting a few hampers, including the diaper pails. Since Naomi, a brown-haired beauty, was as meticulous as they came, she and Beckie were assigned to work together. Beckie was sweet and plenty smart. She just needed to mature, and Sylvia trusted she'd do that one day. But at eighteen, she had a ways to go.

Beckie dusted her gloved hands over the woodbin. "These temps wouldn't be so bad if someone in this room"—Beckie stared at Sylvia, amusement dancing in her eyes—"wouldn't abandon her side of our bed to tend to cows. I woke up lonely and with my toes freezing."

"You could've bedded down beside Ginger. Then you wouldn't have been lonesome or cold."

Beckie peeled out of her gloves. "Ew, gross. I will never be *that* frosty or alone, thank you very much. It's unfair that we ended the day just right, and the next thing I know, I'm in a cold bed all by myself."

Sylvia couldn't help but smile. Beckie and she had slept in the same bed since Beckie was old enough to leave her crib. And as far back as Sylvia could remember, they'd ended most days in the same way, sharing things only sisters did and then whispering, *"Im Gott sei Lieb"*—in God's love—over each other, putting their joys and sorrows in His hands before they fell asleep.

The kitten mewed, and Mamm stopped pouring coffee into a mug.

Beckie gazed into Sylvia's eyes, doing her best to suppress a laugh. Lizzie glanced her way and seemed to purposefully drop a plate onto the countertop in an effort to distract their mother. Thankfully it wasn't breakable.

"Meow." Beckie mimicked the kitten and did a good job of it. "Meow."

Mamm sighed. "Beckie, stop that. I thought I heard a real cat."

"Me too." Lizzie mocked scolding Beckie as she picked up the plate.

Mamm didn't like or trust cats. Rational or not, she worried that they'd scratch one of her daughters' faces and leave scars.

"I can't find my homework." Ruth's whiny voice was a clear indication of how poorly she'd slept last night.

"Coming." Mamm wiped her hands on a dishtowel. "She's so miserable this morning that I don't know if she can go to school."

"I'll see to her." Sylvia hurried toward the doorway of the kitchen. "And she'll be in the mood to go within the hour. I'm sure of it."

"I hope so," Mamm said. "She loves school like you love farming."

"Ah, but she'll grow out of liking school," Sylvia teased before getting to the steps.

"Wait," Mamm said.

Sylvia stopped and turned.

Mamm propped her hands on her small hips. "You need to eat."

"Oh, she's fine," Beckie said. "I'll fix her some coffee and take it to her."

"You girls." Mamm sighed. "Something's going on. I know that much."

"We're just pitching in to help each other like you taught us," Lizzie said.

"Ya, uh-huh." Mamm slung the dishcloth onto her shoulder, a move she repeated dozens of times every day. "You all stick together like peanut butter and jam." She motioned for Sylvia to go. "Well, do whatever you're going to do. But I want food in you within the hour. You were out most of the night, and you also need to get some sleep."

Mamm's correcting tone grated on Sylvia a bit. It never seemed to dawn on her Mamm that by Sylvia's age, she was married and had been running her own home for more than four years. She had one child and another on the way by twenty-two. But as long as Sylvia was unmarried, it seemed she'd be treated like a child.

When Sylvia stepped into Ruthie's bedroom, her little sister was sitting on her bed, crying. The sight of it tugged on Sylvia's heart. She covered her lips with her index finger and closed the bedroom door. "Shh. Don't squeal. But look what I have for you." Sylvia eased the kitten from her pocket.

Ruthie's eyes lit up, in much the same way Sylvia imagined her own did whenever Elam came to the house. "Whiskers." Ruth held out her hands. "She is alive."

"I told you it was just a bad dream." Sylvia placed her hand on Ruth's forehead, checking for a fever. She didn't seem to be coming down with a bug.

"How'd you get Whiskers past Mamm?"

"The little fur ball likes to snuggle in warm places."

Sylvia laid Whiskers in Ruth's lap. She'd no more than gotten Ruth and Whiskers settled and content when Martha started crying, demanding someone get her out of her crib, which woke Salome and Barbie Ann.

The day became a blur of tending to little ones, doing laundry, preparing meals, taking the school-age children to school and picking them up, and helping Beckie make herself another new dress. Sylvia didn't know why Beckie felt she needed one by that evening when she wasn't going anywhere, but they got it done before supper. Sylvia also managed to squeeze in a nap before returning to the barn for the second milking.

The good part was that the busyness made the day hurry by. Sylvia looked at the clock for the umpteenth time. Elam should be here any minute.

Daed had gone to the bank a few hours ago, and he had instructed Lizzie and Lilly to help with the evening milking. When her sisters filled in for Daed, the process always took longer. Darkness fell long before they left the barn for the night, and the stars twinkled brightly.

As they crossed from the barn to her home, she spotted Elam's rig in the carriage house. Her heart went wild. Why hadn't he stepped into the barn to say hello?

She and her sisters went inside the house and peeled out of their coats, scarves, and boots. Kerosene lamps were lit throughout, giving off a warm glow.

Elam's voice filled her soul as it softly rumbled through the house. She followed the sound of it until she found him with her Daed, sitting in the office, looking over papers. With his head bent over a calendar, she was able to study his handsome features unobserved.

Have they been talking business? To her knowledge they'd never done so before. She knew about milking cows and breeding and delivering calves, but she understood almost nothing about the other parts of farming—the finances, the land, growing crops, and what it took to keep the silos filled.

Elam jotted something down. "I think if the weather cooperates and we plant the alfalfa earlier this spring than you have in past years, we could rotate the crop and gain sufficient growing time to have enough silage to increase the herd numbers."

We? Something about his use of the word bothered her. But she knew better than to speak up. If her Daed wanted her input, he would have asked her to join the meeting. Still, it seemed they at least could have invited her to listen to the conversation.

Elam set his notes aside and lifted a stack of papers. "I think this'll work. It might take a few—" He spotted Sylvia standing in the doorway.

Daed glanced up and then returned to studying the documents in front of him. "You were saying?"

Elam rose to his feet. "I have no idea." He closed the gap between them, and a desire to be his thudded inside her chest. "Hi."

"Hello." She longed to kiss him. It'd been so long since their first kiss. She'd never forget it and that quiet evening as the horse and carriage ambled along under the harvest moon. "What are you two up to?"

"Nothing much." His eyes bore into hers with such intensity it was all she could do not to blush. She felt beautiful—wanted—and not at all like an odd duck.

"Elam," Beckie called. "Kumm. Surely it's time you returned to our game."

Elam's smile warmed Sylvia's insides as he winked before peering around her. "Later, pipsqueak."

"You'd better watch out calling her that," Sylvia whispered before Beckie came into the room. At eighteen, Beckie did not like being treated the same as the rest of the brood.

Elam held his hand a few feet off the floor. "It's not my fault she's about this big." He glanced at Beckie while smiling at Sylvia.

Beckie's cheeks flushed pink, and Sylvia wished he wouldn't pick on her. She tended to be dramatic about her petite size and anything else she was teased about.

Elam enfolded Sylvia's hand in his, and her knees felt weak.

Daed moved around them. "Kumm, Beckie. It's their time to be alone."

He pulled the door closed, which was against the house rules he'd made. When a beau visited, he had to earn the right to see his intended in a room by themselves, but even then the door was to remain ajar.

"Alone at last." Elam peered down at her before kissing her forehead.

Oh, how she longed to tilt back her head and let him kiss her lips. The desire overwhelmed her, and she felt like a fallen autumn leaf caught in a windstorm. Her Mamm said that there was nothing wrong with feeling so attracted to Elam, that it was as natural as getting hungry and needing sleep—as long as her feelings didn't turn to actions. But Sylvia wished it'd ease up so she could think with a clear head.

Elam slid his arms around her. "Your Daed has hopes for us, and we've agreed to start working the fields together this spring. But my dreams have nothing to do with farm work. They're haunted by a certain raven-haired beauty." He lowered his lips until they brushed her ear. "I love you. Marry me, Sylvia."

His whisper and his words drew her, but they also jarred her like rock shattering against pavement. Part of her had hoped for this moment since he'd stolen that first kiss last fall. That part nudged her to embrace him and say yes. But she remained still, knowing her whole heart wasn't committed.

She wondered where she fit inside his and her Daed's plans.

She had reservations when it came to the traditional idea of marriage, and she'd told Elam so. An Amish man's life barely changed when he married. His wife looked after him as his mother had—making clothes, cooking three times a day, and doing laundry. He kept doing the same job he always had, whatever it was. But a woman had to be ready to take on the responsibility of running a home and giving birth to baby after baby, sometimes into her forties, as her mother had.

As much as she thrilled at being with Elam, Sylvia wasn't sure she was ready to begin that journey. Something else nagged at her too, and she wished she knew what.

Easing away from him, she tried to gather her thoughts. The papers on the table sat in the light of the kerosene lantern on Daed's desk. She flipped through them, realizing the two of them were revamping the day-to-day running of the farm. "I didn't know you were this interested in our farm."

"I am now. My Daed would have to make room for another son to join him in his timber framing business. But your Daed really needs me."

The farm needed manpower, and Elam had plenty of it. That didn't bother her at all. What bothered her was her ignorance concerning his plans. He hadn't even thought to discuss them with her.

"It seems like you'd talk to me about all this before talking to Daed."

"I speak to him about business matters and to you of marriage. Would you prefer I turn the two around?" He chuckled at his joke.

Sylvia joined his laughter. "Definitely not, and I'm sure Daed appreciates that."

"Ya, me too."

She lifted an official-looking paper that had both men's signatures on it.

"Hey." Elam spoke softly while cupping his hand under her chin. "I just proposed. You did hear me, right?"

She placed her hand over the center of her chest. "I carry you in my heart, Elam, and in my head…all the time. You know that. But at the risk of angering you, I have to ask again. Doesn't it seem out of place that you're making plans for the future, our future, without even talking to me?"

"I was aiming to surprise you, which you don't seem to appreciate. Your grandfather left you his house, and it makes sense for us to live and work here. Doesn't it?"

"Ya. Sure it does."

"Look, Sylvia, I know you have funny ideas about how things should be sometimes. And you have some wild thoughts about what a marriage needs to look like. But I didn't expect this response—or, rather, lack thereof—and I *can* tell you I'm not thrilled about it."

"I'm sorry." She set the paper on the table and eased her hand into his, once again pulled in by his mysterious allure. "I…I was just caught off guard. I'm too surprised to have an answer right away."

"What's there to think about? You want to be with me… I know you do."

"Nothing, really, and I do want to be with you. But I can't say yes this moment. I need a little time to absorb it all."

He stood there, so tall and unbelievably handsome, and she should be melting in his arms. She wanted that, so what was wrong with her?

"You said it yourself, Elam. I'm weird sometimes. The fact is, I don't react to much of anything the way most people do. There's no reasoning it out. Just give me a couple of weeks. I'll be able to explain what's going on inside me then, okay?"

"Ya, okay. There's time, since we don't need to make any plans until spring. But I want to get married this fall, Sylvia."

"This fall?"

He pulled away from her, his features growing hard. "You don't have to say it like it's a disgusting idea."

Sylvia was surprised by his sudden irritation. "I didn't mean it that way. I'm sorry it sounded so rude."

"I'm going now. But you should sort through whatever's holding you back—and as soon as possible."

Her heart fell as he walked out, heading straight for the back door. Despite her conflicting feelings, she hadn't wanted him to leave, especially not while he was upset with her.

"Elam?" Daed rose from his spot across from Beckie, upsetting the checkerboard as he did. "Leaving so soon?" He glanced at Sylvia, silently asking her half a dozen questions.

"I need to go. We'll talk later." Elam paused at the hatrack and grabbed his coat.

Beckie went to him. "But we haven't had supper yet or played a game."

"Another time, Beckie." He put on his black felt hat while his eyes stayed glued to Sylvia. "We'll talk again when I'm not so angry."

Sylvia nodded, wishing he hadn't announced to her whole family that she'd upset him.

Beckie moved to her side. "What's going on?"

Sylvia didn't answer. Some things were too private to share, even with Beckie. But no matter how much Sylvia wanted to keep her silence about this, she doubted she could. She never had been much for keeping truths to herself.

Without another glance her way, Elam walked out the door. Surely after he cooled off a bit, he'd see that her request was reasonable. A little time to think, and she'd be ready to give him the answer he wanted.

The two horses struggled to pull the loaded wagon. Sylvia slapped the reins against the team's back, urging them out of the feed store parking lot and onto the main road. Heavy gray clouds hung low, and a cold wind from the west had begun to blow.

She'd taken her homemade yogurts by Eash's Market, bought groceries, and picked up what seemed sufficient cow feed to get them through the rest of this unusually long winter. That was everything… she hoped.

Sylvia tapped the reins again, urging the horses to hurry. Her thoughts remained on Elam. It'd been three weeks since he'd come to the house. How much longer would he wait before talking to her?

When she'd seen him at the church meeting, he'd seemed unable to take his eyes off her. That had to be a good sign.

She loved him. That she knew for sure. But were they ready to marry? And how could he make plans with her Daed to change the operations of the farm and never once consider asking her opinion?

She didn't expect her Daed to understand her. He lived in a man's world and made do with daughters to help him. But Elam was supposed to know and love the real her, oddities and all.

Now that she understood what had bothered her so much, she was ready to talk to him about it. If he could see her side of it, and if she could see his side, they could work this out.

The house came into sight, and a bitter wind chilled her as she pulled into the driveway.

Elam. Her heart raced as if it'd been tapped by the reins. He and her father were hurrying into the barn. Surely this meant Elam was over being angry at her. It could mean that he'd decided to start working with her Daed in spite of her, but why would he wait until a Friday night?

Gusts of wind nipped her face as she brought the rig to a stop near the back door. She hopped down and ran two bags of groceries inside. "Hello?"

Her Mamm hurried toward her.

"Elam's here," Sylvia said. "Will you get the others to finish unloading the wagon?" She spun on her heels, ready to shout Elam's name and run for the barn the moment she was outside, but her Mamm caught her arm.

"Beckie wants to see you."

"Can't she wait?"

"No. It's best if you go on and talk to your sister. She's in the wash house."

Sylvia stared at her mother, waiting for an explanation, but Mamm simply nodded toward the washroom. Sylvia unbuttoned her coat and went through the narrow hallway that connected the wash house to the main house. Maybe now she'd find out what her sister and their parents had been whispering about for more than a week. Other than a few hints of being excited about something, Beckie had been unreadable, which had never happened before. Her sister had remained silent whenever Sylvia had asked her about it. Whatever it was, her Mamm seemed quite displeased.

"Beckie?"

The moment Sylvia saw her sister, she noticed several things. She wasn't happy, she didn't have on her prayer *Kapp*, and she wasn't making eye contact. Beckie stoked the fire in the small potbelly stove, closed the door to the stove, and set the face of a pressing iron on it.

Since learning what Sylvia had told Elam the night he left, Beckie had been distant and quiet, not offering any words of comfort. And she'd been going out every evening.

Sylvia pulled off her gloves. "You're ironing on a Friday afternoon? What'd you do wrong while I was out?"

Beckie turned to her. "Nothing. I washed my prayer Kapp, and I want it to look just right for tonight."

"Ah, you must be going out again."

Beckie nodded, but Sylvia could read no emotion in her face.

"Mamm said you wanted to see me."

"Ya." Beckie fidgeted with a few loose strands of hair, tucking them carefully back into place.

"And…"

Beckie had obviously done something she shouldn't have—borrowed a dress and stained it or ruined another of Sylvia's prayer Kapps or borrowed money from Sylvia's stash. "Whatever is on your mind, dear sister, can we speed this conversation along? I forgive you. There. It's done. Elam is here, and I want to go see him."

Beckie licked her lips. "He's not here to see you."

"He said that?"

She nodded.

"I guess he's still mad at me after all. Is he here to help Daed?"

"No. Well, maybe a little. But Elam's not upset that you turned him down. Not anymore."

Tightness moved into Sylvia's chest. "I didn't turn him down. You know that. I only said I needed a little time. You reminded him of that, right?"

Beckie shrugged. "I'm sorry, but it's for the best, Sylvia."

Panic began to race through her. What had happened? "Beckie, it's not for the best to let Elam think I don't want to marry him. It's just that twenty-two feels young."

"Nonsense. Most brides marry much younger than that...Amish ones anyway. I don't think you really love him."

"That's ridiculous. What would you know about it?" Sylvia's world tilted. Why was she having this conversation with Beckie? None of it made sense.

Beckie placed a clean towel on the ironing board and gently laid her prayer Kapp on it. "He's...he's here for me."

"Oh, honey." Trying to think of the most gentle way to correct her sister, Sylvia stepped closer. "You must have something mixed up. I—"

Beckie's face turned red, and she shook a finger at Sylvia. "Of course you'd think that! No way could he be interested in a pipsqueak like me, right? Well, he's asked me to marry him, and I wasn't stupid enough to tell him to wait!"

"Elam did what? No!" Her sister's betrayal burned through her, charring everything she held dear.

Beckie's face softened. "I shouldn't have blurted it out. I'm sorry."

"You...you've been seeing Elam?"

"Ya."

Hurt and confusion churned within her, and Sylvia couldn't catch her breath. "I have to talk to him. This is all wrong. He loves me. Wants me."

"Sylvia, no." Beckie moved in front of her, an unfamiliar steeliness in her eyes. "Don't make this harder than it has to be."

Sylvia stepped around her sister, ran out of the wash house, and headed for the barn. Rolling clouds moved quickly across the sky, shrouding the land in winter's gray.

Surely Elam wouldn't... Beckie had to be wrong. The idea of her sister being disloyal hurt too much to bear. And Elam's betrayal? Impossible.

Sylvia hurried into the barn and stopped short. Neither man noticed her.

"Elam."

When his eyes met hers, she was no longer confident that Beckie was mistaken.

"It's not true, is it?" Tears threatened, and she swallowed hard. "Tell me you didn't ask Beckie to marry you."

Her Daed studied her for a moment before he lowered his head and went to the milk house, giving them privacy. Her Daed's reaction made her head spin, and she longed to wake from this nightmare.

Elam walked over to her but fixed his eyes on the floor. "I told you I'm ready to marry this next wedding season."

Part of her felt numb, and part of her burned as if someone had dumped scalding water on her. "You sound as if you don't care who you marry. I thought you loved me."

"I wasn't the one who sounded sick at the idea of getting married this fall." He lifted his eyes, and she could see his contempt. "And the truth is, I don't think you're ever going to be ready."

"That's not true." How had the feelings between them soured so quickly?

"Do you love me?"

"If I said yes, what difference would that make now? You've betrayed me with my sister."

"Let's assume the answer is yes. That means you turned me down in spite of how you feel. Why? That's all I want you to answer—for yourself, Sylvia. Why?"

Dozens of thoughts ran through her, and she didn't know which to voice first. "She's my sister, Elam. How could you do this?"

"If I wait, will you marry me?"

Was he setting her up so he could make more points in his argument, or was he proposing again? Her head pounded. "Are you…asking?"

"I—"

"Stop it," Beckie hissed, interrupting his response. She moved between them, facing Sylvia.

Elam seemed perfectly content to hide behind her sister. Who was this man? Obviously a disloyal liar. As if piecing together a quilt, she began to see a new pattern forming.

On the weekends, after she and Elam finished milking the herd, he'd go into the living room while she showered and put on fresh clothes. How many of those nights had she come downstairs and found him and Beckie cackling over some line in a book or a game of some sort? Often he'd sit between the two of them as they took turns reading aloud. She never once had challenged Beckie about it.

What a fool she'd been. And she feared that her sister was being one also.

Beckie moved closer. "Sylvia, please, open your eyes. I love him so much more than you ever did. Since you turned him down, I see no reason for you to stand in our way."

Sylvia fought to remain standing when all she wanted to do was sink to her knees and sob. "How could you do this to me? You're my sister, and you know how I feel about Elam!"

"I know how *he* feels. He loves *me*, Sylvia. And it's clear that I love him more than you do."

Sylvia looked past her sister, wondering how Elam had managed to steal both of their hearts. Had he kissed Beckie too? Was Sylvia blinded by attraction? "How can you be so sure? I'm no longer sure he has any clue who he loves." She hoped Beckie would hear that truth.

Elam slid his hand into Beckie's, and Sylvia thought she might die from the pain of it. "I asked her, and she said yes. It's done."

The undeniable fact that they'd been seeing each other behind her back scattered the words inside her until she could find none to try to reason with her sister.

The door to the milk house creaked as it opened, and her Daed came toward her.

Sylvia motioned at the twosome. "How can you agree to this?"

Her Daed gestured for Elam and Beckie to leave. "We'll finish up." He waited until they were gone.

Tears ran down Sylvia's face. "How could you be a part of this?"

"I'm not a part of it any more than you are. I've talked to Beckie until I have no more words."

"Do you not have enough loyalty to me to refuse her?"

"Sylvia." Daed pulled out his handkerchief and passed it to her. "I couldn't have stopped what happened." He motioned for her to walk with him as he went to a horse's stall on the far side of the barn and grabbed a bridle. "I can dictate certain things over her, but no parent can predict or prevent something like this. No matter who Elam ended up with, the damage was done before either of us knew what was happening. You have it in you to forgive and let go. Beckie doesn't." He bridled the horse. "You can help your Mamm forgive too. She's fit to be tied, as your sisters will be when they find out."

Sylvia stared at her father, unable to believe his casual attitude toward Elam and Beckie's traitorous behavior. "I can't stay here and watch them marry."

"It'll be tough. I know it will." He put a saddle on the horse and began tightening the girth. "But before Daadi Fisher died, he did something that's never been done before. He left a fourth of the family farm to a granddaughter—you. He bypassed every son and grandson to do it. You were grieving too deeply to know what all was happening, but for a while I thought there was going to be a feud over it. And I wasn't sure the church leaders would allow it, but in the end they did. Don't tell me you'd give up your inheritance over a man. I won't believe it. Besides, if you don't keep giving the dairy farm all you've got, you'll own a fourth of nothing but bills."

"You're not hearing me." She nearly shrieked at him. "I can't stay here."

"You've always said that the old place Daadi Fisher left you is too far from the herd for your taste. Let Elam and Beckie live there. It'll give you some distance, as if they're neighbors. You and I will run the herd and milk production. He and I will produce and harvest crops, keep the silos filled, and deal with the waste management. It's a huge place, and if we handle things right, you won't have to see him often. It's far from ideal, but it's the best I can offer."

She'd never considered living in the two-bedroom house Daadi Fisher had left her, but the idea of Elam and Beckie moving there made her sick.

"Daed, I don't care where they live. I have to get out. Why can't you understand that?"

Hints of anger shadowed her Daed's face before he drew a deep breath. "This is home, and no unmarried daughter of mine is moving away. It's not respectable, and I won't have it. You can find the strength, Sylvia. I know you can."

"Is Elam doing this because of those papers you two signed?"

"No. But if I'd known then how this would turn out, I wouldn't have taken him on as a partner. I'm sorry, Sylvia. Really sorry." He held the leads out to her, giving her permission to go riding until she felt better. "I'll see to it that you can get away for long weekends as much as possible. You can stay with cousins and aunts from other states for weeks at a time during our slow season. But this is home. I can't imagine living here without you, and running away isn't acceptable."

She stared at him, too broken to feel any hope for her future. It was beyond her how either Beckie or Elam could do this, but for both to betray her was more than she could bear.

Daed sighed. "Trust me. It'll all turn out for the best. I know it will."

She took the reins from him, desperate to steal away for a few hours and get as far from the happy couple as she could.

As she rode the horse out of the barn, she didn't bother drying her tears. Her vision blurred so much she could barely tell where she was going, and she knew it'd remain that way for a long time.

Two

Three years later

Faint sounds of someone moving in the next room ended Sylvia's few hours of sleep. It had to be Elam.

The darkness of early morn surrounded her, and she wished she could hide in it forever. She pushed the warm quilts away and sat upright.

Light from a kerosene lantern stretched under the closed bedroom door, flickering softly. The silhouette of two cribs, both holding sleeping little ones, reminded her of where she was—trapped somewhere between love and duty.

It'd taken a while to bury her feelings for Elam after he and Beckie married, but she'd managed it. She'd helped Beckie a lot during her pregnancy and after the twins were born, but it'd been reasonably easy for Sylvia to juggle her schedule and keep a comfortable distance from Elam.

Then, six weeks ago, whooping cough had disrupted their routine. Sylvia had considered that illness extinct. She discovered the hard way that she was wrong. The doctor called it an easily communicable disease, and it'd spread through her family like scattered seed on a freshly plowed field. Sylvia had been vaccinated as a child when a health-care worker came to the house. Elam had been vaccinated as a child too. The doctor believed that was why the two of them remained virus free.

Beckie and their parents were among the first to be hit, and Beckie remained as weak as a newborn kitten, so Sylvia and Elam had no choice but to tend to the farm and family around the clock like a married couple.

His footsteps quietly echoed against the stillness, and feelings she hated burned through her.

Her niece cried out, coughing and whining. Sylvia moved to Rhoda's bed and ran her hand across the mattress until she located the pacifier. She placed it in Rhoda's mouth and patted her back, hoping the infant would go back to sleep before waking her twin brother.

When Rhoda fell asleep, Sylvia went to Raymond's crib and placed the back of her hand against his little cheek. If he still had fever, it wasn't much. She drew a relaxing breath. The symptoms of whooping cough wouldn't last much longer.

The sound of Elam's muffled footsteps made their way through the door. Sylvia grabbed her housecoat and pulled it into a ball against her chest. Thoughts of their long night together, sitting in this quiet room, echoed through her. They'd given the twins a breathing treatment, then talked for hours while rocking the little ones. When he passed Raymond to her, their hands brushed, and desire ignited—the kind that should happen only between him and Beckie.

Her skin tingled. She hoped he wasn't about to enter the room, and yet a part of her wished he would.

A shadow glided under the crack of the doorway and stopped. Her heart pounded. A moment later the shadow disappeared. The familiar screech of the back door opening and then shutting said he'd gone to the barn. She had to join him. He had no other help, not with her Daed, Mamm, and most of her siblings down with whooping cough.

Years of avoiding him, of working opposite milking shifts, had come to an abrupt halt with this illness.

She went to the dresser, lit a kerosene lantern, and pulled out a newspaper ad she'd clipped a month ago. The ad was for help on a dairy farm belonging to an Amish man named Michael Blank, who lived in Dry Lake, a couple of hours southeast of here. Far enough away that she'd never have to see Elam unless she came home for a visit.

She'd shown the ad to her Daed, hoping to convince him to let her go. But he'd bristled at the idea and said he didn't want to hear anything else about it.

He'd never let an unmarried daughter move away from home, and she'd dropped it. But now she clung to the idea of leaving as if it were her only chance of escaping temptation. And maybe it was.

Daed had kept his word, and over the past three years, she'd visited relatives whenever time allowed. She'd gone to singings and dated men from across four states, and not one of them interested her. What was her problem?

Whatever it was, she had to get out of here.

After this time with Elam, living in the main house with her parents would no longer be a sufficient barrier between them. Living a few miles away with a relative wasn't good enough either. She'd still see Elam at church meetings, community functions, and family gatherings.

She peeled out of her nightgown, convincing herself that in spite of whatever had stirred between them last night, today was just another day of farm work and babies. She dressed for morning chores, then quietly opened the bedroom door, went to the mud room, and put on her boots, coat, and hat before heading for the barn.

Cold winter air filled her lungs. The sky's dark majesty sparkled with dots of white light, as if trying to assure her that its vastness covered more than her problems.

As she drew closer to the barn, she heard the faint sounds of Elam moving through the morning routine. Bracing herself, she went inside.

"*Guder Marye,* Sylvia."

She nodded in response to his softly spoken *good morning,* refusing to get pulled into a conversation. If talking could milk cows, he'd never need anyone's help.

She moved toward the wheelbarrow of silage, feeling his eyes on her.

Don't look. Just don't.

Her eyes moved to his, and she felt caught.

He's forbidden. She didn't need the reminder, but the phrase ran circles in her mind.

After filling the troughs with feed, he opened the gate, and the cows nearly stampeded into the milking stalls. As soon as the cows put their heads through the stanchions, she began locking the panels. He grabbed the nozzle of the hose that hung overhead through an elaborate scheme of cables and pulleys and squirted the cows' udders.

"Hey, Sylvia."

She finished locking the devices and grabbed the milking stool. A diesel engine in the milk house ran the refrigerator for the bulk tank and powered the air compressor for the portable milkers, but she had to start the milk flowing from each cow before the machinery could do its job.

"You okay?" Elam asked.

"I'm not getting sick, but I can't say I'm okay."

"Ya, I know. Me either. Just don't be mad."

She wasn't angry. Terrified, maybe. Definitely overloaded with guilt. But too confused about herself to be angry with him.

After she cleaned and primed the first cow, Elam moved next to her with the claw milker and its attached bucket. She tried to get up, grab the stool, and move out of the way before he got too close, but instead she managed to trip into him.

He steadied her, his eyes never leaving hers.

With confusion and desire churning inside her, she went to the next cow. She hated Elam, but she still felt as though he were a magnet, drawing her closer. She longed to feel his lips against hers.

Think, Sylvia, and stop feeling.

"Did you get any sleep after I left last night?"

How she slept was none of his business. "Rhoda's breathing easier." She patted the cow as she stood to move to another one.

Elam's hesitant smile drew her. "I never doubted you'd get the twins through this ordeal safe and sound. You have strength...determination that the rest of us don't." He moved closer.

Every part of her begged to slip into his arms. She passed him the milking stool and took the nozzle, keeping a safe distance.

She had to get out of Path Valley, but she doubted Michael Blank would hire her. She didn't know of one man, Englischer or Amish, who'd hire a female farmhand—not unless she was part of a package deal that included a husband.

Even if Michael Blank would give her a chance, how could she convince her Daed to let her go? He couldn't make her stay, but he could cut off her contact with him, Mamm, and her sisters.

While her mind searched for solutions, she and Elam continued milking the herd. By the time all eighty-two cows were milked, the sun shone brightly through the slats and the dirt-streaked windows. Once the stalls were empty again, she sterilized the milkers and buckets while Elam scraped the grates and cleaned the stalls. After scrubbing the bulk tank, she started spreading white lime sand onto the concrete floor. As soon as Elam joined her, she set the shovel aside and went to the mud sink. He could finish by himself.

When she turned to leave the wash area, Elam stood directly in her path. He searched her eyes the way he had when they were dating.

If she had the guts, she'd ask him what was going on between them. But it'd take so little to dismantle her will. She tried to step around him, but he moved in the same direction.

"Sorry," she mumbled.

He touched her cheek, sending both surprise and warmth through her.

She commanded her body to turn and walk away, demanded herself to break free of his spell, but she couldn't budge. No matter what Bible verse she tried to grab, she wanted what stood before her. "I...I need to...go."

As if the two of them were floating dust particles, they continued hanging in midair and yet moving toward each other. How many times had she dreamed of kissing him again? His lips met hers, and suddenly nothing existed but the feelings that ran between them.

She pushed him away, tears stinging her eyes. Her skin burned with embarrassment. "Get away from me, Elam."

"I don't want to," he whispered. "What are we going to do?"

She knew how he felt. "You have to help me get out of here. Daed doesn't want to let me go, but he'll listen to you."

He brushed a tear off her face, looking weary and sorry and trapped. "Okay."

The door to the barn creaked open. "Sylvia? Elam?" Her sister's hoarse voice sent alarm through her. Beckie's brows furrowed as she looked from Sylvia to Elam. "What's going on?"

Sylvia's heart shattered into a hundred pieces. "I...I tripped, and he caught me." It was a believable lie. Beckie often teased that, when Sylvia was tired, she had all the grace of a newborn calf. Guilt ate at her, and she no longer recognized any part of herself.

Coughing, Beckie grabbed a nearby wall for support.

Elam hurried to her, placed his arm around her, and guided her back toward the house.

Desperate for a moment alone, Sylvia went to the tack room and closed the door. She covered her face with her hands and sobbed, her whole body shaking.

Three

June

Shoving a thick packet of money into his pocket, Aaron left the small bank. He'd emptied his account of ten years' worth of hard work and diligent saving. Even in his worst years, he'd never touched his savings account, and now he had something to show for all that time spent doing what he hated—dairy farming.

He crossed the parking lot to the hitching post, removed the leather reins, and mounted his horse. With the click of his tongue, he was on his way.

Hope tried to spring up inside him, but heavier realities overrode it. A feeling of griminess had taken up residence inside him long ago. His thoughts, emotions, and even the blood that pumped through his veins felt as layered in black soot as the rooftops and porches of homes near industrial smokestacks. He didn't suppose he'd ever be free of it. But he had a plan that would bring as much joy as someone like him could expect.

He stopped in front of the appliance store where he worked, tethered his horse at the post, and went inside.

Aaron walked the narrow aisle, enjoying the business ideas pulsing through him. The cash in his pants pocket gave him a sense of power over his future. A smile tugged at his face. The idea of owning and operating this store fit who he was, and in spite of the weight of his past that he carried, he could see a good life ahead of him.

A middle-aged Old Order Amish couple stood at the sales counter. The man plunked cash into Leo's hand while his wife wrote their address on the invoice so they could have the new wringer washer delivered.

A dusting of eagerness lifted his spirits. He couldn't recall the last time he'd been excited about anything. Owning this business felt more right than anything he'd ever done.

If he signed the papers and put down earnest money today, he could own the shop in about two and a half months. Well, he and the bank. Leo would still hold the note, but he'd retire come September, leaving Aaron as the proprietor. Aaron had to be ready to take over by then.

As he walked through the display area, the wooden floor creaked. Only natural light illuminated the room, and open windows were the sole source of ventilation. Leo wasn't Plain, but he handled his business in a way that made the Plain folk feel right at home. There were living quarters above the store, large enough to house Aaron and his parents comfortably until he could afford better.

Thoughts of his parents dampened his mood. An Amish couple well past their prime with only one surviving child—who'd ever heard of such a thing? If his older sister hadn't died last fall, and if his parents' six other babies had survived, they would have other children to rely on. Aaron didn't doubt he'd still be the black sheep of the family, but at least they'd have white sheep to help them. Instead they had only him.

And he wouldn't let them down. Not again.

Shaking off the negative thoughts, he studied the many types of wringer washers, cookstoves, hot water heaters, and stoves for warming a home. Not one appliance in this store needed electricity. Depending on which sect of Amish or Mennonite the buyers were, they might use solar energy, coal, wood, battery, various types of gas, or diesel fuel. The store had some of those items in stock, and others could be ordered through a catalog.

Though Aaron had been working here for four months, he didn't know much about running a store or about appliances. But he'd grown up on a dairy farm, and he knew how to work hard. Besides, he'd always been a quick study when his heart was in it. And his heart was definitely in this.

Leo shook hands with the customers, promised a delivery time, and told them good-bye. The bells on the door jangled as the couple left.

Aaron stepped up to the counter. "I have the earnest money, and I'm ready to sign the papers."

While putting money into the register, Leo's eyes lit up. He and Aaron had been talking about the possibility of this for at least eight weeks. "A man with a plan and money to back it up—I can't argue with that. However, there's one thing we haven't talked about. My lawyer friend brought it up last night while he was drawing up the papers. A cosigner."

Aaron found it hard to catch his next breath. "But..." He had no one who would cosign with him. "I've brought you more than the agreed-upon down payment, and once I take over, I'll pay you each month from the money I make until I own the store outright. Isn't that enough?"

"Well, it's just prudent to have someone with good credit back you in case of default. You're going home. Get your dad to sign it in front of a notary public, and we'll be all set."

A sick feeling crept into Aaron's stomach. Money he could come up with. His Daed's signature was another matter.

Leo came out from behind the counter. "Let's go to my office and sign the papers between us, and I'll give you the ones you need a cosigner on."

After signing the papers, Aaron mounted his horse and began the ride back to the Better Path. Country stores lined the main street of the small community. The idea of town living sat well with him. He prayed that after he moved here, he'd never live on a farm again.

But first he had to convince his parents to sell and move with him.

Until he left home in January, they had no idea that he was addicted to alcohol and that he'd made a mess of his life along the way. He didn't know how much they knew even now, except that he'd entered rehab five months ago. After being sober for a couple of months, he hadn't returned home. Instead, he'd started working at the appliance store and leading groups at the rehab center where he'd been living since arriving in Owl's Perch.

But he'd realized that he could never truly move on until he acted like a responsible only son by making amends. He figured—no, he knew—that the best way to make up for the past and for his unwillingness to be a farmhand was to get his parents out of that money pit they called a dairy farm.

As his horse ambled toward the Better Path, the sun hung almost directly overhead. Fields were thick with tall, green hay that needed to be cut, dried, and baled for the first time this season. A second and probably a third time were sure to follow.

Farm work. It never ended. And no matter how hard farmers tried, they never got caught up.

Trying not to dread what lay ahead, he put his horse to pasture and went into the rehab housing unit.

He shoved clothes into his canvas bag. He liked the idea of leaving rehab. He was ready.

Well, maybe he was.

He'd certainly learned a good bit about his addiction and how to manage it.

Alcoholic. It had taken him months of rehab and counseling to accept that label. Adding the word *recovering* in front of it did nothing to lessen his embarrassment. But he had to face his past, even if his only goal now was to extract himself from it.

Someone tapped on his door.

"Kumm."

Paul Waddell stepped inside the small room. "Hannah sent you these." He held up a tin. "It has some of the leftover cookies from last night's going-away tribute."

"That's really nice. Thanks." Aaron set the canister on the bed before opening his nightstand and taking out the small stack of letters he'd received from Lena.

Lena—probably the only friend he had left or maybe ever had to begin with. She'd been the one who told him about this rehab facility. He hated the choices he'd made that caused him to come here, but checking himself in was the best decision he'd ever made.

Paul closed the door and sat in the reading chair beside the bed. "Today's the day."

"Ya."

He'd never met a man like Paul—a straight shooter, untraditional, and so very patient. In fact, sometimes the breadth of Paul's tolerance grated on Aaron's nerves. His wife, Hannah, was still in nursing school, but she kept close tabs on everyone who went through the rehab program and even joined the meetings whenever it was family group session day, which took place once every three to four weeks.

There'd been six family sessions during Aaron's time here. He'd invited his parents to every one, but they hadn't come. When they didn't answer a single letter he'd sent them, Paul sent formal invitations on the Better Path stationery, but he didn't get a response either.

"How are you faring?" Paul asked.

"Good and bad, I guess." Aaron moved to the dresser. "The good part is I just signed the papers and put down money on the appliance store."

"You made a plan and followed through. I've seen that strong suit numerous times since you arrived here."

"Unfortunately, I'm losing valuable training time in order to return to Dry Lake, a place I'm definitely not wanted. I'm aiming to be back mid-August, but as long as I'm in Owl's Perch and ready to take over the shop by September first, I have nothing to worry about. That gives me at least eight weeks to do what I should be able to accomplish in four."

"It could be tougher than you expect."

Daed had always claimed the farm was his dream, but surely he'd had his fill of it by now. Despite how Aaron's parents felt about him, he was confident they'd jump at selling the old place and join him in becoming merchants in Owl's Perch. They just needed to warm up to the idea. It would certainly be easier to make a living here.

Aaron put the last of his things into the backpack. He slung the strap over his shoulder and picked up the tin. "I could use a ride to the bus station."

Wiping sweat from her brow and loosening the top buttons on her shirt, Sylvia moved to the open hayloft doors, hoping to feel even a smidgen of breeze on the hot June day. The Blank farm stretched out before her on all sides, and although fence lines divided one pasture from another, no one else's property was in sight.

Another two hours of work in this sauna known as a hayloft and she'd have accomplished her goal. Since breakfast she'd tossed, dragged, and toted bales of hay to one side and straw to the other—all in hopes of making it easier to get at whichever one she needed.

What would possess someone to intermix the two so carelessly?

She leaned against the doorframe, studying the beautiful wild flowers and rolling fields where a contented herd grazed.

Her cows. She didn't own them, of course, but Michael Blank had hired her to tend to them. He trusted her, and she hadn't let him down. When she arrived here four months ago, the herd was in dire need of diligent care. The overall health of the cows matched their milk production— poor. But after working endlessly, she had good reasons to bask in her accomplishments.

She wished it were possible to feel joy again, but she didn't believe she deserved to be happy. Even contentment was beyond reach. She hadn't been able to resist Elam, and the weight of her sin lay heavily upon her. Finding peace was impossible, even with her new start. She alone was responsible for her actions. She knew it. God knew it.

She shoved her hands into her pockets. Elam's life went on as it always had, but she'd had to give up everything.

When her Daed realized he couldn't talk her out of leaving home, he warned her she'd be giving up her portion of the farm and all the money he'd put back as a salary for her over the years. He even said she couldn't write to her sisters, nor would he allow them to write her.

She had left anyway. No one but Elam would ever know why.

Thoughts of home flooded her. She missed her sisters most of all. Any sense of accomplishment disappeared as heaviness tightened its grip. If she thought it would do any good, she'd pray for relief.

Unfortunately, working like an ox came easier than whispering a simple prayer. In the distance the treetops swayed as the humid air stirred, and she wondered if she'd ever pray again. She had called out to God after her adulterous kiss with her sister's husband, but all she could manage was to beg for forgiveness. God's silence bore down on her without relief, and she'd given up praying altogether. She had hope for this farm, but she had no peace inside her, and she missed it.

By the time she milked the cows tonight and tended to the barn, she'd barely be able to lift her feet and walk to her cabin. Freedom to start anew came with a physically exhausting price. If she could sleep at night, it'd help. She would take a long bath before bed tonight, hoping she'd be able to clear her mind and heart.

Soft mews caught her attention, pulling her back to the present. She climbed over several bales of undisturbed straw and shifted a few out of the way before she spotted four young kittens that appeared to be about three weeks old. The mother was nowhere to be seen, but by the look of things, she'd been taking good care of her litter.

Sylvia sat among the bales of hay and pulled the kittens into her lap, stroking each one, hoping to make them more people-friendly than their wild mother. If she had any money, she'd get them fixed and teach them to trust humans. Every barn needed good mice catchers, but a little effort could keep them from being feral hunters.

After several minutes she left the kittens sleeping in the hay and headed for her cabin. It was run-down and small, but each evening as she trudged back to it, the last rays of golden sunlight enveloped it, as if promising that one day the ache inside her would ease.

Until then she found solace in her new home here with Michael and Dora Blank.

Four

Cara studied the Pennsylvania Dutch phrase in the notebook before her, wishing it made sense. The preacher and his wife sat across the kitchen table from her. They'd invited her to come to their home twice a week between now and the end of summer as their gift to help her learn the language. Cara needed to know a little German and a fair amount of Pennsylvania Dutch, and she had serious concerns whether she'd ever get the hang of either of them. But if she didn't, she had no chance of receiving the church leaders' approval to marry Ephraim come fall.

"I don't know." She closed the book and pushed it away. "Male, female, child, adult, singular, plural—nearly every word changes based on who is being spoken to. I can't do this."

Preacher Alvin reopened the book and set it in front of her. He tapped it with his rough hands. "Try again."

His patience and his confidence in her were comforting. She pulled the notebook closer. Studying the phrase again and comparing it with other words, she finally understood. "So *Gott segen dich* is used when the person is talking to only one other person, and *Gott segen eich* is used when the person is talking to at least two people, right?"

"Gut, Cara." Esther's weathered cheeks rose slightly when she smiled. "What do the phrases mean?"

"Both mean 'God bless you.'"

"Wunderbaar." Esther had been teaching German to Amish young

people for nearly fifteen years, but this was her first time to teach Pennsylvania Dutch. She held up a flashcard. *"Saage es,* Cara."

"You said, 'Say it.'"

"Gut."

Cara stared at the image of an infant on the card. *"Bobbeli."*

"Gut." Esther held up another hand-drawn card, this time of a horse.

Cara tapped her pencil on the table. *"Langsam?"*

Esther smiled. *"Letz."*

Wrong. Cara definitely knew the meaning and pronunciation of that word.

"Langsam means 'slow.' It could be a slow one of these, I suppose."

"Horse... Oh, *Gaule.*"

"Gut." Esther put the cards on the table. "Our time's up for today. You're doing fine."

"Denki, Esther." Cara closed her notebook. "But I know how I'm doing, and *fine* isn't the word for it."

"You're doing your best. That's all God asks, and He'll take care of the rest. Just you wait and see."

One could not be fully accepted into a culture if she or he couldn't speak and understand a reasonable amount of the language. As with most things Amish, she could see the reasoning behind that belief, but that didn't make learning the words any easier.

The preacher bowed his head in silent prayer, and she followed his lead.

Peace eased through her. Nearly everything that had happened over the last year had defied logic. Maybe developing the necessary skill in the languages would too. When she came to Dry Lake from the Bronx a year ago, she wanted only one thing—to protect her then seven-year-old daughter from a maniac stalker. But she got so much more. She found Ephraim, a man who'd been willing to do whatever it took to help her. He'd been shunned because of his unrelenting support for her. And in the process, she found God...or He found her. A more mature believer would know which.

Whoever found who, she never would have believed it possible to shake free of her stalker, get out of poverty, and start fresh. The Old Order Amish ways were far from being like a fairy tale, but the love and hope she'd found inside this community had done much to make up for all the years of brokenness.

"Cara?" The preacher's voice interrupted her thoughts, and she opened her eyes.

Alvin rubbed his hand across his mouth, clearly trying to hide his smile. "I said *amen*...twice."

Cara headed for the door. "Well, maybe you cut the prayer time too short." She sounded sassy as she teased, but she knew Alvin and Esther didn't mind.

"Who'd have ever thought extended silent prayer time would bring such a smile to your face?" Alvin grabbed his straw hat and followed her.

Once outside, Cara saw Ephraim in his buggy, waiting for her. He'd gone through Amish instruction and joined the faith nine years ago. Understanding Ephraim was a little like trying to understand God. There was no logic. It made no sense. But his power to change everything for her was undeniable. How Ephraim had stayed single in a society that put so much stock in marriage also defied her understanding.

His strawberry blond hair peeped out from under his straw hat. His broad shoulders and lean body always caught her eye. One glimpse of him and she found it impossible to keep the pleasure of it off her face.

She paused on the front porch. "I wasn't praying as much as thinking of all the things I'm grateful for," she told Alvin.

He put on his hat, making sure it fit snugly. "Feeling gratitude is much like a prayer all on its own. If you thank Him for those things, it becomes a prayer."

"You think so?"

"Ya, I do. You're doing a good job with the language classes. And you did pretty well with the first instruction class too."

Instruction classes. She had eight more sessions to go, and each would take place on a church Sunday between now and fall. The lessons covered the principles of the Christian faith and living Amish.

She heard hesitation in Alvin's voice, as if he wanted to add a *but*. Hoping to avoid that conversation, she thanked him for his time and hurried down the steps and into the buggy. Whatever he saw in her attitude or mind-set that needed to be adjusted would show itself soon enough without her digging around for it.

Ephraim and Alvin exchanged a few pleasant words. After Ephraim said his good-byes, he clicked his tongue, and the horse started plodding along.

Cara moved a little closer to him, keeping the expected respectable distance.

He moved the reins to one hand and placed his arm on the seat back behind her. "This is the rig we used to get you back and forth when you first landed in Dry Lake and hated me."

"I never *hated* you. I just didn't trust you. And I didn't like how much power you held over my situation. And your viewpoint concerning my minor thievery really irked me. And…okay, fine, I did dislike you a little, but only for a short while. You didn't care for me either."

"That's not true." He slowed the rig. "I liked you from the time we met as children."

He was twelve and she was eight when her mother brought her to Dry Lake for a visit. Neither their age nor gender difference kept them from having fun. "That was a great week, wasn't it?"

"Ya. Afterward I kept returning to *our* tree, waiting for your mom to bring you back like she said." He released a long breath. "That was my first heartbreak."

Jealousy crept up her spine. It seemed that he'd spent his years as a bachelor dating nearly every single Amish woman in Dry Lake and the surrounding communities. "Yeah, the first of several."

His hand moved to her back and caressed her. "Ya, just the first." He pulled into a driveway and stopped. "Stay put." He hopped out, went around the rig, and held out his hand. "The second time I had my heart broken was when I went to New York some eight years later to search for you and never found you."

She stared at him from the rig. He had no reservations about telling her how he felt, and she reveled in hearing it, but loving words didn't roll off her tongue. She adored him, but saying so directly seemed impossible.

Shooing his hand away, she climbed down on her own. "You're too good at these verbal games we play. Fine, you win. Maybe you did care."

His smile assured her she hadn't offended him by being sarcastic or rejecting his offer of help.

She peered around him. "What are we doing at Lena's?"

He laughed. "Been paying attention much?"

"Shut up and answer the question."

He placed one hand on the rig on each side of her, capturing her body and her full attention. "I can either shut up, or I can answer your question. I cannot do both." His eyes caught hers and stayed there. "The third and last time I had my heart broken, I was thirty-two years old. You'd waltzed into Dry Lake, stolen my hopes again, and then made plans to leave."

"I didn't *waltz* anywhere." She'd fled in terror from a stalker and stumbled into Dry Lake in utter confusion, with only shards of memories from her childhood. She hadn't remembered Ephraim, not really. When they talked about it later, they figured the lapse was due to the trauma of her mom being killed soon after they returned to New York.

His hands moved to her face. "I love you, Cara."

Her heart constricted, making her wish she could share her feelings as easily. "Of course you do. We're engaged. Remember?"

"I never forget it for a moment. You and the preacher seem to be getting along nicely. That's a good sign."

"He's really not so bad."

"I'm sure he appreciates you thinking so."

Ephraim's closeness reminded her once again that he wasn't like any other man she'd ever known. He was amazing...and she was ordinary. She clicked her tongue and huffed. "Do you intend to kiss me or just keep driving me crazy?"

A throat cleared, and they turned to see Lena's dad with a handsaw gripped in his fist, looking at them. Ephraim released her and eased back, as if an Amish man showing affection in public were normal.

Israel looked amused. "Is there a reason, Ephraim Mast, why you're on my property—and about to kiss your girl?"

"Yeah, there's a reason," Cara piped up, ready to harass Israel. "Ada sent us over to give you a few lessons on how to get a kiss and make it count."

Israel dropped his saw and seemed unable to move. Ephraim flashed Cara a look that said she'd gone too far. She didn't think so. *Good grief!* Israel and Ada had both lost their spouses something like fourteen years ago. From what she'd seen when they were together, they were clearly attracted to each other, but nothing had come of their friendship yet.

Israel cleared his throat and picked up his saw. "I'd like to say, 'Well, then, carry on. I'm paying attention.' But that seems too brash."

Cara burst into laughter. "You just said it, didn't you?"

"Who, me?" Israel feigned innocence.

If she'd had a father growing up, she'd have wanted him to be like Israel. "So where's Lena?"

"On the other side of the house, near the road. She's weeding the flower beds and adding fresh mulch."

Cara brushed a string of her prayer Kapp away from her face and over her shoulder. "How is she managing that with her arm in a cast and a medical boot on her sprained ankle?"

"She moves slower than usual and makes sure to wear at least one work glove."

"How's she really doing, Israel?" Ephraim asked.

"Pretty well, considering a maniac tried to kill her less than six weeks ago. I've not seen any signs of nervousness or bad dreams. Cara, you're welcome to interrupt her for a visit."

"Okay, thanks." Cara headed in that direction and then turned to Ephraim, silently asking him why they'd stopped here.

Ephraim adjusted his suspenders. "Israel, we'd like to pick up Lena if you don't mind."

Ah, now Cara knew why they'd come. Ephraim was helping to arrange a meeting between Lena and his friend Grey. The two couldn't court openly or be seen together very often for several months yet. Cara couldn't really explain the reasons—something about Amish ways and Grey's expected period of mourning. Maybe.

"She'll be glad you've come by to get her. What's the plan?"

"We're going to the shop to do a bit of cleaning, maybe play a game or two."

Cara knew they'd do exactly as Ephraim said—clean and then play games. He wouldn't lie.

"Sounds good." Israel nodded once, giving his stamp of approval. "I imagine Grey is already there and will be glad she came to *help*." Israel smirked and winked at Cara.

Yep, if Cara could have had Israel as a dad, she wouldn't have spent her whole childhood feeling unloved. "Do you happen to need another daughter? I've been thinking of adopting a dad."

Israel moved toward her. "I'd be honored. I take it things didn't go well with your father the other night."

Cara's insides flinched. "I...I... You talked to Trevor?"

"He came to talk to you too, right?" Israel asked.

She shook her head. She hadn't seen the man but once since he'd abandoned her at New York's Port Authority Bus Terminal when she was eight. In April he'd shown up during one of their tourist events at Ada's House. Something he said gave away his identity, and she called to him, but he walked off. She hadn't seen him since. Then she discovered he'd been hanging around for months during several of the outdoor events at Ada's House.

"Oh." Israel looked sorry for bringing up the topic. "I went to the lumberyard in Hope Crossing for supplies a few days ago and bumped into him. We went to the Family Restaurant to eat, and he said he was going to see you that very night. We talked about it for quite a while."

Her good mood drained away like water poured onto desert sand. Resentment unseated her sense of thankfulness. "You bought him food, didn't you?"

"Well, sure."

"Did you give him money too?"

Israel looked sheepish. "Ya, a little."

"So, in essence, you paid him to say what you wanted to hear. That's how it works, Israel." She'd seen plenty of no-account people in her life, and she could almost promise what someone like Trevor would do. "If you see him again, ignore him. Then you're guaranteed to hear all sorts of things you don't want to hear, but at least it'll be honest."

"I think he's changed, Cara."

Fuzzy caterpillars change. Snakes don't. But someone like Israel wouldn't understand the kind of man Trevor was. People like him didn't change, not for the better anyway.

Cara drew a deep breath, determined to keep her thoughts to herself. The church leaders were backing her with their time and patience so she could succeed at the language, instruction classes, and whatever else was necessary for her to join the faith this fall. They were doing their part and more.

And she would do hers. All she had to do was keep control of her actions and her tongue, even where her so-called father, Trevor, was concerned.

Five

The dull hum of the bus had droned relentlessly until Aaron got off in Shippensburg and walked the six miles to Dry Lake. The full moon played hide-and-seek as feathery silver clouds rolled across the sky.

An odd rhythm beat inside his chest as he came closer to his parents' home.

He left the main road and cut through the back pasture near the Amish schoolhouse. Images of his sister being mangled by his bull in this field haunted him. He could see her body flailing into the air and thudding to earth again. The bull stomped her over and over again. As the memory taunted him, his legs almost buckled.

His sister's voice echoed inside his head: *You're their only son. Be a man, get your life straight, and do whatever it takes to help them. They need you.*

He couldn't count the number of times Elsie had said that to him. She'd understood what rheumatoid arthritis had done to their Daed much better than he had. Aaron's drinking had blinded him to everything. But now he'd returned to make things right. Knowing Elsie would be pleased lessened his guilt somewhat.

He crawled over the back fence and kept walking until the homestead came into sight. The old two-story brick farmhouse looked the same as it had when they'd moved here nearly eight years ago.

It seemed awfully early to be in bed, but he didn't see any light coming from his home.

His folks never locked a door, so he went inside. The lingering aroma of his Mamm's cooking filled the air. How many meals had his mother fixed for him that he'd never thanked her for, never showed up for, never cared about?

He set his canvas bag on the kitchen table and lit the metal kerosene lantern. "Mamm? Daed?" He grabbed the lantern by the handle and worked his way through each room. "Hello?"

No one answered.

He looked out the kitchen window toward the barn. It stood dark too, but the cows weren't bellowing to be fed and milked, so they'd been looked after.

A figure cutting across the back field caught his eye. He watched for a moment and realized the person was heading for the cabin. The small building couldn't be seen from here, and at the time he left for rehab, his parents seemed to have forgotten the run-down place existed on their property. But his drinking buddies knew about it.

He hurried outside and took the shortcut through the woods. When he came into a clearing, he nearly ran into a woman.

"Frani?"

Her thin, blond hair fell a few inches below her shoulders, and thankfully she'd put on some weight, but her posture said she carried even less hope than she had the last time he saw her five months ago. She'd always talked about getting sober, but those words had faded over the years— maybe in some ways because of him. She'd been a decent friend, and he'd never once encouraged her to stop drinking. Instead, he'd invited her and the others to bring booze to the cabin night after night.

"Aaron, you're finally back. I had a feeling you'd be here tonight." She held up a six-pack of beer, and he wanted it. All of it. "I brought you a welcome-home gift."

He didn't need to touch a six-pack to feel its magnetism. It woke him during the night and plagued him throughout the day.

He glanced toward the thick row of trees that surrounded the cabin.

He couldn't really see it, but he thought he saw a kerosene light shining from a window. "Are there others inside?"

"Nope." She dug a cell phone out of the back pocket of her jeans, flipped it open, and pushed buttons. "But I'm giving them a call."

The clumsiness of her moves and the slur in her words indicated that she was more than a little intoxicated.

Aaron took the phone from her and ended the call before passing it back to her. "There won't be any more drinking at the cabin, Frani. Not tonight or any night."

"Why not?"

"Because I said so." Trying to explain his new goals was a waste of time in her present condition. He looked toward the hidden parking area but didn't see any vehicles. "Where's your car?"

"Where it's supposed to be. Don't worry. Your folks won't see it."

"Kumm." He headed toward the thicket where his old friends used to park.

"Wait." She stumbled. "Me and some of the gang have been by the cabin lots of times in the last five months. It's neat and tidy every time, but you were never there."

Neat and tidy?

She pushed strands of dirty hair out of her face. "We've missed you."

Before rehab, he might have believed they actually cared, and the power of that would have dragged him wherever they wanted. But now he saw a big enough sliver of truth that he understood. He hadn't been missed—only the right to use the abandoned shack on his property.

He took her by the arm and started walking. "I'll drive you home."

When he got back here tonight, he'd board up the cabin. That should put an end to his old drinking buddies coming around.

When they reached her car, Frani passed him the keys. Before sliding into the passenger seat, she pulled a pack of cigarettes out of her jeans pocket. She groped through the trash on the dashboard until she found a lighter, lit up, and stared out the window while filling her lungs with smoke.

Aaron ran his hand over the steering wheel and started the engine. He'd learned how to drive in this car, cruising dirt roads late at night, drunk with his friends. All of that was over now. He hadn't joined the faith yet, but he intended to as soon as he and his family were living in Owl's Perch.

While Aaron drove, Frani finished her cigarette without saying a word.

He wrestled with what to say to her. He wanted to bury the past. Everything he needed to accomplish—winning his parents' approval, starting fresh, earning a little respect within the Amish community, avoiding having beer waved in his face—would be easier if he didn't have to see her again.

But she deserved to have someone help her do what she'd always dreamed of—getting sober. Maybe she'd forgotten about that hope, but he bet that somewhere inside her that dream still existed. His sister might still be alive today if he'd had the clear thinking of a sober man. He had no way of knowing how the past might have played out if he hadn't been a drunk, but he did know that if Frani stayed on this course, the possible disasters ahead were endless. And she deserved better.

As he pulled into a parking space in front of Frani's trailer, a young woman with a fussy baby on her hip came outside. "Well!" the girl yelled.

"Home sweet home." Frani sighed. "Thanks a lot, Aaron. Now that my sister knows I'm here, I'm stuck." She held out her hand for the keys.

"I'm not walking home for the second time tonight. I'll park your car in the usual spot and put the keys under the mat."

"I'll have to walk that far to get my car back?"

"That's right. You need help getting inside?"

"No thanks."

"Get some sleep, Frani. We'll talk after you're sober."

She got out, taking her beer with her.

He left, determined to board up that cabin tonight. Since his parents were out for the evening, it was a perfect time to kick out anyone in it and to nail the shutters closed.

Once back at the house, he went to the pegs that lined the wall beside the back door. His tool belt still hung there, just as it had before he went away. Had his parents held on to it for him, hoping he'd return? Or had they simply not bothered to move his stuff?

He grabbed the lantern, lit it, and headed toward the path that led to the cabin. The trail was much clearer than when he'd left five months ago. Even if his parents remembered this cabin was here, they had no need to go back and forth from the cabin to their house or the barn. Either vagabonds or old drinking buddies were using it. Whatever the case, they had to go.

He climbed the two wooden steps to the cabin's front door and turned the knob. Locked. The place was dark, so he set the lantern on the porch floor, withdrew his hammer from his tool belt, and tapped on a window-pane in the door. The ancient glass shattered. He reached inside, twisted the deadbolt, and opened the door, taking the lantern in with him.

Frani was right. The place showed no signs of the mess he'd left. No empty beer bottles or pizza boxes scattered about. Instead, three brown cardboard boxes sat in a neat row on the floor along the edge of the wall. He pushed one with his foot. It had contents. Other than the boxes, the rooms were as bare as ever. Except for the trash being picked up, nothing seemed different…until he noticed the table beside the front door.

Flowers? Tiny blossoms, scrunched together and lying on a table. They reminded him of the ones his sister used to pick as a young girl and give to their mother. The depth of Mamm's loss hit him again, and he drew a deep breath.

An aroma of gardenias surrounded him, but the smell hadn't come from the scrawny, uprooted plants. Faint sounds of water dripping echoed against the quietness. He followed the noise, expecting to find a leaky faucet or broken water pipe.

As he drew closer to the bathroom, he noticed reflections on the hallway floor, apparently from candlelight flickering in the next room. The door to the bathroom stood ajar about two inches. He eased it open. A tendril of black smoke looped from an almost used-up candle. Bubbles, mounds of them, wavered in the tub as if someone had been there moments earlier.

He swung the lantern to cast light into the hallway behind him, making sure he wasn't about to get clobbered by a stranger. He saw no one.

Water swooshed, jerking his attention back to the bathroom. A woman's head and shoulders slowly came out of the water. She leaned back against the tub, wringing water from her long, black hair.

It seemed that she hadn't heard the glass shattering or him coming inside. He took a step back, aiming to get out of the cabin before he startled her or before her husband showed up. As he slowly took another step backward, the floorboard creaked.

She screamed. Not a dainty, feminine scream or even a frightened one. She was mad.

He hurried through the living room. Almost at the front door, he tripped over something. His kerosene lantern went one way and his hammer the other. His palms landed in broken glass, sending pain through him. He jumped to his feet, grabbed a couch cushion, and used it to douse the burning wick from the broken lantern.

The woman bounded out of the bathroom, holding the puny candle and wearing a housecoat...*his* housecoat. The one his mother had made for him as a Christmas present a few years back. She stood about five and a half feet tall and looked quite thin under that oversized housecoat.

She picked up his hammer and threatened to throw it at him. "I've told all of you before. Get out of my house!"

"Don't throw that. And this is not *your* house, lady."

She winged the hammer at him full force, and he jumped out of the way, but the tool still smacked him in the knee. "Ouch!" He rubbed his leg. "You're the one who's trespassing!"

"Why don't you idiots try coming up with a new line? I'm tired of that one."

"This *is* my place."

"Yours? Really." Her candle sputtered out. In the darkness she grabbed what sounded like a box of matches and struck one. She held it up toward him and gave him an unfriendly once-over. "That makes you Aaron Blank, I suppose."

"Ya." He wiped his slightly bleeding palm down a pant leg and then held out his hand. She didn't take it.

"Your Daed said you wouldn't be back."

"Nonetheless, here I am."

She tilted the match closer to him as if he might be a vision. "Great. This is just great." She yelped and slung the match from her. Within a few seconds, she'd lit another one. She moved to a gas pole lamp mounted on wheels that stood in the corner. After lighting it, she glared back at him. "Of all the deadbeats I've had to deal with—people removing the screens and crawling through the windows or poking screwdrivers through the screen door and letting themselves in even while I'm standing in plain sight—none of them did this kind of damage." She picked up the couch cushion and sniffed it. "Kerosene," she mumbled and tossed it back onto the floor.

Aaron glanced at the mess he'd made. It wasn't that bad. "Why did you say this is your home?"

Ignoring him, she went into the other room. When she returned, she had on shoes. She grabbed the kerosene-soaked couch cushion, and glass crunched under her soles as she walked to the front door and tossed the cushion outside. "Obviously, you haven't spoken to your parents about the transformation of this place from hangout to homestead."

"They know I used this place as a hangout?"

"Sure. And a lot more. Your Daed caught some of your *friends* here one night soon after you left, and they filled him in on everything."

Aaron shuddered to think of all she must have heard about him.

The wheels on the gas pole lamp clattered as she moved the light closer to study him. She didn't say it, but he clearly heard her: *Drunken louse!*

"And you have their permission to live here?"

"This is a dairy farm. It's not unusual to offer a place to live in exchange for help." She went back into the kitchen.

He picked up the remains of his lantern. "I should be going. You can tell your husband I'll have the glass in the door replaced."

She returned with a broom. The image seemed fitting. All she needed to do was climb aboard and ride it.

"If I were a man, would you assume I had a wife?"

"Well…no. But you said…" He tried to think of exactly what she'd said that made him think she was married. "I guess I thought… I mean, Daed would not hire just a woman to help with the farm work."

"Why? Because *just a woman* would do a worse job than you did?"

"You don't have to get ugly about it. I know I'm no dairy farmer." Aaron raised his hands. "I realize I got your dander up, intruding on you like I did. And rightly so. But can we call a truce?" He moved to the table and lifted the flowers toward her. "Please?"

She gave a disgusted sigh mixed with a faint laugh. "You're going to offer me wilted weeds that I picked myself?"

He shrugged.

"Fine." She took the pitiful-looking things. "Since you're not a dairy farmer, we shouldn't cross paths while I'm doing my job."

"You'd have to take up that request with my Daed. The prodigal son isn't supposed to come home unwilling to work for his meals and a place to sleep."

"Michael and I have an agreement. No one comes into the barn during milking times unless I've invited them."

"Then we don't have a problem." He went to the door. "I'll get the glass fixed tomorrow. Wait. Tomorrow's Sunday. I'll get it fixed Monday."

"No need. But thank you anyway."

"I really think I should." He put a bloody hand on his aching leg. "Mostly as a way to ward off any would-be trespassers. It'll protect them."

He was fairly sure he saw a smile underneath her obvious frustration.

"Any chance you know where my parents are?"

"They said they were going to Abner Mast's for the evening. Some kind of fellowship dinner's taking place there tonight."

"Okay. Denki. Good night."

"Good night."

He wondered if she milked the herd by herself, but he didn't dare ask. If all his father had for help was a girl, talking his folks into selling the farm would be easier than he'd imagined.

Six

Aaron jolted awake and jumped off the couch. Sunlight filled the room, as did the sounds of his mother making breakfast. A familiar ache moved inside him. He'd tried to wait up for them last night. Before nodding off, he'd left a note on his Mamm's pillow, telling them he was home and asking them to wake him when they got back.

They hadn't, so he prayed for the right words and walked into the kitchen. Only Mamm was in the room.

She turned to see him, but no smile crossed her face, and she didn't open her arms to hug him.

"I'm sorry, Mamm."

She pulled three plates out of the cabinet and set them on the table. "You should be." She backed away from him. "How could you just disappear like that? Your sister...died. And we needed you."

He pulled out a chair and sat. "I know. But I couldn't help anybody."

"I didn't even know you had a drinking problem until—"

"I'm better now." Aaron wondered if either of his parents had even opened the letters he'd sent them while in rehab.

His Daed came downstairs, wearing his Sunday best. He walked stiffly past Aaron without more than a glance at him and took his place at the head of the table. Mamm set a cup of coffee in front of him.

"Am I supposed to be honored you've returned?" his Daed asked.

"No. But I'd be honored if you'd hear me out."

His Daed looked at him directly for the first time. "Not on the Lord's Day."

"Tomorrow, then?"

Daed shrugged. "You will ask for forgiveness, and I will have no choice but to give it. But I can't imagine that you have anything else to say that I'll find useful."

His mother set a cup of coffee in front of Aaron and trailed her hand across his shoulders before taking her seat. It wasn't much in the way of affection, but it was better than her reaction a few minutes ago.

They bowed for the silent prayer. Not a word was spoken while they ate, not even an invitation for Aaron to join them for church. Did they not want the community to know he'd returned?

After eating very little, Daed rose. "I'll get the rig."

Mamm put the dishes in the sink and wiped off the table. That's all the cleaning the kitchen would get on a Sunday. "There's leftovers in the refrigerator for your lunch. It's not much."

"It'll be plenty."

A weak smile crossed her lips. "If you were to put on Sunday clothes and get in the buggy, he wouldn't throw you out."

"Denki, Mamm. But it'd be best if I wait until next time." Aaron wasn't ready to face everyone just yet.

She left the house, and Aaron sat back in his chair. The sounds of the horse and buggy going down the long driveway slowly faded.

"Home sweet home." He mumbled the words sarcastically, but he'd known coming back would be tough. He'd embarrassed his parents deeply and hurt them twice as much.

He intertwined his fingers, trying to find words to pray for them and himself, but he only heard the echo of his parents' silence.

A clanging sound came from the barn, drawing him to the window. His knee ached where that woman had hit him with his hammer.

About half the herd stood outside the milking parlor, banging their heads on the metal gate, wanting in. Surely his dad and the girl had milked the cows before church. Was that a person's shadow in the barn? He hustled out the door, trying to ignore the twinge in his knee.

Once inside the barn, he noticed the line of cows in the milking stalls. The woman from last night stood beside a cow, humming. Who hummed while milking?

Her black hair was loosely braided and hanging down one shoulder, but she wore a prayer Kapp. She couldn't be Amish. No way. She had on men's pants, a shirt, and suspenders—all of it looked like his clothes from when he was a scrawny teen. The pant legs stopped an inch or two above her ankles. He guessed she was his age. He had a hundred questions for her, and he intended to ask every one of them before leaving the barn.

She spotted him and nodded. "Aaron." Her smooth tone held a degree of politeness.

"I heard a racket."

"It's just me and the cows."

"And you are?"

She paused. "Oh. I assumed Michael had told you." She wiped her hand down a pant leg. "I'm Sylvia."

He shook her hand, caught off balance by her effort to be nice.

"You agreed last night not to trespass in the barn when I'm working, remember?"

"Of course I remember. I wasn't drunk."

Her eyebrows rose. "If you say so."

"I say so." He took the hose and rinsed the next cow's udder.

She tucked loose hair behind her ear. "I was hoping you and I wouldn't have to argue anymore." Her calm manner made her seem like a different person from the one he'd argued with last night.

"I know how you feel. You made that clear." But he wanted answers.

The best approach was probably to avoid being too personal too quickly, so he'd start out talking to her about the obvious thing—milking cows by herself on a Sunday morning. "Daed went to church this morning, so I guess Sundays are your day to milk alone."

She got the milk flowing with little effort. After dipping the cow's teats in the iodine solution and wiping them off, she attached the milkers. "*Alone* is the key word."

He'd worked by himself on Sundays a hundred times in order to avoid attending church, and he wondered if that was her reason too. "Nope. *Sunday* is the key word."

She rubbed her forehead, probably trying to figure out how to get rid of him.

He adjusted the pressure on the nozzle. "Daed was strong enough today to help milk cows. The two of you could have been done in plenty of time for church, but instead you're here, and he's gone."

The taut lines in her face told him a couple of things. One, he was right about *Sunday* being the key word. Two, she was a fairly easy read. He wasn't particularly good at reading people, at least he didn't think so, but this woman spoke loudly without saying a word.

"Look, I know every evasion tactic when it comes to avoiding church. You don't want to go? No one gets that more than I do. But I'm not leaving you with this herd to milk by yourself. No one has to know I helped. When we're done, you can go have an uninterrupted bubble bath."

She shook her head. "Can't you just respect my wishes?"

"Not today." He went down the line, preparing each cow. When his father's arthritis kicked up, Aaron had been expected to run the farm without anyone's help. His Daed shouldn't ask that of someone outside the family, and Aaron wouldn't allow it.

He pointed at her outfit. "Are you Amish? Or did you borrow that prayer Kapp like you borrowed my old clothes?"

"I was raised Amish, just like you. Much to my parents' disappointment, I haven't joined the faith."

"I get that. So, Sylvia, since we've established that you're Amish and that you avoid attending church, how many visits have you received from the local church leaders?"

"A few."

"Only a few?"

"Preacher Alvin told me about a woman named Cara that the church leaders have been dealing with. They feel they handled her situation too strictly and were unfair to her, so I'm reaping the benefits."

They worked side by side for a good fifteen minutes in complete silence. She refilled the troughs with feed, getting ready for the next group. "Isn't there somewhere else you'd rather be?"

He'd go see Frani later today and talk to her about trying to get clean. He figured he'd need to repeat that conversation numerous times before she began to hear him. But even if she was up, she'd have a monstrous hangover.

"Nope."

"Why come back now?"

He paused, unsure what to say. He couldn't discuss his plan until he'd revealed it to his parents, and they weren't ready to hear it yet. He shrugged. "It's home."

She stopped and stared at him. "You're here to stay?"

"It's complicated. I just... Actually, I'm not sure it concerns you."

"You're right. It was rude of me to ask."

He couldn't figure her out. The agitation between them was like two male cats squaring off, yet she spoke softly and seemed determined to be nice.

"Tell me about yourself. I've never heard of a woman running part of a farm on her own."

"Me either."

"But…" He elongated the word.

"Your Daed needed help, and I needed the work."

"I see."

"If you insist on staying in the barn against my wishes, I'd appreciate it if we could work without talking."

"Oh, come on. I'm not asking about your love life."

She bristled. He'd obviously hit a nerve. His conscience kicked him. He shouldn't be prying into her personal life. But goading people into disliking him came easy. He'd used it for years to keep up his defenses.

"Just explain to me why a young, single woman is handling a dairy herd."

Her hand moved gently down the cow's side. "Amish wives and daughters help run farms all the time. Is it that much of a stretch for me to work on one that doesn't belong to my parents or husband?"

"An Amish feminist. I bet that goes over well with the menfolk."

Her brows furrowed, and he saw innocence reflected in her eyes. "An Amish what?"

"Never mind. So where's your family?"

"Path Valley."

"Where's that?"

"Two hours northwest of here by carriage."

"That's quite a ways."

"I…I think it's far enough."

Was that fear in her voice? The girl he met last night didn't seem prone to being afraid. "So what's his name?"

After a sigh she picked up one of the buckets and headed for the milk house.

Instead of badgering her with questions, he should've been emptying those heavy buckets. He moved toward her, reaching for the sealed bucket.

"I'm fine."

"Please."

She stopped and let the bucket thud onto the ground.

Aaron tried to suppress his smile.

Her face flushed. "Please just get out. What is wrong with men your age? Is it impossible to respect the wishes of a female?"

"Maybe your wishes lack good sense."

She closed her eyes for several long seconds. When she opened them, she picked up a half-empty bucket and its claw milker, went to the next cow, and began humming.

He knew he was acting like a jerk, and he couldn't explain why he was putting so much effort into irritating her. This wasn't who he was. Not really, and certainly not when sober. That question circled his mind as he took two full buckets into the milk house, removed the lids, and dumped the contents into the bulk tank.

With empty buckets in hand, he reentered the milking parlor. Although he didn't spot her immediately, he followed the sound of her humming and found her on a milking stool in the tenth stall.

He started to apologize several times, but he wasn't able to say the words. He sighed and picked up another full bucket to take to the milk house.

"It's obvious that you don't want to be here." She glanced up at him from her milking stool. "Perhaps next time you can follow that instinct and avoid coming into my barn."

Her barn?

He paused, thinking of what he knew about her and had seen in her eyes and actions since the moment he'd found her in the cabin. Last night he'd thought his father had hired only a girl when this place needed a team. There was just one of her, but she had fearless grit and determination, both of which would make his task harder.

But he'd succeed. He had no choice.

No single individual had enough strength to make this place profitable. She'd grow weary of trying or fall in love at some point, marry, and move off. It was inevitable. But he didn't have time to wait for either of those scenarios.

He needed his parents to open their eyes about the farm's condition—and the changes to his character. And his best chance of getting them to agree to his plan was to get Sylvia to quit and go back home.

But how?

Sylvia walked to the creek behind her cabin. Loneliness weighed heavier on Sundays. Only work that was absolutely necessary was allowed on a Sabbath, which meant she could milk the herd and nothing else. All those unoccupied hours gave her time to really miss her sisters, especially Ruth.

Sunlight sparkled off the murky water. The cows were probably upstream, wading in the creek to cool off. The temperature had to be nearing the nineties, and it was only early June. The almanac said this summer would be unusually hot and dry, which would take a hard toll on livestock and crops.

She needed to be working—cutting hay, scrubbing the milk house and parlor for inspection, and tending to the cows' hoofs and udders, for starters. Michael said the farm had a lot of debt, but if she kept her nose to the grindstone, this place was bound to become profitable soon. He hadn't shared the financials with her, but it couldn't be that bad.

Hearing the sound of crunching gravel, she walked to a clearing to catch a glimpse of its source.

Aaron Blank was finally leaving the house.

She'd like to know why he'd come home. Michael had told her that Aaron cared nothing for dairy farming, so he hadn't come back to work.

With him gone for a while, she could visit with Michael and Dora and enjoy the kind of Sundays she'd had since arriving here. She went to the old homestead and knocked lightly as she stepped inside. No one greeted her.

That wasn't normal. She went into the living room. Michael sat on the couch, staring out a window. Dora was in her rocker, holding a book, but she wasn't reading.

"Hello?" Sylvia whispered.

Michael turned to her with a forced smile. "I've been wondering where you were."

He didn't sound like himself.

"*Kumm rei,* Sylvia. We could use a bit of cheering up." Dora lifted her book. "I can't get enough light to be able to see."

"And you can't find your glasses, right?" Sylvia looked around, trying to spot them. She snatched them off the top shelf of a bookcase and passed them to Dora. "Now, who do you think put them way up there?" She eyed Michael.

He smiled again, this time a real smile. "I look better to her when she can't find those things."

Dora put on her glasses and began reading.

Sylvia hadn't seen the Blanks look this sad in months. When she'd arrived, neither Dora nor Michael had any words left in them. They'd been blessed with only two children. Their daughter, Elsie, had died eight months earlier in a terrible accident, and their son, Aaron, had left without a word three months later and entered rehab.

Sylvia, Michael, and Dora had spent their evenings together during the cold winter months after she arrived. She and Michael played games and read. She and Dora baked and sewed. After a while Michael and Dora slowly began to open up. Dora had said that talking to an outsider helped them. And it had helped Sylvia feel as if she mattered. After leaving her parents and sisters, she needed someone to treat her like family.

"What was the sermon about today?" Not that she wanted to know. But talking about religious things always lifted Michael's and Dora's spirits.

Within an hour they were relaxed and appeared to be feeling better, just as Sylvia expected. She took the Old Maid cards out of the drawer, and Michael joined her at the table for a game.

Dora took off her glasses and adjusted the frames. "Michael, did you use my glasses for reading last night?"

"Hush now, Dora." Michael grinned. "You're going to give Sylvia the idea we're a cranky old couple."

"Nothing worse than someone thinking that." Sylvia shuffled the deck.

"We are not a cranky old *couple*," Dora retorted. "He's the only crank."

Sylvia burst into laughter and dealt the cards.

Michael picked up his hand. "Aaron's back."

Afraid he might read her displeasure if she looked at him, Sylvia kept her focus on rearranging her cards. "We met when he came by the cabin last night."

She wouldn't mention his being in the milking barn that morning. Fresh grief had settled over Michael and Dora for reasons she didn't understand, and she wouldn't add to their sadness by insisting Michael keep Aaron out of the barn. Either she'd convince Aaron herself, or she'd have to accept that he did what he wanted.

Michael laid down his pairs. "I talked to Clay Severs last week. I think we can get a good price for our hay if it is an early cut. If we wait, he's likely to buy it elsewhere."

She spread her cards on the table facedown. "I'm ready to start cutting hay tomorrow right after we do the morning milking."

"I wanted to talk to you about that." Michael chose one of her cards and added it to his hand. "While Aaron's here, he needs to work. I'll still help with the milking, but it'll make your day easier if he and I do the hay. After all, you have an inspection to get ready for."

Her pulse quickened. She liked the idea of not having to bale hay but wasn't thrilled about Aaron being the one to help. She could see two possible scenarios. Since he'd left the farm in ill shape, he might unintentionally damage her and Michael's efforts. Or maybe he'd returned to prove that he could be a valuable worker after all. Then he might take over everything important to her...just as Elam had.

Seven

Lena sat under a huge shade tree in her brother's yard, enjoying a lazy Sunday afternoon despite the fact that her arm inside the cast itched like crazy in the heat. Her Daed and all her siblings, their spouses, and their children were here at Allen's. Adults and children sipped lemonade, ate cookies, and played badminton, horseshoes, and games of tag.

Wishing Grey were here, she kept glancing at the bridge that connected his property to her brother's. She held her two-and-a-half-month-old niece, who was fidgeting and fussy, and her Daed sat in a lawn chair next to her. She and her Daed had always been close but even more so after her mother had passed away.

Lena cuddled and jiggled baby Elizabeth. "Your mama will come feed you soon." After a bit of cooing to her, Lena drew a toothless smile from the baby. The warmth of holding a little one brought her such joy and hope that she wondered how it would be possible to love a child of her own even more.

She peered through a gap in the lilac bushes, looking for Grey.

Daed leaned closer. "You can't miss him already. You were together just last night."

"Ya. But we were interrupted, and I want to really *see* him. And to be together without the concern of hurting the Blanks."

She and Grey had enjoyed two hours together at the shop, cleaning it and then playing cards with Cara and Ephraim. But then Ephraim's Daed walked in with Michael and Dora, wanting to show them a cabinetry project. Their pained expressions when they saw their former son-in-law laughing and at ease were too much to bear.

She didn't like sneaking around to catch a few minutes with Grey. She loved him enough to put all of herself into his hands—her soul, her body, her future. And she believed God's goodness had brought them together. But to court openly right now would wound Michael and Dora, and she couldn't do that.

"You're the one who convinced Grey to keep your relationship a secret from the community," her Daed said.

After Grey had saved her life a few weeks ago, then refused to leave her side at the hospital, some folks became suspicious about their relationship, including the church leaders. It felt wrong to hide their romance, as they'd been friends since childhood and hadn't begun falling in love until several months after his wife had died. But Grey and Lena had chosen to protect Michael and Dora's feelings by giving them a year to grieve the loss of their only daughter before Grey and Lena started courting.

Very few people knew about their plan to start courting in the fall: Grey's coworker and friend, Ephraim Mast, and his fiancée, Cara; Lena's brother Allen, who was Grey's closest friend and her closest sibling, along with his wife, Emily; and, of course, her Daed.

"I stand by my decision, Daed, but I ache to go for long rides or walks and talk for hours. When we made our choice, I didn't realize how long spring and summer would last."

"You chose to honor others over yourself. Don't regret that just because it's difficult."

His words worked their way into the deepest parts of her. If anyone knew about being patient for the sake of someone else's feelings, her Daed did. He'd been a widower for fourteen years, and he'd tried to court Ada, without success, for the past five, maybe longer. At least they were occasionally seeing each other now.

She leaned over and looped her arm through his. "I have the best Daed there is."

He squared his shoulders. "I know."

Lena chuckled.

A rig of Amish folks from within the community arrived. They climbed out of the wagon and filled the yard, ready to play games and enjoy a Sunday afternoon.

Her Daed nodded toward the bridge.

Grey's five-year-old son, Ivan, raced over it. Lena looked through the shrubbery that ran along the creek bank to see if Grey was crossing the yard.

Because Grey was a widower and Lena's face was marred with a noticeable birthmark, many would think he was marrying her merely because he needed a wife for himself and a mother for his son. At first, despite how much she loved him, she'd had her own doubts about how Grey really felt and why, but he and God helped her see the truth. Grey had told her, "I know what people are going to think, but we know what is between us. Truth of what exists between couples is all that matters."

When he'd said that, she saw into him, and she knew their love was everything she'd hoped for. And at twenty-four, she'd had lots of time to build her hopes.

She caught a glimpse of him as he stepped into the clearing, and joy coursed through her. When he crossed the bridge they'd built, it was all she could do not to run into his arms.

Grey spoke to her siblings, in-laws, and friends as he'd always done at gatherings, but she knew he was trying to appear nonchalant as he came toward her.

Her Daed stood. "Grey."

Grey walked over to him and shook his hand. "Hello, Israel. Beautiful out here, ya?"

Her Daed glanced at Lena, not the least bit fooled by Grey. "Ya, it is. Sit, please. I'm going to the side yard to check on my grandchildren."

Her Daed had given them a minute to talk.

With his back to everyone but her, Grey approached the chair. His eyes connected with hers, and she felt his love all the way to her toes. "Hi, Lennie." He took Daed's seat and leaned in to adjust the baby's prayer Kapp. As he did, he placed his hand over Lena's for a moment. "I was beginning to think Ivan would never wake up so we could walk over here."

"Ah, so that was the holdup."

He sat back. "He doesn't usually take long naps, so I figured he really needed it."

"Sounds like a reasonable assumption. I dreamed about him the other night. You know, cooking meals for him and reading to him."

Grey interlaced his fingers, looking thoughtful, but he'd barely uttered a syllable when Lena's sister-in-law Emily interrupted them.

"You must be ready for a break."

Lena studied the beauty of her niece. "Never."

"Still." Emily lifted her fussy daughter from Lena's arms.

Grey stood, offering his chair to Emily. "I should probably go play a game of horseshoes."

Lena nodded. If he stayed with her too long, it'd draw attention.

While chatting with her sister-in-law, Lena saw movement on the road. A man. He looked familiar.

Aaron.

She stood and began hobbling toward him. When she reached Grey, she tugged on his arm. "Look. It's Aaron." Her friend had quite a stride, and she needed to hurry before he was gone again. "Aaron!"

Grey put a supportive hand under her good arm as they continued toward the road. "Easy, Lennie."

Aaron turned, and the moment he saw her, he grinned and began closing the gap between them. He engulfed her in a gentle hug.

"Look at you." Lena put space between them.

"I sure have missed you." His eyes moved to her cast and the medical boot on her foot. "I didn't realize you'd been this injured. Your letter only said you were bruised all over."

"I'm mending just fine."

Aaron and Grey looked unsure how to greet each other. They'd been brothers-in-law for nearly six years, but Lena had no idea what their relationship had been like. Strained, she'd guess, with Aaron's drinking.

Aaron held out his hand. Grey took it and pulled him into a hug. "I'm proud of you for going for help like you did, and I'm glad you're home."

Aaron backed away, staring blankly. "I…I appreciate that." After several long moments he turned to Lena. "Are you really okay?"

"I promise. So when did you get back?"

"Last night after dark."

"Tell me how you're doing."

He looked at all the people in the yard. "Not here. Can we go for a walk?"

"I'm barely off my crutches, so I can't do much walking. But we can pull a set of chairs into a more private spot in the yard."

He nodded toward the guests. Several people were glancing his way and whispering.

"Or we can go for a ride in Daed's rig, and you can tell me everything," Lena said. "But first you should say hello to everyone."

"Nobody except you wants to see me." He looked at Grey. "Sorry, but I know it's true."

Grey put his hand on Aaron's shoulder. "That's not true of me. I hold nothing against you. But you and Lennie should go for that ride. If you ever care to come by the house, I'd like that."

"And I'll help break the ice with everyone here." Lena slipped her hand into his and squeezed it. "There won't be a better time than now."

Aaron hesitated, studying the crowd.

Grey squeezed his shoulder. "I'll hitch the horse to the rig for you and Lennie while you shake folks' hands."

Aaron nodded. "All right. Let's do this."

She turned to everyone. "Look who's here." Smiling with confidence, Lena silently dared any of them to give Aaron a lukewarm reception.

Cara had never been a fan of Mondays, but having to study the handwritten pages in front of her made this one worse. She put her elbows on Ada's kitchen table. *"Begreiflich."* She had no doubt she'd butchered the pronunciation, but she should know the meaning by now. Sighing, she turned the paper over to find the answer.

Begreiflich meant "easy."

Yeah, right.

Ada set a cup of coffee and a slice of pie in front of her. "I heard that sigh. Maybe this will help."

Through the kitchen window, Cara saw Deborah hanging laundry on the line. Cara's eight-year-old daughter, Lori, chased her dog, Better Days, with a hose, and he in turn chased her. Cara removed her prayer Kapp and the rubber band holding back her rather short ponytail. She ran her fingers through her hair. "How am I ever going to learn this?"

Ada took a seat. "Well, the good news is the church leaders want you to pass. So they're not going to do any nitpicking."

"But I'm tired of sitting through services that make no sense, though

I do like Ephraim explaining it all later in the day. Why is learning Pennsylvania Dutch so hard?"

"You've only been here a little more than a year, Cara. And look at all you've learned. You've been focusing on the heart of matters. Ya?"

"It's hard to believe I'm the same person I used to be. But if I'm honest with myself about all the garbage I still carry, I can't believe how far I have to go."

"You'll get there, dear, because you're in love."

"So much so it's almost sickening." Cara chuckled. "But for some reason I can't manage to tell Ephraim how I really feel. I beat around the bush and make wisecracks."

"I think he knows. Loving and gentle words don't come easy for you. They don't come easy for me either."

"You say lots of loving things to Deborah and me."

Ada sipped her coffee. "Ya, but you two are like daughters to me. You're each a gift from God, for which I'll always be grateful. Still, I would like to be able to voice how I feel to a man."

Cara leaned back, enjoying Ada's openness. The woman was like a mom one moment, a best friend another, and always a trusted confidante. Truth was, Cara had never been around a mother and her adult children. Was this what it was like? "Just any man or one in particular?"

Ada's eyes flashed with surprise at Cara's question, but before Cara could coax a response, someone knocked on the door.

Ada stood. "I think I've been saved by the bell…or rather a knock. You study, and stop thinking about Ephraim."

"That's impossible," Cara called after her.

As she looked over her notes, she heard Ada talking and then her footsteps coming closer. "Cara."

When she looked up, she saw that Ada's face had lost all its color. "There's a man at the door. It's…Trevor Atwater."

Cara trembled. "Are you sure?"

"I looked at his ID."

Images flooded Cara's mind. Her mother hiding her in the attic to keep her out of his sight. Standing at her mother's casket. Her dad taking her to the bus station. Him demanding that she, an eight-year-old girl, stay put as he turned his back on her and walked off. Horrible emotions pounded her like claps of thunder.

"I'll take care of it," she said. "Thanks."

The hallway between the kitchen and the foyer had never seemed so long.

He stood in the entryway. It turned her stomach to see him in Ada's home. She motioned for them to go onto the front porch, and they went outside. Sarcastic, bitter words came to mind. "Can I help you?"

"Carabean, it's me…Dad."

Only her mother had called her that and only at really tender moments. Cara called her daughter "Lorabean" at such times. But this man had no right.

"Cara," she corrected. Actually she'd prefer "Mrs. Moore." Or better yet, for him never to say her name at all.

He nodded respectfully, looking unsure of himself. "I've been thinking about what your little girl said…"

"You had no right to approach my daughter and ask her leading questions."

He wouldn't have had the chance to talk to Lori if Ada's House, with its outdoor booths and activities, weren't a place for tourists. He'd hung around the booth where Cara sold desserts and drinks, and he'd bought items and talked to Lori and her for weeks before he said something that made her suspect who he was.

"I was trying to figure things out." His eyes reflected bewilderment. "But I understand less now than ever. Your daughter said something about the two of you living in a barn and your not having been here very long. I don't understand, and I need to."

You need? What did she care what he needed?

Sarcasm begged to be unleashed, but thoughts of Ephraim and the need to protect her standing in the community caused her to keep control. "It's a long, personal story, one I'm not interested in sharing with you."

He didn't flinch or show anger. He seemed resigned to her dislike of him. "You have plenty of reasons for being angry with me. But I want to make things right."

She laughed. "Is this some type of reality show? Are there cameras somewhere that I can't see? Surely that's the only thing that would make you say something so..." Ephraim surfaced in her mind again, and Cara shut up. She cleared her throat. "I don't need you to do anything except leave me alone."

"But I have to know, Carabea— Cara. Lori said you don't know the language, but you must have learned some of it while growing up in Dry Lake with Emma and Levi."

As a child, Cara was supposed to have been passed off to Levi, her mom's brother, and his wife, Emma. They were going to raise her, but...

"No comment."

"But I'm your dad."

"My father was a drunk. And Mom hid me from you as much as she could until she died. I was told a car struck her. Is that true? Or did you kill her while I was tucked away in that tiny wall space?"

His expression became defensive. "Of course not. Your mom meant everything to me. She was walking to work, and a car ran a red light, hitting several pedestrians. She was the only one who died."

He rattled off the horror like a well-rehearsed performance, but her body shook the way it had the day she learned her mom was dead. Her mother had loved her and had tried hard to protect her. What had this man done?

She wrapped her arms around herself to keep from striking him. "I needed a lot of things from you growing up, and I got none of them." The words came out hoarse and shaky. "For the first time since Mom died, I have a chance to choose who and what I want and to be happy. But my chance is fragile." She hated being so vulnerable with him. "So can you please just leave me alone?"

"But Emma and Levi were supposed to—"

"You stupid, drunken idiot! Don't you dare talk to me about what Emma and Levi were supposed to do. You left me at a bus station! No one showed up for me but the authorities. I was hauled off to foster care. And here's the kicker: those were some of the best years of my stinking life!"

The man clutched the porch railing. "No. You're wrong. I made sure you were with Emma before I left."

"You dreamed that up so you could live with yourself. With the help of Mom's diary, I found my way here a year ago. A year ago!" She pointed her finger in his face. "Go drown yourself in drink, and leave me alone!"

"Cara." Ada's arm slipped around her. "Kumm."

Nothing felt real, not Ada's tenderness or standing on the porch or finally facing her dad. She could be caught in a dream for all she knew. In spite of Ada's prompting, she couldn't stop venting her fury on the man before her.

"All you had to do was pass me off like some stupid baton in a relay race, and you couldn't even do that. Mom would hate you for that."

"Kumm, Cara." Ada tugged at her. "Now."

She pulled Cara inside and closed the door.

Shaking as if she were having a seizure, Cara paced the floors, ranting. "Idiot. He has no clue. None." When she looked up, Ada wasn't there, but Lori was.

"Mama, what's wrong?" Tears filled Lori's eyes. She ran to her mother and wrapped her arms around her waist. "You're scaring me."

Cara breathed deeply, trying to calm herself, but she felt terrified and powerless. The old, uncontrollable anger had taken over, just as it had when she ran away from foster care, fueling her ability to survive. *Oh, God, help me.* She didn't know anything else to pray.

Cara patted Lori's back. "I'm fine, and so are you. Dry your tears." She pulled Lori free of her. "There's nothing to cry about."

"Cara?" Deborah spoke softly as she entered the room. "Is there anything I can do?"

Cara looked at her daughter. "You stay with Deborah for a little while. I need to go for a walk, okay?"

Lori wiped her eyes. "I want to go with you."

Deborah corralled Lori. "Let's make double-fudge cookies. Big fat ones. When your mom gets back, they'll make her feel better."

A tentative smile eased across Lori's lips. "Okay."

As the two of them headed toward the kitchen, Cara went to the window. Ada stood on the sidewalk, talking to *him*.

She hated him. It didn't matter that she wasn't supposed to. There was no way to get free of what he'd done to her life, just as there was no way to escape her hate.

When she'd seen him a few weeks ago, she'd thought she could cope. She'd known his presence would be a difficult obstacle, but now she knew she couldn't tolerate him. If the church leaders discovered her weakness, they'd tell her she needed at least another year of growing spiritually and learning before she could join the faith.

Ada stepped inside, closed the front door, and leaned against it. "He's gone."

"Forever?" Cara's voice sounded small and vulnerable. She didn't want to feel anything for her dad, not anger or compassion or anything.

"I don't know." Ada drew a shaky breath. "You were merciless, Cara."

"He lived exactly as he wanted, and I'm supposed to walk on eggshells so he doesn't feel too bad about it?"

Ada closed her eyes. "I'm not saying you weren't justified in your reaction to him. I'm sure you didn't come close to unleashing all the pent-up anger you've stored over the years. But if you want to be free of him, you have to extend what he doesn't deserve—mercy and grace."

"I have no clue what that means." Cara flew out the front door and slammed it behind her.

Eight

Aaron stood in the equipment shop, dripping with sweat as he continued to fight with the blades on the hay mower. His fourth day back home, and he'd accomplished nothing. Not clearing the air, mending relationships, taking any stress off his parents, or making headway toward returning to Owl's Perch. He tried to loosen the bolts that would free the blades of the hay mower.

If you'd cleaned it properly last year…

He'd spent yesterday cleaning last year's dried mud and hay off the mower. As soon as he finished removing the blades, he'd sharpen them and put the rig back together, and then, joy of all joys, he'd be ready to start mowing the hayfield.

Disgusted and irritable, he set another blade next to the grinding wheel.

His Mamm was warming up to him some, but his father had little to say. Daed had listened while Aaron asked for forgiveness yesterday, but he'd walked out of the room when Aaron tried to explain about his past behavior and addiction.

He was used to the silence between them. It'd been that way for nearly ten years, except now there was clearly unspoken anger in the silence.

He'd earned their anger and lack of respect, but if they could see their way clear to forgive him, they'd realize that he was trying to do the right thing by them. Farm work was no picnic, but the real problem was the unspoken resentment between him and his father.

However, his folks certainly liked Sylvia. When she walked into the house for meals, Daed became someone Aaron didn't even recognize. He was kind and witty. Aaron didn't blame Sylvia. It wasn't her fault. But she believed that with enough effort the farm could be profitable. Only a fool thought the *Titanic* could be patched with a little elbow grease and kept afloat.

The dinner bell rang.

Despite being hungry, he preferred not to go inside for another round of tactful coldness. But he would. He wiped his hands on a greasy cloth and tossed it onto the workbench.

When he entered the house, he saw his mother at the stove but no sign of his Daed or Sylvia. "Smells delicious in here, Mamm."

She smiled without making eye contact. "It'll be ready by the time you wash up."

Walking up the stairs to his room, he removed his suspenders, unbuttoned his shirt, and peeled out of it and his T-shirt. A two-minute shower would help.

He opened the door to his room and found Sylvia asleep on his bed. She had on a dress, but her prayer Kapp and black apron were lying on the chair.

"Aaron, honey?" his Mamm whispered loudly as she topped the stairs.

He pulled the door closed. "Let me guess. You forgot to tell me she takes naps in my room."

Mamm wiped her hands on a dishtowel. "It's the quietest and coolest room during the day. She was out all night dealing with a calving. You can wash up in our room. I imagine she'll sleep awhile today. She never made it to her own bed last night."

He curbed his desire to remark that she still hadn't managed to make it to her own bed. Was everything that had once been his now hers? "Not a problem."

"There's a basket of clean towels and clothes on my bed."

After a quick shower he went downstairs.

Daed walked in, carrying the mail. "Are you going to be able to get that hay mower in working order or not?" Daed hadn't glanced up to acknowledge Aaron's presence or mumbled one *hello* since Aaron had arrived home, but he wanted updates on his work. Daed sat at the table and began opening the bills.

Aaron moved to his chair. "It'll work—not great, but it'll do its job. The blades still need sharpening. If I can get them to hold an edge, we'll be okay. It's a really thick crop of hay this year."

"Sylvia fertilized the fields with chicken manure a couple of times so we could get a bumper crop."

"Of course she did," Aaron mumbled.

"What's that supposed to mean?"

"She's…different."

"Ya, she is." His Daed didn't seem to mind her strangeness even though his parents were as traditional as they came. Maybe their need for her had stretched their capacity to tolerate differences in people.

"We even managed to get the dent corn planted in the west field." Daed opened a business-sized white envelope. "It'll take time to get us out of the hole we're in, but Sylvia and I are making progress." He stared at the DairyAll bill he'd pulled out.

DairyAll provided equipment for farmers and carried loans for the purchases. His folks had owed them money since the day Daed had bought this place. Daed laid the bill on the table, and Aaron caught a glimpse of it.

"Horse neck." He picked it up and studied it. "We owe that much?"

"We?" His Daed took it from him, folded it, and slid it back into the envelope.

Mamm passed Aaron a glass of icy lemonade. "A cooling tank went out, along with sterilizing equipment and half the milkers. It all had to be replaced last winter."

He set the drink down. "That payment is three months overdue. And it mentions putting a lien on the place in four weeks if a payment isn't made."

"I know all that," Daed snapped. "What do you think, Son, that I'm too stupid to understand what the statement says?"

Aaron bit his tongue and willed himself to speak quietly. "No, of course not. It shocked me, and I was thinking out loud."

"Do me a favor and don't use that super-nice, you're-an-idiot tone with me."

Aaron nodded. Even his effort to sound respectful had managed to annoy his father.

Daed put the bill beside his plate. "If we get that hay in and sold, we can make at least one full payment, maybe one and a half. That will keep the threat of the lien at bay for a while. If the weather cooperates, we might get three harvests this year."

Aaron groaned inwardly. "And you'll face something similar again next year and the next. There are easier ways to make a living, ones that aren't filled with *ifs*." He took a breath. "You could sell the farm."

"That's ridiculous, although I'm not surprised you are suggesting it. I'm a farmer. I farm."

"Daed…could you bear with me and listen for just a few minutes, please?"

"You won't stop at a few minutes."

"Please."

Daed pulled out his pocket watch, opened it, and laid it on the table. He folded his arms. "You have two minutes."

"This place is too much for you. Maybe if your rheumatoid arthritis didn't keep you from working some of the time, it wouldn't be. But it is.

I'm not the same man who left here five months ago. I'm clean. I'm here to help you get out from under this place. There are other jobs you'd enjoy and could do."

"Like what?"

"Well…what about selling appliances to Amish folks?"

"Appliances?" Similar looks of displeasure appeared on his parents' faces.

"I've put money down on Plain People's Appliances. It's a store in Owl's Perch."

"Our family has farmed for as far back as the records show, and you want us to move to town and sell machines?"

"I know it sounds strange to you right now, but it's work we can do together as a family. It'll be much easier on your joints. We'll be closer to doctors and pharmacies and—"

"Sylvia, honey," Mamm interrupted him. "Kumm."

Sylvia stood in the doorway, apron on and prayer Kapp in place, looking at him as if he were a monster.

"Did we wake you?" Daed closed his watch and put it back into his pocket.

"No."

"Gut. I saw that new calf and her mama. They both look strong and healthy. You're doing great."

"Denki."

Aaron was sure she would continue doing great, until Daed wore her out. Then again, Daed acted different with Sylvia. Kinder. Gentler. Was it just an act?

Mamm set the casserole on the table. Sylvia stared at Aaron, shaking her head as if she couldn't believe the kind of man he was. Guilt tried to climb into the pit of his stomach and steal his appetite, but he had nothing to feel bad about. His parents were his responsibility. She was merely the hired help, and he didn't owe her anything.

Sylvia went to the cabinet and grabbed a serving bowl, then dumped peas from the stovetop into it. After a flurry of activity, with the two women getting items from the fridge, oven, and stovetop to the table, all four of them bowed their heads for silent prayer.

His Daed shifted, letting everyone know prayer time had ended. Then he sliced the meatloaf and passed the platter to Sylvia. She took a serving and passed the plate to Aaron. Bowls of vegetables were swapped back and forth until everyone had a full plate.

Sylvia put a napkin in her lap. "We have ten heifers on track for calving between now and September. With any luck we won't lose a heifer or a calf in the process. Then we can get the mamas back in with the milking population and have a few bull calves we can sell."

Aaron had put a new venture on the table for his Daed to consider, and now this girl was casually filling his head with false hope, talking about the herd as if they were turning milk into gold. She'd done a remarkable job on the farm. He wouldn't argue that. But it wasn't enough. When it came to the Blank dairy farm, it'd never be enough.

He downed his drink, wishing she wasn't there so he and his Daed could really talk.

"With that kind of progress, I'm sure we won't need to sell," his Daed said.

Aaron set his glass on the table. "Daed, we should talk about that privately."

"Sylvia's worked here from before sunup to after sundown for four months, and although milk production still has a long way to go, she's helped turn things around. She loves this farm the way I'd always hoped you would and the way I still hope my grandson will one day. It's worth hanging on to for Ivan."

"Ivan, Daed. Really?" Aaron tried to keep the disrespect from his tone. Ivan hadn't even begun school yet, and when he graduated, years from now, Aaron was confident he wouldn't be interested in farming.

Grey hadn't been. Over the years Grey had pitched in if they were in a bind, but he'd never considered quitting his work at the cabinetry shop to make his living on this farm. And Aaron's sister had never asked him to. Their son was like Grey. Even with his disability, he loved woodwork and carving. Aaron believed Ivan would follow in his father's footsteps. Besides, with the financial mess the farm was in, his parents couldn't afford to hold on to it until Ivan was old enough to be of real help.

The hurt in Daed's eyes lasted only a moment. "I won't talk of selling, especially behind Sylvia's back."

Aaron propped his forearms on the table, staring at her. "She's a hired hand, not someone who should've worked her way into your hearts and loyalties."

"Don't you talk to me about loyalty, Son."

"Daed, I'm—"

"We're not discussing this."

"No, of course not."

Daed passed the DairyAll bill to Sylvia. "Aaron saw this, and he thinks we should sell. I don't agree, but it's time you knew the truth of what we're facing."

Aaron figured his Daed was telling her now because if he didn't, Aaron might.

Concern lined her features as she studied the bill. "What's a lien?"

Daed shrugged and pushed his plate away. "Nothing to worry about with the progress we're making."

Aaron wondered if she recognized how absurd it was for his Daed to show her the statement and then skirt around explaining it.

Sylvia turned to his mother. "Dora?"

Mamm's eyes filled with tears, and she shook her head. This was so typical of his parents, shrugging off their problems even when directly asked about them. Aaron didn't consider himself any better when it came to coping skills, though. His tendency had been to drown himself in beer so he didn't have to face his issues.

"We're in default on a loan," Aaron said. "Because of that, DairyAll has the legal right to put a lien on the property. It means they get their money first when the farm is sold."

"We're not selling, so what difference does that make?"

"If they put a lien on the place, Daed will owe more money than the farm is worth. A place can't be sold for more than it's worth."

"But if he's not interested in selling," Sylvia insisted, "it doesn't matter, right?"

"He also can't borrow more money if—no, *when* something else goes wrong," Aaron said. "If equipment goes out and he can't afford to fix it, you'll be milking by hand, and production will drop. And he'll have to buy feed rather than grow it. If he can't sell enough milk to pay the mortgage, he'll lose the farm, and his credit will be worthless. He'll have nowhere to—"

"Okay," Daed bellowed. "She's got the idea."

Sylvia stared at the DairyAll statement. "This is bad news, certainly. But I don't see how it changes anything. Our plan all along was to get the bills paid." She tilted her head, making Daed look at her. "Right?"

"Ya." His Daed sounded weary. "But the pressure is on. It's almost mid-June already, and we haven't made our first cut. We've got to get that hay cut and out of the field. If we have enough help to accomplish that before it rains again, we can get top dollar for it. Can we depend on you?" Daed kept his eyes on his plate, but everyone knew the question was directed at Aaron.

"I'm here to help," Aaron said, "but I think you have to be realistic. The debt outweighs our resources. After the hay is harvested and sold, you and Mamm need to go with me to Owl's Perch and look at the shop."

"No thanks."

"In exchange for your coming to see it and really hearing me out, I'll give this farm my all for the next ten weeks." Aaron figured he had nothing to lose by that deal. He was stuck here regardless.

"Ten weeks?" Mamm asked.

"That's when I need to be back in Owl's Perch." He had nearly two more weeks after that date before he *had* to be there to take over the shop, but there was no sense in telling them. He was going to be in Owl's Perch as close to mid-August as possible. He needed the training time before Leo retired.

His father raised his eyes, studying his son. "There's no way to know if you're telling the truth about helping out through the summer. You lied to us for years, never doing half of what you were supposed to do."

"That's a warped perspective. You were laid up in bed most of the time, unable to work. I really tried, but you got up just long enough to see what I hadn't accomplished, never once mentioning what I had done."

Daed stood, his chest puffed in challenge. "You've always had your own slant, your half-truths and lies. I bought this place for you, and you ran out on us!"

Aaron rose to his feet, daring to meet his Daed's challenge eye to eye. "For me? Really, Daed? You're going to call *me* a liar and then make a statement like that? Did I ask for a farm?"

Daed put an arthritic finger in Aaron's face. "I'm supposed to sell the farm, move elsewhere, and trust you won't up and leave us? I don't trust you into next week, let alone next year."

"I've changed! Maybe if you'd talk to me instead of avoiding me, you could see that. I'm clean now. And I've come back here because it's the right thing to do. I'm the only family you have left."

"You've come back here because you need something from me. I don't know what it is yet, but there's a reason."

Aaron wished he could say no, wished Leo hadn't required him to get his Daed to cosign. Instead he tried to keep a blank face while sidestepping his Daed's question. It'd be best to keep the request for the signature to himself for now.

"Michael." Mamm moved to stand between them. "We need his help, and he's offered us two and a half months in exchange for one day of our attention."

Daed turned to Sylvia. "He'll run off or do shoddy work. You need to know that."

She reached across the table and picked up the pile of bills. "Until then, he'll help us. We need him."

Aaron loved being treated like a pack mule, especially by a young woman who stood to gain too much by his efforts. Then again, he needed her help to keep DairyAll from putting a lien on the farm.

Daed sighed. "Okay. You work through the summer, and your Mamm and I will go see this store."

"And listen while I explain the ins and outs of that kind of business."

"Ya."

"Then it's a deal."

"You two sit." Mamm went to the refrigerator. "It's time for dessert."

They took their seats.

She pulled out a plate and set it in front of Aaron. "I fixed your favorite."

"Peanut butter pie. It looks fabulous." Aaron lifted his fork. "Denki, Mamm."

"So this shop is in Owl's Perch?" Mamm gave Daed a piece of pie. "Where's that?"

"It's in Perry County."

Daed looked a little surprised.

"Ya, that's right," Aaron said. "It's in the valley below that lookout area you've always loved."

Aaron hoped a seed of desire to escape this farm had been effectively planted in his parents' hearts. Now it just needed watering.

Mamm started to pass a slice of pie to Sylvia, but she stood. "I need to check on the calf."

As Aaron watched her walk out, his heart pounded with feelings that made no sense. Maybe this was how it felt to undermine someone's dreams. What he really needed was a way to make her want to go home or to another farm.

Nine

The warm, sudsy water slid over Cara's hands while she scrubbed the pots and pans as if they'd offended her. The worst of the heat was gone for the day as the sun began to set, but she couldn't find any solace in the pink hues outside the kitchen window or the clip-clop of rigs passing by.

Thoughts of the way she'd exploded at Trevor plagued her. If the church leaders caught wind of how she'd treated him—and they could if Trevor chose to go see Emma and Levi and ask why they hadn't picked Cara up at the bus station all those years ago—her plans to marry Ephraim could be jeopardized.

But she doubted Trevor could follow through on anything, so she didn't need to worry about him telling community members about her outburst. And she'd confirmed that Ada and Deborah wouldn't tell. So why couldn't she just forget about the incident? The man certainly had no problems forgetting about her...until recently.

Squeals and giggles from outside drew Cara to the back screen door. The fenced yard was a wonderland to her daughter, who'd been raised in some of the poorest sections of New York City.

Lori tugged on one end of a towel while Better Days pulled on the other. "Look, Mom. I'm winning."

Cara stepped outside, noticing that several items had been jerked off the clotheslines. "Lori Moore! Stop right this instant! What are you thinking?"

Lori froze in place.

Cara clenched her fists, trying to calm herself. This wasn't like her. She wasn't a yeller. They were the mom-and-daughter team that fought against the odds, not with each other. But fury assaulted her just as it had yesterday when Trevor showed up. She swallowed, trying to gain perspective. "Clothes on the line are not toys for you and that dog to rip up."

Her daughter nodded, and Cara wondered what she must sound and look like from Lori's perspective. She hadn't meant for her tone to be so rough, but she burned with offense.

She'd always loved her daughter's silly ways; even the careless or thoughtless ones were a beautiful reminder of childhood innocence. Had Cara let Trevor steal that part of her too? She'd groused her way through last night and all of today, and her anger continued to grow.

She picked up the towel that Lori and Better Days had been playing tug of war with. It was an old one that Cara had given them weeks ago. Deborah had washed it, and Lori had removed it from the line. Cara picked up the other pieces, realizing those belonged to Better Days too.

She turned to her daughter. "Why didn't you tell me?"

Lori broke into tears and ran into the house.

Cara eased into a nearby lawn chair. *God, help me. I'm so angry I can't stand myself or enjoy my daughter or think clearly.*

A few minutes later Deborah eased out the back door and sat in a lawn chair next to Cara. She put her hand gently over Cara's, reminding Cara of the months she'd spent comforting Deborah after her fiancé dumped her and ran off. Deborah had struggled for a long time, but in the end she was glad to be free of him and had slowly fallen in love again—this time with a man worthy of her.

"What am I going to do?" Cara asked.

"Maybe you need to talk to your dad."

"His name is Trevor. Please don't refer to him as anything else."

Ada stepped outside, holding Lori's hand. "It's time for all little girls to get a bath, but I think she needs to see you first."

Cara opened her arms. Lori ran to her, climbed into her lap, and snuggled.

After brushing wisps of hair off her daughter's forehead, Cara kissed it. "I'm sorry, Lori."

"What's wrong, Mama?"

"I think I ate Oscar the Grouch."

Lori's brown eyes stared up at her, but she didn't smile. "I can't remember you ever yelling before. You wag your finger sometimes or count to five, but you don't yell."

Cara had never seen any benefit to yelling. Besides, Lori wasn't the kind of child who required a raised voice in order to listen. But after facing off with Trevor, Cara couldn't imagine taming the beast she'd freed from its cage. Even as she held her daughter, she felt enough pent-up hostility to rip something apart.

She pulled Lori close. "I love you, Lorabean. And moms yell sometimes, just like you get sassy once in a while. It doesn't mean you don't love me, does it?"

"No way!"

Squeezing Lori tight, Cara kissed all over her face and neck until her daughter giggled wildly. "Go on inside with Ada. I need to talk to Deborah."

Lori hugged Deborah good night and skipped up the back steps with Better Days ahead of her. "Ada, you gonna tuck me in and read to me tonight?"

"I'd like that. What are we reading?"

"You mean you don't know?"

Their voices faded as they went deeper into the house.

Cara searched for a way to explain to Deborah the depth of her rage but came up empty. "No one's supposed to join the faith harboring obvious unforgiveness. And this isn't going to fade away."

Deborah played with one string of her prayer Kapp. "I thought you were ready to deal with seeing him."

"Yeah, I thought so too. Until he showed up. Why should we have to forgive people for doing wrong if they'd do the same thing again if given the chance? If the church leaders learn about our situation and believe I should treat Trevor with respect and forgiveness, it'll cause nothing but trouble for me and Ephraim. It'll look like I'm the problem, but I'm the one trying, and I wasn't doing bad until Trevor stepped in."

"I know you're trying, and so do they."

"God revealed Himself to me when I didn't believe in Him at all. If He saved me in this condition, why can't I stay the way I am?"

"Is that what you want—to stay like you are right now?"

Cara moaned. "Oh, dear God, no." She rose from her chair and stared into the evening sky. Was He listening to her right now? "You don't understand."

"You're right. I don't, and I won't pretend to. But you do."

Cara turned. "What does that mean?"

"You understand the emotions stirred in you and whether you want to embrace them as gifts from God or refuse them because they're not something you want."

"I don't get that choice, Deb. Can't you see? They're already inside me—days and weeks and months and years and decades of anger and heartbreak! And I was able to box that up and tuck it away until the source showed up on the front porch."

"But he's here now. And the box has been taken out of its hiding place."

"Your patience and insight are really annoying, you know."

Deborah smiled. "I'm trying my best not to be. Does that count?"

Cara plunked down in her chair, sighing. More than anything she longed to be perfect for Ephraim, but so many obstacles stood in her way. "Can you imagine what he'll think?"

"Who?"

"Your brother. He's such an upstanding member in the church, and he's engaged to me, a holy terror."

Deborah chuckled. "And if you hadn't returned, he'd be single his whole life, dating different women, searching for his one true mate who never showed up."

Cara squeezed her eyes shut, a storm of anxiety raging through her. Forgiving Trevor wasn't possible. But letting Ephraim know of her weakness and anger was.

"Think he's still in his shop?"

"Probably. If not, with all the windows open, he can hear the office phone ring from inside his house."

Cara stood. "You know, for an annoyingly patient person, you can be pretty helpful."

"I'm just glad you didn't get mad at *me*." Deborah raised an eyebrow, teasing her.

Cara took a deep breath. It was just Tuesday, and Ephraim usually visited only on the weekends, but she longed to see him. Maybe he'd hire Robbie to bring him to Hope Crossing tonight.

Ten

Darkness surrounded Sylvia as she slid into a pair of pants and a shirt. She breathed in the early morning air, trying to ignore the concern that weighed on her. The possibility of Michael losing or selling the farm felt like another personal failure.

After putting on her shoes and prayer Kapp, she left the cabin and walked the narrow path toward the main driveway. Only a few stars peeked through the summer haze, and the waning moon gave very little light. A few cows were moseying toward the barn and mooing softly. Before she had the milking parlor ready, the herd would be bellowing at her, ready to be let in, fed, and milked.

When the barn and farmhouse came into sight, tears pricked her eyes. The buildings stood firm against the dark morning, looking like a dream—one she longed to protect.

The Amish who'd come to America hundreds of years ago wanted two things—religious freedom and land to farm. She felt a kinship with her ancestors but understood that farming was a continuous battle that would never be truly won. Was Michael so weary of the fight that Aaron could talk him into selling?

She went into the barn and lit several kerosene lanterns before climbing into the haymow. She counted out ten bales of straw and began tossing them to the ground. Michael would arrive in a few minutes, bringing her a cup of coffee and a kind word before he helped milk the herd.

She dropped another bale to the ground.

"Whoa!" a male voice hollered.

She looked through the hay chute. "Michael?"

A man stepped into view through the rectangular hole. In the dim light she saw Aaron dusting straw off himself.

She grabbed the strings to another bale. "Why would anyone stand under a hay chute while someone is lobbing bales?"

"I wasn't *under* it. I was getting close enough for you to hear me. The bale broke in midair and scattered." He held up a travel mug. "Truce?" He glanced down. "I'm afraid the lid has straw and dust particles all over it now."

"Please step back so I can finish this task."

He did so without argument, which surprised her. She tossed the last few bales, then climbed down the ladder.

Her cup of coffee sat on a ledge. Aaron was using a pitchfork to spread the straw in the stalls. Apparently he hadn't taken seriously her command to stay out of the barn.

"Daed hurt his back last night," he said.

"Ach, no!"

Aaron shrugged as if there were nothing else to say on the topic. He'd explained his presence with a brief sentence, without even making eye contact. She liked that. But she was worried about Michael.

"Is he in a lot of pain?"

Aaron paused. "I didn't ask."

"How badly did he hurt it?"

He went back to spreading straw. "Hard to tell, and I doubt he's got the money to see a doctor."

"What caused it this time?"

"Just bending over to take off his socks."

She cleaned straw off the lid of the mug and took a swig of her coffee. "I can milk the herd by myself."

"Ya, I know. But I can't cut the fields without someone following the mower to keep it free of buildup. If I have to get off the mower every ten minutes to clean it myself, the crops will ruin in the field before I'm finished mowing it."

"So you figured you'd help me in exchange for me helping you?"

"Trust me, I tried to work something else out."

She giggled. "I bet you did."

"Then let's get to work." He forked a mound of straw and tossed it into a stall, then spread it around.

She'd never seen anyone move as quickly as he did. But they both knew if the hay wasn't cut, dried, baled, and put away before rain moved in, they wouldn't get a good price for it.

"You're sure now is the best time to start cutting?" she asked. "I mean, you checked the forecast?"

"Ya. They're predicting seven days of hot, dry weather."

He seemed as determined as she was to get full price for those acres of hay. But he wanted it for a different reason—so his parents could pay off their debts and sell the farm.

She grabbed a pitchfork. "Once we get out from under some of these bills, we'll be fine. You can go run your appliance store, and we'll handle the farm."

Aaron moved from one stall to the next. "You are definitely underestimating the issues here. My Daed has health problems, and the two of you cannot make this farm profitable." He paused, looking sorry about something. "Why is it so important to you?"

"Lots of reasons."

"Like?"

She considered whether to answer or not, but he understood making mistakes, didn't he? "My Daadi Fisher planted the desire in me to be a good dairy farmer. If he were alive, he'd be disappointed in how I handled his farm—slowly giving up and letting someone less qualified take it over.

He'd be even more disappointed in how I handled some decisions. The Blank farm is my second chance."

"Well, maybe the answer is in looking elsewhere for a third chance."

"This is your Daed's dream. And I seem to be *his* second chance."

"Daed has to find a dream that fits his limited mobility. And you can find another farm to work."

"No. You could. I can only go where my Daed allows. He's not thrilled I'm here, and he's made that really clear, but if I went somewhere without his permission, I'd have to be willing to walk away from my whole family and never see them again." She began dumping feed into the line of troughs. "The biggest reason we're not doing better is because all I know is the herd, breeding, and milk production. I've never planted or harvested crops or dealt with bills or filled silos or handled dozens of other things that are part of running a farm."

"Sylvia, come on. The problems here couldn't be fixed even if you had superpowers in all those areas."

"But, given time, I can make this farm earn a profit."

He moved to a straw bale, jerked the strings off, and jabbed another load with the pitchfork. "No, you can't. I'm sorry you're caught in this. But you and Daed have to face reality."

Grey had come to work early, hoping to talk to Ephraim. But it was almost lunchtime, and Ephraim had yet to arrive. Grey had worked at this cabinetry shop for more than ten years, and he'd never seen a day when Ephraim wasn't here before anyone else—except during his rumschpringe when he moved to New York, and then when he was shunned and not allowed to work at all.

It had been the worst shunning Grey had ever heard of, and Ephraim had kept Cara unaware of it for quite some time. Normally, a man was allowed to keep his job, but the leaders wanted Ephraim to understand what it'd be like to lose everything. Ephraim never budged about helping Cara. And in time the church leaders came to see Ephraim's point of view.

Hearing a horse's hoofs against the gravel driveway, Grey glanced out the shop's office window. Ephraim had finally arrived.

Every time Ephraim did something out of character, Cara was at the root of the reason—whether she knew it or not. Grey never would have guessed Ephraim to be the kind of man to turn his life upside down for any woman. But Grey knew one true thing: no one could predict what love would do to the heart, mind, and soul of a man. It might register as mildly and pleasantly distracting. Or it might level a man, like a blazing fire destroying everything in its path.

He figured both Ephraim and Cara fit into the latter category, although he didn't know Cara well. He certainly hoped she felt as strongly about Ephraim as Ephraim did about her.

That was what Lennie had done to Grey—leveled him. But seeing her holding that baby on Sunday had really rattled him. With her having umpteen nieces and nephews, he'd seen her with babies plenty of times. But this was different, and he hadn't slept decently in the three nights since.

Ephraim walked into the office, yawning. "Everything going smoothly?"

"Ya. We're on schedule. I received two calls from people wanting us to come do measurements and talk to them about wood types and estimates."

Ephraim took a seat and yawned again. "I should've called you from Ada's."

"Not a problem. Is everything okay?"

Ephraim massaged his shoulders. "I don't know. Cara called me last night, and we were up most of the night talking." He suppressed another yawn. "I stopped by the house before coming here. Daed said you opened the shop really early this morning."

"Ya. And it's been a smooth day." Unwilling to put more burdens on Ephraim, Grey turned back to his desk and finished filling out the paperwork for the calls he'd taken earlier.

"Good." Ephraim opened and shut a few desk drawers, then stopped suddenly. "Why'd you come in early?"

Grey swiveled his office chair to face him. "It can wait."

"But it doesn't have to, so tell me now."

Grey stared at the floor, battling with himself. "I…I told you that Elsie and I spent years in separate bedrooms."

"Ya."

"Well,"—Grey slouched in the chair—"I eventually found out why. Because of Ivan's missing arm and our stillborn child, she thought we had bad genes, and she didn't want to chance our having more babies."

Ephraim's face wrinkled.

"Ya." Grey sat upright. "She was wrong not to tell me sooner, and it destroyed years of our marriage. After I finally learned what the problem was, I insisted we have tests run. The results didn't come back until after she died, so I burned them. I didn't want to know."

"Why?"

"If I discovered Elsie had been wrong all those years, I'd have wrestled with anger, maybe even bitterness."

"So by burning the test results, you were protecting your feelings toward Elsie."

"Ya. But I never thought I would remarry. I couldn't imagine being willing to." He broke into a smile whenever he thought of Lennie. "Then Lena happened. But when I saw her holding Elizabeth a few days ago, I realized what I've always known—babies mean everything to her. I knew then that I had to tell her. But how?" Grey shook his head. "And what will happen to us when I do?"

Ephraim leaned forward. "Last night I learned that Cara is struggling with some issues that could keep us from being able to marry this fall. Even though I hate the idea of having to wait a year or two—because it may take that long before she can stand in front of the church leaders and honestly say she has no malice against anyone—I'd still choose going through this now, before we're married. What she's dealing with is disappointing and frustrating, but it's also real and honest. I'm not sure I even realized that myself until now."

"Well, it's nice that all my gabbing while on the clock is of some benefit to you too. Thanks, Ephraim. I needed to talk."

"Anytime. I'm glad all those years of you keeping everything bottled up are over. They are over, aren't they?"

"They are."

He just had to find a way to be alone with Lennie so they could talk.

Eleven

The sun bore down on Aaron's aching neck and shoulders as he kept an eye on Sylvia. If she lost her balance and fell forward or if her clothing got caught in the blades, she'd be the victim of a bad accident.

He stood in the mower cart, almost as harnessed as the horses. Sylvia followed behind with a pitchfork in hand.

The ground mower snagged on something, making it jump and jerk. "Watch out!"

Until he yelled, she hadn't noticed what was happening. She took a step back just as the blades jumped upward.

"For Pete's sake, Sylvia! Pay attention!"

She gestured that she was fine and he should keep moving. They'd covered maybe two hundred feet when she yelled for him to stop.

Not again! He ground his teeth and tried to pull the team to a halt, but the horses refused to obey him. He kept a firm but gentle tug on them until they yielded. Then he looked at the wad of hay caught in the mower.

He waited while Sylvia jabbed the pitchfork between the blades and dug out the fresh hay, dislodging the clump. Left in the blades of the ground mower, the mounds of hay would damage the machine, and it would merely run over the hay rather than cut it.

"You know," he said, "we wouldn't be having this much trouble if you hadn't put so much fertilizer on the field."

She peered at him from under his Daed's straw hat, but she didn't respond. He shouldn't have said that. She was doing him a huge favor by helping like this, but exhaustion was getting the best of him.

As she resumed her work, he remembered how she'd started the morning: wearing a dress and apron with a straw hat. They'd begun cutting near the main road, where carriages passed, and she hadn't wanted to stir up controversy if it could be avoided. She was like him in that respect. When they'd moved away from the main road, she'd returned to her cabin and changed into his old work clothes. She had looked awfully cute in a man's straw hat and a dress.

He was miserably hot, tired, and hungry. Who in their right mind would want to own a farm?

She motioned for him to get moving again, and he slapped the reins against the horses' backs. As always, they didn't want to start up. That he understood.

Sylvia moved to the front of the rig, grabbed the harness, and tugged. She patted the lead horse, cooing to it in Pennsylvania Dutch. "Kumm." The two-thousand-pound creature took a step.

They'd barely finished that row when his mother came into sight, carrying a basket.

"Mamm's here," he bellowed, gesturing toward the road.

Sylvia nodded, jabbed her pitchfork into the ground, and headed for her. The moment his mother spotted Sylvia, she smiled and waved. If he could get past his own surliness, he'd admit what a comfort and asset Sylvia had been to his parents in his absence.

While he unhitched the team, Mamm and Sylvia spread a blanket under a shade tree and unloaded the basket. Aaron led the horses to the two five-gallon buckets of water he'd set up for them. After tying them to ground brush, he walked over to the blanket.

The women had bowls of food spread out on the blanket. Plates. Two cups of icy water. Flatware. Bread. Butter. Cloth napkins. Steaming vegetables. And green-bean-and-ham casserole—one of his favorites. In Mamm's eyes anyone working a farm needed the noon meal to be the largest of the day, whether they could make it to the table or not.

"This looks wunderbaar, Mamm. Denki."

Sylvia patted the blanket. "Dora, why don't you stay and eat with us?"

Mamm finished loading a plate of food and passed it to Aaron. "I told Michael I'd take the horses back to the barn and bring a fresh pair while you two ate."

Sylvia rubbed Mamm's shoulder. "How's he feeling?"

Embarrassment and guilt churned inside Aaron. She really did care about his parents. No wonder his Daed had reinvented himself. It was easy to respond positively because Sylvia was gracious to them.

"I can't tell which is worse, the pain or his anger over the injury."

"Well, he'd better rest up," Sylvia said with a grin. "If he thinks I'm letting him win the checker championship just because of a little back pain, he's wrong."

Mamm smiled. "I'll tell him."

After Mamm left, Aaron and Sylvia ate in silence, and the edginess he'd felt while working faded.

"I shouldn't have yelled at you about the amount of hay to cut or paying attention," he said. "I…I'm sorry."

She blinked, her brown eyes showing amusement as she cupped her hand behind one ear. "You're what?"

"Have hearing issues, do you?" He stifled his laugh but not his smile.

"No, not at all." She took a sip of her water. "It's just that those words from a man's mouth are like a foreign language."

"I apologize, and you turn it into an insult of all men?"

"One must make the most of every opportunity on that topic."

He chuckled, and her lips formed a charming smile. She was probably easy to get along with when someone wasn't trying to goad her all the time.

Once again he wondered what had happened to make her leave her farm and come here.

"It's so miserably hot." She wiped her forehead with the back of her wrist. "Enough days of this could make a person black out. Have you ever passed out?"

"You mean while sober?" he scoffed.

She didn't frown or laugh at his wisecrack but just dug into the basket and pulled out two bowls covered with plastic wrap. "Banana pudding." She removed the plastic from one.

He leaned against the tree. "You know, I've been thinking about our conversations since we met, and it seems to me that you have a problem with guys. So tell me, Sylvia, what makes you dislike the male gender?"

"Are you going to pick a fight with me at every meal or just when I say something that's a little personal—like asking about your health?"

"You didn't say anything that bothered me." That was a lie. He didn't like her acting as if they were friends.

She took a few bites of her pudding before setting it aside, then removed her hat, lay down on the blanket with her back to him, and propped her arm under her head. Within two minutes her shoulders moved up and down in a slow, rhythmic pattern.

Who are you, Sylvia Fisher?

Twelve

Sylvia hobbled into the barn, her muscles screaming. The dark morning sky held no charm for her today. She found the kerosene lanterns lit, the bales of straw down from the loft, and Aaron spreading it on the stalls.

He looked up for a moment, then returned to his work. "Coffee's on the ledge."

She tried to walk normally as she went to the mug. Gingerly she picked it up with her aching, blistered hands and took a drink. "Denki."

"You should thank Daed. He won't let me leave the house without it."

She wasn't the only one who was sore. Aaron grimaced as he moved at half the speed he had yesterday. She dreaded the work ahead, but they had at least two days of stirring the cut hay and letting it dry before it could be baled.

"We have four teens coming to do the evening milking until we get the hay out of the field," Aaron said, "and Daed's able to supervise them, so we can keep mowing while they tend to the cows."

"There's no money for that."

"I promised to pay them when we sell the hay."

"But we need that money."

"I know that. But it'll take us another week if we have to do the milking as well. We'll be too tired to keep up the needed pace in the field, and the rains might move in before we're done."

She set her coffee on the ledge. "You're right. As I've said, I don't know much about baling hay."

"Well, this is an awful way to learn."

"Agreed." She grabbed a pitchfork. "My head feels woozy from working in the heat all day, my hands are blistered, and my feet ache all over."

"And it'll be worse before nightfall."

Just what she wanted to hear.

They moved through the milking as if they'd worked side by side for years. While he harnessed a set of horses to take to the field, she went into the house and rustled up snacks and drinks.

Dora should be the one keeping them fed throughout their workday—snacks, drinks, and meals included. She moved better these days than when Sylvia first arrived, but grief over losing her daughter kept Dora from being able to hold to a schedule. She got things done whenever she could manage it.

Sylvia carried the basket of food and a blanket to where they'd begin cutting. They had finished mowing near the road. Today's path wouldn't allow anyone to see her, so she didn't change out of her pants. Last night when she got into the bath, she noticed her legs were covered with scratches, though not nearly as many as there would have been if she'd stayed in her dress all day.

To her surprise Aaron wasn't strapped into the cart. She put the blanket, drinks, and food under a tree before pulling fingerless gloves out of her pants pockets. Even with gloves, she'd earned several blisters yesterday.

"Kumm." Aaron motioned for her. "You're in the cart today."

"Why?"

"If we're going to survive the next two days, we have to swap jobs. Each position works different muscles."

"My sisters and I used to do that with our vegetable garden."

He helped her get the team's rigging around her shoulders and firmly placed in each hand. "How many sisters do you have?" he asked as he adjusted the straps.

"Eight."

"Any brothers?"

"No."

"Do all your sisters have the same rule about who can enter the barn during milkings?"

"I don't want to talk about my family."

"Of course you don't." He tugged on the straps around her. "Does that feel okay?"

"It's fine."

"The horses don't like stopping, but if you pull back too hard, you'll split their mouths."

"Horses I know."

"Okay, let's get this glorious day under way." He sounded sarcastic, and she ignored him.

Time seemed to drag as the sun moved across the sky, and the heat was more suffocating than the day before. Her body ached as if she'd been beaten.

They changed the worn-out horses for mules midmorning, and Sylvia passed Aaron a hunk of coffeecake. The mules proved so stubborn and frustrating to work with that Aaron traded them for a set of horses they'd used yesterday. They shared a lunch and then worked through the hottest hours of the day. By the time the sun flirted with the tree line, Sylvia's legs shook with exhaustion, and her peripheral vision burned with brown spots.

"Whoa!" Aaron yelled. He wiped sweat from his brow and freed the blades of thick hay. He held his back as he slowly stood up straight. "It's time to call it quits."

"There's at least forty more minutes of daylight."

"We're done for today. End of discussion!" He threw the pitchfork to the ground.

Part of her wanted to cheer, not just because he had insisted they quit, but also because he wasn't afraid to say when enough was enough.

He loosened the horses and passed the reins of one to her. "I shouldn't have yelled."

"Forget about it."

"You still like farming?" he asked as he stepped into the lead position.

"The only thing I don't like about farming is working with mules."

His laughter echoed off the hills.

She trudged through the thick, uncut hay to get the canteens, lunch containers, and blanket. Just before reaching them, she tripped and fell, seeing snatches of images on her way to the ground—the trees, the ocean of ripe hay, a ladybug on a strand of dry grass, and finally the ground. Everything turned brown for a moment, and she fought to inhale, but she couldn't catch her breath.

"Sylvia!" Aaron ran to the last place he'd seen her just before she seemed to disappear into the ground.

He found her lying facedown in the grass, and she didn't appear to be breathing.

He gently sprawled his hands along her back. She moved, and relief made his knees go weak. "Sylvi." It felt right to refer to her as Sylvi, to call this odd woman by a name that no one else used.

She tried to roll over, but he had to help her. The movement caused her to jerk air into her lungs. Apparently, the breath had been knocked out of her.

"You okay?"

Seconds ticked by as she lay there blinking, as if trying to focus her vision.

"What happened?" he asked.

"I...I don't know."

"Don't try to get up." He ran to the picnic basket and returned as fast as he could with a canteen of water.

He sat beside her and lifted her head to help her get a sip. "You really scared me. One moment I saw you marching across the field, and the next you were gone. I thought maybe you fell into an abandoned well, like you sometimes find on old farms. You know, the kind that farmers dug long ago and then boarded up when they went dry. The thought of them makes me shudder."

She took another sip, then mumbled, "No more."

He gulped down a drink, closed the canteen, and set it next to her.

Relieved that she seemed to be all right, he put a piece of hay in his mouth, trying to look relaxed and unperturbed. "I can't do this stupid, overfertilized field by myself, you know."

She stared at the evening sky with its streaks of pink and gold. "I really don't like you."

He chuckled. "Ya, back at you." But he didn't really feel that way. He wished she was more unlikable, but how could he not enjoy someone as sincere and focused as Sylvi, even with her oddities? "But you're a good worker. Never seen better."

She slowly raised herself to a sitting position. When she tried to stand, he got up and helped her. She wavered a bit, no doubt feeling the effects of a day of manual labor in soaring temps.

"Maybe you should stay put for a little longer."

She rubbed her temples. "Not here. I'm bug food in this grass." She teetered, and he grabbed her arm.

"Kumm." He steadied her as they slowly walked back to the blanket. He helped her sit and passed her the water. "Did you really think you and Daed could have done all this alone?"

"I thought we could hire some help. He didn't tell me how much debt there is. I knew money was tight, but it is for most farmers."

He nudged the canteen, encouraging her to drink. "Was it tight on your farm?"

"Some years were really tough, but my grandfather's father owned the farm outright. It's been passed down and divided up for generations, but there hasn't been a penny borrowed for decades. When milk prices drop and equipment prices go up, money is tighter, and we hire fewer workers, so the days are longer. During good years equipment is bought or repaired, we grow the herd, and we save up."

"Your folks have the ideal situation."

"You couldn't convince my Daed that having nine daughters and no sons is ideal for a farmer."

He doubted that losing six babies, having their only daughter die, and raising a son who'd been nothing but a disappointment was any better. He opened a container of fruit and offered it to her. "This'll help."

The sounds of evening grew as they ate a few grapes and waited for her strength to return. He didn't feel antsy or annoyed sitting with her. Truth be told, he liked having an excuse to talk to her and almost regretted that he needed her to leave the farm.

He nudged the grapes toward her again. "How did you land here?"

"Your Daed put an ad in the paper, and I responded. Our fathers spoke on the phone a few times, and then the three of us met halfway between the two places. The men talked until my Daed felt sure I'd be safe, and I came home with Michael. But I paid a high price."

"You mentioned that earlier. How?"

"In many ways my Daed feels the same about me coming to work this farm as your Daed does about you leaving home when you did."

"Parents always think we're the problem, which in my case is only true about ninety-eight percent of the time."

She laughed. "Michael said you guys moved here from a farm in Ohio about eight years ago."

"That we did." He let his mind wander back over the years. "I was seventeen. Daed assured me time and again that this would be our promised land. Before we moved, night after night he talked about this place and had me totally sold on the idea."

"Why'd they leave a farm in Ohio to move to Dry Lake?"

"If they didn't tell you, I won't."

"Seriously?"

Irritation stirred within him. "You think that because they've told you every embarrassing thing about me, I'll share their problems?"

"We all have embarrassing things. Your folks needed to talk, and I listened. Much of the time they reminisced about Elsie. And about how you hate this farm and how they found out that you drink—I mean, drank."

"They'll talk about it, but they refuse to say the word *addict*, let alone admit I am one."

"Is that important?"

"I'd like them to understand at least one or two things about me. Real forgiveness would be nice too. Not that forced 'I forgive you' that Daed gave me while meaning the exact opposite. Isn't that what family is about? Forgiving unconditionally?"

Sylvia's forehead wrinkled, and she stared into the distance. He wondered what had happened in her family to cause her to leave home and attach herself so strongly to someone else's parents.

When she turned back toward him, he saw tears in her eyes.

"You sure you're feeling okay?"

"Ya." She swiped at her cheeks with the back of her hand. "I miss my family, that's all. But part of the reason I'm here is that I don't want to see…some of them, especially one sister."

"That must've been some fight."

"No one in my family even knows how to get here, so I accomplished my goal. I guess that means you and I are both a twisted array of faults."

"I guess so, but unfortunately I still win by a long shot."

She gave him a slight grin. "You know, you're almost tolerable right now."

"*Almost* being the key word."

"Will I have to hurt myself again to see a repeat performance?"

Heat flushed his cheeks. "No."

"I'm glad to hear it."

"Ya, if you get hurt again, I won't be the least bit tolerable."

She broke into laughter. "That was mean, Aaron Blank."

"You wouldn't want me to be too nice. You might go into shock or something."

They had ten weeks of working together ahead of them, and it would make it easier if he could enjoy her company. But the issue that was most important to him—getting his parents to sell the farm—sat between them like an immovable boulder.

He picked up another piece of hay and chewed on it for a while before tossing it aside. "Do your sisters like farming too?"

"No, none of them. Beckie is married, so Daed now has a son-in-law working beside him."

"Is she the one you argued with?"

Sylvia's features melted into a pool of sadness. "Aaron, I know I started this conversation, but I don't want to talk about that. Ever."

"Sure. Okay."

But they didn't need to talk about it again. He now knew what to do. He'd write to her sister Beckie, sending a detailed map and inviting her to visit. Once Sylvia talked things out with her sister, she'd want to go home. Maybe not right away, but at least she'd be willing to help him get this place ready to sell. After she left, his Daed and Mamm would see the wisdom in moving and owning a shop with him. It was best for all of them. Even Sylvia.

All he needed was to find her home address in that mess of papers on his Daed's desk.

Thirteen

When Grey stepped out of the shower, he heard voices in his kitchen. He wrapped a towel around his waist and opened his bedroom door a crack. "Mamm? Is that you?"

"Ya. We brought supper. Hope you don't mind."

"Ya, actually I do. So we must destroy the evidence as quickly as possible."

His Daed laughed. "I agree."

"*Dabber,* Daed," Grey's five-year-old son pleaded. *"Ich bin hungerich!"* Ivan urged his Daed to hurry, but cheerfulness was evident in his voice.

Grey had left work a little early that afternoon and taken Ivan fishing, which he did sometimes on Fridays. They'd had fun, but by the time he'd cleaned the fish, bathed Ivan, and then taken a quick shower, they'd both grown quite hungry. Besides, whatever his Mamm had prepared would be better than anything he could fix, including freshly caught fish. He was glad his parents had come over. The house was too quiet most weekend nights.

"Ich kumm glei naus." Grey assured his son he'd be out soon. He'd been teaching Ivan more English, as Lennie had suggested. Ivan was catching on well, but Pennsylvania Dutch was still much more comfortable for him.

After Grey dressed, he walked over to his nightstand and slid the letter he'd been writing to Lennie into a drawer under his T-shirts. He'd finish

that later. He didn't mind his parents knowing, and when they did find
out, they'd be happy for him. But in the fall, when he and Lennie began
courting, he didn't want his parents put on the spot if someone asked when
the relationship had begun. As for himself, he didn't care who thought
what. He'd been faithful to his wife in every nuance of the word even years
after she'd shut him out of her life.

Walking into the kitchen, he rubbed his hands together. "Edible food.
There's nothing quite like it." He took plates from the cabinet and began
setting the table.

His Mamm laughed. "Ivan says you cook pretty good."

"I'm not bad but nothing like you, Mamm."

They were halfway through the meal when someone knocked on the
front door.

"Kumm."

Ephraim stepped inside and bid everyone a warm hello.

Mamm fetched a plate. "Kumm. Eat with us. There's more than
enough."

"I can't stay. Cara's expecting me at Ada's House." He shifted, looking
a little uncomfortable. "I didn't mean to interrupt your dinner."

"It's no problem," Grey said. "What's up?"

Ephraim handed him a paper that showed the layout of a room.
"Israel needs some measurements taken for a set of cabinets he wants built
in his shop. I was hoping we could get the information logged this weekend and begin work next week, but I can't get to it. I was busy doing the
books for the shop and lost track of time. I should've been in Hope Crossing an hour ago."

Grey looked over the diagram. "There's no description of the type of
wood."

"Israel said to check with Lena. He's wanted this done for a while, and
the two of them can't agree on exactly what's needed."

Ephraim had brought Grey exactly what he needed: a legitimate reason to be at Lennie's—one that would hold up no matter who dropped by unannounced.

Mamm scowled. "I have a question."

Grey's Mamm always had questions, lots of them.

She put her elbows on the table and folded her hands. "Israel makes furniture for a living. Why would he hire you to build a set of cabinets?"

"Probably because we can build it faster and better," Grey said. "That is our skilled area, Mamm, just like Israel could build a kitchen table and chairs faster and better than we could."

"Okay. That makes sense. So, Ephraim, have you and Cara set a wedding date yet?"

He shook his head, maintaining a casual posture. "We're hoping for fall, but the languages are giving her some trouble."

"I 'spect so," Grey's Daed said. "If I'd had to learn our languages from scratch as an adult, it would've made me think twice about even trying to join."

"Ya. She's pretty frustrated right now. And I'd better be going before she's frustrated with more than just the language."

Grey's parents laughed.

Grey walked out with Ephraim. Robbie sat in his truck, waiting. "I appreciate this, Ephraim."

"I think she stayed home tonight, although that could've changed if one of her friends dropped by."

Lennie had a lot of energy and even more friends, so it was very possible he'd arrive and she'd be elsewhere. Grey went back inside. He saw his parents nearly every weeknight, and he enjoyed their company, but right now he wished they'd head home so he could go see Lennie. The minutes dragged into two hours before his parents left with Ivan.

Grey hitched his horse to a rig. Pitch black painted itself across the summer sky, and he thought he heard thunder rumble in the distance as he drove toward Lennie's. When he arrived, he couldn't see any light coming from her home or her Daed's furniture shop. Disappointment bit.

He pulled farther onto the driveway. The greenhouse glowed dimly, reminding him of a full moon against a field of damp, ripe hay. After tethering the reins to a hitching post, he strode toward one of Lennie's favorite havens. It tended to be muggy inside the greenhouse in summer, but she'd put in screened doors and windows so she could enjoy working in it at night, free of the day's overbearing sun and the night's pesky mosquitoes.

He went to the door and started to knock, thinking that'd be less startling than just barging in. When he heard a man's voice, he went inside, expecting to find Lennie and her Daed.

Instead, Aaron sat on one of the long workbenches, talking seriously. Lennie stood at another workbench, her back to Grey and her side to Aaron. An oversized pot sat in front of her, and Nicky lay on the dirt floor nearby, watching and wagging her tail.

It felt right to see Elsie's brother like this. Grey knew firsthand the struggles the young man had been through, and right now he looked better than Grey had ever seen him—healthy, sober, as if he'd found an inner compass. But a twinge of concern pricked him.

"Grey." Aaron nodded casually.

Lennie wheeled around, a beautiful smile greeting him. Her gloved hands were covered in potting soil, although he couldn't imagine what needed to be potted in mid-June. Her eyes moved to his and stayed. "Grey." Pulling off her gloves, she walked to him. "What brings you here tonight?"

When she moved in close, he couldn't find his voice. He pulled the work order from his pocket.

Pleasure danced in her gorgeous bluish green eyes as she took the paperwork from him. "Oh, for Daed's shop?"

"Ya." He pointed at the schematic. "But he's asking for an abundance of storage space for the amount of room we have to build in."

"We've talked about it before, but it's been a while. Give me a minute, and I'll walk over with you." She went to her workbench. "Are these cabinets going to be open faced?"

"It's my understanding that he's leaving that up to you."

"That's because he's playing chicken." She opened a tube of glue, spread it on the edge of a broken pot, and squeezed two pieces together before passing it to Aaron. "Hold it just like that. If you do, I'll come by your place tomorrow and invite Sylvia to an outing tomorrow night or Sunday."

Aaron mocked frustration. "But you already agreed to do that."

"Ya, and now I've added a price tag. Stay put. I've wanted that pot glued for quite a while. Now that you've volunteered to hold it just so for the next several hundred minutes..."

"Lena." Aaron elongated her name, fussing and laughing. Then he shifted his attention. "Grey, any chance you'd be willing to help milk the cows once in a while?"

"I'm willing. I helped your Daed whenever I could right after you left. But then he hired a young woman..."

"Sylvia Fisher."

"Ya, that's her name."

"And I bet she asked you not to come anymore."

"She was nice about it, but ya."

"See, Lena, I told you. Sylvi is weird. Who turns down good help in exchange for the grand prize of working seven days straight, week after week?"

"Sylvia, I suppose."

Grey listened to the banter, and the concern tugged at him again. "Lena."

She looked surprised, but he didn't know why. She pointed at Aaron. "You stay."

"Yes, ma'am."

When she opened the door, Nicky bolted ahead of them. Lena left the greenhouse, carrying a lantern. Grey followed her, and she gave him the light.

"You called me Lena," she whispered as they walked across the dark yard toward the small shop behind the house.

"So?"

Laughing softly, she dug a skeleton key out of her pocket and shoved it into the lock on the shop's door. "I don't know that I've ever heard my real name come from your lips."

"What are you doing?" His muted voice fell against the humid air.

Jiggling the key, she looked up at him. "Currently I'm fighting this door. In a moment I'm hoping to be kissed."

He took over the key but couldn't make it open the lock. "I don't think you realize how much Aaron likes you. He's home and sober, and maybe he's looking for a girl."

"He's doing no such thing. Not by coming here, anyway."

The door jarred as he finally unlocked it. "You've been his only connection within this community for months. He wrote to you at least once a week. And you answered, right?"

"Sure. But this is Aaron. I know him, and he'd never think like that toward me." She set the lantern on a workbench. "We're friends."

"Just be a little more…distant in your responses to him." He slid his hand into hers. "For his sake."

"Okay." She tilted her head back. "I miss you. It was so much easier to get quality time at Allen's back when we were just friends."

"I even let you win at checkers." Her scent of lavender mixed with roses and violets drifted into his soul.

She smiled up at him. "Evenings and mornings and weekends will be ours soon enough."

He squeezed her hand and lowered his lips to hers. The soft sweetness of her called to him.

The screen door to the greenhouse banged shut, and he knew Aaron was heading their way. "Aaron," he whispered, brushing her cheek with a kiss.

She caressed his hand before putting several feet between them and then motioned toward the empty wall. "How deep does Daed want the cabinet?"

"Hey, Lena," Aaron called as his footsteps echoed off the small wooden porch of the shop.

"Ya?"

He opened the door and walked in. "I think the pot is secure enough to hold together while it finishes drying, and I need to head out. It's been thundering, and I have to get back so I can promise Sylvia it won't rain."

"You can't promise that."

Concern flashed through his eyes. "Well, I can't make it come true, but I can and will promise it."

"Why?"

"Because she knows the hay we've cut will lose at least half its value if it rains before we get it baled and out of the field."

It sat well with Grey that Aaron seemed to care how the farm was doing. He'd never seen that in him before.

"Grey, would you give him a lift home?" Lena asked. "After cutting hay all day, he walked here."

Grey folded the papers and shoved them back into his pocket. He knew that underneath Lennie's request to give Aaron a ride was her desire for Grey to spend a little time with his son's grandparents. After the way Michael, as head of the school board, had refused to stand up for her last year, he found it illogical that she cared so much about him and Dora. But he appreciated that she did.

"Sure."

Fourteen

From the dessert booth in Ada's front yard, Cara kept an eye on the road, looking for Ephraim. When the sun finally went down, the temperatures dropped, but humidity clung to the air as thunder rumbled. The street-lights illuminated the area surrounding Ada's House, and shots of lightning blazed across the distant sky. The storm seemed to be skirting them.

After a day of helping Deborah and Ada bake in a hot kitchen, she soaked in the cool reprieve. Deborah ran the register, and Cara boxed up the orders as they sold one dessert after another. Customers buzzed everywhere.

She noticed an unfamiliar rig come to a halt about halfway down the block. Amish friends in carriages didn't park down the block. They used the hitching post or the barn behind the house.

The bishop got out, and a strongbox of heaviness seemed to open inside her. Maybe Sol had stopped by to get a fresh view of Ada's thriving business. Or maybe he'd come because Trevor had tattled on her.

Ephraim had said not to worry about the fallout. If it became an issue, they'd deal with it one step at a time. Was it any wonder she loved him so? Deciding not to give Trevor another thought, she placed two boxes with shoofly pies on the counter.

"Deb." Cara taped the order on top of the boxes and grabbed another ticket to fill. "I want to do something really nice for Ephraim."

"Ya, like what?"

"You're his sister. I was hoping you'd know."

"Not a clue. Before moving to Hope Crossing with Ada, I cooked a few meals, did his laundry, washed dishes, and cleaned his house when I wanted to do something nice for him. Those are things guys appreciate."

"We agreed I wouldn't go in his house for more than a minute or two when I'm in Dry Lake, not until after we're married." She watched the bishop slowly wind his way toward her. "No sense inviting trouble, especially since I'm a magnet for it."

"I could go with you."

Cara shook her head. "Cleaning or cooking for him isn't the kind of gift I'm looking for."

"What are you looking for?"

Ada hurried out to meet the bishop and redirected his steps.

"I don't know. Something…" She gazed up at the evening sky. By nightfall a new moon would be somewhere, invisible to the naked eye. How long had it been since she and Ephraim had enjoyed the night sky through his telescope? He had set it up in his hiddy, which was off-limits to her for now because of its secluded nature. "Oh, I've got it!"

Deborah jumped, dropping some of the customer's change on the counter. Laughing, she picked it up and handed it to the man. After thanking him for his purchase, she turned to Cara. "What's your idea?"

"Let's have a picnic tomorrow night. All of us—Ada, Israel, Lena, you, Jonathan, Ephraim, Lori, and me. We'll go up to the mountain, spread out blankets, eat lots of food, play some games, and stargaze."

"He'll love that…I think. Won't he?"

"Are you saying I know your brother better than you?"

"You know him better than anyone."

Cara elbowed her gently. "Good answer, Deb. And, yes, he will totally enjoy an evening like that." She slid half a dozen cookies into a bag. "There isn't a problem with us doing all that on a Sunday, right?"

"No. It'd be a fellowship for singles, not much different from people having a singing at their home. And we'll have the necessary chaperones because Ada and Israel will be there."

"How will we get everything up that mountain?"

"I'll get Jonathan to bring us a cart."

"Perfect."

Cara kept watching for Ephraim. She'd made supper for him, and it waited in a warm oven. When he arrived, they'd take the food to one of the picnic tables set up for customers under the large oak in the side yard, and she'd sit with him while he ate. But the desire to do something really nice for him had been on her mind since he'd left on Wednesday morning, physically and mentally exhausted. In the three days since, they'd only been able to chat for a few minutes here and there on the phone. At least his cabinetry shop and Ada's barn had phones.

"Cara, sweetheart," Ada called.

She looked around and spotted Ada standing beside the bishop near his carriage, motioning to her. Her chest tingled. The conversation must require privacy, and seclusion was hard to come by at Ada's House on a Friday or Saturday.

Whatever was going on, she wasn't going to let Trevor Atwater do any more damage than he already had.

"Wish me luck," Cara mumbled.

"Luck?"

"Yeah, like, 'Break a leg, Cara.'"

Deborah's face scrunched into confusion. "What?"

"You people really need to watch more television."

Deborah grinned, realizing what Cara was talking about. "Oh, ya? Why don't you tell the bishop that?"

Cara headed for Ada, wishing she knew some trade secrets about acting.

"Hey, Cara," Deb called.

Cara turned.

"Break a sweat." Deborah suppressed a smile, feigning innocence. They hadn't stopped sweating night and day for weeks.

"Thanks."

Before Cara got halfway to the rig, Ada met her. "He'd like to talk with you, alone." Ada straightened Cara's apron, looking her straight in the eyes. "Mind your manners, and think before you speak." She said the words lightly, but the motherly look in her eyes conveyed much more. Ada hugged her, then excused herself. Cara walked to bishop's rig.

"You've been good for her," he said.

"She's been good for me too."

"When Mahlon left the way he did, I wasn't sure how we could help her or Deborah survive it. You pulled off a marvel. And I want you to know I've seen a good heart in you, as good as any Amish person I'm responsible for."

"Did you know Ada prayed for me from the moment she heard my mom was pregnant? I think her prayers are the only reason I found my way to Dry Lake."

"Very possible. I know they were part of God's plan to get you here." He straightened his suit jacket. "I also think God had more in mind than changing just your life when He brought you here. We've all been changed for the better...all except your Daed."

Trevor had told on her. But to whom?

"What do you mean?" She had a good idea, but she didn't want to assume anything and end up volunteering information.

"I understand Trevor Atwater came by here earlier this week and learned news that was very upsetting."

"It's old news, and the fact that he discovered it twenty years after the event shows how careless he has been with following up."

"Perhaps we should all meet together and talk."

"Why? It's settled. He wanted to know what happened, and I told him."

"Did you forgive him?"

"He didn't come to be forgiven."

"True. But when he discovered the truth—that you had been abandoned—I'm sure it was difficult for him."

For him? She was the one who'd had to survive her childhood. All he had to do was hear about it.

"He needs your forgiveness, Cara, and it's the godly thing to do. You understand that, right?"

The idea sickened her, but how long would it take to say the words—a few minutes, an hour at the most? She could do that with her worst enemy.

"Are you ready to forgive him?" Sol asked.

No. A thousand times no. But she couldn't tell him that. If she had a choice to say anything other than yes, she would. Her mouth went dry. "Yes. I am."

"Good."

Ephraim got out of Robbie's car, and her heart turned a flip. He'd be relieved that she'd agreed to face her father and meet the bishop's expectations.

"Perhaps it'd be good for you to spend a little time with him," the bishop said.

What? No way! The words begged to leave her mouth, but she didn't let them.

"He is your Daed, and you've been separated from him for twenty years."

Ephraim came up to them, and Sol shook his hand.

"How's everything going?" Ephraim asked.

"Good, I think. Cara?"

"Yeah. Good." Her chest tightened again. Lying didn't come as easily as it used to.

"Cara and Trevor are going to spend two or three evenings together over the next few weeks."

Ephraim's eyes widened, and disbelief was written across his face.

Cara's hand moved to her hip, and she kept telling herself to lower it. She clutched at the only straw she could think of. "Don't you people have some sort of regulation against an Englischer spending too much time in an Amish home?"

"He's hurting, and you've added to it, Cara. You need to do what is necessary to send him on his way in peace. And then peace will come to you and your home."

"Why would you want me spending time with an alcoholic?"

"He said he hasn't touched a drink in more than ten years."

"And you believe him?" she spat. "Forgive me. I'm just not sure he's capable of being honest. If he thinks I'm as naive as my mom was, he's mistaken."

Sol ran his hand down his beard. "What Trevor says may or may not be true. But the other night when he showed up at Emma Riehl's, Preacher Alvin witnessed a man broken by the words of one of our own, and we must make things right."

"Oh, come on." She put both hands on her hips. "He's upset that Emma and Levi never came for me like they agreed." She pointed a finger at him. "No one is laying Trevor's remorse and so-called brokenness on me."

Sol glanced at Ephraim and took a deep breath. "It's not just for Trevor but for you too. It's also for Emma and Levi. They've struggled with guilt since you found your way here. Can you imagine what it was like for them to realize that the confusing conversation they had with your dad twenty years ago was a serious request to come pick you up at the bus station?

After agreeing to come, they discounted the conversation, thinking he was drunk, and chose not to follow through. If you can't forgive your father, you're saying you haven't forgiven them. And all three of them *need* your forgiveness."

Cara did feel bad for Emma and Levi. But the bulk of the misunderstanding was Trevor's fault, not theirs. She huffed. "Fine. I'll sit with him for a couple of evenings, but I won't mollycoddle him."

He smiled. "That's not at all the attitude I was hoping for."

"I'm trying." A lump in her throat made it hard to talk.

"Keep fighting the good fight, Cara, and you'll win. So I'll bring your Daed here tomorrow?"

"No!" She jolted at her tone. "I…I'm not ready."

"Monday, then?"

He had no idea what he was asking. She couldn't stand the idea of looking Trevor Atwater in the eyes and apologizing. Not yet. She needed time to brace herself…or at least learn how to be a decent actor.

She nodded. "On Monday."

Fifteen

In the steamy bathroom Aaron applied shaving cream to his face. He ran his razor under the hot water before swiping it down his cheeks.

He and Sylvi had finished cutting the hayfield yesterday, and tomorrow he'd begin the rounds of stirring it until it was dry enough to bale, but today had been a peaceful between Sunday. Nonchurch Sundays always had an extra restfulness about them, but he'd be ready to attend next week's meeting.

He'd asked Lena to invite Sylvia to a gathering of some sort so she could make some friends and have an evening away from this blasted farm. When Lena had come by last night, he'd taken her to the cabin to introduce her to Sylvi, and Lena had invited her to come to Ada's House today for a group picnic on the mountain. Aaron hadn't expected Lena to invite both of them to such a nice event.

When Sylvi balked at going, Aaron told her that he'd asked Grey to help Michael with the milking today so they could have this Sabbath day off. He wasn't surprised that she was frustrated by his changing the milking roster without asking her, but he had thought she'd be more open to the idea of getting away for a night.

Instead, she seemed uninterested and distant. She was polite, but she carried an unusual coolness about her.

Sylvi hadn't come to the house for breakfast this morning, and he'd gone to Frani's just before lunchtime. He wanted to be a friend to Frani as he should've been years ago when she first started talking about getting sober. She couldn't do it on her own any more than he could have.

Aaron checked the clock. It was almost three, so Lena and her Daed would arrive soon. Since hiring drivers wasn't allowed on Sundays, they'd travel by carriage to Hope Crossing. He finished shaving and put on his Sunday pants and shirt. When he stepped outside, he saw Sylvi walking into the barn. She probably wanted to speak to Grey about the evening milking.

Aaron hurried across the triple-wide driveway that separated the house from the barn. "Hey, Sylvi." He stepped out of the heat and into the milking parlor. She turned. "You're going tonight, right?"

She backed away, looking at the horizon as if trying to block him out. "No, but denki."

The sound of gravel under the wheels of a carriage let him know Lena and her Daed were approaching.

"You need to get away for a few hours."

She glanced at him, but rather than frustration he thought he saw fear or concern. "I'd rather stay here and help with the evening milking."

He'd had an easier time reading her that first morning in the milking barn than he was having now. What was going on?

Israel brought the open carriage to a halt near them. "Afternoon."

Aaron turned. "Hi, Israel, Lena. We need a few moments."

"Gut." Israel climbed down. "I want to speak to your Daed, and Lena brought your Mamm flowers." He went around and helped Lena out of the carriage since her medical boot and the cast on her arm made the process awkward.

"Daed, this is Sylvia." Lena shifted the pot of flowers she held. "Sylvia, this is my Daed, Israel."

A few niceties passed between them before Lena walked to the house and Israel went into the barn.

"You need a break," Aaron said. "We worked hard last week and have another tough one coming up."

"Why do you care what I do? Can't I spend the day however I like?"

"There's a real person inside you, not just a farmhand. I think you do your best to keep her locked up under a constant work load. Am I wrong?"

"I don't—"

"I know. You don't want to talk about it."

From the corner of his eye, he saw Lena and his Mamm come out of the house and cross the driveway.

"You've isolated yourself long enough. Someone should have insisted you meet a few people before now. You're letting Daed use you for his benefit, and I'm using you to get this farm sale-ready, and it all starts again tomorrow. Now, please, get in the rig."

"You can't insist I go."

"Then can I bribe you?"

She looked at him as if his behavior disappointed her. "No."

"It's a simple evening out. Why does it have to be a big deal?"

Grey, Daed, and Israel came out of the barn, talking. Lena and his Mamm drew near and waited.

"We're ready," Aaron said loudly and motioned for her to go to the rig. Sylvi didn't budge.

"Aaron." Daed moved forward. "Is there a problem?"

"We shouldn't ask so much of her. And she shouldn't give it. Seven days a week is too much."

"Actually, Dora and I were talking about this last night. We have asked too much." Daed winked at Sylvia. "I hear that Ada's House is never dull."

While his Daed spoke softly to her, she glanced at Aaron, those beautiful brown eyes expressing hundreds of thoughts he'd like to be privy to.

What he'd really like to know is why he cared what she thought or felt. In spite of a few pleasant conversations here and there, they weren't friends. They weren't exactly enemies, but they were close to it—in a civilized, respectful sort of way. Her patience and gentleness caused him to drop his normal obnoxious shield.

Sylvia turned to Lena. "I didn't mean to be rude, and it really is a nice invitation."

"You know," Grey said, "I can come every Sunday evening to help Michael."

"And I could come by every Sunday morning," Israel said.

Daed shrugged. "I don't know. That's an awful lot to ask of—"

"We'll take the help." Aaron shook Israel's hand and then Grey's. "Sylvi will be off every Sunday. Daed and I will rotate Sundays. Denki. Now that it's settled, it's time to go."

Anger flitted through Sylvia's eyes. He'd stepped far over the bounds of dealing with what she considered *her* herd. But he didn't care. She needed one day of rest a week, and now she had it.

He opened the door to the carriage. "Sylvi, get in, please, or I'll tie you to one of the horses."

She got in, but her tight mouth and stiff movements indicated she was not at peace, nor was she eagerly anticipating the evening.

Sylvia felt like an overstretched rubber band—taut and at the breaking point. Frustration with Aaron banged around inside her, but he was right. She had kept herself buried under a heavy work load. She had since Beckie and Elam had betrayed her. Before that, work was enjoyable but just one aspect of who she was. Now work was everything. She hadn't expected anyone to figure that out, least of all Aaron Blank.

When they finally arrived at Ada's House, Aaron helped Lena out of the rig. Before he could turn to help Sylvia, she jumped down. He was so pushy.

The white clapboard house looked huge and homey and inviting. A hand-painted wooden sign out front read "Ada's House, Baked Goods and Seasonal Activities."

A woman in her late thirties or early forties opened the front door. "Welcome. Welcome. I'm Ada. Since yours is the only face I don't recognize, I'm going to say you're Sylvia."

Sylvia nodded, unsure whether to offer her hand or not.

Before she could decide, Ada hugged her. "I'm so glad you came." She turned to Aaron with obvious pleasure. "Look at you. You are a sight for sore eyes, young man." She engulfed him in a hug too. "I bet your parents are glowing."

"Not so much."

"Don't worry. They'll come around."

Ada's eyes moved to Israel. "Good evening."

He removed his hat. "Ada. It's always nice to get another invite."

"And you're always welcome, but tonight is Cara's doing. She and Deborah and Lori are taking a load of items up the mountain. She'll be back shortly."

"Ada," Lena said, "how about giving Aaron and Sylvia a tour?"

"Sure. Kumm."

They went through the house and walked the grounds. Five days a week—Tuesday through Saturday—Ada, Deborah, and Cara made desserts, and five nights a week they sold them, along with Amish-made items like jellies, canned goods, wall hangings, dolls, and furniture Israel made. People paid for tours, hayrides, and various events that changed with the season—like going through a corn maze in the fall and cutting fresh ears of corn off the stalk, shucking them, and cooking them in an outdoor kettle.

Sylvia couldn't imagine wanting to see so many strangers every day, but Aaron had lots of questions and seemed quite taken with the idea.

When they went into the kitchen, a young woman came in the back door. "Ada, did you—" She stopped short. "Oh, we have guests."

"Cara, this is Aaron Blank," Ada said.

"Blank?" Cara repeated, clearly trying to place him. "Oh, Lena's friend."

Aaron laughed. "There are so many descriptions you could have used just then, and you happened to choose my favorite."

Ada put her hand on Cara's shoulder. "This is Sylvia. She's new to Dry Lake."

"Ah, someone newer than me. Good."

"You live in Dry Lake?" Sylvia asked.

"No, but I stayed there for a few months. My fiancé and his family live there, so it'll be home for me…one day. Ada and Deborah are from there. Of course, everyone is related or connected somehow. It drives me nuts trying to figure it all out. Do you know everyone already?"

"Not at all. Aaron and his parents mostly."

"Mom!" A little girl jerked open the screen door and ran inside. "Can Better Days go with us when we go up on the mountain?"

"I don't think so, honey. We'll have picnic foods spread out on the ground, and you know how uncontrollable he gets."

"Please?"

"I'll think about it."

"Hello?" a man's voice called out.

Cara's eyes lit up, and she and Lori headed for the front door.

Ada laughed. "That'd be the fiancé."

Sylvia met Ephraim, his sister Deborah, and Deborah's beau, Jonathan. Everyone grabbed something—a game, a snack food, or a drink—to take up the mountain. Sylvia carried a blanket. She hadn't seen this much

bustle of activity since leaving home. As she thought of her sisters, she
longed to see them again.

Ephraim put Better Days on a leash and passed it to Lori. Lena sat on
the back of the cart with her feet dangling toward the ground. They began
the trek up the hill.

Ephraim and Cara walked to the far left of the group, talking quietly
together. Deborah and Jonathan went ahead of the cart, walking hand in
hand. Israel led the horse, and Ada walked beside him, leaving only Lori
and Sylvia behind the cart.

Aaron walked up beside her. "Are you talking to me yet?"

"Only if you make me or embarrass me in front of a group of people,
which you seem to insist on doing."

His shoulders slumped slightly. He walked to the cart and jumped
onto the back beside Lena.

Sylvia determined to look in any direction except his, but she could
feel his eyes on her. In a moment of weakness, she looked at him, and he
held her gaze.

She wasn't sure what his relationship was with Lena. When he'd
brought her to the cabin last night to invite Sylvia to come today, she'd
been confident they were seeing each other, though Michael and Dora had
said nothing about a girlfriend. It was part of the reason she didn't like his
invitation to come tonight. She had no interest in being a third wheel.
Besides, he didn't act like he had a girlfriend, and that bothered her. A man
should talk about his girl. Be clear about his feelings for her.

But this evening Aaron and Lena seemed more like friends. However,
Sylvia wasn't good at reading signals between men and women. She'd had
no clue Elam cared for Beckie, yet he loved her enough to carelessly and
quickly throw Sylvia aside. It became obvious that while Elam and Sylvia
courted, he and Beckie had been having *moments* together—the kind that
looked innocent but entered the soul and drew one human to another.

She turned her attention to Lori and Better Days. Lori slid her hand into Sylvia's and smiled up at her. The simple gesture warmed Sylvia's heart.

"'From and Mama are getting married, and I can't wait."

"That's nice."

"I don't remember my daddy. Mom says he died when I was two. I think 'From needs us. He lives all by himself."

"I live by myself too."

"I think that's sad. I like living with lots of people in the house, especially my mom. When I'm old like you, I'm gonna have lots of friends live with me." Lori splayed her hand. "And five dogs."

Sylvia chuckled.

The more they talked, the more Sylvia longed to see her sisters. Lizzie would turn twenty soon. Naomi had just begun her rumschpringe. Next year Lilly would be sixteen and of age to attend singings. Would her youngest sisters begin to forget her?

Aaron got off the back of the cart and moved somewhere ahead of it and out of sight. Several minutes later he returned with a handful of wildflowers and held them out to her. "I know I was out of line, and I'm sorry I embarrassed you. Truce?"

She took the flowers, feeling as confused about who this man was as she had the night he'd broken into her cabin.

When they reached the picnic spot, she spread out her blanket and helped Ada lay three others side by side. They all ate together, and the food was delicious and the conversations entertaining. Lori moved from adult to adult, clearly welcome in every heart.

Each woman came over and sat with Sylvia at some point, welcoming her warmly and chatting or inviting her to play games. Sylvia joined the group for badminton and volleyball.

Aaron partnered with various people at those same games, including her. Until tonight she'd had no idea he had such a deep, wonderful laugh.

The sun slid below the horizon, painting the sky with streaks of purple and pink. The men built a small fire, and the women roasted marshmallows. Ephraim set up his telescope, but Sylvia lay on her back, watching the stars. The dark sky looked like a beautiful, dazzling ceiling when in reality it was openness that went on forever. A longing to talk to God washed over her, but she didn't know what she could say that He'd be willing to hear.

Aaron sat beside her and lay back. He was silent for so long that she wondered if he'd fallen asleep. When she turned her head to look, his eyes were open, staring into space.

If anyone could handle how she felt about church without totally disrespecting her, Aaron could. Connecting with God through prayer and songs used to be fun—seven days a week, but especially on church Sundays. Gathering with loved ones and focusing on the creator of all things had made her soul sing. But how long had it been since then? Since she betrayed God, or since He let Elam betray her?

"You've freed up my Sundays, but I can't go to church," she said.

Aaron rolled on his side, facing her, quietly thoughtful for several long moments. "Why?"

She shook her head. "I...I used to love going before..."

"Yeah, I figure anyone who can tolerate milking cows twice a day, seven days a week, wouldn't feel the services are too long or boring."

"You didn't go last week either."

"I was embarrassed to see people when I first returned. Lots of reasons to feel that way—all of them my own fault. We haven't talked about this, but I know you've been told that I'm partially responsible for my sister's death. Everyone knows it, but no one says a word to me."

"I don't think anyone blames you, certainly not your Mamm or Daed."

His brows furrowed. "Sure they do."

"No they don't. Michael blames himself."

"But he never said…and I thought…" His voice sounded hoarse.

Before Aaron had returned, Michael had said a lot of things about him. Things she wouldn't tell. It wasn't her place. But it sickened her to know how much Michael cared and how little he showed that to Aaron.

"Talking with parents doesn't come easy," she said, "for them or for us."

He cleared his throat. "Some are better at it than others. Watch Lena and her Daed."

Sylvia wondered if Lena's close relationship with her father was one of the things Aaron liked about her. A wave of envy rippled through her, catching her by surprise. Did she really care what he admired about Lena?

Shaking off the unwanted thoughts, she said, "Speaking of Lena, she told me a few minutes ago that my invitation to this event was your doing."

"I figured it was about time you had a little fun."

"It was nice of you."

"That happens every once in a while. Catches me off guard every time."

She laughed. "I can't remember when I've had a better time. Everybody's been friendly and fun. Authentic…which is nice."

"Well, everyone here has their own troubles. Lena's been in hot water with the school board this past year. Ephraim was shunned. Ada's son was once engaged to Deborah, but he left without a word to anyone. Church leaders asked Cara to leave Dry Lake. I don't know about Jonathan or Israel, but since they're human, I'm sure they've received and given hurts and have embarrassments they can't erase."

"From what little your parents told me about you, I didn't expect you to come back."

"Me either. But the more time I spent in prayer, the more I knew I had to do two things—come home to face everyone and be a decent son to my parents."

"Prayer?"

"Hard to believe, isn't it? Before I hit bottom, the only words I said to God aren't repeatable. My parents have their faults and all." He paused. "But they deserve better than what I've dished out to them."

Cara sat down on the other side of Sylvia and lay back on the blanket. "It's time to stretch out and enjoy the sky with the naked eye."

Ephraim lay beside her, and soon a long line of folks were lying on the blankets, staring at the sky.

Lori squeezed between Cara and Sylvia. "Let's sing. Sylvia, do you know any good songs?"

"I bet I know one you're familiar with. 'Miss Mary Mack, Mack, Mack.'"

Lori bolted upright and sat with her legs crossed. She held up her little hands. "You know the clapping game?"

Sylvia sat up. "I most certainly do."

"Think you can keep the pace?" Lori bobbed her head, exuding confidence. "Mom says I'm the best!"

They sang the song and changed up the clapping game as they went along.

"Your mom's right," Sylvia said. "You can move at this. But can you sing it in Pennsylvania Dutch?"

"I don't know enough of those words yet."

Sylvia sang the Pennsylvania Dutch lyrics, and they clapped hands to the rhythm.

Cara moved closer. "Say that first line again—'all dressed in black'— in Pennsylvania Dutch."

Sylvia repeated it, and Cara followed suit. Then Sylvia taught her the pronunciation of the next line.

Within a few minutes Cara had the song down pat. *"All* is *all.* And *dressed* is *gegleed.* And *black* is *schwarz."* She reached behind her, patting

Ephraim on the arm. "Songs. That's our answer to my learning the language!"

He sat up, clearly interested.

"Sylvia, do you know any English songs?" Cara asked.

"A few. Mostly Elvis songs."

Everyone broke into laughter.

Aaron had a strange look on his face, an expression somewhere between amusement and confusion. "Elvis?"

"I owned a used iPod in my rumschpringe, so I listened to whatever songs were already on there when I bought it—until it fell to the ground during a milking and a cow stepped on it."

"Stupid cow," Lori said with a giggle.

"How'd you keep it charged without a computer?" Cara asked.

"The Englischer guy who picked up our milk recharged it for me."

"Do you know any Elvis songs?" Ephraim asked Cara.

"Oh, yeah. 'Heartbreak Hotel,' 'Don't Be Cruel,' 'It's Now or Never,' 'Jailhouse Rock.' And you'll love this: 'You ain't nothin' but a hound dog cryin' all the time.'"

He laughed. "I think I've heard that one somewhere."

"Think you could teach me some more Pennsylvania Dutch words for songs I know?" Cara asked Sylvia.

"Sure. Why?"

"I have to learn the language, and I need help."

"Oh. I'm glad to try, but when?"

"I go to Dry Lake on church Sundays for instruction class, and I meet with Esther and Alvin on Tuesday and Thursday afternoons to study Pennsylvania Dutch and German. I can easily come to your place on any of those days and other ones too, I'm sure."

"The hay will still be drying Tuesday, so that'll work this week. After that we'll figure out our days week by week."

"Ever milked a cow?" Aaron asked Cara, chuckling.

"I'm certainly willing to learn."

"Speaking of cows…," Aaron said. "Four o'clock in the morning comes awfully early."

"Just one more game," Deborah said. "It won't take more than twenty minutes, and everybody can remain right where they are. Think about the person you walked up the mountain next to tonight, and tell the first thing you remember that person saying when you met."

"I'll go first," Lena said. After a short silence she said, "I'm done, because I didn't *walk* up the mountain with anyone."

The laughter made Sylvia feel lighter than she had in many months. Well, that and Cara needing her. And having a pleasant conversation with Aaron. And having an evening with new friends.

"Ephraim, you're next," Deborah said.

"I was twelve and Cara was eight when we met. The first thing I remember saying to her is 'Are you a boy or a girl?'"

Cara cackled. "That was closely followed by 'Do you fish?'"

"Hey, she had on jeans and had really short hair. I was confused."

The laughter didn't stop.

"Cara, what's the first thing you remember saying to Ephraim?" Deborah asked.

"Oh, man, we're going back twenty years, but I think it was 'You got a name?'"

"And the next time you saw each other?"

Ephraim chuckled. "Fast-forward twenty years, and I didn't recognize her while trying to get her out of Levina's old barn and off my property. I remember asking her if she was from around here. I was trying to be polite before insisting she move along. To which my lovely wife-to-be replied…" He gestured toward her with his palm upward.

"'Is that the Amish version of "Haven't we met before?"' You should have seen his face turn red with embarrassment and anger."

Amid the chortles Sylvia longed to know more of their unusual story.

Deborah proceeded to ask each couple. Jonathan told of Deborah's early days in school and some of the stunts he pulled on her. Deborah talked of the first time she began to be drawn to him.

"Aaron, what's the first thing you said to Sylvia?"

"I don't think that's such a good thing to talk about."

Sylvia scoffed. "He's a chicken because he's afraid to mention that the first time we saw each other, one of us wasn't dressed."

"Not dressed?" an echo of voices said.

"I can't believe you just shared that," Aaron said.

Among the hoots and claps, Sylvia stood and gestured for them to quiet down. "I was in a tub with mounds of bubbles the first time he saw me. When he went into the other room, I put on a housecoat, so I was fully covered by something at all times."

Deborah smiled. "And what's the first thing you said to Aaron?"

"Get out of my house!"

The group howled and clapped.

"To which Aaron said, 'Lady, don't throw that.' To the best of my memory, the next thing he said was 'Ouch!'"

"She threw a hammer at me!" Aaron's eyes stayed on hers. "My poor knee hasn't recovered yet." He stood, mocking a fresh limp.

The roars of laughter filled Sylvia with a joy she thought had died long ago.

"You all can stay," Aaron said, "but we have to head home. Sylvia's usually out cold hours before now. Can we borrow a horse and rig from someone?"

Israel stood. "Not necessary. We need to call it a night too. You can ride back with us."

Sylvia gathered the blanket, thinking that Aaron made little sense. He pushed her and insulted her—like when he complained about her putting too much fertilizer on the hayfield—but then made sure she was invited tonight, caring very much that she got a night off. And he talked about God as if he'd shared a cup of coffee with Him or something. No condemnation or gnashing of teeth, just trust and faith in Him. How did someone who'd been where he had freely talk to God? And why did Aaron care that she be a part of tonight?

Sixteen

Aaron rubbed an oversized cotton handkerchief across his face, wiping away the sweat. The horse pulled the hay rake up and down the field. Stirring the hay wasn't anything like cutting or baling it. He'd been in the field less than three hours, and he'd almost completed the job. He'd stir it again tomorrow. Praying the rains would stay away was a daily thing, much like asking for the strength to stay sober.

Desire for a drink pounded him. Unbridled. Unmatched. Unwanted.

Most days he could ignore wanting a drink. It was like his own shadow. It never went away, but as long as he didn't try to outrun it or give up because it was always there, he knew he could win the battle.

Today the shadow taunted him, and he didn't know how to free himself of it. Not one ounce of faith seemed to stir as he petitioned God for help.

"Aaron," Sylvi called to him, yelling above the creaking and groaning of the hay rake, the swooshing of loose alfalfa, and the racket of the horses pulling the contraption.

She stood at the edge of the field with a picnic basket in hand. He brought the horses to a stop. Until this moment he'd barely caught a glimpse of her today. His Daed had helped her milk the cows this morning, and stirring hay required only one person.

By the time he unhitched the horse and walked to her, she had a blanket spread out and was unloading the basket.

"Your Mamm brought this out to me and asked if I'd find you. Your Daed's asleep, and she doesn't want us waking him. She's on her way into town to get supplies." She put a piece of oven-fried chicken on a plate. "I gave my word, so tie the horse to some shrub and come eat."

He did as she said.

She met him with a bowl of water, soap, and a towel. He washed up, dumped the water, and followed her back to the blanket.

She paused, watching him. "You okay?"

"Just one of those days."

"What's that mean?"

"You wouldn't understand. It goes with the territory of once being addicted to something."

"I might understand more than you think."

His interest was piqued. "Do you have a poison?"

Innocence radiated in her eyes. She had no clue what he meant.

He couldn't help but smile. "Never mind."

He ate while she stared at her plate.

She set the dish on the blanket. "I'm not an addict, but I've struggled in other ways—unable to think of anything else night or day. It drives and molds you until you slowly become someone else, someone you don't like. But it doesn't matter because you don't care. In your mind you know it makes no sense to want it, but that does nothing to ease your craving."

"Ya, exactly." Maybe she did understand. But he wouldn't ask her twice what tempted her.

She pinched bits of bread off her roll and ate them. "We can get top dollar for this hay, and we should be able to get three, maybe four cuttings without reseeding, right?"

"Ya, that's right. If the weather is good all summer, not too dry or too wet."

"Then wouldn't we make enough money to end the threat of a lien?"

"That'd get Daed caught up on every bill with some money left over. But we can't sell everything we plant. We have to store some hay for the winter. The acres of corn in the west field could become a cash crop too, but we have to use it to fill the silos."

"Isn't there any way for us to get ahead, even just once?"

Aaron wished she hadn't asked, wished she'd make his life easier and accept defeat. She wouldn't abandon the farm with the work that needed to be done to sell the place. He knew that. But if she could let go of hoping for the impossible, he'd feel much better about the situation. "There might be a way. But help just once would not be nearly enough."

"It might be. What did you have in mind?"

"If Daed asked for enough hay, straw, and silage from other farmers to get him through to next spring, and if the farmers had enough to share, and if we managed to get three harvests of hay to sell—the combination of those things could give you the boost you desire."

She pursed her lips and sighed. "That's a lot of *ifs*."

"*Ifs* and farming are looped together like strands of fiber in a hand-woven basket." The disappointment in her eyes bothered him. "I don't want you to get hurt in this, Sylvi. You can help get the farm in proper shape to sell and stay until it sells, but you need to plan to move on when that happens."

She stared out over the land as if willing it to meet her needs. "I know you're telling me like it is."

"No reason not to."

"I don't think anyone's ever done that for me before. My Daed and… other men I've known seem to think they need to keep certain things cloaked when it comes to the big picture."

Her openness unnerved him, making his defenses rise. "Don't get the wrong idea. I'm not your answer to anything. And I'm not interested in helping you find answers."

"I know that." She said it matter-of-factly. "But you seem to be transparent with me. And I want us to be that way for each other."

If she wanted transparency, he could pull her to her feet and lecture her on getting real about the farm. But just then he noticed someone near the edge of the woods. He stood, watching an Englischer woman with an infant on her hip draw closer.

Frani.

When he glanced at Sylvi, her doe eyes reflected a genteel spirit of absolute resolve. She had strength, no doubt, but she couldn't handle what was real for him.

"I need to go. Thanks for lunch."

He turned his back on Sylvi and headed for Frani.

Cara stood in her bedroom, staring into a mirror, assuring herself she could do this.

Who was she kidding? She couldn't express regret and pardon to the man who'd abandoned her. Been a mean drunk. Made her mother's life miserable. Been a no-account father. Shown up here on false pretenses. Then run to Emma and Levi and tattled about her outburst at him. Why was *she* the one who had to apologize?

Her relationship with Ephraim was not the reason she had to meet with Trevor. She'd planned to join the faith back when she mistakenly thought Ephraim loved Anna Mary. So she'd be in this fix whether Ephraim was in the picture or not.

This war raging in her had to be dealt with, but how?

She moved to the side of her bed and knelt. "Dear God, I know it's wrong, but I *hate* him. And I can't act my way out of it."

Memories flew across her mind like stones from a slingshot, one after another, hurting her as if they had just happened. Trevor had been worse than useless when her mother was alive and completely useless once Cara entered foster care. Biting coldness moved inside her. That frozenness used to define her. It didn't now, but she wasn't free of it.

"Cara." Ada tapped on the door before opening it. "They're here. Ephraim too."

Cara remained on her knees, unable to move. A tingling sensation ran through her fingers and toes. "I'll be down in a minute."

Ada closed the door.

Cara's mind went numb too, but at least the memories had stopped. She remained on her knees, a silent lump of screaming pain. She closed her eyes and rested her forehead on the edge of the bed. No tears fell as emptiness overshadowed her other emotions. Emptiness and rage were strange bedfellows, but the two went together—at least they did for her as far back as she could remember.

She thought she heard someone knock on the door again, but she wasn't sure. Too drained to respond, she ignored it and kept her face buried. She didn't know how much time had passed since Ada had come to her room, but she kept waiting for the strength to apologize to Trevor. Her jaws ached, but she hadn't yet whispered a prayer.

The door clicked open. Just like when she was a little girl in the homes of strangers, she couldn't make herself look. She used to keep her eyes shut tight, unwilling to stare into the eyes of people paid to keep her, and tell them good night. She'd lie there, trying to remember what her mother had looked like and hoping to see her in her dreams when she fell asleep.

A warm, strong arm slid around her shoulders.

Ephraim.

She kept her eyes closed, unable to look at the love or understanding or expectation or disappointment in his eyes. He placed his hand over her folded ones.

"I can't do it. You weren't there. You don't know how he ruined my life."

He didn't say anything, but the warmth of his embrace began to ease the ache inside her. She folded her arms on the bed, placed her forehead on her wrists, and wept. His gentle, silent love touched her deeply, and his presence seemed to reach into the wounds of her childhood. He couldn't touch her past, of course, but he offered her a future filled with love and respect. Suddenly love was tangible, as if she could hold it in her hands, as if it could be shaped and molded at will. And the monstrous ache and hatred of the past could be absorbed into the love he gave her today.

The battle of dealing with anger and resentment at her dad wasn't over. It had probably just begun. But she felt equipped to fight…and for the first time had hope of eventually winning.

Her tears stopped, and she wiped her wet cheeks. "Thank you." She rose, opening her eyes.

Shock pierced her, and she gasped.

No one was in the room with her.

Seventeen

Sylvia walked into the Blank home, knowing she was late for supper. Michael sat at the dinner table, hidden behind a newspaper. Dora stood at the sink, shoulders slumped while she stared at dirty pots and pans. Aaron leaned against the edge of the counter. He seemed irritated, but he offered her a half smile.

Dora pulled a plate of food out of the oven and set it on the table. "Here you go, dear."

Sylvia moved to the table and took a seat. Michael jerked the newspaper away from his face and folded it. She bowed her head in silence.

After she took a few bites, Sylvia turned to Michael. "Daisy's gone to the briars in the east pasture. Unless it's a false alarm, I'm sure she'll deliver by morning. I'll sleep in the hayloft tonight. That's the best place to hear her if she starts bellowing."

"See?" Michael gestured toward her as he glared at Aaron. "That's how it's to be done."

Sylvia glanced from one to the other, sickened that Michael was using her in his attack on Aaron. Michael had been cold and difficult with his son since he'd arrived home. She'd started out treating Aaron much the same way, but Michael's hot and cold temper grated on her nerves.

"Daed,"—Aaron took a mug from the cabinet—"this conversation has nothing to do with my farming skills."

Sylvia looked down and examined the plate before her, wondering what she had interrupted.

"If you'd given heed to what needed to be done over the last eight years and spent less time indulging your whims, we wouldn't be in this mess."

Aaron poured himself a cup of coffee before sitting at the table. "You've said that over and over in the last few hours. Can we change the subject?"

"I should've known you had someone in Dry Lake." Michael smacked a palm against the folded newspaper. "Now I understand why you've come back. Well, that girlfriend of yours and her child can't live on this farm. I won't have it."

Sylvia felt as if a cow had kicked her. *Girlfriend?*

"She's not my girlfriend," Aaron said. "She's a friend who's lost her job, and if she can't find another one right away, she'll lose her trailer in the next couple of weeks. If that plays out, she and AJ will have nowhere to go. I won't let that happen. She can help out around here. I'll pay her expenses. And we have an extra bedroom."

"Where are her own folks?" Dora asked.

"They're not willing to help her right now."

"Go figure!" Michael barked.

"Maybe they're justified, but I won't let her and AJ go without a home to live in."

"Is he...yours?" Dora's hands shook while she held a napkin over her mouth, as if trying to take back the words she'd spoken.

The question rang alarms inside Sylvia. An uncomfortable dusting of jealousy settled over her, but the emotions made no sense. Beyond her own confusing feelings, she knew conceiving a child with an outsider was an unforgivable sin in the sight of many in their community. The mistake couldn't be hidden or managed. Or even solved by marriage—unless he left the faith altogether.

"Are you more likely to let her stay here if I say yes?" Aaron asked.

"Answer your mother."

"No. She's not my girlfriend. Not now. Not before," Aaron said quietly through gritted teeth. "I have been visiting her since I returned but just as a friend. She needs someone who understands to talk to her."

Michael's fists pounded the table. "If you'd been the man you should've been, you wouldn't be friends with that kind of trouble."

"Keep saying it, Daed, and maybe your yelling will turn back the hands of time, and I can do everything right the second time around."

Sylvia ached for all Michael couldn't see. In his blind anger he didn't trust anything Aaron said. She saw integrity and faults in each man, but what could she possibly say to make a difference between them? Should she remain quiet, as Dora did?

"Look," Aaron said, "I'm sorry you disagree with me, but Frani needs help. I'm only asking for a little time to try to convince her to go to rehab."

"Why you?"

The lines on Aaron's face grew taut. "Because we're friends. Is that so hard to absorb?" He sighed. "I think she'll listen to me, so maybe I can make a difference. And, honestly, I feel a little responsible for ignoring her when she used to say she wanted to get sober."

Sylvia studied Aaron, wondering if he'd always had a good heart in this type of situation or if he'd grown one because of his own journey.

Michael looked at Sylvia and motioned to Aaron. "My son thinks I'm going to fall for his lies all over again just because he's been here helping for a few days." He jabbed his finger at the tabletop as he spoke. "I can't prove what you're really doing when you *visit* Frani, but I've played the fool for you once, Aaron, believing your excuses and lies about where you were and what you were doing. I'm not falling for it twice."

Aaron slumped, seeming resigned to both his Daed's anger and his Mamm's indifference. But if Sylvia knew him at all, his patience was wearing thin, and his ability to curb his typical sharp retorts wouldn't last much longer. And she didn't blame him.

"Michael, I know you missed Aaron when he was gone, and yet now that he's back, you're angry with him all the time." Sylvia swallowed hard. "You have me on a pedestal and him in a ditch. Neither image is accurate."

Michael paused, and for a moment he appeared to waver in his anger. "I've talked to your Daed, Sylvia. I know you'd never pull an ounce of what he's pulled over the years."

Sylvia drew a breath. "When I was a young teen, I made a decision to handle myself carefully. The preachers spoke at every service about pure living, and my soul latched on to their words when I was very young." Her insides turned cold, and her hands began to shake. "I didn't drink or lie or do anything I needed to hide from my parents. I even decided I'd never kiss a man unless I was willing to marry him." She took a sip of lemonade, hoping to stop her voice from quivering.

Michael nodded. "That's as it should be. Respectful of your parents."

"I agree, only that's not the end of the story. I fell in love, and the young man asked me to marry him. But...he changed his mind, and we never married."

Her head pounded, and tears threatened. The words felt trapped inside her chest, but she wanted to free them, to give Aaron some relief—and herself. "Unfortunately, the last time I kissed him"—she closed her eyes, wishing there was a way to erase what she'd done—"he was married to someone else."

She drew a ragged breath, lacking the courage to confess the whole ugly mess of how she'd betrayed her sister. "When I imagine God...I think of Him shaking His fist at me, angry and unforgiving. But I can't undo what I've done." She cleared her throat, determined not to burst into tears. She stood. "If you'll excuse me..."

She dashed out of the house, ran across the driveway, and was well into the pasture before she slowed, gasping for air. After walking through the field and across a footbridge to the creek, she came to Daisy's hiding spot. The cow stood very still, panting. Labor had begun. Sylvia left her alone and walked along the muddy, winding creek.

If Michael shared her revelation with her Daed, the explosive reaction to her sin would ricochet around her forever. But that wouldn't be the worst part. Beckie learning the truth would be far worse, more than Sylvia could bear to imagine.

Trembling, she returned to the footbridge and sat, watching the creek amble through Blank land and keep right on going. Had she helped Michael see that she was no better than Aaron? Or had she just sealed her own fate? She drew her knees to her chest and wrapped her arms around her legs, wishing she could erase her image of God as one who was as angry and unforgiving as Michael. She longed to see God the way Aaron saw Him.

Eighteen

Lena hurried around the kitchen, finishing preparations for supper. She'd had another doctor's appointment. This time they'd replaced her arm cast with a shorter one. Afterward, she'd pursued a new job prospect and gotten so distracted that she'd lost all track of time. Excitement pumped through her.

When the school board had let her go, everything she'd worked so hard to achieve had been taken from her. Now that her name had been cleared, they'd hire her again. But women teachers weren't to begin a school year if they knew they'd marry during it, so even though her relationship with Grey was a secret for now, she would not reapply for her old position. She could teach and make a difference without being in a classroom.

A rig pulled into the driveway and headed for the barn. Her Daed was home. She couldn't wait to tell him about her job interview. She wished she and Grey could talk, but she'd write him later tonight.

"Lena?"

Nicky bolted from her bed in the corner of the kitchen, wagging her tail as she went to greet Daed.

"In the kitchen."

She put a thick towel over her cast and grabbed a hot pad with her other hand, then opened the oven door. She pulled out the casserole dish and, by balancing it on her towel-covered arm, moved it to the top of the stove. "Daed, where have you been?" She dumped a loaf of freshly baked bread out of its pan.

The familiar screech of Daed's turning on water in the mud sink near the back door echoed through their home. She wondered how long she'd live in Grey's home before it carried any of the wonderful sentiments that this one did.

"I had an errand to run," Daed answered.

"Well, I have good news, and you weren't here to share it with." She spoke loudly while setting the chicken spaghetti on a hot plate on the table. "You won't believe this." After grabbing two goblets containing his favorite gelatin salad out of the refrigerator, she turned.

"Try me." Grey's voice caused joy to skitter through her.

She broke into laughter. "Benjamin Graber! What are you doing here?"

"Your Daed came and got me. Seems he intends for me to do the work I didn't get done last Friday."

Her Daed entered the room, grinning. "It is perfectly respectable for me to be seen bringing him here to do some work. We can't get away with it often, mind you."

She wrapped her uninjured arm around her Daed's neck. "You're the best."

He didn't make a retort of any kind, which wasn't normal. When she pulled away, he looked sad in spite of his smile. "I don't know why I encourage this relationship. I can't imagine what it will be like once you've moved out." Behind his jesting, there was a flicker of raw pain she hadn't seen since her mother had passed away.

She hugged him again, but words failed her.

A little unsure whether to embrace Grey in front of her Daed, she motioned for him to take a seat.

Grey removed his hat. "You have a new cast."

"I do." She held it up. "It's called a short cast, and it's definitely more comfortable than the last one." She wiggled her fingers. "But my hand tingles."

"What'd the doctor say?" Grey asked.

"It's normal, and he gave me instructions for new exercises that will strengthen my shoulder. He'd like me to start walking without the medical boot for a few minutes each day and work up to a couple of hours, but never if it causes pain."

"Everything is healing as it should?" Her Daed studied her, as if trying to be sure she was telling them the whole truth.

"Ya. I have to keep going back for routine checkups, but he thinks I'll be out of my cast and boot by the end of the summer."

"I know you're tired of seeing the doc so often, but it makes the two of us feel better." Grey winked and moved toward the stove. "Can I help?"

"Slice the bread for me, would you?" She poured them each a glass of icy water.

After everything was on the table, she and her Daed put their hands on the table. Grey seemed unaware they were waiting on him to do the same.

"We hold hands during prayer," Lena said. "That is, unless Daed has frustrated me to the point that I won't hold his hand."

"A word to the wise," Daed said with mock sincerity. "Don't come home for dinner when she gets that way."

Grey chuckled and enfolded her hand in his, and she didn't want the silent prayer to end. Little in this world seemed as perfect as praying with Grey, but it lasted only a minute before Daed shifted, ending the prayer time.

"What's your good news?" Daed scooped chicken spaghetti onto his plate.

"I have a new job."

Mild alarm took over Daed's expression. "Without talking to Grey?"

"As you know, it's extremely difficult to talk to him."

"Ya, but, Lena, you could have written to him and waited for an answer. I know you've been raised without a mother most of your life, but not even to communicate with him about it is unheard of."

She studied Grey. "Do you mind?"

"Not at all. I trust your judgment."

Her Daed got up from the table and looked for something in the refrigerator. "Still, Lena, right is right."

"Israel." Grey held up the bowl of freshly grated Parmesan.

Her Daed returned to the table and took it from Grey's hand.

Grey wiped his mouth on a napkin. "You seem concerned that Lennie was raised with just a father. Maybe you're afraid she's too independent and more set in her ways than your other daughters were because she's several years older than they were when they married. I like her the way she is, Israel. She won't be a perfect wife. And I won't be a perfect husband. I don't want perfect."

Lena knew what he did want: friendship—the deep, mysterious kind that only happened between a man and woman who loved enough to marry.

Daed cleared his throat. "I guess I was out of line. I suppose that means I'm not perfect either."

"You're close enough for me," Lena said. "And Ada too, I think."

One corner of her Daed's mouth lifted, revealing his pleasure in what she'd said. "So tell us about this new job of yours."

"I found an ad in the newspaper from an Englischer woman who teaches her children at home. I went to see her. She's expecting her seventh child this fall and would like help with both teaching her children and running her house. We'll take turns. One of us will teach while the other tends to the littler ones and meals."

"You like this idea?" Daed asked.

"It's perfect for me. I can teach and hold babies, and my hours will be really flexible. She will pay me almost as well as my position at our Amish school did. And I can continue helping her throughout this year even *if* I were to marry." She didn't like using *if*, but any talk of marriage with someone other than Grey was improper at this point.

"It sounds like a good fit for you." Grey said the supportive words, but was that concern she saw in his eyes?

They discussed the weather and how business was going at the cabinetry shop. When the sunlight waned, Lena lit a kerosene lantern.

Grey got up and began clearing the table. "We need to talk, Lennie."

Her Daed stood. "I'll leave you two to chat." He clicked his tongue, and Nicky hurried toward the door. "I'll be in the shop whenever you're ready to discuss the cabinets I need built." Her father's footsteps faded, and soon the screen door slammed shut behind him.

"He's struggling with the idea of letting you go."

"I know. It's weird. One can never tell how a person will feel when faced with new circumstances."

"Speaking of facing new situations, I...we..."

She waited, but he didn't continue. Instead, he set a pile of dishes in the sink. She'd seen him this way a few times since they'd fallen in love but never before that. They'd been friends forever, but when it came to the intimate side of sharing, he struggled to talk to her.

"What's the topic?" she asked.

"Us."

"That's my favorite subject."

He folded his arms and leaned against the sink, facing her. "It won't be tonight."

"I doubt that. So what's up?"

He stared at the floor, and she could feel the war going on inside him.

"Grey," she whispered as she moved directly in front of him. Hope for their future danced inside her. She placed her hands on his face, drew him close, and kissed him. "Tell me what's bothering you." She caressed his beard. "Whatever it is, I care about you more than *it*."

His silvery blue eyes bore into hers as if looking for the strength to tell her. He took her hands into his. "Remember when I told you last month that my marriage was troubled and that Elsie and I had taken a few steps toward a second chance right before she died?"

She nodded.

"One of those steps involved medical tests. See, it's possible that..." He stopped again.

When she realized how burdened he was, she led him out the back door and sat on the steps. This had been their place to talk years ago. "When I was a young teen, we talked for hours. You were my confidant. I was so smitten with you I couldn't stand it."

He sat beside her and propped his forearms on his legs. "Lennie."

She looped her uninjured arm through his and laid her head on his shoulder. "Whatever it is, we'll deal with it. Now, take a deep breath and spit it out."

He jerked air into his lungs. "There might be something wrong with my DNA. It may not be possible for me to have healthy children."

Fear jolted her body, but she held on to his arm and didn't lift her head. The desire for children had always been a part of who she was. Her need to nurture children was why she had become a teacher. She had a list of children's names in her hope chest. Silently she cried out to God.

He'd told her that his marriage had been difficult. He hadn't wanted to betray Elsie by telling others about their struggles, but he also didn't want any secrets to come between Lennie and him. Apparently he'd held on to this one.

"I had tests run last fall, ones that would confirm if there are certain hereditary issues."

"What did the results show?"

"I don't know. I burned them."

She fought to keep her voice from faltering. "Why?"

"It doesn't matter."

"So we don't know *if* there's a problem." Tears threatened, not just for herself, but for the heaviness Grey had been carrying. This gentle, loving man lived inside a prison. "But the doctor will have a copy of the results. After you contact him and learn the truth, we can go from there."

"It sounds easy enough, doesn't it?"

The grief in his voice pressed in on her until she finally understood. Learning the truth had a finality to it that he didn't want to embrace. He'd ignored and repressed his concerns until he no longer had the strength to do so.

"Grey, we can work through anything. Where is your faith?"

He removed his arm from hers and interlaced his fingers. Staring into the distance, he said nothing for several minutes. "You don't understand. You're young and full of ideals about what marriage will be. But I can tell you, the inability to have children has the power to destroy us."

"No it doesn't. I'll never, ever regret falling in love with you."

"You're starry-eyed and in love." His shoulders slumped. "But time could change that. You were lugging around baby dolls before you could walk—and every year after that until you turned thirteen and started baby-sitting. It's a part of your makeup."

Sitting up straight, she gazed into his eyes. "You can't honestly believe that if the tests come back with disappointing results, it's the beginning of the end of us."

"I didn't know that's what all my reservations boiled down to until this moment. Either I lose you now or years from now."

She knelt on the step below him. "How can you talk to me as if we're doomed because we may have serious problems to face? Life dishes out what only God can get us through." As the words poured forth, she knew it was more than just her speaking. She felt His Spirit moving in her. "About two months ago we were standing on opposite sides of the creek where the bridge is now. We hadn't talked for weeks because I wasn't sure you really loved me. Remember?"

He traced the birthmark across her cheek and down her neck. "I'd been bearing my soul through letters, and finally you came to look me in the eyes."

"While we talked, I saw an image in my mind's eye. I believe God Himself was showing me how you really felt, encouraging me to accept as truth what you'd said and written to me. To finally believe that you loved me."

The gentleness in his eyes warmed her. "What did you see in that vision?"

"Us. Married and in your bedroom. Moonlight painted the room with a silvery glow. You were leaning against pillows, and I was lying across the foot of the bed while we talked. We were so happy, and in that snapshot I felt what could never be seen with the human eye or understood by logic—the magnitude of our friendship. It was rich and deep and beautiful." Even now she could feel the power she'd experienced when she saw that image. "Only you or I have the power to take that from us, Grey."

He held her hand, stroking it but saying nothing. The summer evening sounds of crickets, June bugs, and frogs surrounded them.

She hurt for all he'd been through and his worry over their future. "I will grieve for a season if we can't have children. But my dreams will break for all time if I can't have you."

"It's not that we can't have children. It's that we mustn't. If the DNA tests confirm there's a problem, we could conceive child after child with severe handicaps."

Heat prickled her skin at the image, and she thought of Ivan, who'd been born missing part of one arm. Ivan was quiet like his Mamm had been, but having tested him last year as a forerunner to starting school this fall, she knew he was brighter and more of a problem solver than most.

"Earlier tonight you said you didn't want us to be perfect. But you want perfect children?" she asked.

"Not perfect, but at least with a fighting chance to be whole."

"Special children are a blessing, and I trust God with those things. Always have. And once we're married, you'll be by my side too, protecting, strengthening."

"Lennie, full-term babies die with the kind of issues we're talking about. I can't protect you from the brokenness that will take place."

She remembered his and Elsie's grief-stricken faces when they buried their stillborn son. "Grey, you've been through so much in the last six years. Has it caused you to forget how to trust God?"

He lifted her hand to his lips and kissed it. "I should have seen this before, but it's clear now that it's not God's ways or this fallen planet that I'm afraid of." He caressed her hand. "It's losing you."

"Think about who I am. Is that really possible?"

An unsure smile slowly grew more confident. "Are you saying it's not?"

"I am."

"You're not taking this the way I thought you would."

"I don't like your news, but I love you. That won't change. You've been letting worry talk, and you've been listening."

"Ya, I guess so."

"And there are ways to prevent getting pregnant. I learned about them in public school."

"The bishop would never allow that."

"Are you going to ask him?"

Grey blinked. "I thought… Never mind." He cleared his throat. "Personally, I believe the union between husband and wife stands before God on its own. If you agree, then whatever decisions we come to on this will be between Him and us."

"I trust God, and I trust you to hear Him."

A smile tugged at one side of his mouth. "Pray with me. Then whatever we think our next move should be, we'll do it in agreement."

With their heads bowed, she cried to God. The idea of burying their babies hurt deeply. But with Grey holding on to her hands, she already felt strength pass between them.

Nineteen

With a rolling pin in hand, Cara flattened a double portion of piecrust against the countertop. Lori sat on the floor beside her, lightly prancing her homemade cloth dolls over Better Days's ribcage as he lay still, wagging his tail.

When she'd come downstairs Monday night to meet with Trevor, the bishop, and Ephraim, she didn't have any anger left in her to lash out with, which was a welcome improvement. But she didn't apologize either, not really.

Her memory of coming down the stairs and into the room where the men were seated was fuzzy. The God event that had taken place before-hand seemed to have displaced her, as if only part of her were there.

She clearly remembered talking to Trevor. "I'd intended to pretend my way through this," she'd told him, "but I can't. And I won't lie. So if I've said things you didn't deserve or treated you worse than I should have, I'm sorry. Personally, I don't see how my honesty comes close to comparing to what you did to me, but apparently you think so. And the church leaders seem to agree with you."

Feeling woozy, she had taken several deep breaths. But as she'd stood there, she'd felt empowered to speak her heart. "I actually do hope I can forgive you one day, for my sake more than yours. That's all I can offer you right now, and it's a ton more than I want to give. But I'm willing to aim for some type of bearable reconciliation."

He'd stepped forward, shaking the way old alcoholics tend to do. "Thank you." His eyes had misted, a half-starved man gratefully accepting the meager scraps being offered.

Hatred had melted from her, leaving a strong residue of dislike in its place. She should have been more specific about how often he could visit, but it hadn't dawned on her at the time. He'd rented a room in someone's house not too far away, which made dropping by easy for him.

The front screen door closed with the familiar rhythm of two thuds, one thump, and numerous taps. Someone had either come in or gone out. Footsteps echoed against the wooden floor. Heavy ones.

He had entered the house. He'd come Monday and yesterday. Would he visit *every* day until she put a stop to it?

She had no idea what to call the man who was technically her father. Before the mandated visits, she'd called him Trevor a few times. But now even that seemed too personal, and just thinking the word *Dad* made her physically nauseous.

Answering the door when he showed up and having to let him in without really welcoming him was awkward—as if her pride kept her from being able to perform that simple task. So she'd told him not to knock.

Now that seemed like a mistake. This was the only real home she'd had since her mother died, and she'd allowed him to come in at will. Not only did she not know what to call him; she didn't know how to deal with him.

He opened the swinging door to the kitchen. "Morning."

She returned his nod. "Hello."

He knelt beside Better Days and smiled at Lori. "How are you this morning?"

"Okay," Lori whimpered before getting up, moving to Cara, and wrapping her arms tightly around her mom.

Her behavior reminded Cara of the trauma her daughter had experienced after she'd witnessed the police handcuff Cara and threaten to haul Lori off to foster care. Ephraim had arrived and intervened, despite his reservations. Later that evening, in an effort to soothe Lori's panic, he'd brought her favorite puppy from the litter in the barn. Lori had taken to Ephraim immediately, but she didn't like her own grandfather. Cara had no doubts that Lori was picking up on her mother's feelings toward Trevor.

She kissed the top of Lori's head and gently unlocked the girl's arms from her waist. "Why don't you take Better Days outside for a while?"

Lori picked up her dolls, skirted as far around Trevor as possible, and went outdoors with Better Days.

"Would you like some coffee?" Cara asked.

He shook his head. "I thought maybe we could go for a walk, all three of us."

"I have lots of work to do."

He didn't respond, and she refused to look at him. She cut out miniature piecrusts, wishing Deborah and Ada would get back soon from making deliveries to bakeries and picking up supplies. Someone running interference would be very helpful.

He leaned against the sink and folded his arms. "What are you making?"

She leveled a look at him before focusing on the dough in front of her. It was obvious she was making piecrusts. Thoughts of her mother scurrying up the stairs with her and hiding her in a cubbyhole behind the wall of the attic screamed at her.

Two days. That was all that had passed since her odd encounter while kneeling beside her bed. It was God who'd held her, wasn't it? It seemed impossible that He cared that much for someone like her. At times she found it easier to believe the whole thing had been her imagination. But, in spite of herself, she knew it had happened.

She tried to apply those feelings of love and acceptance to the man in the room with her, but it wasn't working. Not yet. Maybe never. God's intervention had touched her mind and heart deeply, but it hadn't done much to free her of bitterness and rage.

"Look, Cara, I know this is hard for you," Trevor said. "From the things you said Monday evening, it's obvious you think I ran to Emma and Levi to complain about your outburst. I didn't, but I have no words to describe what your news did to me. It's my own fault. I know that. But all these years I've believed you were happy and safe here with them. I had to know what happened, to separate facts from fiction. I'm sorry that the bishop got involved and that now we're both stuck going through the motions."

"If you don't want to be here, then why not make our lives easier and just go away?"

"For me, I want to be here. For you, I'd leave if I could. But we both need to prove to the church leaders that you're ready to join the faith this fall. If I walk away now, it'll make your efforts to become Amish harder, won't it?"

She hadn't thought about that, but he was right. Now that the bishop knew about her outburst and her bitterness toward Trevor, if he left without their coming to some sort of peace, she'd not be allowed to join the faith—a faith that believed in gentleness toward those who'd wronged them and forgiveness at all costs.

"I guess it's best you're here…for practical reasons."

"I'm glad we understand each other about this." He watched her cut another miniature piecrust. "Can I help?"

"I guess."

He went to the sink and scrubbed his hands.

When he returned to the work station, she passed him a disposable pan. "Lay it upside down on the dough, and slice around it. Getting them up in one piece takes practice, and I don't have time for mistakes."

He pressed the pan onto the dough, following her instructions care-fully. His eyes rose to meet hers, and she realized they shared the same eye color—golden bronze. Why would he act so humble and willing to follow her directions? What did he hope to gain?

The rolling pin hit the floor with a thud, breaking in to her thoughts. She picked it up, scrubbed it, and dried it. When she turned around, her father had set a row of pie tins along the countertop, brushed each one with oil, and begun putting piecrusts in them. Moving from cutout to cutout, he efficiently fixed each one, including the decorative edge.

"Where'd you learn to do that?"

"Your mom."

Cara wished she hadn't asked.

"Don't you remember any of our Sundays together?"

She shook her head. "I can barely remember what she looked like."

He pulled his billfold out of his back pocket and passed a small picture to her. "It's awfully faded."

The photo showed all three of them in what looked like a park. Trevor was holding her, and she had her arms wrapped around his neck, giggling by the looks of it. Her mom's smile radiated back at her.

But the image in her hand washed out and was replaced by a more familiar one. "Cara," Mama whispered, touching her lips with her index finger. "Don't make any noise." She turned on the flashlight and put it in Cara's hand. "You sleep here unless I come back for you." Cara clutched her doll in one hand and the flashlight in the other.

"Melinda!" Her father's footsteps echoed like a monster invading their home. Her mother closed the small door to the attic wall.

Cara passed the snapshot back to him.

"You don't remember?"

"I recall plenty. Do yourself a favor and don't ask me about it."

"It wasn't all bad, Cara."

She swallowed and managed a nod.

"You know," he said as he washed his hands again, "there are perks to my being around. I have a car. It's beat-up, but I could make it easier for you to get back and forth to Dry Lake."

"Don't you want to get a job?" Since it was obvious he'd be around for a while, she liked the idea of his doing something that would keep him out of her hair.

"I had one as a school janitor until recently. I get the shakes so bad at times I can hardly stand up, and they let me go."

"Years of drinking can do that to a person."

"You have your mama's sense of honesty."

"I know of a couple of people who need a farmhand. Aaron Blank and Sylvia something."

"Friends of yours?"

"I just met both of them Sunday evening. She's going to help teach me the Amish language starting tomorrow."

"Another obstacle to joining?"

He acted so interested and caring. If she told him he was a fake, he'd look hurt and argue. Maybe she should test him a little, let him see his own insincerity.

"Yeah, but I can't let her do that for no cost, and money is always tight for me. If you want to make up for the past so badly, how about paying for the lessons? That's what dads do, isn't it?" She talked to Better Days in this same tone when he misbehaved.

A sweet-looking smile crossed his face. "I'll speak to Aaron Blank about that job opening."

He wouldn't last long doing farm work, especially in this heat. But it'd keep him from having so much free time on his hands.

Aaron climbed the ladder to the haymow, looking for Sylvi. He'd gone to the cabin and the pond behind it as well as to the milking parlor but hadn't found her. The old wood moaned under the weight of his body.

Five days had passed since she'd told him and his parents about having kissed a married man. She had revealed her wrongdoing for his sake, to try to make his father understand that people make mistakes but can change. And other than a brief "thanks," Aaron hadn't mentioned a word about it to her. They'd worked from sunup to sundown Wednesday through Saturday, but they'd only spoken when necessary and avoided any mention of that topic.

He'd kept to himself more this week, thinking silence would build a thick partition between them. Instead, an invisible connection had formed—at least for him. No matter how much he tried to deny, ignore, or sabotage the bond, it only grew stronger. He had no idea what she thought or felt other than determination to hold on to this abomination she called a farm.

A quick glance into the haymow said she wasn't there either. He climbed into the loft, hoping to spot her in one of the pastures. Instead, he found her sound asleep on a blanket against a mound of loose hay. Four kittens were bunched up in her lap, sleeping.

He sat, leaning against the frame of the barn, and watched her.

He was drawn to her, fascinated by her, and thirsty for more time with her. He'd never before been pulled like this by anything—except alcohol. The realization scared him senseless. He'd already proven he lacked good judgment about what attracted him.

So why was he here?

On Friday, with Trevor Atwater's help, he and Sylvi had finished baling the hay, and yesterday they'd loaded it onto several wagons. It now sat inside the barn, waiting to be sold. His excuse for searching for her was that he had a buyer, a person that he had begun talking to a couple of days ago. The man had come by earlier today, but since it was Sunday, Aaron was limited to agreeing to sell it to him tomorrow. And the man had agreed to a top-dollar price. She'd like that.

After all their work getting the hay in before the rain came, they should've celebrated last night—had a feast with special desserts or something. Instead they did what they always did when work or mealtime was over—they went their separate ways. Then again, how could they celebrate together when they saw the completed task as accomplishing opposite goals?

She stretched and drew a deep, relaxing breath. When she saw him watching her, she frowned and rubbed her eyes. "Hi."

"You're not an easy woman to find." It struck him how true his words were. Anytime he thought he saw her—figuratively speaking—she shifted and revealed something different. Like a mirage, she appeared, only to disappear.

She sat up, rearranging the kittens. "What do you want?"

"I have good news. A man has offered top dollar for the hay."

"Clay Severs?"

"No, a different man. Clay's idea of a fair price was way too low."

"You shook hands on it with this other man?"

"Ya. He's picking it up and paying for it tomorrow."

"That's great." She closed her eyes tight before blinking a few times. "What time is it?"

"Five."

Her eyes grew large. "I knew I was tired. It was all I could do to stay awake during church this morning. I think Cara pinched me three times."

"You should've stayed home and slept instead."

She huffed. "Very funny."

He'd knocked on her cabin door an hour before time to leave for church, then returned in a rig to pick her up. She wasn't pleased. To convince her to go, he agreed to do one favor of any sort for her if she'd get in the rig. Without another word, she got in.

"So have you decided what favor I owe you?"

"You shouldn't ask that when you're sitting near an open hayloft door three stories above ground."

He laughed. "I wouldn't recommend tossing me out until we get the next field cut and sold."

She moaned. "Next field? Oh, Aaron, don't use such mean words. I can't stand the thought of more hayfield work right now."

"Sorry. I didn't mean to ruin your Sunday afternoon."

A tabby kitten climbed up Sylvi's chest and snuggled against her neck.

"There's something else I'm really sorry about. I shrugged off what you did to try to help Daed and me get along better. Time will tell, but I think your story has given him a new perspective. It took guts to share your past, and I should have thanked you properlike."

Her brows wrinkled a bit, and he wondered if she found him as difficult to understand as he found her. "Why didn't you?"

He gathered a small handful of hay off the floor and tossed it out the doorway. "I don't know. Maybe because I know I haven't earned your kindness. And we have opposing visions. It's like we're enemies, and yet we're not."

She put the three sleeping kittens on the blanket. Keeping the other one in her hands, she moved to the hayloft door next to him. "I can see that." She sat, dangling her feet toward the ground. "There's always been plenty unsaid between my Daed and me too. It's the way he is with all his daughters. Good man. Diligent and faithful to God, family, and community, but..."

"You wanted more."

"I longed for him to understand me. I had that kind of relationship with my grandfather. And Daed seemed fine with my voicing an opinion or questions—in small amounts. Based on what I'd said, he even changed certain aspects of how we farmed. But I kept my mouth shut as much as I could stand. I didn't want to ruin what we did have."

"I hate how tough it is to build a good relationship and how easy it is to ruin it."

"You and Michael could win an award for what's left unsaid between you two."

He cleared his throat. "When I was a kid and even well into my teen years, we talked about everything. But after we moved here, he and Mamm changed. They'd been through hell in Ohio, and every hope they had was centered on this farm in Dry Lake. Within weeks of moving, Daed started feeling exhausted and weak, and the knuckles of his thumbs hurt. Within a couple of months, all his joints ached, and shortly after that he was diagnosed with rheumatoid arthritis. He made it worse because he stopped trying to use his hands. He'd spend weeks in bed, and when he got up, he'd start in on me about everything I hadn't done. The farm was going to seed…and it was my fault."

"Is that when you started to hate farming?"

"Probably. The next few years I worked like crazy trying to live up to what he wanted." He ran his fingers over the dust on the rough-hewn planks. "It never happened. I was so miserable that I'd do anything for a break from the weight of it. From that first beer, the experience was…an escape. So I started partying with anyone who wanted to come to the cabin and bring drinks. I couldn't get enough. It's not Mamm's or Daed's fault, but they made it easy. Never checked on me. All those times I didn't come home at night, they thought I was sleeping in the barn."

"Maybe if you really opened up with Michael as humbly and unaccusing as you just—"

He put his index finger to his lips. "Don't, please." He stared at the rolling hills dotted with grazing cows. The sight might look beautiful to her, but it made him feel like a slave to a bunch of completely stupid creatures. "Can we change the subject?"

She nodded. "How's Frani?"

"She's a mess. More pigheaded than I am. But there's hope that she'll decide to get help."

"When your Daed hired me, he said I could share the cabin with anyone I wanted...as long as it wasn't a man, of course. I think he had my sisters in mind. But if it comes to that, she can stay with me for a while."

"Thanks. That's really generous of you." Aaron chewed on a piece of straw, mulling over whether to ask her a question or two. "What happened between you and the man you..."

"Elam." She stared at the horizon. "We fell in love, but when he asked me to marry him, I wasn't ready. I wanted another year, maybe two. Three weeks later he asked...someone else. A few years after they married, the emotions between us resurfaced. That's why I came here."

The depth of grief in her brown eyes made a twinge of physical pain run through him. Maybe he shouldn't have written that letter. He hadn't known this was her reason for leaving Path Valley. He'd thought she was here because of a feud with her sister. That was what she'd said, wasn't it?

The upside was that she had no idea Beckie had ignored his letter. So far.

"Hey." She tossed a little hay at him. "Just because I don't want to talk about that doesn't mean you can't talk at all."

He wrestled with the idea of asking her to go for a buggy ride. At almost twenty-six, he'd never asked a girl to go anywhere. It'd be nice if he had some experience to rely on. He wondered how Elam had asked her out the first time and what she might expect from a beau.

Idiot! What am I thinking? They couldn't get all cozy. He intended to sell this place and leave. She was bent on convincing him not to sell and probably wished he'd just leave. The key word in either scenario was *leave.*

Sylvia moved closer and dusted off the hay that she'd thrown on him, quickly brushing her hands over his shoulder before picking a stray piece out of his hair. "There, now you look all perfect and handsome again."

Did she think him handsome? He liked that idea, although he knew he shouldn't. He took the lone piece of hay from her and quietly placed it on her head. They laughed before she plucked it off and dropped it out the window.

"Oh, I almost forgot." She passed him the kitten and rubbed behind its ears. "During the after-service meal, a couple of the single girls invited me to a singing tonight."

"And you said yes? That's unexpected." His eyes locked on hers.

"Not that much. I've been to singings all around Pennsylvania, some in Ohio too."

"Really?"

"I used to get away from the farm for weeks at a time, staying with cousins. We went to singings and outings."

"That's a side of you I wouldn't have banked on."

"It was fun. I never found another guy I liked, but I met lots of interesting people. A girl named Mary is coming to get me. Do you want to go with us?"

His heart beat a little faster at the idea, but he wasn't the kind of person to attend the overly chaperoned event, boys on one side and girls on the other. A fair number of the parents seemed to want a spotless attitude to shine from every youth, and he wasn't a mask-wearing type of guy. "Spare me."

She laughed. "That's a definite no." Then she hustled down the ladder.

Seeing the top of her head vanish, disappointment settled over him. He could have talked with her the whole evening and enjoyed it more than doing anything else. It was apparent she didn't feel the same way.

Twenty

In the upstairs bathroom Cara held a washcloth under cool water, hoping to find some relief from this awful heat wave. She wrung it out and wiped it over her face and neck. The old mirror hanging in front of her matched the banister, moldings, doorknobs, and other fixtures in Ada's House—worn, but classic.

This house had character and stamina. It gave shelter from the elements, provided a place to be a family and meet each other's needs, and even offered a way to make a living. In a metaphorical way, she wanted to be like that too—protective, hospitable, and a unique asset.

But she couldn't stop rehashing the hurt and misery her dad's choices had caused her. She wanted to be free, not just so she could settle the issue with the church leaders, but so she could focus on healthier things.

He'd lived as he wanted to, making poor choices all along the way and not caring one iota about her. Who she was today—the ugly, awful past Ephraim helped her shoulder—wasn't her fault. If Trevor had stopped indulging himself in liquor long enough to make sure his daughter was in safe hands, she would've grown up being the kind of woman Ephraim deserved.

"Cara?" Deborah tapped on the bathroom door.

"Come on in."

Deborah opened the door, moved to the sink, and picked up her toothbrush. "Jonathan found this neat little ice cream parlor about two miles from here. It opened earlier this summer, but he just discovered it a few days ago. Since we're closed this evening, we thought we'd put our night off to good use. Would you and Lori like to go with us?"

Deborah and Ephraim didn't favor each other as much as some siblings, but they'd both stolen her heart. "You sure Jonathan wouldn't mind? Maybe he'd like a little time alone with you." Jonathan helped around Ada's House nearly every night and worked as a traveling blacksmith to Amish farms during the day.

A beautiful dusting of pink shaded Deborah's face as she loaded toothpaste onto her brush. "He's the one who said to ask."

"Really? I knew I liked that young man of yours." Cara stepped aside to let Deborah brush her teeth. After Cara removed her prayer Kapp, she pulled the bobby pins out of her half-fallen hair and brushed it in an effort to recapture all the loose strands.

Deborah had been seeing Jonathan for quite a while, and their relationship had been tested. Mahlon, her ex-fiancé, had come back for her and promised to do whatever it took to win her back. But instead his visit had convinced Deborah that the kind of man she really wanted was the opposite of Mahlon—a man who embraced life and people, who gave because he enjoyed it, who didn't need her to keep him in line or to make sure he had enough reasons to want to live.

And Deborah had all that in Jonathan.

Deborah rinsed her toothbrush. "Here, let me." She ran a brush through Cara's hair. "Since Amish women don't cut their hair, I didn't realize it grew in again so slowly. You've been growing it out for more than a year, and it's not even to your shoulders yet."

"That's partly because it started out shorter than most men's hair. And maybe my hair grows really slowly."

"Why'd you keep it so short?"

"It was convenient and cute, in my estimation. When I saw all the

Amish women with their hair pulled back, I thought that was silly. If you're going to keep it hidden, why not cut it short?"

"I can see thinking that way." Deborah looped a covered rubber band around Cara's hair and pinned it in a bun. "So are you going with us to the ice cream parlor?"

Cara put on her prayer Kapp again. "Sure." She went to Lori's room, where her daughter sat on her bed, reading aloud to Better Days. "We've been invited to go with Deb and Jonathan for ice cream. Care to—"

"Yes!" Lori hopped up and gave Cara and Deborah a hug before bounding down the steps, Better Days running ahead of her.

"The dog stays, Lori."

"Aw, Mom."

"He'll eat your ice cream, mine, Deborah's, and Jonathan's."

"Well," Israel said.

Cara spun around.

"Good thing he's not eating my ice cream."

"Israel." She wanted to hug Lena's dad, but that suggested a closeness she didn't really have with him. "I didn't know you were here."

"I wasn't. Now I am. What's all this talk about Better Days eating ice cream?"

Lori hurried over to him and took his hand. "You seen Ada yet?"

"I most certainly have." He pointed up the stairs.

Ada stood behind the banister, peering over it. She wore a clean dress and apron and a beautiful smile. She looked more youthful than ever as she slowly made her way down the stairs.

"So where's Jonathan?" Cara asked.

The sound of footsteps on the wooden porch made them turn toward the screen door.

He stood there.

Israel glanced at Cara, waiting to take a cue from her. But she stood in a pool of hurt, unsure how to cope with *his* presence. It was as if each time she saw him, she dealt with the same raw, unbound pain she'd grown up with.

"Trevor." Israel motioned for him to enter. "Good to see you."

When Trevor stepped inside, Lori took a step back, withdrawing her hand from Israel's. She moved beside her mother and wrapped her arms around Cara's waist.

Jonathan came in the front door. "I've connected the hayride wagon, minus the hay. Now we have room for everyone." When he spotted Trevor, he looked at Cara as if checking on her.

She wanted to shake her head, but something stopped her. Maybe she should feel sorry for Trevor. He looked out of place, standing in the middle of a group obviously bent on going elsewhere.

In the eleven days since he'd begun working at the Blank farm, he hadn't been around much. And she'd enjoyed every moment of his absence. Nothing like dairy farming to keep a person constantly busy.

"I'll just be going." Trevor looked at Cara. "Have fun. I'll see you later."

When he walked out, everyone stood there awkwardly, looking anywhere but at her.

"Okay, fine. I hear you." She stepped onto the porch. Her father's shoulders were slumped as he went down the sidewalk.

An image of herself at sixteen, scantily dressed and dancing at a bar, flashed before her. Circumstances had trapped her into making choices she wasn't proud of. Had they trapped him too?

"Wait." Cara hurried toward him.

He turned.

"You could go with us."

"That's okay, Carab—" The hurt reflecting from him tugged at her. She closed her eyes. "I want you to come with us."

"No you don't."

"So you're giving up?"

He barely shrugged. "I'm not much of an arguer."

"Was Mom?"

He shook his head. "She had a strong will, but like most of her people, she wore it quietly and politely."

Cara's eyes misted. "I still miss her."

He nodded. "So do I. Every day, all day long."

His words stunned her. He used to say that to her before bedtime on a good evening. They'd had good times? The realization made her shudder. "You...read to me on the couch while Mama sat in her chair mending clothes."

A faint smile eased some of the sorrow from his eyes. "Yeah, that's right."

She remembered that when it was time for her to go to bed, she'd say, "I love you," and he'd say, "I love you more. Every day, all day long."

She'd gag on those phrases if she tried to speak them now. "You should come with us."

"You really want me to?" The disbelief in his voice rattled her.

She nodded.

"Lori won't like it."

"I'll let Better Days go with us, and you can give the dog a lick of your ice cream. She'll like that."

He scrunched his face. "Do I have to eat the rest of the cone afterward?"

She stood speechless for a moment until she realized he was teasing her. She chuckled. "Is it okay if I call you by your first name?"

"Of course."

"How about a horse-and-wagon ride to the ice cream parlor, Trevor?"

"I'd like that."

She turned toward the house. "Deb, you guys ready?"

While everyone piled into the wagon, Cara stepped inside the house. "Come on, Better Days." The dog bounded out the door, to the wagon, and onto Lori's lap. Cara climbed into the wagon, and Lori beamed at her mom.

Israel drove with Ada beside him. Trevor shifted, his thin frame looking uncomfortable on the wooden slats. "Where's Ephraim?"

"He doesn't usually come to Ada's House during the week."

"Why not?"

"He logs a lot of hours at his cabinetry shop in Dry Lake."

"He seems like a good man."

"He is." She bit her bottom lip to keep a goofy grin off her face. "I first met him when I was eight. As an adult he came to New York, looking for me."

They spent the ride in stilted, uncomfortable conversation. But at least she was able to talk civilly to him.

The ice cream parlor had walk-up windows and picnic tables under huge shade trees. Everyone except Trevor picked out a favorite flavor, then moved to a table. Trevor stayed in the wagon with Better Days.

Cara ordered three cones and sent Lori back to the wagon with Trevor's. After gathering some napkins, Cara handed Lori her ice cream, and she hurried to Deborah and Jonathan's table.

Cara moved back to the wagon and sat on the tailgate. "If cameras were allowed here, I'd fill a photo album a month with pictures."

Trevor licked his ice cream while trying to keep forty-pound Better Days at bay. "You could probably snap some privately of those closest to you and keep them tucked away."

"Yeah, maybe. But I'm already on the bishop's most wanted list, though I've managed to stay off the deacon's list. I'd like to keep it that way."

"The deacon coming to see someone is a bad thing?"

"He visits when a person is in violation of an Amish rule. From what

I've seen, the bishop tries to intervene in situations and steer folks the right way. If the deacon is called in, he drops the gavel—no debate allowed."

"Guess it'd be best for you not to be caught with a camera."

"I wish they'd at least allow one family picture every four or five years. Nothing fancy but something like the shot you have of Mom and me."

"I look at it every day."

"I don't have a single photo of Lori's dad to show her."

"Why not?"

"I needed to get out of New York fast, so I took Lori and left everything behind except the clothes on our backs…and her book bag."

"Maybe you could return to New York to get your things."

"Oh, I can just see the Plain folks finding out I'm running over to New York for a couple of eight by tens."

"I guess not. Those pictures meant a lot to you, though, didn't they?"

"Certainly not more than our safety. But they would mean a great deal to Lori. She doesn't have any memories of her dad, and he loved her so much—both of us, really. I think she'd cherish having photos of them together. Even more so when she gets older. I realized that when I saw the picture of you and Mom."

"Where in New York did you live?"

When she told him the name of the apartment building, his eyes lit up. "I know right where you're talking about. I used to work as a handyman at the apartments across the street."

"Really?"

"The manager of your apartment building would've had cleaners get rid of anything left behind."

She shrugged. "Yeah. Probably."

"Anyone who might've salvaged your stuff?"

Her heart glimmered with a touch of hope. "Lori's baby-sitter lived next door. It's possible she grabbed a few things and is holding on to them."

"You should write to her."

The hint of excitement faded. "I can't. It's best if my whereabouts remain a secret."

"Creditors?"

"Worse. I'd rather not talk about it."

Better Days lunged forward, taking a swipe at Trevor's ice cream. The sudden movement made him drop the cone, and Better Days lapped it up.

"And Lori wasn't even here to see my great sacrifice," he said.

His humor caught her off guard, making her realize she saw him as less than human, which he wasn't. Maybe building some semblance of a relationship with him was possible after all.

Twenty-One

Grey rinsed off the last of the flatware, but his mind remained on Lennie and their future. She loved so deeply and had enough resilience to cope with disappointments and grief without turning against him. No one would ever understand what that meant to him, but he was still unsure what his next step should be. He placed the handful of utensils into the dish drainer.

It had been two weeks since they'd talked. Except for the one church Sunday, he'd not even caught a glimpse of her. He still wasn't sure what he should do about the test results. Grey released the water from the sink and began to dry the dishes.

This decision wasn't about what he wanted. Lennie trusted him to hear God in the matter, so he kept setting aside his personal feelings while praying.

His son came inside with a small, hand-carved horse in his hand. After telling Grey that Israel was coming, Ivan asked for two things: a cup of cold water and permission to go across the bridge to Allen's house.

Grey glanced out the window and saw Israel cross the backyard. He'd used the bridge, which might mean Lennie was at her brother's this afternoon. Since today was the Fourth of July and all of Israel's family loved watching fireworks, they might be having a midweek gathering. It would be nice to see her, even if they'd be among a large group and would have to keep their distance.

Grey poured Ivan a drink and gave him permission to go to Allen's. He opened the screen door. "Hello, Israel. Kumm rei. What brings you here?"

Israel walked in. "I have a proposition for you to think on."

Grey took a glass out of the cabinet and filled it with icy water. He passed it to Israel. "Have a seat and tell me about it."

Israel pulled out a chair and sat. "I haven't talked to anybody but Ada about this, and I'm not ready for others to know just yet."

"Now I'm curious."

Israel grinned. "I asked Ada to marry me, and she said yes."

"Congratulations. That's great news."

Israel grinned while staring at the table. "I didn't know a man with grown children could feel like this. It's taken a long time for things between Ada and me to work themselves out. To say we're really happy about it doesn't begin to tell the tale."

"Lennie may be just as excited as you two when she learns of it."

"I suspect so." Israel took a drink. "We'll tell everyone soon enough, but one of Lena's first questions will be where we'll live, which is why I'm here." Israel smeared the condensation on his glass, fidgeting for no apparent reason.

Grey waited.

"I don't mean for my idea to interfere with your plans or hopes for your and Lena's future. You'll be the head of your household, so I'm coming to you with my idea. If you don't like it, I won't mention it to Lena. It's just an offer, one you can turn down, and I won't take it personal."

"Okay."

"You built this house, and maybe you and Lena want to move in here, but I'd like for you to think about moving yourselves and Ivan into my house when the time comes."

Israel had one of the nicest and prettiest places in all of Dry Lake. "Your place? Why?"

"Lena loves that old home, and I can build furniture anywhere. But Ada can't run her business here in Dry Lake. We don't get enough tourist traffic, and she loves operating Ada's House. So what I propose is a sort of house swap. You get my place, which has several rooms for a growing family, acreage, barns, and Lena's beloved greenhouse, and I get your place to put up for sale. Eventually that money will go to my other children to divide equally."

That was a really generous offer. Maybe too generous.

Israel slid his glass one way and then the other. "I'd do just about anything for Lena. I guess you've figured that out by now. And it's hard on a woman to enter another woman's home and build a life with someone, especially if she's never been married before." Israel sighed. "Am I butting in where I oughta stay out?"

"No. I agree with what you're saying. But how would the rest of your family take it? It's more their homestead than it is mine."

"If anyone minds, they'll get over it within a few days. Lena's been running that home since her mother passed, and it's hers. No one will deny that. Ada thinks if you two will be living there, it will make planning the wedding even more special for Lena."

"Ada knows about Lennie and me?"

"Ya. I had to talk to someone about giving up Lena. I know I'm not supposed to feel that way. Lena's nearly six years older than her sisters were when they married, but the idea of letting her go isn't coming easy."

"I'll take good care of her."

"Oh, heavens, I know that. And she'll do the same for you." Israel took a long drink. "Just think on my idea and let me know. This plan does have one stipulation."

"What's that?"

"The whole family is to gather there at least once a month in cold weather. We've always done that, and it's the only place that has room for all the children, spouses, and grandkids. Allen's place works in the summertime because we can overflow to the outside."

"You're right about Lennie and her home, and I'm sure the idea of moving into this one would give her some trouble." Grey had built this home, but it held a lot of memories. He really liked the idea of Lena and him getting a fresh start elsewhere, but he'd never entertained the idea because it wasn't affordable. "It's quite a gift."

"I'd appreciate your taking me up on my offer."

"Lennie would love it." Grey could imagine the excitement mirrored in her bluish green eyes. They might not be able to fill the rooms with children, but living there would always give her joy. "Of course I accept, Israel. Denki."

"Gut. Ya, that's gut." Israel finished his drink. "We'll talk to her about it as soon as Ada and I are ready to announce our news. I think Ada's right. Lena likes to know what's ahead when she can. It gives her time to get her feet under her."

A quiet calmness fell over Grey, hushing all the confusion and uncertainty inside him. He knew what he needed to do now. He'd get the test results. Whatever they learned, it would give Lennie and him time to get their feet under them.

Lennie had never failed to find contentment with any situation. It might take her a little while sometimes, but she put her will to work when it came to being happy. He'd seen her do it dozens of times, like when the school board removed her as a teacher even though that was all she'd ever wanted to be. Now, less than three months later, she'd found something else to joyfully fill her days this next school year—helping a homeschooling mom.

"Hey." Israel stood and set his glass in the sink. "We're having a spread of cold cuts and fruit at Allen's tonight. After supper we're going to load up in a few wagons and go watch fireworks in Shippensburg. I think you should join us."

Grey wouldn't go with them on the outing. That was for family members. But he could visit for a while before they left.

And he'd find a private moment to tell Lennie that he intended to find out the test results.

Twenty-Two

The aroma of dinner filled the air, and Sylvia's stomach growled. She stood in the driveway, waiting to see how many pounds of milk the cows had produced since the buyer's last visit two days ago.

The Englischer pulled a receipt off his ledger. "I think you'll like what you see."

She glanced at the numbers. "Oh I do. And I won't be the only one."

Milk production had increased consistently over the last several pickups, and Aaron had gotten top dollar for the hay. Both were very encouraging pieces of news.

"I'll see you day after tomorrow," the man said.

"The milk will be here. Bye." She folded the receipt and headed for the farmhouse. Since Aaron's apology in the hayloft more than two weeks ago, they'd managed the farm together without too many disagreements, although he didn't like her letting expectant cows find their own birthing spots. He preferred putting them in a large, clean stall.

She stepped inside the farmhouse but stopped cold when she saw Aaron walking around the table, setting it for dinner.

"Oh, good, you're here," Dora said, stirring a pot on the stove.

Aaron looked up. "You're late."

"Indeed I am." She laid the receipt on the counter before washing up to her elbows in the mud sink. "So...you're placing the flatware? What universe have I been transported to?"

"Can't a man pitch in without you making a big deal out of it?"

She dried her hands and arms. "Do you know how many men it takes to replace a roll of toilet paper?"

He shook his head.

"No one does. It's never been tried."

He laughed. "Do you know how many women it takes to make a man sorry he attempted to pitch in?"

She shook her head.

"One." He pointed at her. His demeanor was light and playful.

She stuck her tongue out at him. "Where's Michael?"

"Fetching the mail." Dora put the large pot in the center of the table.

Aaron poured a glass of water and handed it to Sylvia. "I wish he wouldn't wait until suppertime to do that. He opens it on the walk back, and the contents never make for good mealtime conversation."

Michael walked in, sorting through a handful of mail. He passed Aaron a letter. "This one's for you."

Aaron opened the envelope, read the letter, and laid it to the side.

Dora sliced huge chunks of homemade bread and placed one on each plate. She glanced at the envelope. "That looks like another letter from the place where you stayed."

"The Better Path," Aaron said. "Did you ever open any of the ones they sent to you?"

"I did once," his father said. "That was enough." He held up another envelope, showing it to Dora. It was from the Better Path and addressed to her and Michael.

Dora picked it up.

"If you're going to read it," Aaron said, "I'd suggest doing so later."

Ignoring her son's advice, Dora tore into it. "It's an invitation." She passed it to Michael. "Is that place like Alcoholics Anonymous?"

"I've never been to an AA meeting, but it's probably similar. It's designed by a Plain Mennonite, and it's for people in the Plain community."

Michael shook his head. "It's sad that Plain people need that kind of facility."

Aaron's anger flashed in his eyes. "It's even sadder when people know they can't cope well, yet they refuse to get help."

Embarrassment clouded Michael's features. "I handle things just fine. And I'm not getting into an argument tonight."

Sylvia loved the Blanks, but Michael's anger and Dora's submissiveness to him when it came to Aaron continued to disappoint her.

Dora poured a ladle of stew over the bread on each plate. "Why would we get an invitation to visit the Better Path since you're no longer there?"

"I'm supposed to attend the meetings at least twice a month, but I haven't gone since I came back here four weeks ago. This weekend is a group meeting, where everyone who's part of the program can have family or friends come. Since you never responded to my letters, I've never had anyone attend the group meetings for me."

Michael tossed the envelope toward the trash bin. "I'm not going this time either."

The disappointment on Aaron's face was minimal. No doubt he'd known what his Daed's reaction would be and had braced himself.

Dora finished pouring the stew and sat down. They bowed their heads for the silent prayer. Michael followed with an "amen."

Sylvia pulled the cloth napkin into her lap. "When is the meeting, Aaron?"

"This Saturday."

"Are you going?"

"I need to."

She turned to Michael. "I can handle a day of milking while you go with Aaron."

"Let it go, Sylvi," Aaron said.

She studied him, disappointed in the apathy she heard in his tone and saw reflected in his eyes. If every person who attended that day would have at least one family member or friend there, Aaron should too.

The clinks of flatware against plates resounded in the quiet room. When the meal was over, Aaron excused himself and left the house.

Sylvia turned to Michael. "I think you should go to the Better Path on Saturday."

"It's bad enough he's going. I won't embarrass myself by stepping into that place."

There were so many arguments on Aaron's behalf that she wanted to voice. But it wasn't her place. Michael was her father's age, and even though the feelings between Michael and her were often like that of a parent and an adult child, she was just a hired worker. She looked to Dora, silently begging her to speak up.

Dora rubbed her forehead as if it hurt. "Michael." She spoke softly and waited for him to look at her. "You won't stop reminding Aaron of his past mistakes. You won't help him when he tries to make up for previous wrongs. And you won't attend a meeting that might help him with his future. What exactly are you willing to do for our only son?"

Sylvia longed to grasp Dora's hand and shout "denki!" Instead she remained still and silent.

Michael's face reddened. "Why should I do anything for him when he'll just up and leave again? And when he does, there'll be no note. No warning. He'll be here one day and gone the next."

Now that she knew Aaron better, Sylvia couldn't imagine him doing such a thing. He'd left home to get straightened out and had returned a hard-working, focused man.

Dora lowered her head. "If he'd asked your permission to go to this place and get help, would you have let him?"

Sylvia waited, but Michael didn't say anything. "Is this how you feel about me now too?"

He closed his eyes and put his head in his hands. "I've thought on your story about you and that married man, and you were wrong to do what you did, but that's different from what Aaron did. Your incident happened once, and you fled the temptation. Aaron wallowed in his sin and hid it from us for years. It's not my fault he needed such a place."

With Michael having that kind of stubborn attitude, Sylvia didn't understand how Aaron could remain so loyal to his parents. She'd given Elam the best of her heart, and he hadn't been loyal to her. He hadn't been loyal to Beckie, either. Yet Aaron had been good to his folks in spite of the way they treated him.

"I've been working with Aaron for a month now. He's not perfect." She reached across the table and put her hand over Michael's. "But he deserves someone who believes in him."

Dora ran her fingertips along the edge of the table, keeping her eyes lowered. "Does he know you began looking for someone you could hire to help him months before he left here?"

Michael shook his head. "He wouldn't believe me, and if he did, he'd say it was too little too late."

"It might let him know that we care. Would it be so horrible to admit we were wrong too?" Dora asked. "To let him see that we need him as our son, not just as a laborer?"

"I...I can't."

Sylvia was suddenly drained of all energy. She knew Michael felt deeply. During the months before Aaron returned home, she'd spent long evenings in the living room with Michael and Dora and had come to understand how much Michael loved his son. He needed Aaron far more than he needed a farmhand, but things she didn't understand, maybe pride and hurt, kept the two of them at odds. She couldn't help but wonder if Michael would open his heart before it was too late.

Dora moved to a chair closer to her husband. "If we went, we could go see that appliance store too. You promised we would."

Michael stood, looking frustrated and unsure of what was taking place. He sighed. "Okay, fine. We'll go." He looked at Sylvia. "All three of us. Grey won't mind stepping in to help on Saturday."

"But…" Sylvia saw no reason for all of them to attend.

"We're all going. But no one tells Aaron in case something happens that keeps us from making the trip."

She wished she could convince Michael to let her skip the outing. She had no problem supporting Aaron at the Better Path, but she didn't want to witness Michael and Dora walking through the appliance store. What if they liked it and the idea of moving began to grow on them?

Twenty-Three

Cara sat at the treadle sewing machine, making another cloth doll. Lori had gone with Ada and Deborah to deliver special order cakes to two shops. In a few hours customers would fill Ada's House, but at ten in the morning, it was quiet and peaceful.

Better Days went to the door, wagging his tail.

"Hey there, little pup." Trevor's raspy voice flowed through the empty home. He tapped on the door and then walked inside, carrying a brown bag about the size of a tissue box. He saw Cara working near a window in an open area off the foyer.

"He's not a puppy," she said. "Had his first birthday in April."

"Don't kid yourself, Cara. This dog is quite the puppy. Not an ounce of him is a watchdog, though, unless you count watching people walk right in your front door."

"He's a good fit for Ada's House. Can you imagine having a territorial dog with all the customers who come in during a week?" Cara snipped threads. "You're not working at the farm today?"

"Morning milking is done, and the barns are cleaned out, so I'm on break for a few hours." He pulled a treat out of his pocket and fed it to Better Days.

Trevor didn't seem to mind running back and forth regularly between Hope Crossing and Dry Lake. As dilapidated as his car was, it never gave him a lick of trouble, and he acted as though he enjoyed carting her around. That made it easy for her to go to Sylvia's to study...and to drop by the cabinetry shop to see Ephraim for a few minutes on the way. Cara liked Sylvia and appreciated the lessons, but her favorite part of going to Dry Lake was seeing her fiancé. Having Trevor around actually made her life easier, but taking his help was almost too effortless, and she chafed over it.

Trevor stopped petting the dog. "I wanted to come by and let you know I'm going away for a few days."

In spite of how far they'd come, she felt a burst of hope at the idea of his being gone, even briefly. "When?"

"This weekend."

Cara couldn't decide if she wanted to know where and why. "Looks like I'm going to be without a free ride this week." She sounded as if she were just using him, and part of her balked at being so distant toward him while allowing him to be of service to her.

"I'll probably be back before Tuesday."

Probably? She stopped messing with the material in her hand and stared at him, wondering if he might not come back at all. She couldn't deny that he had begun to matter a little, and that bothered her.

"I brought you something."

She took the package from his hand and peered inside. A used book. *The Hiding Place* by Corrie ten Boom. It seemed odd that she and Deborah had used the phrase *hiding place* when talking about Cara's anger with Trevor, and now he'd brought her a book with that title.

She read the back cover. He'd bought her a biography of a Holocaust survivor. She loved reading, but she hadn't read a biography since dropping out of high school.

"I bought it at a used bookstore a couple of miles from here. I gave your mom a copy for Christmas one year, and it became her favorite book. I'm not sure what happened to her copy."

"Did she love to read?"

"There isn't a word to describe how much she enjoyed it."

She opened the book. "Ephraim, Lori, and I love reading." Inside the front cover was a handwritten sentence. "Did you write this?"

"No. I didn't even see it there."

She ran her fingers over the cursive writing. *Never be afraid to trust an unknown future to a known God.*

Emotions rolled over her. "It's a saying of some sort." She passed him the book.

"That's a quote by Corrie ten Boom."

Never be afraid to trust an unknown future to a known God. "I like it."

"Good."

She skimmed through the book, catching just enough to know what she'd be doing tonight after everyone else went to bed. "Thank you."

He didn't answer, and she glanced up.

"Hello?" Jonathan called as he came in the front door. His almost white-blond hair looked like sunlight beaming under his hat, and his hazel eyes carried a gentle confidence. Deborah could look forever and not find a man better suited to her.

"Hey, Jon." Cara gestured from one man to the other. "Trevor, you remember Jonathan Stoltzfus. He and Deborah are courting."

"Yeah, he's been here several times while I was here," Trevor said. "Good to see you again."

Cara knew they'd met, but so many people came in and out of Ada's House that she didn't want to assume Trevor had everyone's names straight yet. "What are you doing here?" she asked Jonathan.

He peered into the other room. "Is it just us?"

"Yeah. Sorry. Deborah's making deliveries with Ada and Lori."

"Gut."

"Good?" She laughed. "That's a surprising answer. What's up?"

"I thought I had timed it right to miss her. I want you to come with me so I can show you something. I need your expertise."

"Mine? I know nothing about everything."

Jonathan chuckled. "Now that's just not true. You have great hunches and a good grasp of the big picture. Besides, you have Deborah pegged better than anyone else I know."

Cara found his opinion of her too lofty, but she lowered the needle into the cloth and released the presser foot. During one of her many sewing lessons, Ada had said that was the position to leave the machine in—the needle in a piece of cloth and the presser foot resting on it. "I'm game." She glanced at Trevor. "You?"

His eyes widened. "You're asking me to go too?"

She stood. "I am."

Trevor turned to Jonathan, wordlessly asking for his response.

"Ya, sure. I bet you know a thing or two about older homes."

Trevor pulled out his keys and dangled them. "Need a ride?"

Jonathan shook his head. "It's a stone's throw from here."

It surprised Cara how excited she was for Deborah. She hadn't realized it until now, but in some ways Deborah resided in her heart much as she imagined a sister would. "A house?"

He nodded. "I'm only checking into it right now. And I'd like to keep it a secret until I'm sure that it's the right house and that I qualify to buy it."

"Oh, Deborah's going to like the sound of that."

"Not a word, Cara. I know how you two stay up and talk half the night sometimes."

Cara made a zipping motion across her lips. A dreamlike feeling surrounded her. Before she landed in Dry Lake, she'd had only shards and fragments of relationships. But today with her *dad* beside her and her future brother-in-law inviting her to share in his excitement, she sensed a wholeness she'd never known before.

Aaron carried a fifty-pound bag of milk replacer into the calf barn and plunked it onto the ground. Trevor had already begun to muck out the stalls. Whatever the man was like at one time, he was now a hard worker. Aaron pulled at the nylon thread to break the bag's seal, but the cord broke instead.

"Here." Trevor hurried to him, reaching into his pocket. He pulled out a knife, whipped the blade open, and slit the bag.

"I need to get one of those."

Trevor smiled. "My beat-up old car and this knife are the only things I own that are of any use. It's a folding Buck with a lockback design." Trevor closed it with one move of his thumb. "Take a look."

Aaron held it. "It's got a nice weight to it."

"A man of means like you wouldn't have any trouble buying one of these."

Aaron passed it back. "I'll think about it."

It'd be rude to say he had less cash than Trevor. The man owned almost nothing, and the Blanks owned hundreds of acres, but they were up to their eyeballs in debt. However, people who lacked didn't want to be told how tight money was for a landowner with cattle, horses, crops, several carriages, and two houses.

"I could use a ride to Owl's Perch this weekend," Aaron said. "If I paid you, could you take me?"

"Actually, I was gonna ask for this weekend off."

"Oh, okay. I can get a ride elsewhere." Aaron had no idea if that was true, but it was the polite thing to say.

"Where's Owl's Perch?"

"Perry County, not far from Duncannon."

"I'm heading to New York on Saturday. I'd have to pass close to Owl's Perch. What time do you need to be there?"

"About two."

"Your dad and Sylvia doing the milking by themselves?"

"Ya. It was just the two of them for several months. They'll be okay."

"I can drop you off. But you'll have to figure out another way home."
Trevor slid his knife into his pocket.

"So what's going on in New York?"

"Were you here when Cara arrived in Dry Lake?"

Aaron hated being reminded of all he didn't remember. "Technically,
I'm sure I was."

Trevor filled the ten-ounce measuring cup with powdered milk and
dumped it into a sterilized calving bottle. "Technically?"

Aaron turned on the warm water at the mud sink. "When you came
here to ask for work, you said you're a recovered alcoholic."

"Yeah. Been sober nearly twelve years." He pointed at the bottle in
Aaron's hand. "Uh, I wouldn't do that if I were you."

"I'm just preparing the bottles for the calves."

"Sylvia will want to feed them herself. I just get the bottles ready with
powder and set them on the shelf." Trevor fixed a second bottle and put it
on a shelf near the sink.

"Not today she won't. Mamm roped her into helping can corn and
green beans." Aaron added two quarts of water to each bottle before turning off the water.

Trevor had been down the same rough road as Aaron and had been
sober much longer. Aaron wanted any words of wisdom the man might
have.

"I've been sober about six months."

Trevor moved to a fresh bale of hay and forked a hunk of it. "So you
were here when Cara arrived more than a year ago…and yet you weren't."

Aaron put the nipples and rings on the bottles and shook them. "Pretty
much. I don't remember her coming to the community, but at some point
I heard Ephraim had been shunned concerning her."

"What'd he and Cara do that caused Ephraim to get shunned?"

Aaron moved to the calves' pens and stuck the first bottle through the gates. A calf latched on hungrily. "I heard she and Lori were living in a barn, social services came for them, and Ephraim stepped in and took them to his home. He was sleeping in his shop, but when the elders confronted him and told him to get her out of his house, he refused."

Trevor spread hay in the stall while the calves were occupied and out of the way. "I can see why Cara and Lori trust him so much."

"That's all I know, just stuff I heard. I have years that are a jumbled, fuzzy mess inside my head."

"Cara told me that when she moved away from New York, she left everything behind. I'm going to see if the apartment manager or a neighbor might've held on to anything of theirs. I'm hoping somebody kept photos and maybe some special knickknacks."

"Sounds like a nice gesture. Does she know?"

"I want to keep it a surprise. So how are you doing with your sobriety?"

"Still sober. Still tempted not to be."

"Trust me on this one thing, Aaron. It's a battle worth fighting every day and every night."

A calf nudged the bottle, trying to get more milk to flow, and Aaron almost lost his grip on it. "Cara must've been, what, sixteen or seventeen by the time you sobered up?"

"I lost contact with her when she was eight, but, yeah, I was sober before her seventeenth birthday."

"You lose a lot, don't you? Booze lures...and then destroys."

Trevor climbed out of the last stall. "It does that. But it ruins far more than just *your* life."

Aaron's heart thudded against his chest. He knew the truth of Trevor's words. "The possibility of taking up the drink again scares me."

"Good. Fear keeps us from sticking our hands into a fire, walking through briars barefoot, and all sorts of stupid stuff. When being afraid of it goes away, you'll likely think you can handle a drink or two or a night or two out drinking. Don't believe it. People like you and me can't ever afford to believe that." Trevor put the pitchfork away and began cleaning the mud sink. "Both of my parents drank, and I started young. My mom once said she put a tablespoon of whiskey in my baby bottle every night so I'd sleep. But I thought I'd gotten free of it by the time I turned eighteen. That's when I met Cara's mom."

Trevor's confession rolled over Aaron like a threshing machine.

The calves had drunk all the milk, and Aaron tossed the bottles into the sink.

Trevor turned on the water and began disassembling the milk jugs. "I drank most of Cara's childhood away, and she's got the scars to prove it. If you ever have a child, you'll know that the word *love* doesn't begin to cover how you feel about that little being." Trevor dipped his head. "Not that Cara would ever believe that, and who can blame her? There's not one shred of evidence that I ever cared. To rebuild a relationship, there's gotta be something you can point at and say, 'Remember when I helped you build this or helped you make a good grade on that or taught you to swim?' Something…anything."

Aaron's skin felt clammy. Trevor spoke of honest, giving, caring love—the kind that couldn't be his if he ever started drinking again.

Trevor turned off the water and set the bottles upside down in a rack to dry. "When Cara came along, her mom and I thought we'd hit the jackpot." Trevor pursed his lips and released a heavy breath. "Yes, sir, we thought our ship had come in, you know? She was just that precious to us."

"Can I ask what happened that started you drinking again?"

"We had some issues. Melinda's heart was still broken over another man when we married, and I wasn't sure if she loved me or was just a loyal woman. But I kept trying, and so did she. Bills were never ending, and I lost a couple of jobs. Between all those things and how I grew up, I carried the constant feeling of being worthless. But there were some great times in spite of the pressures. I finally got a job that really suited me—as a handyman at an apartment complex. It came with free rent and enough money so Melinda could stay home with Cara."

Trevor grabbed the bag of milk replacer and put it inside a huge wooden barrel. He put the lid on it and tapped it down, ensuring no mice could get to it. He seemed to be buying time so he could gather the strength to finish the story.

"One day while I was fixing a light fixture in another family's apartment, a toddler wandered into the room. He grabbed hold of my ladder, smiling up at me, and I didn't think nothing about it." Trevor wiped tears from his eyes. "Next thing I knew, my metal toolbox fell off the top rung of the ladder and hit that little boy on the head. He died almost immediately."

"And you couldn't cope with the guilt."

Trevor shook his head. "It destroyed me. I always knew I was of no account as a drunk. But when I saw that I was of no account when sober and doing my best, I lost all will to fight. Poor Melinda did everything to reach me and give me strength."

Tears ran down Trevor's face. He put his hand on Aaron's shoulder and cleared his throat. "Whatever you do, stay sober. All those years of drinking made everything a thousand times worse, and the people I loved paid the highest price." Trevor let go of him and walked out the back of the barn into the pasture.

Aaron whispered a prayer, asking God for the ability to hold on to Trevor's words. Surely the tragedy of Trevor's story would strengthen his own resolve to remain sober. Addiction didn't bow to logic. It didn't yield to a man's dreams. It never surrendered to anything easily, including the will. For him, it took a combination of tools: determination, patience, and, most of all, the ability to surrender to God while fighting his own instincts.

What Trevor had just given him, the viewpoint from the bottom, and what the Better Path gave him, the truth of his condition and a community of support, were about all an addict could hope for. And he was grateful for every bit of help.

Twenty-Four

Sylvia looked out the side window of Robbie's car and then at the invitation in her hand. Michael sat up front, talking to Robbie. Dora and she had said little since the ride began more than an hour ago.

According to the time specified for family and friends to arrive, they were a little late. Trevor had picked up Aaron about four hours ago. But she'd had to find a missing cow and her calf while Michael milked the herd, and then she had to shower and get ready.

"This is the Better Path?" Michael asked.

Robbie pointed to a shingle hanging from one side of the porch.

"It's a house," Dora said.

"Appears so."

Three horses with carriages were tied to nearby hitching posts. Sylvia was sure the sight of Old Order Amish buggies made Michael regret his decision to come. He didn't want other Plain folk to see him going into a place like the Better Path.

"I have to go into Harrisburg and run some errands for Ephraim," Robbie said. "I should be back about the time you're ready to leave here and go to the appliance store."

"We appreciate your driving us," Michael said.

"Ephraim's needed me to get to Harrisburg for nearly a month. It's working out just fine."

Sylvia got out of the car and climbed the wooden steps to the porch, trusting that the reluctant Michael and Dora Blank would follow her. The house looked historic, but it wasn't in need of paint or fixing up. The sign on the glass part of the door invited folks to enter, so she did.

She walked into a large room with wooden floors, a huge staircase, and lots of doors off to the sides. The room was filled with people holding small paper plates of food and clear plastic cups filled with ice water or soft drinks. The air-conditioned room felt marvelous. Nothing like a sweltering summer to make one appreciate places with electricity.

She held the door open for Michael and Dora as they trailed in.

She noticed photos of Mennonites hanging on the wall, and she could tell with one glance which sect each person belonged to. Outsiders often thought all Plain people dressed alike, but every Amish and Mennonite group had its own style of dress and head covering.

A young Mennonite woman walked toward them. "Hi." She smiled, welcoming them as if she was glad to see them regardless of who they were or why they'd come. "May I help you?"

"We're looking for Aaron Blank," Sylvia said.

"Well, you're in the right place." She motioned to a room off to the right. "I was just chatting with him. I'm Hannah Waddell."

"I'm Sylvia Fisher, and these are Aaron's parents, Michael and Dora."

"It's a pleasure to meet you." Hannah shook hands with each of them, then raised a finger, took a step back, and said, "Paul?"

She'd not said it loudly, but a man several feet away immediately looked at her. She smiled at him. He excused himself from the person he was talking with and headed straight for her.

"Paul, these are Aaron's parents, Michael and Dora, and a friend, Sylvia Fisher."

Paul shook Michael's hand, then Dora's, welcoming them. When he came to Sylvia, she said, "I don't think he'd say I'm a friend."

Michael frowned. "I thought you two were getting along."

Sylvia didn't know what to say to that. Aaron didn't snipe at her as much as at first, but they were in a tug of war over the farm's future. It was possible that Michael didn't realize he was the rope.

Paul glanced at Hannah, a warm smile passing between them before he returned his attention to the newcomers. "We're really glad you're here. Let's find Aaron and let him know. Then maybe we can all chat for a bit."

"I didn't come to talk," Michael said.

"What did bring you here?" Paul asked.

"Sylvia, mostly."

Paul shifted. "Aaron's quite a man, but the more support he has, the better he'll be at fighting the good fight."

A baffled look covered Michael's face, but he said nothing. Sylvia let Michael and Dora follow directly behind Paul, then fell into step after them. They walked into a room where there were twelve chairs arranged in a circle. Aaron was one of a half-dozen men sitting and talking.

"This is our group counseling room," Paul said. "Men and women come here to share their experiences—temptations, failures, and victories. Right now they're just visiting." Paul moved toward Aaron, with Michael and Dora right behind him. He touched Aaron on the shoulder.

The initial shock on Aaron's face soon turned into a smile. He stood. "I didn't think you were coming."

Dora hugged him, whispering something Sylvia couldn't hear.

Michael backed away, clearly indicating that he didn't want to be embraced. He nodded at Sylvia. "This was her idea."

Aaron's eyes met hers. "Why?"

She glanced at his parents before shrugging.

"Why don't you help yourself to some food and look around?" Paul said. "Then we'll all go someplace where we can talk more privately."

Hannah directed Michael and Dora to a table spread with snacks, but Sylvia hung back. Paul was talking to Aaron, and when he turned to face her, she smiled briefly and went to the far end of the room. She looked out the window. This was someone's farm at one time, and the rolling hills and pastures were gorgeous.

"I don't understand you," Aaron said, startling her. "If fences are mended between my parents and me, that will make it easier to convince them to move."

"Some things are bigger than you and me and that farm."

"Why, Sylvia Fisher, I do believe you've committed blasphemy." Standing there grinning, he—with his broad, powerful shoulders—demanded her attention. "Would you like a tour?"

She didn't regret coming or pushing Dora and Michael to do so, but she felt confused by the emotions Aaron unearthed. "No, thanks. I'm fine right here."

He took her by the hand. "Kumm."

The warmth and power and gentleness of his grip confused her even more. When they were outside, she pulled her hand free. They walked the grounds, and he showed her what he called the dorm rooms. Then they toured the stables before taking a seat at a picnic table.

"If it won't bother you," Aaron said, "I'd like to ask Mamm and Daed to go by the appliance store while they're this close."

"That was Michael's plan from the start."

"He said as much?"

"Ya, but I wouldn't put too much stock in it. We're in the area, so it makes sense."

"I take it that going there wasn't your idea."

"I bet it smells of rubber and grease and diesel fuel." She wrinkled her nose. "I'll feel sick at my stomach before we're through."

"This from a girl who drinks her coffee while milking cows."

"It's true. I'll feel closed in, like I can't breathe."

"Good grief. There are windows."

He seemed to think she was kidding. But being in a store often gave her a headache. Maybe it was the dyes or fumes that emanated from the items. "I'm not saying my reaction isn't weird, but I always feel that way in a store. Nauseated and suffocated."

He laughed. "You're serious, aren't you?"

"Very."

Michael and Dora came outside, each with a plate and drink in hand. Michael sat next to Aaron. "This place isn't at all what I thought it would be. I expected something like a hospital but a lot dirtier."

"I wrote about the Better Path in my letters, describing it. It's a clinic that does its best to meet the needs of the Plain community—mental and physical."

"And the problem you deal with—is it mental or physical?"

"It's sort of both. Alcohol is habit-forming both physically and psychologically. I'm sure Paul can explain it better."

"But you knew it was wrong when you began."

"I didn't get into it or out of it because it was *wrong*. Black-and-white reasoning may work for you, but it doesn't for me. Drinking brought relief, but I had to get out because the escape turned into a nightmare."

"So what happens when you want relief again?"

"I'll take a vacation."

Michael set his sandwich on his plate. "Be serious, Aaron."

"I hit bottom, Daed. And while I was there, I found God. There's power between Him and me, and I rely on that. Even so, I can't promise I'll never mess up. I can assure you that if I do, I won't waste any time getting help."

"I'm supposed to trust that's enough?"

"No. I can't live up to your expectations. But you're supposed to trust that God is enough. That no matter what else happens, He's sufficient to forgive and strengthen."

"I guess when we go to talk to Paul, I'll be blamed for lots of stuff."

"That's not what we do here." Aaron grabbed a potato chip from his mother's plate and munched on it. "Not long after I began rehab, I saw myself through God's eyes, or at least a little of how He sees me, and the power of His love compared with the ugliness of who I'd become changed me. Then I saw what I'd done to you and Mamm through your eyes, and I came home to try to make amends. That's what Paul will do—help you see me from a different perspective than your usual disappointment and anger."

"I don't—" Michael's growl was interrupted when Paul came to the table.

"Would you rather meet out here or in my office?" Paul asked. "It won't be long—maybe fifteen, thirty minutes."

Everyone looked to Michael for an answer, but he said nothing.

Sylvia stood. "Either way, this chat needs to be between Aaron and his parents."

"She's right." Michael stood. "In your office."

Sylvia glanced at Aaron, who gave her a slight smile before the four of them left.

Michael was talking about what had brought Aaron here. That was good. She wanted to be glad only for Aaron's sake, but somehow whatever mattered to him mattered to her too.

Her interest didn't stop at the normal kindness extended from one human to another. She cared for him. She liked who he was and who he'd chosen to be.

And it had her rattled.

Twenty-Five

Cara sat on the couch reading *The Hiding Place*. It had been her constant companion for days, and whenever she had a few minutes, she read more of it. She'd never loved a book this much. She read and prayed and then read some more. This Corrie ten Boom had a handle on how to walk in forgiveness, and Cara had benefitted from reading her story.

"Hey, Mom." Lori ran into the living room and held out the familiar gray blue hardback of *Shoo-Fly Girl*. "Time for you to read to me! We're almost to the end of the book."

"Yeah, for the umpteenth time this summer."

"Please finish it for me again."

Cara set her book to the side and tapped her own cheek. Lori kissed her several times before Cara engulfed her daughter in a hug. "Love you, Lorabean."

"Love you too, Mom."

Lori snuggled against her. The heat didn't matter. Cara had her daughter in her arms, and she'd never mind that, no matter how high the mid-July temperatures soared. Per her daughter's request, they had on matching dresses. Better Days lay on the wood floor, panting.

Later in the day customers would begin arriving at Ada's House, but for now dinner, which for the Amish was the largest meal of the day, regardless of when it was served, was done. The kitchen was clean, and all sorts of baked goods and handmade items were ready to be sold. Since

Trevor wasn't here to take her to see Sylvia, she'd studied the languages on her own that day. At the thought of how well she was learning of late, joy bubbled up inside her.

She opened the book Ada had given Lori and continued reading *Shoo-Fly Girl* aloud. At the end of the last chapter, she bent her head to kiss her daughter's forehead and discovered that Lori had twisted the strings of their prayer Kapps together.

Cara looked up and was surprised to see Ephraim standing there, quietly watching them. Better Days stood next to him, nudging his hand for attention. Cara gently bumped Lori's shoulder, getting her to look up.

"'From!" Lori tried to run to him, but their intertwined prayer Kapp strings stopped her.

"Ow!" Cara yelped and quickly unraveled them.

The moment Lori was loose, she ran to Ephraim. He picked her up and hugged her.

Cara rubbed her scalp where the head covering had been attached to strands of her hair with a straight pin. Those pins kept the Kapp on no matter the work or the weather, but *ouch.*

Lori clasped her arms tight around Ephraim's neck and kissed his cheek before hopping down.

Ephraim embraced Cara and took in a deep breath. "My favorite part of the week."

"Tuesdays?" Lori asked.

"No." He touched her on the nose. "Anytime I'm with my two favorite people."

"What are you doing here in the middle of the week?" Cara asked.

"My sister called me at the shop about an hour ago. Said she had news she wanted to tell both of us and asked if I'd come. So I dropped everything and had Robbie drive me."

Cara slid her hand into his. "Would you like some lemonade while we wait for Deborah?"

"Anything cool in this heat would be great."

Cara led him through the hallway.

Ephraim held Lori's hand too. "You don't seem very surprised that Deborah has news for us."

Cara shrugged. "Nope."

"Is it what I think it is?"

"You can't ask me that."

"Sure I can. Listen carefully. Is it what I think it is?"

She chuckled, opening the swinging door to the kitchen without answering his question.

Ada stood at an ironing board, carefully easing a flat iron over a prayer Kapp. "Hi, Ephraim. This is a nice surprise."

"I need to show up unexpectedly more often," he said, smiling.

"You do that." Cara grabbed a glass for him from a cabinet. "Of course, you know that after a couple of times it won't be unexpected anymore." She poured a glass of lemonade and gave it to him.

"Hello?" Deborah called from the front door.

Ada put the iron facedown on the stove. "In the kitchen."

Deborah and Jonathan entered, hand in hand and glowing. "We have news to share." Deborah stared at Jonathan, radiating love. "Jonathan has asked me to marry him."

"And she said yes," Jonathan added.

Chatter filled the room as hugs were exchanged. Then Deborah paused in front of her brother.

"Ya," Ephraim whispered. "Totally, one hundred percent."

Deborah hugged him.

Cara would have to learn the history behind that conversation later.

"But that's not all," Deborah said to the room at large. "Ada, I know you wanted us to move in here, but he's buying us a house."

"As long as you're happy, Deborah."

Cara knew Ada's words were true, but she also had to be disappointed.

Cara would move to Dry Lake once she and Ephraim married, and now Deborah was moving. But Ada adapted to the changes as a mother would, even though neither Cara nor Deborah was her daughter. Whatever aches Ada felt didn't match the joy of seeing her "children" happy.

"Do you want to see it?" Deborah asked.

Ada moved the iron to the cooling shelf on the back of the stove. "Absolutely. Is there time to get there and back before we open for business tonight?"

Jonathan rubbed his chin. "Hmm. I'm not sure. I say we give it a try and see."

Ada moved directly in front of her nephew. "What's this smirk on your face?"

"We're buying the house next door."

Ada's eyes grew large. "What?"

He leaned against the countertop. "You two are in business together here, so it made sense. But if you prefer, I suppose I could buy a place in Dry Lake."

Ada pushed his shoulder. "Don't you dare." She hugged him. "Which one is it?"

Deborah took Ada by the hand and headed for the front door with the rest of the group following.

Cara couldn't help but think about what God had given Ada through the love between her and Deborah. Ada had lost her husband more than a decade ago, and her only child had left last year, cutting her off from him. When Deborah and Jonathan had children, Ada would be able to live out her days as if she were their grandmother.

The beauty of it awed her. Heartache stomped its way into everyone's life, but it seemed that love never stopped planting seeds or harvesting crops.

And forgiveness. The thought came to her as if it wasn't her own. But it made sense that forgiveness had to be planted in the midst of hurt. Since Trevor had given her *The Hiding Place,* she'd been praying almost constantly about forgiving him. If Corrie ten Boom could forgive the Nazi soldiers and prison guards who had so severely mistreated her and her sister during the Holocaust, surely Cara could manage to forgive Trevor.

"Look!" Deborah pointed to the house across the empty lot to the right.

Ada's eyes grew large. "You wouldn't tease an old woman."

"I just might," Jonathan said, "if I saw one."

"It gets better." Deborah tugged at Ada's hand, and they all headed down the sidewalk toward the house. "It seems my husband-to-be has bought half of the land we've been renting for the corn maze, picnic tables, and hayrides."

"I had no idea you were rich," Ada teased.

Jonathan laughed. "Far from it. But I've been pinching pennies ever since I finished school and started working full time. With the money I had, I made a down payment and signed a contract for a small mortgage. And it was all worth it when I saw the look on Deborah's face."

Deborah held open the door, motioning for everyone to walk through. The conversations echoing through the house felt warm and rich to Cara's mind and soul. She held Ephraim's hand as they made the tour, soaking in being part of a family. Lori ran up and down the steps half a dozen times.

The property even had an outbuilding that Jonathan could convert into a smithy shop. A day or two a week he'd still put all his blacksmith equipment in his work wagon and travel to Amish farms to shoe horses, but he'd work out of this shop the rest of the time.

After walking through the house, talking about possibilities, hopes of babies, and an extension of space to Ada's House, they started the trek back.

While going up the front walk at Ada's, Cara spotted Trevor sitting on the porch steps. A small box sat beside him. The sight of him didn't bring up hurtful images and stored resentment nearly as much as it had a few weeks earlier.

"Lori," Cara whispered, "go tell Trevor about Deborah's good news."

Lori stared up at her mom before looking to Ephraim.

"I think that's a good idea," he said.

Lori shrugged. "If you say so." She ran ahead. "Hey, Trevor, guess what?"

A rare but warm smile crossed his face. "Hmm... It's cold in Antarctica?"

"No, silly. Deborah's gonna marry Jonathan and live right there." She pointed.

The smile on Trevor's face broadened. Lori had talked to him the way she did to everyone else. He looked at the newly engaged couple. "Congratulations."

Ada, Deborah, and Jonathan chatted with him briefly before going inside. Lori went in with Deborah, prattling the whole time about having a sleepover at Deborah's house one day.

"Trevor,"—Cara motioned toward the house—"care for some lemonade?"

"Not right now. I brought you something."

"You don't need to keep doing that. Besides, I haven't finished the book you already brought me. It's really good, though."

He picked up the open corrugated box and held it out to her.

Ephraim leaned in. "Looks interesting."

Cara took the box from Trevor, walked inside, and set it on a side table. Familiar frames filled with family photos startled her. "Where did you get these?"

"I went to your old apartment building and talked to the manager. He looked up which place had been yours, and he knew who'd rummaged through your stuff before he threw it out."

She studied the images, glad to have them again in her hands, but at what cost? "You shouldn't have."

"It's not that big a deal," Trevor assured her. "New York's less than five hours from here."

She couldn't believe he'd done this for her, but fear threatened to seep out from under locked doors. She looked at more of the pictures. "Who had these?"

"A woman named Agatha Brown. She said she used to baby-sit Lori sometimes."

"Yes, she did." Cara pulled out the last frame, which held a picture of Johnny, Cara, and Lori as a toddler. She showed it to Ephraim, and when his eyes met hers, she wished he could see through them and into her mind to understand the concern building inside her.

He took the picture. "Trevor, did anyone ask you about where Cara is living now?"

"Mrs. Brown did. She wanted to hear all about Cara and Lori."

"She's the only one?" Ephraim asked.

"Yeah, why?"

"A man from Cara's days in foster care used to stalk and threaten her. That's why she left New York with nothing and lived in my barn for a while."

"I...I'm sorry." Deep hurt mirrored in Trevor's face. "But, Cara, honey, it's one of the largest cities in the world, and I was in your building for only a couple of hours. No one but the manager and Mrs. Brown knew I was there. Besides, surely that fella has lost track of you by now and probably lost interest."

Trevor made sense, and her fear retreated. "You're right." She looked at the back of a frame. "I need a screwdriver or butter knife."

Trevor pulled a knife out of his pocket and popped open the blade before she could blink. "I can use the blunt side of this to push those clasps out of the way. But why do you want to?"

"I never had enough frames, so I stashed older pictures behind newer ones. I put duplicates there too."

He took the back off the frame and pulled out two hidden photos.

Cara held up two pictures with Johnny in them—one when Lori was a newborn and one when she was almost two.

"You're pleased?" Trevor studied her.

"I am. Look." She moved closer to Ephraim, pointing out a stuffed puppy in Lori's hand that looked very similar to Better Days.

Her stalker, Mike, had done so much damage that it was natural to feel overwhelmed at just the thought of him, but Trevor was right. She had nothing to fear, and he'd done something for her no one else could— driven to New York on his own, found her old apartment building, and brought Lori pictures of her father.

She should hug him and really thank him, but she couldn't make herself go that far.

"Come on." She motioned to Trevor. "Let's show these to Lori."

Twenty-Six

Aaron closed the pliers over the loose strand of barbed wire and twisted the metal around and around, tightening it. More than a thousand feet of fence ran behind and ahead of him. It had taken him two days, but he'd almost finished repairing the half mile of fence line. A horse stood nearby, hitched to a work wagon loaded with topsoil. Sweat trickled down his face and neck as he used all his strength to tighten the eight feet of thick wire from one fence post to the next. His arms shook with weariness, and his legs felt weak.

He jerked the post back and forth to test it. It held tight, so it didn't need fresh dirt packed around it. He withdrew a pad of paper and a stubby pencil from his pants pocket and jotted a note.

Farming wasn't as miserable when he knew other people were on the property, helping him keep up. He stood straight, working the kinks out of his back.

Seeing Sylvi cross the field toward him caused his insides to do a little jig. It was a beautiful sight to behold—a dark-haired woman in a purple dress walking across green pastures. She held two half-gallon thermoses in her hands, but as thirsty as he was physically, he was thirstier for a conversation with her.

Aaron moved to the next fence post.

Sylvia had done more than dismantle the walls he'd tried to build between them; he found himself wishing she'd go with them when this place sold. Not that his Daed had agreed to sell yet, but he was moving in the right direction. Ten days had passed since Sylvia and his parents had gone to the Better Path and then to the appliance store. Aaron couldn't control how he felt about Sylvia any more than he'd been able to control his desire for alcohol. Terrifying situation, really.

"Hey, Sylvi." He clamped the pliers onto the wire. "Mamm too tired to walk this field again?"

She came to a halt near him. "No."

He exerted muscle power to twist the wire, which was what Sylvia did to his insides with no effort at all. Her presence had him curious, though. She usually didn't bring him drinks or food unless Mamm couldn't do so.

Sylvi set one thermos on the ground and opened the spout on the other. She held the jug out to him.

He shoved the pliers into his tool belt, removed his work gloves, and took the thermos. The icy water tasted wonderful as it cooled his whole body. He wiped his mouth with the back of his hand. "What's up?"

She got the large tin bowl out of the wagon. "Remember the favor you said you'd do for me if I'd go to church without arguing?"

"Is it finally time for it?"

"Ya." She filled the bowl with water from the other thermos.

"So what can I do for you?"

She walked to the horse and set the bowl of water in front of it. "There's a farming issue."

"There are hundreds of farming issues. You only earned one favor."

Technically he owed her far more than that, but he'd rather not admit it openly.

The lines of tension in her face didn't fade even a little as he teased her. She walked over to the back of the wagon and sat on the tailgate. "Men never want to talk to a girl about farming."

The embarrassment on her face bothered him. She was smart enough to understand whatever the issue was, even though no one had taught her the financial ins and outs of farming. It angered him that someone had treated her as if her opinion didn't matter.

"What's the problem?" He removed his tool belt, put it on the tailgate, and sat beside her.

"Some men from the EPA showed up about twenty minutes ago."

What little energy he had left drained from him. He'd heard stories of government agencies stopping by farms to enforce new regulations. "Someone from the Environmental Protection Agency is here?"

"Something about the fence lines along the creek banks being in the wrong place."

The thought of moving all the fencing along the waterway made him want to crawl into a hole. "Where are these men?"

"They're driving along the fence line in their truck. I asked Michael to have them start in the east field so I'd have time to talk to you."

He liked having her respect, though he longed to rail against the futile pursuit of farming. "So what's the favor, Sylvi?"

Her brows knit and her eyes searched his, looking as if she thought her request had been clear. "To listen as if you have my heart for the farm and then help me understand what the problem is and how it can be fixed."

He heard the fear in her voice. If she had no understanding of the problem, she had no chance of finding a solution. And he realized afresh how much she loved this place.

Sylvia kept searching the horizon. "There are the men from the EPA." She pointed to a knoll a couple hundred feet away.

He looked across the field and saw a truck headed their way. He dreaded the two possibilities that could come out of this conversation—the work it would cause him or the standoff it would bring between him and this branch of government.

"I'll go see if your Mamm needs anything." She took the jug from him. "Will you come to the house to talk to me after they're gone?"

"No." He pulled a handkerchief out of his pocket.

"Why?"

He removed his hat and wiped sweat from his forehead and the rim of his hat. "You're not going to the house. You're staying right here."

Her eyes met his, and a smile lifted her face.

The truck came to a stop, and two men got out.

Aaron put on his hat and looked at Sylvia. "If you have a question, ask it."

They hopped off the tailgate.

"Aaron Blank?" one man said.

"Ya?"

The men stepped over clods of uneven ground. "I'm Dusty Randall." Aaron shook his hand. "This is Brian Clayton. We're with the Environmental Protection Agency. We understand you run this farm."

"About half of it, actually. This is Sylvia Fisher. She runs the other half."

Randall blinked. "Oh. I owe you an apology then." He held out his hand to Sylvia. "I didn't realize... Mr. Blank said I needed to talk to his son."

Sylvia didn't say a word as she shook his hand.

"What's the problem?" Aaron asked.

"You're in violation of federal regulations. Someone from the EPA came through here years ago and explained to all the farmers the regulations concerning fence lines and fresh waterways. According to my records this farm wasn't in operation at the time. The sale of it to your father and his reestablishing it as a working dairy farm flew under our radar. We're not sure how that happened, but we're here to work with you to fix the problem."

Randall began explaining about the Clean Water Act and the laws that governed where fences could and couldn't be put and where animals could and couldn't trod or graze. He pulled out a stack of papers stapled together. "There's more information in here, but the bottom line is, we need to get these fences moved as quickly as possible. You can keep the old fences up for property-line purposes, but the new fence has to keep the cows a hundred feet from the creek."

"A hundred feet." Aaron mentally calculated how many hours of work it would take, how many miles of fence line would have to be moved, and how many acres of grazing land he'd lose. "What about the pasture on the other side of the creek? How are the cows supposed to get to that land to graze on it?"

"A culvert will need to be built, and the fence will attach to the railings so the cattle can't get to the water."

Aaron moaned. Did these men have any idea the amount of work and money it would take to build a cattle crossing of that type? "Then we have to find a new way for the cows to get water."

"We'll help you as much as we can."

"How?" Sylvia asked.

"When the paperwork's all filled out, you should qualify for a grant."

Sylvia stepped forward. "What's a grant?"

"It's money given by the federal government for a specific purpose. It's not a loan. If you qualify, the money must be used for its intended purpose, but you won't have to pay it back. Our help is part of the package deal. We'll bring in the manpower and the machines to dig the postholes, place the concrete or metal culvert, and run some or all of the line. You can get your own supplies with the grant money, or we can provide them. You can be here directing or leave it all up to us. If you don't feel you can accept a government grant to help offset the costs, you don't have to. You have the right to do it however you want. If you do it on your own, you'll have ninety days to comply. If you want our help, it'll have to be done in thirty days. We have other projects on the schedule after that." Randall passed Aaron the stapled papers.

Aaron looked at the fat stack. "What's this?"

"Details outlining regulations and offering solutions. This farm is clearly struggling with outdated equipment. A modern system that helps handle waste management would make your days much easier and protect the environment too." He turned to the other man. "Would you get him an information packet?"

Clayton grabbed a thick manila envelope out of the truck and handed it to Aaron.

"Everything you need to know is in there," Randall said.

"Excuse me," Sylvia said. "Will moving the fence fix all the problems?"

Randall drew a deep breath. "There could be penalties for the years of violation. Either you or your father might need to go before a board and explain why you weren't compliant to the laws."

"How stiff a penalty?" Sylvia asked.

"Hard to say. The regulations take into account the number of cows and each day you've been in violation."

Her face went ashen. "A penalty for each day, and it's been years?"

If she'd seen farming through rose-colored glasses before coming to the Blank farm, those glasses were being ripped off her face. That wasn't a bad thing, but Aaron wished the men would leave and give her a chance to absorb the news.

"We'll need time to read this information and think about what we're going to do," he said.

"Sure." Randall pulled a phone out of his pocket. "Today's July 24. Allowing time for all the work you do, it'll probably take you close to a week to read through everything and fill out the necessary forms, so I'll be back out July 30. But, like I said, if you want our help, we only have thirty days from today to resolve this issue. And the sooner you show cooperation, the better the penalty assessment will go."

"I understand."

The men climbed into their truck and drove off.

Sylvia eased onto the tailgate. "How could we farm all this time and not know about this regulation?"

"I'm sure the answer to that is in here." Aaron tapped the stack of papers.

"Has anything like this happened before?"

"No. Usually there's no grant money to help out. This could be easier to deal with than most of the problems that come up on a farm."

"If we qualify, will Michael accept money from the government?"

"I don't know. Taking government money isn't a comfortable position to be in. I'm not even sure how I feel about it. Are you?"

She shook her head. "No."

"Whatever is decided about the grant money, the fences have to be moved. This place can't be sold as a working farm if it's not in line with federal regulations. To get around that issue, we'd have to sell the herd, and I'd have to drop the price so low we couldn't pay off the mortgage."

He expected her to tell him she needed the fence moved in order to keep the feds from shutting down their operation, but she said nothing as she walked to the spot where she'd left the thermoses, gathered them, and put them in the wagon.

"I'm heading back," she said.

Watching her strength evaporate was more than he could stand. She took the horse's water bowl and dumped the remaining contents on the ground. Tears welled in her eyes. He didn't know what to say. She'd taken a hard hit. Why did he feel as if he'd been the one to issue the blow?

"How about I give you a lift back to your place or the barn?"

Passing him the bowl, she offered a tender smile. "I'll walk. Denki."

He fought the temptation to offer comfort or put his hand on her shoulder. The lesson had to be learned, and softening it for her would be a lie. She slowly made her way across the field. Why did this godforsaken money pit matter to her so much anyway?

Seeing her now was like watching someone drown, and he could do nothing about it.

Could he?

Twenty-Seven

Lena stood at the counter of the doctor's office, paying her bill. Dr. Stone had removed her cast and kept her medical boot. Her arm tingled a bit, especially her fingertips, but mostly it just felt weird not to be wearing a cast. The doctor had said she was doing really well but that the damage to her arm had been extensive. He'd lined up months of physical therapy.

She'd hoped her hand and arm would be completely healed by now. But considering that Dwayne's goal had been to kill her, she was beyond grateful.

Just as she reached the exit, a man opened the door for her from the outside. When she looked up to thank him, she saw Grey wearing a knowing smile.

"I spotted your horse and rig when I pulled in and wondered if I'd catch you. I see the cast is off."

Lena held up her hand and wiggled her fingers. "Ya."

He gestured toward her carriage.

She went to the hitching post and untied her horse. "Today's the day you find out what the test results were?"

"It is. Dr. Stone agreed to examine the genetic specialist's reports and interpret them for me."

A nervous shiver ran through her as she stood at the hitching post, playing with the leather strip she'd used to tether the horse. "Good. I'm glad. This has bothered you long enough."

"It could bother me even more before it's all over. I didn't sleep well last night."

"It's a weighty thing." She wouldn't tell him she'd lost sleep over it too. "Do you know how much I'm looking forward to our years together? Whatever you find out in there does not change that." She opened and closed her hand, trying to rid it of the tingly feeling.

"Do your fingers feel funny?"

"Ya. Dr. Stone said the stinging and numbness should go away over the next few weeks. I begin physical therapy tomorrow. But I can't wait to get my gloveless hand in potting soil."

"I think you simply like to play in the dirt, Lennie."

"Remember when we booby-trapped the door to my greenhouse?"

Grey laughed at the reminder of the time they'd placed a bucket of soil on top of the doorjamb. "The look on your Daed's face when all that dirt landed on him was priceless."

"And as soon as Daed was gone, we reset the trap, remember? But my brother still didn't come through the door. However, the very expectant preacher's wife did."

Grey rubbed his chest, a gesture she'd come to understand in the last few months that meant a heaviness was lifting from him. "She didn't appreciate your joke one bit."

"Oh, *my* joke, was it? May I remind you I was only nine, and you were a savvy fourteen-year-old?"

"Ya, that's it. I was savvy." His laughter slowed, and he studied her, his eyes radiating affection. "And the community wonders why all your girl-friends started pulling stunts on each other. I knew why the first time I heard about one of those tricks."

"You never told on me." She went to her carriage and got in. "We'll be fine no matter what the results are. Although I do have concerns for the rest of the community."

"You're something else."

She winked at him. "Don't you forget it, or you'll find yourself on my hit list."

"I won't forget." He held up his hand as if taking an oath. "Is there any way we can talk once I'm done in there?"

"Jonathan asked me to meet him at Ada's after my appointment here. Since you're so close to Hope Crossing, why not go there when you're done? So many Amish come in and out that no one will think anything of your dropping by."

"We might not have much privacy, but I'll come by when I'm done here."

Lena pulled onto the main road, praying for God's mercy over their future.

Cara put the photo of Lori's dad, Lori, and her into a frame she'd bought at a consignment shop downtown. Her daughter had carried the picture around for weeks with no signs of losing interest, so Cara had no other option. If she didn't frame it, Lori was going to ruin it.

She ran her fingertips across the cool, metal frame. It was hard to imagine ever having been the woman in that photo.

The stairs moaned softly as someone walked up them.

Ada stopped at Lori's bedroom door and then came and sat beside Cara. "He looks like a good man."

"When I met him, he gave me something I'd spent years looking for: protection from Mike. Did you know that's what brought us together?"

"No. You've never talked with me about it."

"I was a waitress in the diner he managed, and when he caught wind of what Mike was doing, Johnny had no qualms about killing the man, if necessary, to protect me." Cara set the frame on Lori's nightstand. "When I think about all that God has done to protect me rather than about the hardships, I see everything differently. Even my landing here is because Mike was relentless."

"God used that man's evil intent for good."

"Does He do that?"

"Ya. The first mention of it is in Genesis, when Joseph's brothers sold him into slavery. Keep your eye out for it in the New Testament. Over and over again, evil men heaped unspeakable torment on good people, and God brought good out of it. All those men who hung Jesus on the cross meant it for evil too."

"Deborah?" came a voice from outside the room.

"That's Lena." Ada went to the door and called, "She's not here at the moment. I'll be right down."

The pitter-patter of Lori's feet echoed through the old house as she ran from the kitchen to the foyer to welcome Lena. Ada dusted off her apron and ran her fingers roughly over her cheeks to give them color.

Cara straightened Lori's bed. "Why do I get the idea you're hopeful that Lena's handsome Daed is with her?"

Ada grinned. "I have no idea."

"You really like Israel, don't you?"

Ada grew serious. "Tell me one thing not to like about him."

"Well, if he's not here, you won't like that about him."

"True enough."

They both walked down the steps to greet Lena. Ada stepped into the foyer first. "Deborah's out with Jonathan, having a bit of lunch."

"Guess I'll wait," Lena said. "I'm supposed to meet him here."

"Is your Daed with you?" Cara asked.

"Not today. I came here from Dr. Stone's." Lena held up her cast-free hand.

Ada gasped. "Well, look at you. I didn't even notice."

"Her mind was elsewhere," Cara teased.

"Shush now, Cara, or I'll put you to work."

"And that's different how?"

Ada laughed. "It's not, but it sounds tough. Lena, how about some lemonade?"

Lena sat on the steps of Ada's front porch, waiting for Jonathan. Lori sat beside her and peppered her with questions about the Amish school in Dry Lake. Cara and Ada were in one of the porch swings. But the picturesque image of good friends gathered on a peaceful summer's day drinking homemade lemonade didn't line up with the concern beating out a strong rhythm inside her chest.

Grey's tests had been bothering her more than she'd expected, and right now her mouth remained dry no matter how many sips she took of her drink.

"Lena Kauffman." Jonathan appeared from nowhere. His grin made her jump to her feet and scurry toward him. He met her halfway up the sidewalk and embraced her. "My goodness, I don't see enough of you anymore."

She squeezed him tight. "Well, that happens when a girl's best guy friend gets a girlfriend."

He backed away. "Look at you! No cast. No medical boot. And no limp."

She held out her hands and turned around. Jonathan applauded as she finished her full circle.

Deborah stepped in front of Jonathan and gave Lena a hug. "You look healthy and perfect."

"Well, the healthy part I'll believe. Where have you two been?"

"We found a little place to have lunch," Jonathan said. "I want to show it to you."

"Now? You can't be hungry again."

"Kumm." Jonathan bent his arm at the elbow and held it out to her. She looped her hand around his arm, and they began walking.

Lena paused. "Deborah, aren't you coming?"

"You two go. He wanted to visit with you alone for a bit, and if I go, I'll talk the whole time."

They hadn't walked more than thirty steps when he stopped. "We're at our destination. What do you think?" He waved toward the house.

A well-kept Victorian home stared back at her. "Oh no, you did not."

"Oh yes I did." Jonathan took her on a tour of the house. "It was built in the mid-eighteen hundreds, and it needs work on the inside, but Deborah and I love it." He told her of their plans and how he'd proposed. She adored seeing him completely happy.

He'd been in love with Deborah for years. He'd courted other women while Deborah planned to marry Mahlon, but tears welled in Lena's eyes when she thought of how patient and hopeful he'd remained. Even in the face of apparent defeat, he'd waited without complaint to see if God would give him a chance with Deborah.

"Hey," Jonathan scolded her. "There are no tears allowed over this."

Years of memories of their friendship and his loneliness for Deborah melted her, and a sob escaped.

"Okay then," he growled. "Cry like a girl." He hugged her. "I knew no one would understand what this means to me like you would. Now all we have to do is find the right person for you."

She wiped her face and touched her lips with her index finger. "I do have someone."

"Who?"

She heard Deborah's voice and went to a window. Deborah and Grey were walking toward the house. "It's Grey."

Jonathan grinned. "I should have known. You two will be good for each other. How long will you wait to court openly?"

"October, probably the middle of the month. I...I need a few minutes to talk to him if you could help manage it."

"You got it."

Deborah walked inside. "I gave you twice the amount of time you asked for. Was it enough?"

Grey followed her in.

"Perfect timing," Lena said.

Jonathan pulled out his pocket watch. "Deborah, did you finish making that batch of cookies you promised Ada?"

"No, but she won't mind."

Jonathan slid his watch back into his pocket. "And when Lori notices you didn't keep your word, what will you tell her?"

Deborah made a face and gave Lena another hug. "I gotta go. You two finish showing Grey the house."

"Lena, I want to go with Deborah." Jonathan pulled out a key and passed it to her. "Lock up when you leave."

"Not a problem."

Deborah and Jonathan walked hand in hand out the door and down the sidewalk.

Grey removed his hat and hung it on the newel post of the banister. Lena waited, hoping for good news, but unwilling to ask. The empty old house was too quiet. Not even a clock ticked.

He looked deep into her eyes. "The subject of chromosomal issues is a complicated one, and I'm sure I won't use all the right jargon, but according to Dr. Stone, the test results indicate I don't have any of the issues he was concerned about. The specialist only tested for certain hereditary issues, but he saw nothing that would cause deformities of any kind."

Unable to speak, Lena straightened his already straight collar. He drew her hand to his lips and kissed it.

"You're finally free." She wrapped her arms around him and laid her head on his chest. Relief and expectation over their future wrapped around her as they stood in this unfamiliar home that she knew they'd visit for decades to come.

Twenty-Eight

Aaron sat at the kitchen table reading the documents the EPA men had left. He'd begun right after lunchtime. Now supper was over. The cows were milked—no thanks to him. And Sylvi and Trevor were probably done bottle-feeding the calves. Yet the pages about government regulations, grants, and teamwork between farmers and the EPA went on and on.

He'd thought some of those self-help books that were required reading at the Better Path were dry. This stuff was so parched it could make a person die of thirst while sitting in a pool of spring water. But as he read, he realized there might be ways to get the much-needed help for this farm, the one-time boost that Sylvia had asked him about. The thought made him queasy, yet he intended to share the idea with her, not just because it was the right thing to do, but also because he wanted to quiet her fears. To see her excited.

When he heard a car pull up to the house, he headed for the door, glad for the interruption. As Frani got out of her car, he walked down the steps to her.

"You know how I kept telling you my folks weren't willing to help me?" Frani asked.

"Ya."

She leaned against the car. "You've made your bed, now you can lie in it," she mimicked, wagging her finger.

He laughed. "Sounds familiar."

"Well, they made a deal with me."

"What kind of deal?"

She rolled her eyes and sighed. "Said they'd help me in all sorts of ways if I agreed to go to rehab. Even offered to keep AJ while I'm there."

"And?" He waited.

"I'm going."

"Frani, that's great." He hugged her. "You won't regret it."

She grabbed his shirt and held him tight. "I can't believe how scared I am. What if I mess this up like I have everything else?"

He backed away, wishing he knew the right thing to say. "Make sure you don't. You have to fight for yourself and for AJ. Where are you going?"

"Some place in Baltimore that Mom knows about and trusts. My parents said if I come home clean, I can move back in. Like I'm looking forward to that. But if you can stand it, I can. I might even go back to school." Her cell phone rang. She pulled it out of her pocket and looked at it. "It's Mom. I told her I'd just be a minute." She hit a button that made it stop ringing and shoved it into her pocket. "I gotta go. I don't suppose you got a number where I can reach you?"

"No. But you won't be allowed to call anybody for a while anyway. You can write me."

She tilted her head. "Where? Aren't you selling this place and moving?"

"Well, yeah, but not for at least a couple of weeks, maybe four." It struck him that his time was running out. But more than that, he wasn't in a hurry to get off this land and move to Owl's Perch. "Write to me here. And then I'll send you my new address."

"I don't want to lose touch."

"Then don't. The farthest I'm going is no distance by car."

"I don't understand, Aaron. Why did you try so hard to get me to go for help?"

He shrugged. "I should've heard you years ago when you drank the night away but kept talking about getting sober. You wanted it long before I did. And this has sort of been like reaching into that part of my life and grabbing hold of one redeemable thing."

"Aw." She hugged him. "That was really sweet."

He patted her back and stepped away. Hugging her was like embracing a cousin. A small scrunch was plenty.

She smiled. "I won't ever forget what you've done for me over the last couple of months—yakking at me about God and my future. It took someone who's been right here, someone who knew the real me and still believed I had a fighting chance, to get me this far."

"It's not near far enough."

"I know. But it's a start." She tugged on his shirt before hopping into her car. "See ya."

He waved as she drove off, glad she'd chosen to follow the once-buried hope of getting and staying sober. They might write a few letters here and there. Maybe they'd see each other a couple of times a year, but other than the days they'd spent drinking, they had little in common.

Longing for time with a woman he did connect with, he wondered if Sylvi might go with him to Shippensburg to get an ice cream. It was a long shot, and he couldn't say it was a particularly wise idea for them to spend more time together, but he didn't care. He was going to ask anyway, right after he showered and shaved.

But whether she agreed to go or not, he'd tell her some of the new farming ideas that were forming in his head.

Annoyed and irritable, Sylvia soaked her aching body in the bubble bath. She'd scrubbed the milking parlor and tank room for hours, getting ready for tomorrow's inspection. For what? To give the place a little more value when it came time to sell it?

Her usual way of ridding herself of frustrations wasn't working, so she got out of the tub, dried off, and dressed. It was time to own up to the facts. Aaron had come home with a plan, and he was slowly accomplishing it. Michael's defenses and anger continued to fade. Not that he'd admit it openly, but she saw subtle changes in him—the look of pleasure on his face instead of resentment whenever Aaron came to the table.

What really had her in a foul mood was seeing Aaron all cozy with Frani out in the driveway. And Sylvia had volunteered to let the woman live with her! She was such an idiot. He clearly wanted a different kind of life—one that didn't involve a woman who sometimes smelled of Holsteins. She seemed to care only for men who wanted something or *someone* else. Did all men have to connect with women on an intimate level behind other women's backs?

Maybe some food would make her feel less grumpy. She wandered into the kitchen and looked through her mostly barren cupboards.

Someone tapped on her screen door, and she turned to see Aaron. He held a large manila envelope in his hand, and his smile stirred fresh irritation. She had no interest in hearing about other ways to make the farm more valuable when he put it up for sale.

"Sylvi, I have something to show you."

She pulled a jar of peanut butter out of the cabinet. "Great."

He stepped inside. "Is something wrong? I mean, other than the bad news we got about the fence?"

"No." It was a lie, but how could she tell him the truth?

Aaron set the envelope on the small kitchen island and sat on a barstool. "I think I understood you better when you threw that hammer at me."

She opened the jar of peanut butter and grabbed a knife. "So, does Frani need to move in here?"

He leaned his forearms against the island. "Actually, she doesn't."

She faced the counter, her back to him, determined not to let him see any sign of the swell of relief moving through her. "Good. I'm sure having her own place will make your relationship with her easier."

He sighed. "I've already explained my connection to Frani." He tapped the manila envelope. "Look, I brought you some information that may be useful in your quest to keep this farm. I thought maybe we could talk about it. But I guess you're not in the mood."

He stood and headed for the door, and it thudded behind him.

Until she saw him with Frani, she'd thought he was totally honest with her. So why did their hug make her think otherwise? Her stomach turned. *Jealousy.* Unwarranted and unfair to him.

"Aaron, wait." She hurried out the door and tried to catch him as he strode up the lane, but her bare feet slowed her. "Aaron, please."

He turned, and she gingerly made her way to him on the gravel.

When she looked into his eyes, she knew a simple apology wasn't enough. "I saw you and Frani smiling and hugging, and I…" She shook her head. "You still frustrate me, with your defenses and contradictions. But…"

His anger faded, and he sighed. "It's not like that between Frani and me. Sylvi, think about it. Have I done anything that says I'm in a relationship with Frani?"

She crossed her arms and held herself tight. It was time to come clean with him. "When Elam asked me to marry him and then asked someone else so soon afterward, I realized he must've shared moments with her while courting me. I had no idea, and I felt like a fool not to have known."

"Moments?"

"I'm sure you feel it when we have a moment—when we share a laugh or talk about something meaningful, and our friendship grows stronger." Her face flushed.

"I like our moments."

"I do too. But I won't be so foolish again, having them with someone I shouldn't." She scooted dirt around with her bare toe. "I've been on the other side of that fence too. I was close to the woman Elam married, and because of the moments he and I shouldn't have shared, I ended up betraying her."

Aaron brushed strands of loose hair out of her face. "And yourself?"

Tears filled her eyes.

"You know forgiveness from God is there for the asking."

"I did ask. Over and over until I gave up."

"If you asked, He forgave you. Walking it out until you feel that forgiveness inside you—that's often a different issue. But you have to accept that He forgave you. It's a done deal."

Her tears refused to stay at bay. She wanted so much to believe that.

"You seem to be carrying enough guilt for you and Elam both. Some of this belongs to him, you know. I mean, you didn't chase him down and hogtie him, did you?"

She couldn't help but chuckle. His kindness and humor warmed her.

"Frani came to say good-bye because she's going into rehab at some place in Baltimore. The night I returned home, I saw her headed for this cabin, and I figured God had put her in my path for a reason. I now see that I needed her too. As I talked to her, I got fresh perspectives on all the reasons sobriety is so important. When her rebellion reared its head, I understood more of my own. And as it turned out, it was sort of like getting to reach into the past and salvage someone else's life." He gently brushed a strand of wet hair from her face, looking at her as if he truly cared. "She and I both needed that. But she's nothing else to me."

"I shouldn't have gotten upset with you. It's just—I can't figure out how I feel about you."

He gazed down at her. "I'm confused about how I feel too. Seems all we really know is how we feel about this homestead."

She laughed. "It's a stressful mess on the Blank farm, isn't it?"

"Uh, ya."

She swiped at her wet cheeks. "So you brought me hopeful news, and I dumped my baggage on you."

He flexed his biceps, which looked rock solid under his short-sleeved shirt. "I can carry it." He lowered his arm. "You were carrying most of my load before I ever showed up."

Looking him in the eyes, she saw a true friend standing in front of her. She knew that much. "You're doing that *almost tolerable* thing again."

He shrugged. "Blanks aren't tolerable. We're difficult. You don't have that figured out yet?"

"Well, you're all rather confusing. I've got that much clear. I mean, you care about your parents, and they love you, but no one can admit that. You stormed back here, fuming about dumping the farm and trying to corner *and* bribe your parents to go with you, but you haven't sat down and told them why it's so important to you."

"You want me to confess that I think they're not capable of knowing what's best for them or of accomplishing anything even if they did know?" His half smile and tone signaled his dry sense of humor at play.

"I want you to admit the truth to yourself and them—that you feel deeply and you rarely know what to do with it. Your parents are the same way, Aaron. And each of you is hiding behind the walls you've built."

"I hate to disappoint you, but you're seeing this all wrong. They care deeply about *you*, and I'm glad for you and them, but that's where their affections end, Sylvi."

He wasn't convinced that they were invested in him, but he was on the farm to do the right thing, and she admired that loyalty in him. It was past time that someone told him they cared, but she had little proof to back up her statements.

"Michael put the want ad for farm help in the paper last September," she said.

Disbelief registered on his face. "In September?" He mulled that over. "That was even before Elsie died."

His forehead remained tight as he stared at her, processing what she'd said. That meant Michael had known Aaron was struggling with the work and had tried to find a solution. It was a tiny peek inside the usually locked door of Michael's heart.

Aaron rubbed the back of his neck. "Are you sure?"

"Positive. My dream of coming here began then, but my Daed wouldn't hear of it."

"You have scary dreams, Sylvi."

She laughed. "You never once considered the freedom to farm this land and work with this herd a worthy goal?"

"Ya, actually I did, but that was a long time ago. A better question is, why didn't Daed tell me he was trying to get help? Why keep that a secret?"

She shrugged. "Remember your first Sunday home when you refused to leave the barn? You were angry that your Daed would let me work on the Sabbath by myself, but you couldn't see that Michael was purposefully giving me the freedom I'd asked for. Later you insisted I have Sundays off, as a break, and even did your part in helping me make friends. That's not your Daed's way. If I want to be left alone, that's what he's going to give. It doesn't mean he's heartless. For him, it means the opposite. You're all each other has, and I can't understand why you let your thoughts and feelings push you away from each other rather than drawing you closer."

A shadow passed over Aaron's face, and she wondered if she'd said too much.

She gestured toward the porch. "Care to sit?"

He nodded, and they sat on the steps.

Sylvia drew a deep breath. "Maybe I'm out of line to tell you this, but I've been holding my piece, giving your parents and you time to open up on your own."

"Not so sure the earth will last that long."

She couldn't help but chuckle when Aaron turned on his parched humor; it wasn't always what he said but the way he said it that made her laugh. "You may be right about that. But Jesus said, 'Blessed are the poor in spirit: for theirs is the kingdom of heaven.' And clearly there's a lot of inner poverty between you and your folks. Dirt-poor, honestly."

"Ya, I guess so. I always thought we fit the part in the Sermon on the Mount about those who mourn and hoped we'd find comfort, but that hasn't worked out so well either."

"Mourning? Because your sister died?"

He sighed, gazing down the narrow footpath that led from the cabin. "Throughout their marriage my parents lost six newborns, which is why they had only two children...and now just one. Instead of the losses drawing our family closer, each one scattered us to the wind, emotionally."

Sylvia studied his handsome face, realizing anew how deep his thoughts ran and seeing the magnitude of the mismanaged feelings that had pulled him toward drinking. "Michael and Dora are very tender-hearted people, even with thick walls guarding that tenderness. They're sensitive, much like you. Maybe Elsie was too. I don't know, but it seems that for gentle people such losses here on earth are even harder to bear."

His eyes searched hers. "You think we have a gentle spirit?" He sounded skeptical.

"I see your heart, Aaron. It is tender. You build up your walls with drinking or with biting comments, and now you're trying to pull them down. Perhaps Michael is so critical of you because he recognizes he's still hiding behind his walls. I've known a few men in my life who didn't have that tenderness of heart, who lacked sensitivity. No good comes of it. But after watching your family, it seems to me that when people feel deeply and try to bottle it up, it makes a mess of every relationship."

"I agree that our lack of communication has created chaos." He turned to her. "But here's something that is true. More than coming by to talk about the farm, I wanted to see if you'd care to go for a buggy ride into Shippensburg for some ice cream."

It was a bold request. He was making himself vulnerable. As she sat on the steps under the canopy of trees in the cool of the evening, she couldn't conjure up one scenario where it would hurt to spend a little personal time with him. If he sold the farm, she'd have a few good memories to take with her to the next place. If he set up a business in Owl's Perch and left her here with his parents, she'd have spent an evening building a bond with the owner's son.

She had to admit that beyond her logical reasons to go with him, her heart weighed in heavily. Spending time with Aaron satisfied some part of her she couldn't understand.

Despite his feelings about the farm, she wanted a chance to enjoy a romantic relationship with him. She admired his steely determination, his humility in admitting when he was wrong, and his desire to change for the better. His tenderness in understanding her pain and truly caring. His loyalty in returning for his parents and his unwavering faithfulness to them.

Not to mention his newly found strength of character. It had been seven months since he'd chosen to free himself of alcohol, and regardless of all the problems that had reared their ugly heads, he kept walking that path. She knew his journey wasn't over, but she felt confident that he would remain honest about the struggle.

Was she finally seeing him for who he really was? How would she know if she didn't give herself at least one evening out with him?

She stood. "I can't think of anything else I'd rather do."

Twenty-Nine

Cara pulled a sheet of cookies out of the commercial gas oven. She set the pan to the side to cool and slid another one into the stove. Worry kept pricking her conscience, but Cara attempted to wrestle it into silence. So far her emotions listened to her about as well as Better Days did.

For several nights she'd dreamed about not being allowed to join the faith for years. Now thoughts of not qualifying hounded her. Instruction classes got harder each session, and in spite of Sylvia doing a great job of teaching her the language, Cara had a long way to go.

Trevor jerked open the back door. "Need a hand?"

"Uh…" She looked around for something he could help with. "How about squeezing some lemons?"

"Sure." He went to the refrigerator and took out a basketful.

He used the glass hand juicer to squeeze several lemons while she sliced whole ones into thin strips and dropped the pieces into a vat. Sweat trickled down her chest. She was finally able to respond to her father with patience and compassion—not a ton of it, but enough that they could struggle through the awkwardness.

Trevor poured the pulp-filled juice into the large vat. "You've been quiet the last few days."

"Just thinking. I do that sometimes."

"I see."

She rinsed a rag in cool water and wiped the back of her neck. July temperatures and constant baking in a home without electricity made for a hot kitchen even with the sun dipping below the horizon. But living and working here was one of the best things to have happened to her.

Voices of children playing outside and of adults browsing in the gift shop down the hall surrounded her. God had brought her back to Ephraim through the oddest of circumstances. Surely she could pass instruction classes and learn enough of the languages to join the faith and marry him *before* he gave up or they were too old to have children.

Trevor dumped the lemon rinds into a tin bucket. She and Lori would dry them in the sun along with rinds from oranges and limes, then add them to a mixture of homemade potpourri.

She moved back to her work station and stirred sugar into a large container of lemonade before putting some of it in a glass pitcher.

"Your mom used to make lemonade with slices of lemon. Don't know that it helped the flavor, but it sure makes it look tasty." Trevor wrung out a washrag and wiped the work station where they'd made the lemonade. "I...I got a letter today."

She set a mixing bowl on the counter and measured out butter and sugar, wondering who would've written to him here.

He held out an envelope. "The lady from your apartment building sent you a letter."

Cara snatched it, studying the postmark. Trevor had been back little more than a week. The envelope was postmarked a few days after he'd left New York. She ripped it open and pulled out a letter and a newspaper clipping.

"What does it say?" Trevor asked.

Scanning the letter, her eyes caught the name Mike Snell, and a wave of dizziness made her sit. Agatha's words seemed to move about the page.

"Cara?"

"It…it's about…my stalker. Agatha didn't want to say anything to you, but…"

Mike had moved into her apartment the night she left. He'd stayed there until the rent was due, waiting for her to return.

Her hands trembled as she skimmed the newspaper page, trying to figure out what piece of information Agatha wanted her to see. Then she saw it: an obituary for Mike Snell. It listed his date of birth, parents' full names, and the borough where they lived. It was definitely the same Mike Snell who'd stalked her for more than a decade.

But she felt no relief, only nausea.

She returned to reading the letter. Agatha wrote that she wasn't sure if the letter would reach her, but she hoped it found her safe and happy.

She laid the letter, news clipping, and envelope on the table, then rose and went to the refrigerator. She pulled out eggs, cracked several on the edge of the bowl, and added them to the butter and sugar before throwing the shells into the sink.

"May I?" Trevor held up the letter and news clipping.

"Yeah."

She shoved the blades of the rotary mixer into the batter and turned the handle, round and round, faster and faster. Her knees were wobbly. She'd see Ephraim tomorrow after another language lesson, and she wondered if the news would have any effect on him.

"You're upset." Trevor set the papers to the side. "I don't understand."

"Yeah, me either." She took the hand mixer out of the bowl and slammed it down on the counter, spattering cookie dough. "I spent so many years wishing he was dead…wishing I could kill him. And now I…I feel like I can't breathe. A man's life is over."

"Did you expect to rejoice?"

"The old me would have…I think." Since she was young, she'd known the finality of death. Nothing was as changeless or hopeless as life leaving a body and never returning. After it happened to her mother, nothing was ever the same again. But why did she find the finality of Mike's death so disturbing? She stared at the letter and newspaper, wondering what he'd died of.

Relationships were often complicated, disappointing, or even a source of pain, but until someone died, there was always a possibility for change. Whatever condition Mike's relationships were in when he died, they would remain that way forever—including whether he ever came to know God.

The bond with her dad wasn't what either of them had wanted, but they were here and working on improving it.

Where was Mike?

It was absurd to compare the two. They were nothing alike. Yes, Mike should have been in jail where he couldn't wreak havoc. But dead?

She'd been worried and melancholy over whether she'd join the faith this year or next or the following year, but she had hope—both in this life and the next one. What did Mike have?

She'd never once thought of praying for him. If Ada hadn't spent a lifetime praying for her, where would she be?

She blinked, realizing her dad had gotten the cookies out of the oven and had finished mixing the batch she'd begun. "Trevor," she whispered.

He stopped stirring the dough. "Yeah?"

She wanted to say that she forgave him. That she was enjoying getting to know him and looked forward to his being around so they could continue making progress. Instead she shrugged. "I'm glad you went to New York and brought back pictures for Lori." She couldn't even manage to tell him "thank you"?

He put a dollop of cookie dough on a pan. "Anything like that you need, I'm here to do it, Carabean."

Tears pricked her eyes. She cleared her throat. "So, are we still on for you taking me to Sylvia's tomorrow?"

Thirty

Tired of trying to grasp the complicated solutions, Sylvia folded the papers on farming that Aaron had brought to the cabin. She tucked them under the edge of the quilt on the ground beneath her and lay back, staring at the billowing gray clouds. Two kittens were curled up in her lap asleep, and two played beside her. She'd carried them in her picnic basket along with a jar of water, a sandwich, the blanket, and farming information to study. Bringing the cute balls of fur to this private spot had been her best effort to make this nonchurch Sunday as pleasant as possible.

But the day stretched out like warm taffy, looping round and round and seemingly growing longer with each spin. As a child she'd once seen taffy being made in a candy shop. She hadn't liked the smell of it, and when the candy maker cut off a piece for her, she didn't like the taste of it either. She had to laugh at the fact that working in a barn didn't bother her, but the aroma of artificial flavoring and mass amounts of sugar did.

That appliance store of Aaron's had made her feel much worse. It smelled like fumes from an old bus, and that always made her headachy and nauseous.

She believed a lot of things about her were odd, but she'd never minded it until Elam chose her sister over her. Beckie was beautiful and dainty and, she guessed, all the things men looked for. Truth was, Beckie could have had her choice of men.

Trying not to think about it, she focused on the sky. The clouds moved across it, hinting at a possibility of rain. She'd been desperate for the weather to stay dry while she and Aaron baled hay, but now, seven weeks later, she felt as much angst wishing it would rain.

They hadn't gotten a second cutting of alfalfa yet. They would soon, but it'd grown slowly because of the lack of rain, and she doubted they'd get a third cutting before fall. The field corn she and Michael had planted days before Aaron returned had suffered too. They needed a good yield from it to help fill the silos for the winter, but it looked rather scraggly from a distance, and she couldn't make herself walk into the field to see it up close.

The good news was that, being part of the silage, the kernels themselves needed very little moisture in them. Surely this current weather pattern would help in that department…maybe. She didn't really know. All she knew was that Michael's resolve to keep the farm seemed to be evaporating along with the ponds and the creek bed. Not that he'd actually said those words. But she'd walked into the Blank home a few days ago and had seen him reading a newspaper ad for nonelectric appliances. They didn't need a new appliance of any kind, so he was probably entertaining the idea of a lifestyle change.

"Sylvi." Aaron's voice echoed around her.

She sat upright. This little spot, nestled in a patch of trees between an unused field and a pond, was supposed to be too secluded for anyone to notice her.

Aaron crossed the field, carrying something in each hand. Her heart beat a little faster at the sight of him. Something about his ways made her want to know his thoughts and opinions, even if they were his frustrations about the farm or his parents.

He stopped at the edge of the quilt, holding a thermos in one hand and a plate covered with aluminum foil in the other. The fact that he'd gone out of his way to locate her gave her some much-needed assurance that he was worthy of her growing fondness for him.

She hid her smile, not wanting to give her thoughts away. "How did you find me?"

"I think I know all your favorite resting places now." He held out both items.

She wanted to respond, but suddenly she felt shy in light of his efforts toward her. On mornings when Michael didn't come to the barn before milking, Aaron always brought her a cup of coffee. But Michael had insisted on that. Three days ago he'd brought her helpful information about farming. She hadn't had time to figure out what all the gibberish meant; still, it showed his willingness to share the burden of the farm with her.

"It's not a marriage proposal, for Pete's sake."

His sarcastic humor relaxed her, and she moved the kittens to her other side and patted the quilt before taking the items from him. "Denki."

"Not a problem."

He bent his knees and put his forearms on them, reminding her of the one thing she kept trying to overlook—that he was, above all else, a man. One who seemed different from any other she'd ever known. And the relaxedness of between Sundays looked good on him. Actually, his appeal was just as strong the other days of the week. Her trying to stay too busy to notice hadn't worked. But it wasn't, by any means, just his appearance that made him look good. What attracted her came from deep within him and radiated through his eyes and showed in the determined way he carried himself.

She opened the thermos and poured icy water into the lid. She brought the drink to her lips and enjoyed the coolness as the liquid filled her mouth and slid down her throat. After setting the cup on top of her picnic basket, she peered under the aluminum foil. "Bread pudding! I love this stuff."

"Mamm said you did."

"You even brought me a fork." She dug into the gooey confection.

"Mmm." The sweet, soft, cinnamon-flavored bread melted in her mouth. "Delicious. And still warm. Care for a bite?" She held a forkful up to him.

"Not me, thanks. Never been a fan of bread pudding."

"Your mom has a new recipe. You ought to give it a try."

He didn't look convinced, but he opened his mouth, and she eased it past his lips. "Oh, wow." He chewed and swallowed. "That's actually quite good."

"Isn't it?" She took another bite. "Dora made a batch for me with her old recipe last winter." Sylvia mocked a cough and shuddered. "I had to tell her the truth, and I passed on to her a much better recipe, one that belonged to my great-grandmother." After taking another bite, she held a second one out to him.

Aaron leaned back on his elbows. "This spot is sort of nice."

"Close your eyes."

His chestnut eyes held a spark of challenge, but he closed them.

"Now feel, hear, and breathe in everything around you."

He lay back and propped his hands under his head. He took a deep breath, and a trace of pleasure showed on his face.

Sylvia remained sitting upright, but she closed her eyes too, hearing a crow caw, a fish in the pond jump, and wind rustle through the trees. "Everything you sense, Aaron, has been here long before this country began, yet every bit of it is new, right here today, for you." Her eyes refused to stay shut, and she watched a smile caress his face.

"You do have a way of making a person value a day." He opened his eyes and looked at her. "But the joys of nature can't make a small dairy operation like ours less of an uphill battle."

"I wasn't trying to change your mind, only open it to the world around you."

"Is that what you like about dairy farming, the romantic view of it?"

"Oh, please. No real farmer can keep a romantic image of the job. Besides, I never said I was in love with cows."

He sat upright. "Yes, you have."

"When?"

"Well, not in words. But your actions have said it."

"My great-grandparents were dairy farmers, as were my grandparents, and now my Daed. And they made a decent living doing it."

"I don't know your family's operation, Sylvi, but times have changed. You have to have substantial growth to compete these days, and this place isn't set up to sustain that kind of expansion."

"Your Daed has barns, cows, and milking equipment—everything a farm needs for a healthy dairy business."

"The profit margin isn't equal to the work load, especially considering what we'd need in order to grow. If they were equal, I wouldn't feel like it's such a waste of time."

Unsure what to say, she took another bite of the bread pudding and then gave him a bite. She took a deep breath. "Between Sundays are actually sort of nice."

Aaron took the fork and plate from her. "Your turn to close your eyes."

She stared at him.

"Go on. I did it for you."

She closed her eyes.

"Feel the ground under you and the breeze on your skin," he said. "Pay attention to all the sounds—the birds and the wind. Smell the aroma of hayfields, flowers, and distant rain."

She relaxed and relished the nature surrounding her.

"God is everywhere, Sylvi." Aaron's whisper sent chills over her body. "You can't avoid Him by refusing to attend meetings. You only avoid acknowledging Him." He brushed his fingers across her back. "You don't have to go to church to find Him, but you can't hide from Him by avoiding it. I learned that the hard way. I show up in my rig at your place every other Sunday because I want you to find peace with your mistake, with yourself. It seems you need to face the church folk during Sunday meetings." His hand rested on the center of her back. "The answer you need won't be found in running any more than mine was found in drinking."

Sylvia wished going to church would magically erase her shame, but it magnified it. Ready to put some emotional distance between them, she shifted away and huffed. "I think you're in cahoots with the church leaders."

"When I began running from God, I wish someone had been willing to make me angry if that would have kept me from doing things my own way. Caring people aren't the enemy, Sylvi. Apathy is."

Aaron didn't seem to have an apathetic bone in his body. She didn't know why that was so important to her, but she truly valued it. And whether he liked it or not, he'd just confessed that he cared about her.

"I need to mention a few recent changes I've worked out. You want to hear them now or later?"

"Now, of course."

"We're not planting or harvesting any more crops," he said. "I've rented the fields to Mennonite farmers who own tractors and modern equipment. It's the right thing to do for both our sakes."

"What about the field of corn that's almost ready to harvest?"

"I've worked that out too. They'll harvest it for a percentage of the crop. We won't make as much money, but we won't work ourselves to exhaustion either."

Michael had given the running of fields over to Aaron, and she wouldn't argue. If they weren't in such a tight fix for money, she'd be thrilled with the idea.

He dug something out of his pocket. "I brought you more than a dessert."

The white envelope was thicker than if it held a letter. "What is it?"

He shrugged. "Hopefully not the cause of a fresh argument."

She licked her lips before taking the envelope and opening it. "Money?"

"Did you forget what it looks like?"

She closed the envelope and held it out to him. "Michael and I have an agreement. I receive pay after the overdue debts are paid."

"Ya, I heard, and I've already gone a couple of rounds with him on this. Here's the deal, Sylvi. If you work on the Blank farm, you get paid. End of discussion."

"Where did you get this?"

"It took some juggling, I'll admit. But the bills are paid, and nothing's been borrowed."

"The overdue bills are caught up?"

"No. I'm not a miracle worker. But we've paid enough that the threat of immediate liens and repossession of equipment is over...for now. Take the money, Sylvi."

A lump formed in her throat as if the bread pudding had stuck there. He was settling up debts. Did that mean he'd found a buyer for the farm without having to put it up for sale? "Have you accepted a down payment from someone?"

"No. We wouldn't do that without telling you."

We? "So your Mamm and Daed have sided with you about selling?"

He leaned back on his elbows. "Take a breath, Sylvi. I brought your favorite dessert and a long-overdue payday. That's all."

She turned the envelope over, saddened by its contents. He had four weeks before he had to take over at the appliance store, and he was doing all within his power to get there by then.

With the issues on the farm—the drought, Michael's arthritis giving him fits, and being in violation of EPA laws—Aaron only needed to wait a few more weeks, and his parents would be more than ready to sell and move to Owl's Perch with him.

The farm wouldn't be sold by the time he took over the appliance store, but it would be on the market.

Sadness pressed in. He'd told her all along that this was the way things would work out, but mourning the loss of another farm was going to take its toll. She'd believed she could make a success of this place. And she realized for the first time that somewhere inside her had been a faint hope that her coming here had been some kind of fate. As if there was a slim possibility that God would give her a second chance.

Thirty-One

Aaron poured a cup of coffee and added cream and sugar, hoping he had the right amount of both. Cup in hand, he walked down the driveway toward the path to the cabin. Every morning about this time, Sylvi returned from milking, washed up and changed out of her barn clothes, and came to the house for a midmorning break. Warm winds stirred the summer air, and thunder rumbled across the cloudy sky. The first of August would arrive the day after tomorrow. His time here was dwindling rather than dragging.

Sylvi came out the cabin door, looking scrubbed, with a few loose strands of damp hair hugging the nape of her neck. She walked his way without looking up. His heart beat like crazy as her presence caused an avalanche of emotions.

She was about ten feet away when she finally noticed him. "Well, hi there." Her energetic, willful smile mesmerized him.

He paused under a canopy of rustling trees and held out the coffee.

"Denki." She took it from his hands. "To what do I owe this treat?"

"I wanted to talk to you for a minute, and we can't talk easily with Mamm and Daed around."

She brought the mug to her lips. "Mmm. That's delicious. Did you make it?"

"Ya."

Closing her eyes, she took several more sips.

"I altered it from the way Daed does it. I've noticed that you like desserts with cream, so I added extra."

"I expect this same concoction again, you know. It's a good thing I work hard enough to burn off all these calories." She stretched a bit, as if working a few kinks out of her shoulders, then let her free arm fall to her side. When the back of her hand brushed his, he stroked her soft skin and dared to slide his fingers between hers. Her eyes bored into his, and she took a step back before wrapping both hands around the mug. "What did you need to talk about?"

He shrugged, unable to think of anything except kissing her. It'd be a dangerous move, altering everything between them. But it could be worth it. Stepping closer, he leaned in, pausing mere inches from her. She smelled delicious. "Let's forget the farm for a minute, Sylvi. Be here with me, just us and nothing else."

She didn't argue or turn away. That had to be a good sign. But he waited, hoping for some indication that he was welcome.

"Convince me," she whispered.

He placed his mouth on hers. The delicate softness of her skin was beyond what he'd imagined. But she didn't return the kiss. She held firm to the cup of coffee between them.

He kissed her again, and this time she responded.

A good ten seconds later, she tucked her head. He kissed her forehead while catching his breath. He'd never dreamed that a kiss could mean so much.

He straightened and put a bit of space between them.

She drew a deep breath and ran her fingers along her lips. "I've never… wow."

Never and *wow* had to be good, right? Aaron laughed. "My thoughts exactly."

Her cheeks flushed, and she headed toward the main driveway. He fell into step with her. He knew he shouldn't stare, but he did anyway.

She sipped her coffee. "This confuses things."

"Ya, I know." His voice was husky. "But I'd do it again."

"Me too. But in light of our differing goals, it seems rather short-sighted."

For the first time he wondered if maybe they had the wrong goals. "What did you want to talk to me about?" she asked again.

"The grant money. I spoke to Daed, and he believes we have no other choice than to accept it. The fence line has to be moved, and we don't have the money to do it ourselves."

"Are you okay with taking grant money?"

"I want to verify with Dusty Randall that it doesn't come with strings, but otherwise, ya, I am. What do you think?"

"I can't say the idea of taking government money is easy to accept. But I'm not sure we have a choice. The government is demanding something we can't do on our own."

They stepped onto the main driveway and turned toward the house.

"Was there anything else you needed to talk to me about?"

"There is one thing I've been wanting to ask." He shoved his hands into his pockets, and they walked in silence. The minutes dragged by as he fought to ask a question he wasn't sure he wanted answered. "Do you still love him?"

"Who? Elam?" She rolled her eyes, looking disgusted. "No. A woman can't remain in love with a man she doesn't respect." She took a sip of her coffee. "Old feelings and unfulfilled dreams tugged at us. But even then I knew what I felt for him wasn't love or respect or anything else worth having."

"It sounds as though you really spent some effort trying to under-stand your feelings. Until I went into rehab, I'd always tried to bury my emotions instead of examining them." He didn't know if he was mak-ing sense, but it was part of the reason he'd started drinking. It wasn't that his parents had been unfair or that he hated being a farmer. He drank to bury emotions that needed to be felt, dealt with, and released or expressed.

She grabbed him by the suspenders, and they both stopped walking. "Be that as it may, you are a good man." He smiled down at her, loving the way she thought. And the way she expressed her heart to him. "I like who we are together."

Something unfamiliar to him flickered through her eyes before she released his suspenders and stepped around him.

He fell in step beside her. "I know we've muddied the waters. But let's take a little time to think, and then we'll talk."

Dust billowed on the driveway toward the main road. A vehicle was heading their way. Their time alone for the day was coming to an end too quickly.

He'd made no promises, and she'd-asked for none. But he was connected to her more than he'd known was possible.

"Aaron," Dusty Randall called while pulling his truck to a stop beside them, "you ready to discuss moving fence lines?"

"You want to go with us?" Aaron asked Sylvia.

"No. You need to head up the fence-line project. I'll take care of the rest of the chores."

With a nod to Brian Clayton in the front passenger seat, Aaron opened the door behind Randall and climbed into the cab of the truck.

He couldn't stay on this farm. That much he knew. If he asked, and if he gave Sylvi time for the idea to grow on her, would she be willing to leave with him?

Thirty-Two

The rain pounded on the roof as Cara wrote "Happy Birthday, Sylvia" in yellow icing across the cake's chocolate frosting. Ada walked out of the room, carrying a load of freshly folded towels.

Ephraim dipped his finger in the bowl of frosting. "So I finally make it here again midweek and on a perfect night, since Ada's House has no business on rainy days, and you're leaving. What's with that?"

Cara passed him a spoon with remnants of the gooey chocolate. "Poor planning on your part?"

He took the spoon from her, gazing into her eyes. "It's your loss, you know."

"Hey, no being mean to me. It's bad enough I'll miss out on enjoying a rare night off with you. Between your workweek and the weekend busyness at Ada's House, I feel deprived enough already. Of course, you could go with us."

"To an all-girl event? No thanks. Besides, there's only one of you I wanted to spend time with tonight." He pulled her close. His lips had almost touched hers when Lori ran into the kitchen.

"Ew!" she screamed.

"Cut it out, you two." Ada's laughter-filled voice came from the other room.

Ephraim backed away and passed the spoon of frosting to Lori. Her eyes grew large, and she ran to show Ada. Ephraim focused on Cara, moving his eyebrows up and down. "Now where were we?"

Cara closed the gap between them. "About here..." She held his face, but just before she kissed him, Deborah walked into the kitchen.

"Oh, sorry." She went to the refrigerator. "I forgot to mix up a pitcher of lemonade for tonight's gathering."

Cara released him and shrugged. "Who'd have thought a simple kiss was too difficult a task to accomplish—in private, no less!"

Ephraim shrugged. "Eventually there will be only one interrupter in our house—Lori."

Deborah set the lemons and hand juicer on the island. "But not for long." She sang the words.

Ephraim grinned, and although he'd not said much on this topic, Cara knew that he really looked forward to having children. She did too. Still, it was strange being around men who looked at marriage as an honor and a multitude of children as a gift. Unlike newly married Englischer couples, Amish ones hoped to conceive as soon as possible—just another way that the ideology still felt foreign to her.

When Cara had found out she was pregnant with Lori, she feared her husband would be angry with her. He wasn't, but he hadn't wanted children until that moment. And after Lori was born, he didn't intend for them to have a repeat performance. She understood and had embraced that line of thinking herself, but here, where family wove itself together like a huge safety net, her view on conceiving was completely different.

Deborah cut a lemon in half and nudged it and the juicer in front of her brother. "If you want me out of here, get busy helping."

Ephraim made quick work of his job, and soon the two-gallon jar of sweetened lemonade was ready. Deborah left it on the counter and headed for the swinging door.

Trevor walked in as Deborah walked out, and Cara's eyes met Ephraim's. Maybe they'd have to move the refrigerator to block the door.

"Nice work, Cara." Trevor pointed at the cake. "I left the Blank farm about fifteen minutes ago. Everything is calm and quiet. The cows and calves are tended to and the barn scrubbed, and Sylvia went to her cabin for the night rather than working on a puzzle or playing a game with Michael."

Cara put the cake into a dessert box. "Good. She'll be surprised when we show up."

Ephraim and Cara walked onto the porch with their hands full. The cloud-covered daylight had little power behind it, but it wouldn't be dark for another two hours. Ephraim held a large umbrella over Cara, and streams of water ran off it as they huddled by Trevor's trunk, loading the birthday items.

Cara caressed Ephraim's face. "I feel sort of bad about messing up your plans."

"Don't. I like what you're doing."

"But you had a driver bring you and made arrangements for him to pick you up four hours from now."

"I'll cancel with Robbie. He'll be more than glad not to come get me. And Trevor can drop me off on his way to taking you and Deborah to Sylvia's."

"We're going by Lena's to get her too."

"You're enjoying yourself with your girlfriends. How could I possibly mind that?"

She leaned in and stole a kiss. "I like you, Ephraim Mast."

"I was hoping for more than *liking* me."

She rested her head on his chest, wanting to tell him how she really felt, but saying the words *I love you* seemed impossible. Not all that long ago, she'd recalled as a child telling her dad that she loved him. Maybe that was her hang-up—she and her dad had openly said they loved each other, and then he'd abandoned her. In truth, she didn't know what her real problem was, but unless she was talking to Lori, those words turned to ash inside her throat. Telling Lori she loved her was easy. That was what moms did, and she had told Lori the first time she held her. But that was different. Cara wasn't vulnerable in that relationship. In other relationships she always skirted actually saying those words.

Always.

Even when she and Ephraim first spoke of marriage, she didn't tell him that she loved him. When he said it to her, she said things like "Well, duh" or "Of course you do." He knew she loved him, but she'd like to be able to say it.

The front door to Ada's House slammed, causing them both to glance that way. Trevor and Deborah stood on the porch, wrestling with an umbrella. Her dad wasn't anything like she'd expected. He seemed to have an understanding of commitment and love.

Cara walked Ephraim to the front passenger side door and then took the umbrella. "I'll be right back."

After going inside and giving Lori a hug and extracting a pledge that she'd be good for Ada, Cara piled into the car with the others, and they headed out. Ephraim was dropped off first. Then Trevor stopped at Lena's house.

Lena hopped into the front seat where Ephraim had been minutes earlier. "I'm so glad you thought of this, Cara. Is it an all-girls night, or will Aaron be there too?"

"He might drop by. I see him for a few minutes fairly regularly when Sylvia's teaching me songs in your language. But he won't stay long. He never does."

"Is there anything between him and Sylvia?" Deborah raised her eyebrows quickly several times, obviously hopeful of Cara's answer.

"Sometimes I think there is," Cara said. "Other times I don't."

One thing Cara had learned about riding in a car with the Amish was that they seemed to forget the driver was listening.

Trevor glanced at her in the rearview mirror and smiled before focusing on the road. He looked at her and treated her differently than any other man she'd ever known. Then it dawned on her. He responded to her like a dad.

His daughter. The words churned inside her brain. It wasn't such a horrid thing to think of him as Dad, was it?

He stopped a couple of hundred feet from Sylvia's cabin and turned off his lights. The rain had quit, and Cara got out of the car quickly. They took the items out of the trunk as quietly as they could and sloshed along the muddy path. Before they reached the porch steps, Cara unboxed the cake, and Deborah lit the candles. They stood at the bottom of the porch like Christmas carolers, singing "Happy Birthday."

Sylvia walked outside, took one look, and broke into a huge grin. "Cara Moore, what have you done?" She hurried down the steps.

"Make a wish."

Sylvia closed her eyes before blowing out all the candles. "You're the best student I've ever had." She hugged Cara.

"Uh, yeah, I'm the *only* student you've ever had."

Sylvia hugged Deborah and Lena. "Is she always this sassy?"

"No," Deborah said. "Sometimes she sleeps."

Her friends chortled, and Cara stuck out her tongue.

The idea of Trevor driving off without even a "thanks" from her bore down heavy. They were making progress, and she should show her gratitude.

"You guys go on inside." Cara passed Deborah the cake. "I'll get the lemonade and join you in a minute."

The three women went up the porch steps, chatting feverishly as they peeled out of their muddy shoes. She couldn't hear all of what was said amid the laughter, but she caught bits about cutting huge slices of cake.

By the time Cara returned to the car, Trevor had already lifted the jug out of the trunk. "Here you go. I'll pick you up around nine?"

"Perfect. Sylvia turns in early."

"You would too if you got up at four. Ephraim would probably still be up then. You want to stop by and see him?"

"Yeah, uh...thanks." There, she said it.

"Be here then." He climbed into his car.

He treated her like a beloved daughter, and she treated him like a servant. What was she, fourteen? Yet she still hated the idea of really thanking him.

He started to pull away.

"Trevor."

He stopped the car and got out. "Did you need something else out of the trunk?"

He had the track record of a drunk and the heart of a father. What did he really want? If she fully forgave and embraced him, would his work be done and he'd leave?

No longer able to justify withholding love, she set the jug of lemonade on the hood of his car. "I forgive you." As the words left her mouth, her chest felt weird and prickly. "Do you think maybe you could forgive me too?"

"You're my Carabean. I'll always forgive you."

"You scare me." Her voice cracked, a lifetime of longing trying to force its way free from where she'd locked it up years ago.

"You're the only good thing I've ever done."

For a moment she saw an image of what had to be his life—a barren wasteland, miles and miles of parched, dried earth. Then she saw herself, not as an oasis, but as this man's one lost pearl.

Words failed her, but she put her arms around him. He held her.

She backed away. "You'll pick us up at nine?"

"I'll be here, Carabean. Whenever you need me, for as long as I'm able, I'll be here."

She swallowed hard. "Thanks, Dad."

Thirty-Three

With the morning and early afternoon chores done, Sylvia made her way to the cabin. Birds sang, and the wind rustled the thick canopy overhead. After the heavy machinery the EPA had brought in had droned on and on for two weeks, they'd finished earlier today and were finally gone. Now only gentle sounds echoed in her ears.

While the laborers ran various types of equipment, she'd put up with the noise and odors of modern-day progress, though it had taxed her nerves until she barely recognized herself. But now that the work was done, she hoped to feel more like herself within a day or two.

The job had taken much longer than expected, mostly because the list of necessary improvements kept growing as the men worked. New fences were built on each side of the creek, a huge open drainpipe that ran from one side of the creek to the other was set in place, and concrete had been poured to secure the pipe. The rains forced the men to run double rows of silt fences on both sides of the creek as well. When the fields dried and the freshly seeded earth yielded grass, the cows would use the newly con-structed concrete-and-earthen bridge to get from one part of the pasture to the other. For now a temporary barrier was in place to keep the cows off the fresh seeding.

She went inside the cabin and spotted a sink full of dishes. She never could figure out how that happened when she ate most of her meals in the Blanks' kitchen. It'd be nice if Cara came by for another language lesson.

Sylvia needed the distraction and the friendship. But no one—not Cara, Aaron, or Michael and Dora—could fill the void that missing her sisters left inside her. Some days she felt their absence more acutely than others, and she was having that kind of day.

She shuddered and bit back tears. Busyness was the answer, so she went into the wash house at the far end of the cabin. Since it had been raining so much, she had mounds of laundry that needed to be washed and hung out to dry.

While sorting clothes, she heard the familiar sound of a rig—either going up the Blanks' driveway toward their farmhouse or coming down the much smaller path to the cabin. For a brief moment she imagined it was Aaron coming for a visit, but she knew better. He didn't drive a rig to her place except on church Sundays and sometimes on a weekend night when asking her to go for a ride. Besides that, she'd not seen much of him in the last couple of weeks. He'd been spending long days with the EPA workers.

It could be Cara.

A pounding on her front door made her stop sorting laundry and leave the wash house. She entered her kitchen, craning her neck to see who stood at her screen door.

Beckie!

Sylvia's heart stopped, and she was rooted to the floor. Her sister's face was somber. Did she know what had happened with Elam?

Beckie spotted her and broke into a smile. "Sylvia." She flung open the door and ran to her. "Oh, I did find the right place, and I made it all on my own. Can you believe it?" Beckie swamped her in a hug.

Sylvia breathed in the aroma of her little sister, wanting to wrap her arms around her, but her body wouldn't budge. "How…"

"I'm fine." Beckie took a step back. "Let's look at you." She brushed a few stray hairs from Sylvia's face. "Still the same, aren't you? Your hair always needs a fresh combing and pinning midway through your workday, but do you ever redo it?"

Sylvia pulled away from her. "Would you care for something to drink? A glass of water?"

"What's going on? You don't seem the least bit happy to see me."

Sylvia put her hands on her sister's shoulders, trying to look pleased. "I...I'm just surprised."

"You should be. I mean, *me* taking on something like this by myself? You always told me I could do whatever I set my mind to. I never believed you until today."

Sylvia managed an encouraging smile, but hypocrisy stuck in her throat. "How about that drink now?"

"Ach, ya. Denki. It's so hot today."

They went into the kitchen. Sylvia grabbed a glass and moved to the refrigerator.

"Looks like you've had lots of rain of late," Beckie said.

"Ya." Sylvia handed her the cold water.

"Kumm." Beckie took her hand and led her to the living room. "Tell me about this place and what's so great about it that caused you to leave your sisters."

Sylvia's palms sweated. "It was time for me to go."

"Well, I'm sure we wore you out. Everyone down with whooping cough except you and Elam." Beckie took several long sips of her drink. "But surely you're ready to come home by now."

Plagued with guilt, Sylvia rose. "You had a long drive. I should water and feed your horse." She headed for the door.

"Oh, Shady can wait." Beckie followed her outside.

The horse frothed, and sweat soaked his body. "Oh, Beckie. Look at him. He's been in this August heat on black pavement for hours."

Beckie growled. "You drive me nuts, always thinking of the animals first."

Sylvia chafed. If Beckie had any good sense, she'd have waited a month for cooler weather or made arrangements to get a fresh horse at a midway point. There were Amish folks along the way who'd have gladly met that need. "Beckie, I'll just be a few minutes taking care of Shady. I'm sure you need a little time to freshen up and rest."

"I guess…but I made this trip to visit with you."

Sylvia could barely think. How was she supposed to have a conversation with her sister? She envisioned her guilt being tattooed across her face. "What about?"

Beckie frowned, looking confused and amused. "Have you been here so long that you've forgotten we need no subject to talk on? We just get started, and it stops when one of us falls asleep. But I do want to talk about your coming back home."

"Falls asleep? Are you…staying?"

"Of course, silly. I brought my overnight bag. Remember when we used to pack our bags to spend the night in a homemade tent in the kitchen?"

Overnight bag? Sylvia jerked open the door to the carriage.

"Are you just going to stare at it?" Beckie giggled.

As if Sylvia's world had slowed to the pace of cold molasses, she removed the bag from the carriage and passed it to Beckie. Her sister had a set of very active twins at home, and she intended to spend the night away? Sylvia looked at the bulging sides of the bag, wondering how long Beckie intended to stay.

Her eyes flashed with excitement. "I'm so proud of myself for making it here. I kept asking Elam to bring me, but you know what he's like. When he wants something, there's no stopping him, and when he's not interested, there's no motivating him. He simply tuned me out. When I said I'd go by myself, he kept coming up with reasons I shouldn't make the trip. But here I am."

A dozen memories of Beckie as a little blond-haired, blue-eyed girl all excited about birthdays or having tea with their dolls ran through Sylvia's mind. No one lit up a room like Beckie.

Sweat spattered when Sylvia patted Shady. "The barn is a little ways from here, so I'll be a few minutes. The rest room is in the hallway to your right, and there's stuff for sandwiches in the pantry and refrigerator."

Beckie smoothed her hands down the front of her dress, revealing a bulge. She smiled radiantly. "I might doze off. The little one and I have had quite an amazing day."

Without another word Sylvia took the horse by the reins and began walking. She wished Aaron was there to talk soothingly to her and to keep her company until she felt her strength return, just as he had that day she fell in the field. But he was somewhere along the fence line, double-checking things, taking notes, and looking for any scraps of barbed wire.

Beckie waved. "Hurry back. We have so much to talk about."

Sylvia wanted to beg God to help her keep the awful secret. Beckie was a long way from home and expecting. Sylvia had to make the visit pleasant. Her inability to lie, even through silence, was poor and part of the reason she'd fled the Fisher farm as quickly as she could after the incident with Elam.

Her mind racing, she led the horse into the equine section of the calving barn. Hoping she'd catch a glimpse of Aaron, she watched for him while removing the rigging, walking Shady some more, and wiping him down. But what could Aaron say other than she had to get through the visit?

The horse's rib cage continued to expand and contract in quick succession. Sylvia feared she might walk into the barn tomorrow and find the poor creature dead from heart failure. After giving him small portions of feed and water, she promised she'd return to give him more within the hour. She had no choice but to go back to the cabin.

Walking down the main driveway, she saw Trevor driving toward the farmhouse. He must have come early for the afternoon feeding. They exchanged waves.

The lane back to the cabin had never been so short. When she walked inside, Beckie was stretched out on the couch. She moved her arm from resting over her eyes. "This cabin sits off all by itself, surrounded by a patch of woods. I could never get any sleep in a place like this. Do you share it with someone?" Her sister sounded relaxed, as if maybe she'd dozed off.

"No."

Beckie sat upright.

Sylvia tried to steady her nerves. Maybe she needed to stay busy. She went to the kitchen sink.

Beckie followed her and leaned against the counter mere inches away. "Are you okay? You don't seem like yourself."

Sylvia poured dish detergent into the sink and turned on the faucet, wishing she could drown out her guilt. "I'm fine."

"Elam said I shouldn't come." Beckie reached over and turned off the water. "I was so mad at you when you left. I know you came to help a man hold on to his farm, but how could you leave us like we didn't matter? And why didn't you write? I don't care if Daed was angry that you left and forbade you to write the girls. I have my own mailbox. He would have never known."

Beckie was always keenly aware of what she felt and wanted, but she seemed unable to imagine what others might feel or need. Hadn't Sylvia remained by her side as a faithful sister while Beckie and Elam married and had babies? But Sylvia's difficulties because of that situation never seemed to bother Beckie at all.

Sylvia turned on the water again. "I've been busy. When I left home, this farm was struggling, and my only help was a man with health issues." If she couldn't get Beckie out of here soon, that would be the first of a hundred white lies she'd tell before this visit was over.

Beckie put her hands on Sylvia's shoulders and faced her squarely. "But there's more help here now, right? Aaron Blank?"

Some of Sylvia's ability to think returned to her. Who'd given Beckie directions to the farm? Their Daed had come only halfway, so he couldn't have written directions for her.

And who told Beckie about Aaron's return? Had Michael given up on keeping the farm and contacted her sister in hopes of encouraging Sylvia to return home?

Sylvia gently pulled away from her sister's grip, turned off the faucet, and plunged her hands into the soapy water. "If you intend to spend your visit trying to convince me to come home, I'll go fetch a driver for you now. We have one on site, and I'll pay the fee myself."

Beckie looked stung by the sharp words. "Why would you rather live like this than on our farm, surrounded by a family who loves you? Daed does, you know. He's angry that you chose to go elsewhere to work, but he loves you."

He wouldn't love her if he knew what she'd done. None of them would.

"I need you to let this go, Beckie." Sylvia jerked her dripping hands out of the sink, dried them on her black apron, and went into the wash house. She attached a hose to the mud sink and laid it in the wringer washer. Nothing was as noisy in an Amish home as the diesel-powered air compressor that ran the wringer washer. She flipped the switch, bringing the machine to a roar.

Beckie came to the door. "Sylvia!"

"I'm not coming home."

"And what will you do when these people don't need you anymore?" Beckie shouted above the racket.

"I'll find another farm that does."

"You think Daed's going to allow that?"

Sylvia tossed dirty dresses and aprons into the tub, and it jerked them in tiny movements one way and then the other—much like her insides felt.

Right now she didn't care what her Daed would allow. She was twenty-six years old and not a member of the Amish church. The only power he had over her was whatever she chose to give him.

Beckie skirted around Sylvia and turned off the machine. Immediate silence fell.

"For months since you left, Daed has hinted that I asked too much of you. That I relied on you constantly. I didn't want to believe him, so I tried getting by without anyone's help. All I managed to do was prove him right." She exhaled, deflating like a balloon. "It got so bad that Elam called his sister. She's living with us now, and it's awful. If I promise to do better and let you have a life of your own, will you come back? Please?"

Brackish water sat in the machine full of still-dirty clothes. "No." Sylvia turned off the hose and withdrew it from the washer. "For once, Beckie, respect my answer and drop it."

"I have to know why! Do you hate me that much?" Beckie stomped her foot, and tears fell from her eyes.

Anger swept through Sylvia and caught her in its rushing current. "Because I refuse to be stuck in a barn alone with your husband ever again! Is that a good enough reason for you?"

Sylvia's own words didn't register until she saw the horror on her sister's face. Beckie took a few steps back, stumbling over a pile of clothing. Sylvia grabbed her to keep her from falling.

When Beckie regained her footing, she jerked free. "What are you saying?"

Tears burned Sylvia's eyes, and she couldn't mutter one word. What had she done?

Beckie shook her. "Tell me what happened!"

"I'm sorry, Beckie. We never meant…" She wiped her tears and drew a breath. "We kissed."

"You kissed my husband?"

Sylvia lowered her head, unable to admit it a second time.

"Wh-what? No! When did this happen? I trusted you!"

"No you didn't. You *needed* me."

Beckie gasped for air, tears streaming down her face. She ran out of the room and toward the front door, gaining speed as she went.

"Beckie, wait. Please." Sylvia ran after her. She caught up to her at the bottom of the porch steps and grabbed her arm. "I didn't mean to blame you. It's my fault. I know that, and it's why I left. I'm so sorry. That kiss meant nothing to Elam, I promise you."

"We both know better than that," Beckie screeched. "I hate you for this."

Sylvia wiped her tears. "What can I do? I ran away from him—from all of you—as soon as I could."

Beckie held her stomach protectively while taking in a sharp breath. "All this time I've missed you, and Elam kept ignoring my pleas to visit, saying that he had no time and that you needed a life of your own. You both make me sick."

"We made a terrible mistake, Beckie. We didn't tell you because we didn't want to hurt you. He loves you."

"I want to go home."

Sylvia hesitated. Now that the truth was out, she wanted Beckie to stay and talk to her, to find a bit of peace. She knew her desire to fix the situation was unfair but couldn't help longing for it.

"Now!" Beckie's scream flew through the air. "I want to leave now!"

"Okay. Just sit on the porch steps for a minute and breathe. I'll get Trevor to drive you home." She'd have to figure out how to get the horse and rig to her later.

Tears blurred Sylvia's vision as she ran to the barn. She spotted Cara's father in the calf barn, scrubbing bottles. "Trevor, I need a favor."

He looked at her with narrowed eyes. "You okay?"

"Will you take my sister home?"

"Sure. I'll be done here in—"

"She doesn't want to wait."

Trevor set the bottles in the mud sink and dried his hands on his pants. "Okay." He pulled keys out of his pocket. "You want me to pick her up at the cabin?"

"Please. I'll ride with you."

They went to his car, which sat under a shade tree, its windows open.

When the cabin came into view, Sylvia saw her sister, overnight bag in hand, sitting on the top step.

"You going too?" Trevor asked.

"No. Wait here."

"Not a problem."

Beckie rose, looking pale and shaky.

Sylvia took the bag for her. "He'll need directions."

Beckie lifted her apron, revealing the pocket underneath, and pulled out two items: an envelope and a folded piece of paper. She opened the paper. "And to think I was so proud of following these directions to get here."

"I'm sorry." Sylvia kept repeating the phrase, but it held no power, no source of relief for her or Beckie. The handwriting on the envelope looked like Aaron's, and her guilt began to mold into suspicion and anger. She pointed at it. "Who wrote to you?"

Beckie handed the directions to Trevor, then threw the envelope on the ground and hurried to the car. Sylvia put her bag in the backseat.

As Trevor drove out of sight, Sylvia's dam broke, and she fell to her knees and sobbed.

When she could breathe again, she picked up the envelope from the mud. The return address told her what she'd hoped wasn't true. Aaron had written to Beckie.

Thirty-Four

From inside Ada's fenced backyard, Cara dipped an oversized wand with dozens of holes into a vat of homemade bubble mixture. She held it at arm's length and slowly made a circle. Hundreds of bubbles floated through the air, making Better Days bark with excitement while Lori danced through them.

"Watch me, Mom!" Lori stretched high and gently caressed a bubble in her hands without it bursting. She blew into it, making it larger.

"That's beautiful."

"This is the best bubble recipe ever, huh, Mom?"

"The best, Lorabean."

"Look!" Lori hollered and started running.

Cara turned to see Ephraim coming out of Ada's house. Lori leaped into his arms, and he lifted her into the air before settling her near his waist.

Cara crossed the yard. "When we're married, I'm going to jump into your arms whenever you arrive."

Ephraim grinned and reached for her with his free arm. "Do I have to lift you over my head?"

"Maybe." She hugged him and Lori at the same time. "We won't be busy tonight, and I'm not going anywhere, so is this my second chance at a midweek date?"

He set Lori's feet on the ground. "Show me how well that bubble stuff works."

Lori hurried to the vat of mixture.

"The bishop and deacon are on their way," he said quietly. "They're not more than a minute or two behind me. As far as I know, it's just a routine visit to see how you're doing now that you've had time to work through some of your issues with Trevor."

"I'm not in trouble for using secular music to learn the language?"

"How would they know that?"

"Preacher Alvin and Esther noticed a huge, sudden improvement in my comprehension and speaking skills. When they asked, I told them the truth."

Deborah stepped outside. "The ministers are here. They're waiting in the living room."

Cara went ahead of Ephraim, straightening and smoothing her clothes. Being in a test period was no fun, and she looked forward to the day when all this was behind her.

The two men stood in the living room, talking and chuckling.

"Cara." Sol held out his hand. "I hope we're not coming at a bad time for you."

"No. This is fine."

"Gut." He motioned to a chair at one end of the room. "Have a seat." She sat facing the couch and chairs. "Mostly we just want to ask you some questions and keep up with your progress."

Mostly?

The men, including Ephraim, took seats facing her.

They bowed their heads. Ephraim winked at her before closing his eyes. A minute later he cleared his throat, and she opened her eyes to see the others waiting for her to finish her prayers.

"Cara," the bishop began, "are you getting along with your dad?"

She was in a sticky situation here. It was her nature to want to tell these men to mind their own business. "What you really want to know is if I've forgiven him and how well I'm working that out."

"Ya, that's right."

Saying the words to her dad had been hard enough, and she didn't do it because these men said she had to. She'd told Ephraim, but only because she wanted the man she loved to share in the joy of reconciliation with her.

Ephraim got up and moved to the chair beside Cara. If anyone understood how difficult she found this kind of meeting, Ephraim did. He took her hand into his. "I think you should just talk about what the last two months with your dad have been like."

She took a deep breath. "Well, I started seeing Trevor as a man who struggles with his weaknesses, his longing to undo the impossible, and the loss he's sustained by his own hand. I've begun to feel compassion and understanding. It wasn't because of any one thing, and I have to be honest that his kindness has made forgiving him much easier. If he was as sharp-tongued with me as I've been with him at times, I'd still resent him. So I haven't done anything worthy of accolades. I'd like to get to where I can do what I'm supposed to without the other person having to meet me halfway, but I'm not there yet. I'm sorry if that's not good enough, but it's where I am."

The bishop looked at the deacon and received a nod. "Cara, you still have to complete the instruction classes and be able to converse reasonably well in German and Pennsylvania Dutch. As the leader for the instruction sessions, I can say that everything looks good for you to successfully complete them within the next few weeks. I talked to Alvin, and he assures me you're doing remarkably well with the languages."

"What?" She wanted to look to Ephraim for confirmation, but she was afraid he'd fade into nothingness and she'd wake to find herself in bed.

The bishop leaned forward. "Cara, what we've come here to say is that we expect you and Ephraim to be able to marry this coming wedding season."

Her heart leaped, and she jumped up. "Really? I'm doing that well?"

"You are."

She wanted to dance, but instead she balled her hands into fists. "Yes!"

Ephraim got up and hugged her like a long-lost friend. After several minutes of celebration, she wondered why they were telling her this now.

She and Ephraim separated, still holding hands. "I haven't completed everything or been baptized yet."

"True," the bishop said. "But Ada brought it to my attention that you and Ephraim have made no plans for a wedding this coming season. Since that is no easy feat to pull off, we feel you should be free to begin making plans."

She knew next to nothing about Amish weddings. What she'd heard about the feasts and the daylong ceremony made little sense to her. She'd never even seen one. "I don't suppose we could elope?"

"No," the ministers said in unison, then chuckled at their response.

"Sorry to pounce," the bishop said, "but no one elopes. If special arrangements need to be made, we do a small wedding in a quick manner."

"I like the sound of that," Cara said.

Ephraim leaned in and whispered, "He means if a couple comes up expecting before they're married."

"Oh. How many people will we need to invite?"

"Hundreds of people in this community have been looking forward to the day when Ephraim marries," the bishop said. "They will feel cheated if they don't get to attend the wedding."

Cara's mouth went dry, and she glanced at Ephraim. "Hundreds?"

"If we're careful with the invitation list," Ephraim said, "I imagine we could keep it down to six hundred guests."

Cara laughed. "Six hundred? And we're to feed them two meals, cakes, drinks, and whatever else the day calls for? I hope God still multiplies fishes and loaves." She knew she had loved ones who'd enjoy sharing the work load. She wasn't sure how she'd foot the bill, but after all it'd taken to get to this point, coming up with the money was nothing. She gestured toward the kitchen door. "This calls for a celebration. May I fix you a plate of our best desserts and something to drink?"

Aaron walked the silt fence line with a mallet in one hand and the horse's reins in the other, making sure the stakes were driven deeply enough to hold against the torrents of rain predicted for tomorrow afternoon.

He had hours of double-checking ahead of him, but if he could get done today, he could help Sylvi with the routine farm work tomorrow. Then maybe they'd both have enough energy to go out that night.

An odd sensation skittered over him, causing him to stop and scan the field. Finally he spotted Sylvi marching toward him. The intensity of her steps caused him to mount his horse and ride to her.

"Hello there."

She shook something at him. "Explain this to me."

He slid off his horse, and she thrust an envelope at him. One glance and he knew what it was. "Did she mail it back?"

"No. She came here." Sylvi's eyes swam with tears. "How could you do something behind my back like this? I trusted you."

Her body and voice trembled as she spoke. He'd known she and Beckie would probably have a rough meeting at first, but she was beyond upset. Something had gone very wrong. "I shouldn't have sent it without your permission."

Sylvia balled her hands into fists, crunching the paper into nothing. "She didn't know!" Sylvia sobbed. "Not until today."

"Didn't know what?"

She bent slightly, looking as if she might collapse. "She's Elam's wife!"

A jolt thundered through him, and then the scope of the situation

became clear. This was why Sylvi struggled deeply to forgive herself. "I
didn't know."

"But you knew enough. You knew I'd come here willing to end all
communication with my family." She walked off.

He ran after her. "I thought it was because of a spat of some kind."

"You thought you could get rid of me by bringing Beckie here. It'd be
all you needed to get Michael and Dora to sell this place, wouldn't it?" She
hurried away.

"Sylvi, please."

She turned. "Say it, Aaron. Look me in the eyes, and tell me the real
reason you did this."

The betrayal reflected in her eyes made him sick, and he couldn't
defend his actions.

She tightened her fists and screamed toward the sky—a painful, broken cry. Then she folded her arms and slowly gained control of her tears.
"You wanted me gone, and you didn't care what it took to accomplish it."

"Maybe when I sent the letter," he admitted. "But not now."

"I thought you were honest with me. You never once mentioned having written my sister. Every moment between us was a lie!" She stormed
off. "Stay away from me!"

Aaron watched her slowly disappear past the dip of the rolling fields.
Questions ran wild inside him, and he couldn't find one solid answer he
could trust.

He made his way to the barn. His thoughts jabbed him mercilessly as
he readied the stalls. Was she right? Had he lied to her this whole time?
Initially, he hoped Beckie would visit, the two would make up, and Sylvi
would want to go home. But what had he been hoping for since falling in
love with her? And did it matter? She wanted nothing else to do with him.

Half of the cows were milked before Trevor showed up.

"I took Sylvia's sister home."

"I figured as much."

"They both seemed really upset." Trevor released a set of milkers from a cow and grabbed the bucket. "Is there anything I can do?"

Aaron shook his head. He had no idea what he could do himself. He thought of Trevor on the ladder inside that apartment building and the toolbox falling on that little boy's head. The toolbox had just fallen on Aaron. Or maybe he'd shoved it onto Sylvia. Either way, there was no undoing what had been done.

Thirty-Five

Aaron lay on his bed, staring at the ceiling. Darkness and heat clung to the early morning. Hours from now Sylvi would walk through the blackness to the milking parlor, and he'd meet her there, hoping she'd forgive him.

He'd spent the night lying here, trying to sort through his motivations. Sure, at the time he'd wanted Sylvi to go away. He'd come home with a goal, and she stood in his way. He had expected her and her sister to argue, but he'd banked on Sylvi's more gentle nature taking over and enabling the two to settle their differences. She'd then pack her bags and be on her merry way, leaving him free to convince his parents to sell the farm.

He'd never once thought the letter might rip their lives apart.

He sat up, putting his feet on the floor and his head in his hands. The image of Sylvi's brokenness brought another round of fresh pain.

He caught a glimpse of an insight and latched onto it.

He'd broken an unspoken rule—one person did not reach into another person's life and make decisions for her...or him. It seemed this was a lesson he should have learned long ago.

As his thoughts followed that trail, he understood something else. It wasn't his place to pry his parents' grip free of this farm. He wasn't wrong in showing them options for a different life or in sacrificing his time to help them. But his way was overzealous.

He was doing for them what he wished they'd done for him—see the problem and get involved. But they were mature adults with the right to hang on to this black hole until they or the bank said otherwise.

He'd offered them a good, sound plan to move to Owl's Perch. It made sense for him and his parents to stay together since he was their only surviving child. Since Daed wasn't easy to get along with, asking both parents to move into the living quarters above the appliance store and his Daed to help run the shop was a huge sacrifice. But...

He'd learned in rehab that a spouse, friend, or parent can't make someone want to get clean. And he couldn't make his parents want to leave this place. He'd banked on having more influence over his parents than he really had. It was now mid-August, and his Daed trusted him a little more but not enough. He hadn't expected his Daed to be grateful for what he was trying to do, but he'd thought his Daed would cooperate more by now.

After moving to his desk, Aaron lit a kerosene lantern and looked through the informational documents the EPA worker had left. He found the page titled "The Struggle to Make Small Farms Profitable." Unfortunately, it all hinged on one thing—getting that boost Sylvi kept looking for. He took out a notebook and began writing down information.

By the time he heard his parents moving around downstairs, he'd come up with a couple of plans that might work. After putting each idea for a specific section of the farm into its own folder, he gathered his work, tucked his small notebook and pencil into his pants pocket, and went downstairs.

A sense of nostalgia tugged at him as he gazed at his parents in the kitchen, dimly lit by a kerosene lamp. His Daed stood at the counter with the percolator in front of him, making coffee. His mother kneaded a bowl of dough, probably preparing a batch of cinnamon buns. They had legitimate reasons to struggle with coping. Mamm had carried eight children to term, and only two had survived past the first few hours or days of life. They left Ohio under duress, and then they lost his sister in a horrific accident. But his sympathy for those terrible events and for Daed's battle with arthritis didn't offer any solutions. Answers for the future were what mattered, not heartbreak for the past.

He put his plans on the kitchen table. "We need to talk."

His Daed lit the eye on the gas stove and set the percolator on it. "What's that?"

"A new set of plans that I believe represent your best chance for making this farm both manageable and profitable."

"Is it something we can do and afford?"

"You'll need money and some restructuring to get it started. I should be able to get out some of the cash I put down on the appliance store—it was more than what was needed anyway. I'll get back as much of it as I can."

His mother moved toward him, eyes wide with hope. "Are you staying?"

"No."

Sylvi didn't want him here, and he'd done what he came to do—face his parents and give them his best until it was time for him to take over the store. Surely they would cosign the loan papers, even if they didn't go with him, so that his agreement with Leo would be satisfied.

Anger shrouded his Daed's face.

"Daed, you can't do to Sylvi what you did to me. If you want to keep this farm, you have to be willing to do your share or hire full-time help for her."

"You do more bellyaching than a girl."

"This isn't about me. I'm here on Sylvi's behalf. You drew her in on promises, much as you did me when you wanted to move here from Ohio. You bought this place because you had a dream, but then you gave up and blamed me for every failure. You can't do that to her."

Daed grabbed a newspaper off the counter and threw it across the room. "How dare you—a strong, healthy man in your twenties—judge me! I've been through hard times you know nothing about."

"I'm sure that's true. But you need to decide whether you're capable of pitching in to achieve your dream—or if you even want to. If you can't or won't, then free Sylvi before all this hard work breaks her."

"You always think I'm not fair. Life isn't fair. I'd think you'd know that by now."

"You need to be honest with Sylvi. If you don't want this place enough to pull your weight or hire the needed help, say so."

"I do want this place! But I don't have the money to hire help, and a man with back problems can't work that milking barn twice a day every day."

"The barn can be redesigned with a ramp for the cows so you don't have to bend so much. And once the overdue bills are paid, you can start setting aside money to buy supplies."

Daed wagged his finger. "I may not handle as much around here as you think I should, but I've never run out on this family. You abandoned us. After your sister died, milk prices plummeted, the cost of feed and veterinarian bills skyrocketed, and you left!"

"So did you. You crawled into your bed and became just as unavailable as I was when I went to rehab."

"We moved here for you."

"Hogwash."

Daed had left Ohio because his own father had divided up his farm based on the number of grandchildren in each of his children's households. Daed's brothers ended up with hundreds of acres. Daed was left with only forty acres and the right to use the dairy barn.

For years his parents had carried the grief over their six lost babies. When Daadi Blank divided the land based on living grandchildren, it was as if he'd cursed them in front of all their relatives and friends. It was too much for them to handle, so they found this farm in Dry Lake and moved.

His Daed picked up the folders and flung them. "Why don't you keep your money and your plans and just go? We don't need your help. Sylvia and I were managing just fine without you."

"No, Michael, you weren't. Besides, he's our only child." Mamm turned to Aaron. "He grieved for you constantly, and I prayed day and night that you'd come home again. Please don't leave now."

"Don't beg him. He made up his mind years ago." Daed jerked a chair away from the kitchen table and sat, but his harsh words and movements didn't hide the pain in his eyes. "You want to go, go."

Aaron took the seat beside his father. "Daed, I know you have hurts, really deep ones. But you shouldn't have dumped your agony and garbage on me. We've become just like you and your dad—only worse. Well, I'm tired of making excuses for you, and I'm finished trying to fix your problems."

His Daed stared at him, eyes filling with tears. "Then leave."

Spiteful words coursed through Aaron until he thought they'd explode from him. He marched out the back door, slamming it behind him.

Black skies hovered, and the cows mooed, ready to be let into the barn and milked. He stomped across the wet fields. He'd always believed his Daed loved him, but now he wasn't so sure. Pain throbbed inside his chest. He'd taxed his parents for years, lied to them, and embarrassed them in front of the community. But Daed's hardness wasn't rooted in Aaron's behavior. His father didn't like him, plain and simple.

He wished he could talk to Sylvi, but she wanted nothing to do with him right now and for good reason.

Even with the hostility between his Daed and him, he didn't regret coming home. He'd do it all again a hundred times over for the chance to get to know Sylvi. And to let his Mamm know he loved her and was sorry for bailing on them the way he had.

Hurt swirled around inside him, picking up other hurts as it went. At least now he understood a little better why he'd felt the need to escape. And he wanted that escape right now. A six-pack would take the edge off. Two would do a better job. What else could he do? There were no answers, not to his and Sylvi's relationship, not to his and his parents'. He walked the fence line, using the moonlight to avoid the huge tractor ruts wherever he could.

Everybody used something to escape, right? His Daed crawled into bed for weeks at a time. Sylvi left home and worked herself into exhaustion. What was so wrong with his way?

The mud and earth shifted under him. A cracking noise rumbled, and suddenly the lower half of his body dangled in a hole. He tried to dig his fingers into the ground, but the mud came loose. He grabbed onto wet grass, trying to find something that would keep the rest of his body from being pulled into the hole.

He slid farther. "No. God, hear me, please!"

The grass yanked out by its roots, and Aaron plummeted. Everything around him went pitch black.

Sylvia woke with her eyes burning, her body aching, and the same pressing question that had kept her up most of the night—what should she do now? Darkness filled the room, and she wished she could hide in it forever. It didn't matter that she'd cried herself to sleep. Nothing had changed. She owed God and her sister a price she could never pay.

Thoughts of Aaron crowded her mind, confusing her even more. She pushed herself upright, determined not to think about him. She didn't know who'd handled the milking last night, but she needed to get to the barn this morning. Heaviness pressed down, as if she were trying to carry a newborn calf on her shoulders.

Without putting a match to a lantern, she slid into her clothes and made her way along the shadowy path. Light shone from inside the barn. If Aaron was there, she'd leave.

She stepped inside. The stalls were already bedded, feed sat in the troughs, and the doors were open to let the cows enter.

Trevor looked up. "Morning."

"Is it just you today?"

"Yeah. Aaron had me come in early."

Good. At least she wouldn't have to see him.

Tears welled again, and she turned away to grab the spray bottle, paper towels, and stool. How many times would she believe in a man only to be made a fool of? She sat beside the nearest cow, cleaned her udder, and prepped her for milking.

Trevor paused near her. "I don't know what's going on, but whatever it is, please don't run from it. Face it, Sylvia. I give you my word it's the only way. New cities can be built on top of old ruins. Did you know that?"

Maybe she shouldn't bare her soul, but she had to talk to somebody, and Trevor didn't seem like the kind who would judge her unfairly. "But I knew right from wrong. I walked right into the middle of lust and stayed there."

"God forgave Paul, who called himself the chief sinner. From what I understand, he tortured, imprisoned, and killed people in God's name. What makes you think you're better than he was?"

"Better? I don't think that."

"Sure you do. God forgave the worst sinner. The Bible says so. Only thing I can guess is that either you think you're too good to take the same grace Paul took, or you think God is too weak to supply it."

Tears spilled onto her cheeks. She didn't want to agree with him, but his bluntness held wisdom. Needing fresh air, she walked outside and looked into the dark sky. Was it really possible to make things right between God and her?

"God, please…I can't undo what I've done. If I could relive it, I'd never let myself or anyone else get me in that same situation, but I did let it happen, and I'm sorry. What can I do now? Please, I need Your guidance and strength."

As her muted whispers pierced the quiet around her, energy and hope trickled into her. And she knew what had to be done. She had to go see her sister.

She returned to the barn. "Trevor, I need a ride to Beckie's. I don't know how long I'll stay or if my Daed will let me come back. But I have to talk to Michael and then go."

Thirty-Six

Sylvia's stomach clenched and her fingertips throbbed with an odd numbness as Trevor drove down the narrow road toward her home. The trip to the Blank farm had taken Beckie more than two hours by horse and carriage, but it had taken Trevor less than thirty minutes to drive here.

It was well past lunchtime. Since she didn't know what she'd face when she arrived home, she had spent the morning talking to Michael and Dora, doing laundry, and packing all her clothes.

She hadn't seen Aaron. He was probably still working the fence line, which was just as well since she didn't know what to say to him.

One battle was all she could handle today.

Trevor passed her brick homestead. The red milking barn still needed a new coat of paint. The herd stood grazing in the lush fields. A little farther down the road, he pulled into the driveway in front of the eighteenth-century gray stone house where Beckie and Elam lived.

In spite of looking like her home, it didn't feel like it. It had lost its homeyness the day she learned that Elam intended to marry Beckie. With a little time, she could have adjusted to that disappointment easily enough if not for two things—Elam's backstabbing sneakiness at dumping her for someone so close to her, and her inability to get away from him. The real shame was that the mess had given a mediocre man too much power over her emotions.

Trevor put the vehicle in Park. "I think the best way for you to reach me when…if you're ready to come home is to call Ephraim's cabinetry shop. Either I'll get the message from him, or he'll bring it to the farm." He passed her a piece of paper with Ephraim's name and phone number scrawled on it. "How far to the nearest phone?"

"Unless the bishop has approved one for someone closer, it's two to three miles away." She opened the car door, her head swimming. "I can get to it easily enough when I'm ready. Thanks for the ride."

"Glad to do it."

The tires crunched against the gravel driveway as Trevor left.

Movement near the pasture, some two hundred feet away, caught her eye.

Elam.

As he walked toward her, her legs felt more like flimsy rubber bands than muscle, sinew, and bone. But the reaction came from dread of facing her family with her sin exposed, not from any feelings for Elam. Nothing about him interested her anymore.

Still, memories of their best courting days ran through her mind. Whatever she'd found so special about him eluded her now. He'd been charming, to be sure, and everyone flocked to him as if his boyish good looks and handsome smile inflated his value. Aaron was far more attractive to her, and he thought nothing of his looks. But Elam relied on his appearance and hid his disloyalty behind it. He'd been slowly maturing for years, so maybe he'd changed, but the person she knew was self-absorbed, conceited, and manipulative. She'd seen those flaws when they were courting and had foolishly been willing to overlook them.

Elam stopped within five feet of her, looking drained and subdued. There wasn't a hint of the bold-faced, overconfident man who had married her sister.

She cleared her throat. "I didn't intend to tell her."

"I'm glad it's out."

His words gave her some much-needed hope.

He studied his home, sadness radiating from deep within. "I wanted to tell her so many times, but I couldn't make myself. It seemed unreasonably selfish—even for me—to lighten my load by dumping it on her."

She needed to make sure every speck of unfinished business and all secrets between them were attended to. "You were right when you said I was never going to marry you. It never would've happened."

"Why?"

"You don't want to hear it."

"I need to know."

Elam waited, and thoughts of Aaron tugged at her. "You had no sense of loyalty. No ability to care about what I needed over what you wanted."

Within a week of knowing her, Aaron had more respect for her position on *his* farm than Elam ever had of Sylvia's place on a farm she partly owned. Aaron understood her better than she had herself—her avoidance of church and her drive to overwork. He put effort into planning breaks for her. The man in front of her had no understanding of being someone's equal partner, and she wondered if he had the capacity to really love someone. Aaron did. She'd seen it in the way he treated his parents and Frani.

And her.

A new ache for her sister banged around inside her.

Sylvia turned to face the house Elam and Beckie called home. "My regret is deep, and I need to tell Beckie that. But I don't know if she'll hear me."

"Maybe she will. Even if not, I think you're right to try. I knew when she got home yesterday that she'd found out. She took to bed immediately, made me swear I wouldn't tell her parents or sisters what was going on, and kicked me out of the bedroom until further notice."

It surprised her that Beckie hadn't told their parents or sisters. Beckie held the power to make them all hate her while gaining sympathy for herself for years to come. Wasn't she going to use it?

Sylvia started up the brick walkway.

"Sylvia."

She turned back to Elam.

"I'm sorry for the way I broke up with you, for the way I took over your responsibilities of running the farm, for taking advantage of your loneliness when you were just trying to do the right thing by Beckie and your family."

Her heaviness lifted a bit. But she'd thought it had been her idea to give up her farm duties piece by piece to avoid coming into contact with him. It sounded as if he'd planned that.

Aaron would never have done that to anyone, least of all her. Even when he had no feelings for her, he'd made sure she understood his plan. No manipulation. But plenty of stubborn concern—that she worked too hard, kept herself from making friends, and had turned away from God. And he worried where she'd land when he sold the farm.

Her anger had blinded her. If he'd thought contacting Beckie would have been truly bad for her, he wouldn't have done it.

She tried to free her thoughts of Aaron. "I've asked forgiveness from God, and I'll give it to you." She hoped God liked her a lot more than she liked Elam. "I'm going to see Beckie."

As Sylvia walked toward Beckie's home, Lilly rounded the side of the house with a bowl in her hands.

"Sylvia!" Her face lit up. She hurried to the steps and set down the bowl before running to Sylvia and engulfing her in a hug. "Oh, you're home." She squeezed her tight. "For good?"

Sylvia returned the warm embrace. Concern that her father would refuse to let her leave again—and that he'd insist on gaining control of her once he learned of her sin—lifted. She wasn't staying. "No, just for a few days."

Lilly took a step back. "Don't you dare leave again without giving me your address. If I have it, I might be able to talk him into letting all us girls write. If not, I'll wait until I'm in my rumschpringe. He won't even try to stop me then." She glanced back at the house. "Beckie came home yesterday so sick she went straight to bed. We figured the heat was too much on her, driving that distance and being pregnant. I was bringing her some of Mamm's famous chicken noodle soup."

"I'll take it to her. Where are her little ones?"

"We're keeping them at our house until she feels better."

"Tell Mamm and Daed I'll be up to see them later, but I need to see Beckie first."

Lilly's eyes shone bright. "I'll make your favorite dinner. Will you be ready to eat in a few hours?"

She doubted it, but she squeezed Lilly close. "Absolutely. Denki, Lilly."

Sylvia took the bowl of soup into the house with her, grabbed a spoon from a drawer, and went to Beckie's bedroom door. She tapped and heard movement, but Beckie didn't respond. Sylvia eased the door open. Beckie lay curled in a ball, staring at the wall.

"Beckie, honey?" Her sister stirred a bit. "Are you hungry? Mamm made you some soup."

Beckie slowly worked her way to a sitting position. She still wore the clothes from yesterday as well as her prayer Kapp. But it was a good sign that she hadn't screamed at Sylvia or thrown anything—yet.

"What are *you* doing here?"

Sylvia set the bowl on the table. "I came to beg forgiveness."

Beckie scowled. "Get out."

"I'm not leaving. If you need to drag me in front of the whole family and humiliate me so your anger will subside, then do so. But I won't leave until I've eased your pain…and forgiveness would be really nice too."

Beckie stared at her. "I have no words to begin to tell you what you've done to me."

Sylvia knelt beside the bed. "I can't begin to explain the depth of my sorrow."

Beckie looked the other way, clenched her fists, and crossed her arms tightly. The minutes ticked by, and Sylvia remained on her knees.

"Im Gott sei Lieb," Sylvia whispered. *In God's love.* It was their phrase, the one they used to say in bed after talking about everything—their joys and hopes and fears and anger.

Beckie jumped as if Sylvia had startled her. Tears welled in Beckie's eyes, but she said nothing.

Every night, no matter what was happening around them, they had put it all in His hands and had fallen asleep believing every good thing came from His hand and every bad thing that happened or that they did could be engulfed by His love. They weren't little girls anymore, and their ability to sin seemed to have grown along with their bodies, but had God's love gotten any smaller?

Beckie patted the side of the bed. "Get off your knees, Sister."

Sylvia moved to the edge of the mattress. Beckie struggled to speak. Her hair was a mess, which was unlike her. Sylvia went into the bathroom, retrieved a hairbrush, and sat on the edge of the bed next to her. Her sister shifted, allowing Sylvia room to get behind her. Sylvia removed the straight pins that held the Kapp in place, then took out the various hairpins, slowly unwinding her golden locks.

Sylvia brushed her sister's hair. "It'd be nice if we could untangle life the way we can untangle the knots in our hair."

Tears fell from Beckie's eyes. "I started something with Elam because I wanted to steal him from you."

Sylvia's heart jerked wildly, but she continued to brush her sister's long locks.

Beckie wiped her nose on the wadded mess of tissue in her hands. "My plan worked out well, don't you think?"

Sylvia kissed the back of her sister's head. "He loves you, Beckie."

Silence hung between them while Sylvia pinned her sister's hair into a bun. Then Sylvia picked up the bowl and spooned up some broth.

After Beckie took a bite, she wiped her mouth with the back of her hand. "I don't hate you like I said. I know I carry some of the blame too."

Her sister's graciousness caught Sylvia off guard, but it explained why Beckie hadn't told their parents and sisters.

She swallowed another spoonful of soup. "I need you. Now more than ever."

"I can't stay. We both know that. Besides, you're a grown woman well capable of taking care of yourself and your family." Sylvia continued to spoon-feed her sister.

"It's true what Daed said, isn't it? I relied too heavily on you."

Needing a moment to adjust her thinking, Sylvia set the bowl to the side. "Ya, and I let you."

Beckie smoothed the sheet across her lap. "Can you and me and Elam work this out somehow…enough so you could come home?"

"This isn't my farm anymore, and I don't want it to be. Besides, I don't belong here. I started out with a dream." Understanding began to trickle in, and she longed for it to pour like last week's gullywashers. "Actually, I started out with what I thought was a dream. I wanted to be a strong, capable woman unlike any other Amish woman I knew. But what I really wanted was to find someone who respected my thoughts and skills. Someone who wanted an equal partner, not a farmhand." She took Beckie's face into her hands. "I'm so, so sorry."

Beckie passed her a tissue. "I knew better than to try to take Elam from you. What kind of a sister does that? I'll tell you—one who's spoiled and selfish and jealous and a host of other things it's taken me years to figure out."

"And love was mixed in with those reasons too, ya?"

"I'm not convinced it was." Beckie's eyes moved to the bedroom doorway and stayed there. "For either of us."

Sylvia turned toward the door to see Elam standing there.

"Sylvia,"—he removed his hat and entered the room—"I need to talk with Beckie alone, please."

Sylvia rose and quietly slipped out of the house.

Thirty-Seven

Cara tapped the reins against the horse's back as she headed for Ephraim's. He wanted them to come to the shop around lunchtime today, so she and Lori had spent the night at Lena's. With her dad working extra while Sylvia was gone, it was easier to stay in Dry Lake than to try to get back and forth.

"You're getting better at handling a rig, Mom."

"Denki."

Cara had spent the travel time finally admitting that Trevor wasn't just a man the church leaders wanted her to be nice to. She also explained to Lori who each person in Ephraim's family would become to her after the wedding. Since arriving in Dry Lake and learning she had relatives here, Cara had continually balked at telling Lori about family relationships, in part because it was painful to explain and in part because it was so confusing. Most of all, Cara never trusted how long these people would remain in their lives. Why tell Lori about Trevor if he might up and disappear, hurting her in the process? But now Cara knew that as long as illness or some other unforeseen issue didn't interfere, Trevor would always be near, and she was actually thankful for that.

Lori wiped sweat from her little nose. "I didn't have any grandpas, and once you and 'From get married, I'm gonna have two."

Cara mulled over the Pennsylvania Dutch language until she came up with the right words for *You have one Amish grandfather and one Englischer grandfather.* "*Du hab eens Daadi un eens Grandpa.* Ya?"

Lori's eyes grew large, and she giggled. "Wunderbaar, Mom! 'From will be proud of you." Lori brushed a fly away from her face. "I don't think I'll always call him 'From. After you marry him, he'll be my Daed."

Her daughter sounded so mature. Cara couldn't help but enjoy the idea of having babies.

After pulling into the driveway, she brought the carriage to a halt. Lori jumped down and ran into the shop. In a few months her daughter would be as comfortable with Ephraim's family as if she'd been born into it. For that, Cara would be eternally grateful.

Grey stepped outside. "Hi, Cara. Ephraim's finishing up a business call." He took the horse by the reins. "I'll tend to her."

"Thanks." She stepped close to him so she could speak softly. "How's Lena?"

His grin gave him away. "As beautiful and amazing as ever, even from a distance. I expect I'll have a letter from her in my mailbox when I arrive home this evening."

"I'm glad you and Lena at least have the mail to make your relationship a little easier. How much longer before you two can court?"

"Seven weeks. Maybe a little more if Lennie feels Michael and Dora need it." He didn't sound the least bit perturbed at having to wait for his former in-laws to be ready.

"And you don't mind her calling the shots on the timing?"

He smiled. "Lennie has insight and instincts that I'd be a fool to discount. Besides, she'll trust me without question in other areas over the years." He pointed toward the shop where Ephraim was talking to Lori. "He's off the phone."

"Thanks, Grey."

Ephraim walked toward her, holding Lori's hand. "How about if the three of us have a late lunch in the hiddy?"

"I didn't bring any food."

Lori covered her mouth, snickering.

A conspiratorial look passed between Ephraim and Lori. He lifted his straw hat for a moment and wiped his brow. "I knew I was forgetting something." He replaced his hat and held out his hand. "Kumm."

Cara refused to take his hand. "What's going on, 'From?"

He looked at his empty palm and then to her. "I never would've taken you for a stick-in-the-mud."

She slid her hand into his. They crossed the wide berth between his shop and his home. Once on the far side of his house, they went toward his hiddy. It stood surrounded by hedges on three sides and open to a pasture on the fourth. A porch swing hung from the branch of a huge tree. He used this hidden place to relax and stargaze, and she looked forward to the day when they could come here at will, without concern for how it might look to others.

Lori ran through the man-made opening in the hedges. She gasped and clapped her hands. "Yes!"

Cara eyed Ephraim. He'd done something. He shrugged and motioned for Cara to enter ahead of him.

She stepped through the opening and spotted a blanket spread on the ground with two picnic baskets on it.

"Look, Mom. It's a surprise."

Cara turned to Ephraim.

He smiled. "Surprise."

"Uh, yeah, but why?"

"My stepmom made it for us. It's filled with traditional foods served at weddings."

Ada had been explaining Amish wedding dishes to Cara. "This was really thoughtful."

Ephraim sat on the blanket beside Lori. Cara joined him.

They tasted all the different foods, and Ephraim explained what they were. The roasted chicken and mashed potatoes seemed usual enough, but she'd never tasted cooked celery. It was sweet and had the consistency of a relish, only she couldn't imagine eating a relish as a side dish. There were several types of salads along with cheeses, cold cuts, breads, and lots of desserts. She could see why these foods were served at weddings.

The meal was simple and delicious. They talked and ate. This would be home in a few months.

Ephraim winked at her. "We did it, Cara."

Cara loved him enough to last a dozen lifetimes. "Yeah, and all it took was a shunning, a reconciliation, a salvation, learning two languages, forgiving Dad, and a partridge in a pear tree."

"And a God who knew how to weave it all together."

She inched her fingers across the blanket until they found his. "I love you."

His eyes searched hers, telling her he knew her well. "I know," he whispered hoarsely.

She intertwined her fingers with his. "Even though the words may never come easy, loving you does. And I'm determined to find other ways to let you know how much I love you every day for the rest of my life."

The cabinetry shop echoed with the taps of hammers and the rasping of hand sanders. There was no hint of finishing early today, even though it was Friday.

Grey opened the leather pouch that held his set of carving tools. He picked out a 35 mm bent gouge and began making a design on a cabinet door. One of the many things he appreciated about this job was that it made good use of his artistic skills.

He hovered over the walnut panel, carving an intricate pattern reminiscent of something from the eighteen hundreds—per the customer's request. Wood shavings curled as he carved, and he brushed them to the floor.

"Grey," Ephraim called to him.

"Ya," he answered without lifting his head. He finished sculpting the tiny section he'd begun and then looked up.

Ephraim stood in the double-wide doorway, talking with Michael Blank. If Michael had come to the shop specifically to see Grey, the topic must be important. Grey wiped off the tool with a clean cloth and slid it back into the leather pouch, then walked toward them.

The last time Michael had come to speak with him, he was displeased with Grey for not agreeing with him and the rest of the school board about letting Lena go. Michael had been Grey's father-in-law for six years, and Grey knew he easily recognized when others were wrong but rarely saw his own part in an issue. They had politely butted heads on more than one occasion.

Before Grey closed the gap between them, Ephraim said his good-byes and returned to sanding an oak cabinet.

"Michael." Grey extended his hand.

Michael took Grey's hand and pulled him close. "Have you see Aaron?" he whispered.

"Not today. Is there a problem?"

Michael stepped back, holding his forehead while staring at the floor. "We...argued." He cleared his throat. "But that was before daylight, and I haven't seen him since."

It was almost time for the shop to close for the day, so Aaron had been gone at least twelve hours. "He's not been here. If he needed to talk, you might try Lena's place."

"I've already gone there. She hasn't talked to him. I spoke with Trevor too. He didn't take him anywhere."

"What does Sylvia think?"

Michael glanced behind him, clearly checking to see if anyone had moved within hearing distance.

"Kumm." Grey motioned toward the office. They went inside, and he closed the door. Michael still looked uncomfortable. Grey closed the blinds on the windows between the office and the shop.

Michael's hands trembled as he removed his hat. "Sylvia is devoted to the farm, but she left early this morning, saying she needed to visit her folks. She wouldn't explain why. She's not even sure if she'll be able to return. I don't understand."

Grey motioned to a chair.

Michael shook his head and paced the small room. "Aaron said him and me are just like me and my Daed, only worse." His eyes revealed pain and confusion. "Is it true? Am I just like my father?"

"I've only seen him a couple of times." The man had come to Grey and Elsie's wedding and returned for her funeral. Elsie never said much about anything, including the family they'd left in Ohio.

Michael dropped into a chair and stared at the ground, his shoulders stooped. "My Daed made decisions, and you could agree or get out. Is that how Aaron sees me?"

"Maybe he just needs time to cool off." Grey knew Michael feared that Aaron had left for good or that he'd started drinking again—or both.

Michael shook his head. "This morning Aaron said he was going to get money out of the appliance store and give it to me, to help the farm run better. Now I can't find him."

"Let's call the appliance store and the Better Path. Maybe he got there another way." Grey picked up the receiver and dialed information. Once he had the phone numbers, he placed the calls and pressed the button for the speakerphone so Michael could hear the conversations.

Neither Leo nor Paul had seen Aaron in a month. Grey thanked the men and said good-bye.

Michael took short, choppy breaths. "What have I done?"

"You've been the best father you could be. Paul just said you even went with Aaron to talk to his counselor and to see the shop he wanted to buy. Those are good things."

Michael rubbed his eyes with the palms of his hands. "Dora pushed me to go. And I knew if I didn't, Sylvia would never have the same respect for me. I wouldn't have gone otherwise."

Grey didn't know what to say, so he kept silent.

"Aaron used to love farming. Did you know that?"

"No." Grey took a seat, knowing that Michael needed to talk.

"When I started looking to move here from Ohio, he was just a teen, but he was already an amazing farm manager and worker. I was impressed, and I wanted to give him something he could be proud of—a farm with enough land to expand the herd as he saw fit." Michael closed his eyes. "But he hates it now." He rose and walked to the far corner, his back to Grey. "I have to stop lying to myself. It's true. I'm as exacting and difficult as my Daed, maybe worse." He turned, tears welling in his eyes. "You know when I began to see it?"

Grey shook his head, silently praying for Michael.

"When I saw myself through Sylvia's eyes."

"Sylvia's?"

"Before Aaron came home, she respected me. But when she saw how I was with my son, my anger and nagging, she began to look at me differently. I kept telling myself she just didn't understand, but I'm the one who's been blind." He blinked as if he'd just realized something. "I told Aaron he had no right to talk to me the way he did this morning or like he's done in the past. But the truth is, he was trying to get me to understand him. And I couldn't—or wouldn't." He slumped into the chair and put his head in his hands.

Elsie had been similar to her father—they both felt deeply and shared little. Because of that, Grey had some insight that might help…if Michael would hear him. "No one in a household can decide what's right for everyone else—not a husband, a wife, or a parent of grown children. But if everyone's willing to listen, they can talk things out and find a compromise."

Michael sighed. "I'm afraid we've never lived like that. After burying six babies, Dora and I were a solid block of grief by the time we moved here. All I wanted was to give Aaron a farm he could develop. When he got fed up trying to turn a profit, my grief turned to anger. Nearly every word my son spoke added to my hurt and rage." Tears spilled down Michael's face. "I asked myself countless times why he abandoned us to go to Owl's Perch. The real question is, why did he care enough to return with an offer for us to move back there with him?"

"You'll never know unless you ask."

Michael drew a deep breath and stood. "I have to find him."

"Want me to come with you?"

"No, not yet. I need to do this on my own." Michael opened the office door and paused. "There is one thing you can do."

"Anything."

"Pray."

"Absolutely."

Thirty-Eight

Aaron stared at the hole twelve feet above his head. The blue sky above him faded, turning to a charcoal gray. Soon it would be as black as it had been when he'd fallen into this pit before daylight. The thought of facing a full night underground seemed intolerable, but for the first time in his life, he had no alternatives.

He sighed, too exhausted to hold another raging vigil. He'd screamed in anger throughout the day—yelling at Daed, life, and most of all this stupid abandoned well. Now he sat in silence, staring upward, wondering if he'd die down here.

His hands trembled, and his body felt heavier than it should—the toll of not having any food or water since last night's dinner.

Sylvi was the only one who might come looking for him. His Mamm might go to the porch and scan the farm, but she'd never think to wander a field in search of him. His Daed might consider it, but he'd never do it. He'd assume what was easiest to believe—that Aaron had run off.

He wasn't physically hurt, other than a few bruises and aching joints from landing so hard. But the pain in his heart was severe.

He hated what it would do to Mamm if no one found him. She'd spend her life praying for him to return.

Sylvia would blame herself, thinking that she'd run him off or that she'd caused him to take up drinking again. If she kept working the farm, she'd find him one day—or his bones. Then she'd know the truth…and blame herself more.

Without water, he'd die in a matter of days.

A crow cawed as it crossed the sky above him.

Aaron's mind kept running down various trails of thought, scattering like a handful of hay dropped from a high loft. He had no reason to reel in his imagination, so he let it meander.

His father's problems were bad. He needed room to grieve the loss of six cases of infant death and the death of his twenty-seven-year-old daughter, Elsie, as well as his disappointment in Aaron. And he needed to find ways to cope with his arthritis. But Daed's bottom-line problem was that he was never grateful for what he did have. When each new loss hit, Daed took on more pain without ever having freed himself from the previous hurts. Aaron understood how it happened but vowed that he would cope differently.

He closed his eyes, listening to the wind move across the summer grass. He breathed in the aroma of the rich soil and remembered the conversation he'd had with Sylvi about seeing God in the nature around her.

"Okay, God, I hear You."

As clearly as if he were talking with Sylvi, he could hear God inside him, chastising him for all his years of feeling sorry for himself. Being truly thankful would give him power over his desire to escape. It was the ultimate freedom from the day-to-day heartache and grind of living.

He leaned his head back against the cool, craggy earth and began telling God everything he was thankful for, beginning with the walls around him and the ground under him. As the hours passed, his faith grew.

He began to see the farm the way Sylvi saw it—beautiful and strong. A heritage that their forefathers sacrificed for, regardless of the cost. They understood the toil it would take and yet were grateful for the chance to work the fields.

While it made no sense, trapped as he was, he'd never been more content.

"God, please get me out of this pit. I want...I need a second chance with Sylvi."

Aaron said that prayer countless times in between his lists of things to be thankful for.

"Aaron!"

Chills ran over his body, and he stood up. Was he imagining things? The voice sounded like...his Daed's.

"Down here! Daed, can you hear me? I'm down here!"

His Daed continued calling to him, and Aaron kept screaming. Daed called. Aaron answered. And nothing happened.

How many times had they been this close and yet unable to see or hear each other?

"Daed!" Aaron screamed with all his might.

His father's voice faded into nothingness, leaving only the sound of the wind crossing the fields above him. Aaron closed his eyes, trying to hold on to hope. Wanting to believe he'd get out of this prison. In his mind's eye he saw the farm—the green pastures, growing crops, and meandering herd. Sylvi's cabin. The main house.

They looked different from down here.

Digging a fingernail into the packed dirt, he breathed in the smell of rich soil, and he could feel this place inside him now. Sylvi felt it so deeply, and he wanted a chance to give it back to her.

"Aaron?" His Daed's voice returned, sounding hoarse. Aaron couldn't believe he hadn't given up. Maybe he didn't know his Daed as well as he'd thought.

"Daed! I'm down here, in a hole in the ground! Can you hear me?"

Silence. Aaron prayed. He cupped his hands around his mouth. "Daed!"

"I hear you. But where..."

"A hole. Look for a hole." He could hear noises, scrambling of some sort. Dirt from above fell on his head.

"Aaron?" His Daed set a kerosene lamp near the edge of the hole.

"I'm here. You found me." Relief and excitement ran like a stampede through him. He'd been given a second chance—or maybe it was his third or fifteenth. How would a former drunk know? How did anyone know?

Daed's face poked over the top of the hole as he reached as far into the well as he could. "Are you hurt?"

Aaron reached for him but couldn't come closer than two feet from his fingertips. Still, he found peace in the near connection. "No. I just need a way to get out."

"I'm so sorry, Son." His Daed sobbed.

"It's okay."

"No, it's not. You told the truth, and I knew it when I heard it. We'll get you out of there and really talk. I love you, Son. Hang on, and I'll be back as quick as I can with a ladder."

Aaron sank to a sitting position again and began making a fresh list of all he was grateful for.

Lena sat on her bed, writing to Grey. Months of his letters surrounded her. Most nights she opened and read every one of them, but she hadn't seen him, except at a distance, in nearly a month. Nicky lay on the cool floor, panting.

Michael had come by yesterday, looking for Aaron. Thankfully, Aaron dropped by earlier this morning to assure her he was safe. He didn't stay long enough to tell her much of anything, only that he wasn't missing and that a driver was waiting to take him to Owl's Perch.

"Lena?" her Daed called as he tapped on her door.

"Kumm."

He opened the door, but he didn't enter. "I came to tell you that there'll be a family meeting downstairs within the hour. Your siblings and their families will start arriving in about forty minutes."

Excitement scuttled through her. "A meeting on a Saturday night? This must be really important. What's up?"

A grin made creases around his eyes. "You don't want me taking time to answer your questions when I brought someone to see you." He moved to the side.

Grey stepped into her room, and happiness flooded her.

"Grey!" She flew into his arms.

Daed laughed and closed the door behind him.

Grey caressed her cheek, and the warmth of his hand strengthened her. "Hi."

He pulled her into a hug and held her for several long moments before he raised her chin and kissed her.

She gave a final squeeze before going to her reading chair, removing a few articles of clothing hanging over it, and gesturing for him to sit.

She sat on the edge of her bed. "Do you know what this family meeting is about?"

He nodded. "I won't stay for it. It's for family, and your Daed assures me most of your siblings still don't know about us."

"True. Are you sworn to silence about the meeting?"

"No. Actually, your Daed and Ada think you should know before hearing it with everyone else."

"Daed and Ada?" She resisted the desire to let out a holler of excitement. "He must've asked her to marry him."

"He did, and she said yes."

"This is fantastic!"

"It is." He grinned. "But there's more. Israel wants to give you this house."

Lena's heart leaped. Marrying Grey, raising a family with him, *and* living here would be the fulfillment of every dream she'd ever had. "How do you feel about that?"

"We have so many great memories here—a lifetime, really. I can't think of anywhere I'd rather live."

She crossed the room and knelt in front of him. "You're not just saying that because you know it would thrill me?"

He trailed his index finger along her jaw line. "If my only reason for doing it was for you, that'd be more than enough reason."

She soaked in his assurances, knowing he loved her just as her mother had promised her before she passed away: *When the time is right, you'll be drawn to the right man. And he'll be drawn to you. And he'll love you deeper and higher than most men are capable of. I promise you that.*

Thirty-Nine

Sylvia sat on the porch with her parents and Lilly, rocking the glider back and forth. Thoughts of Aaron swam through her day and night, even in her sleep. She'd been so angry with him before she left, and she longed to find him and talk it all out.

The sun hung low in the sky as Sunday drew to a close. This was the kind of Sunday she'd missed so badly her first few weeks on the Blank farm. But now her family surrounded her, and she'd never been so lonely.

She'd been here since Friday afternoon. Whenever the family shared a meal, Sylvia had to answer dozens of questions about living on the Blank farm. She kept pointing out to Daed how safe and happy she was there, but he still wanted her to stay home.

Beckie didn't want Mamm or Daed or any of their sisters to know what had happened between Elam and Sylvia. Sylvia didn't ask why, but she hoped that the reason had more to do with keeping peace among the family than personal embarrassment on Beckie's part. Maybe her little sister was finally maturing.

Sylvia had spent two days thinking about her future and Aaron. She knew without a doubt what she wanted. "Daed."

He propped his arm on the back of the porch swing he and Mamm shared. "What's on your mind?"

"I'm going home in a few days."

"This is home."

"It's the home I grew up in. And I'll keep it in my heart every day. But it's not *my* home. Remember when I was little, you'd always say, 'Someday you'll have a home of your own'?"

"I want you here. We can make this work."

"No, Daed." As she spoke, she could feel the impact Aaron had had on her. "Just because you want something from me, that doesn't mean it's reasonable to expect it."

Lilly squeezed her hand. "Hmm, I think those words must be from the book of Aaron."

She and Lilly had stayed up late last night talking, and Sylvia had told her all about Aaron.

"You shouldn't have insisted I stay here after Elam married Beckie," Sylvia said. "I *needed* to go."

Daed glanced at Mamm before nodding. "I've had time to think while you've been gone. I was trying to keep my family together and all my daughters safe." He shrugged, looking pained that he'd lost the battle. "But now I can see that sometimes home isn't the best place for a daughter to be." He sighed. "So is the Blank farm home from now on?"

"No."

"What?" He frowned. "Then where are you going?"

"Wherever Aaron goes. If he'll have me."

Lilly squealed. "I thought you must be in love with him."

Sylvia knew she might have quite a road ahead of her to win him over. It might take a good bit of patience, but Aaron was worth it. "We'll most likely live above an appliance store, at least for a while."

"You hate stores," Mamm said. "You're barely willing to go in a store to sell yogurt or pick up an item or two. You've never bought fabric because it takes too long to pick it out, and you feel sick by the time we're through."

"I'll use my will to get over it or ask a doctor for an allergy pill or something. It has to be something like fumes or dyes that bother me, right?"

Daed smiled that gentle, knowing smile that defined him so well. "You're determined. I see it in your eyes. You go, Sylvia. Wherever you land, we'll come visit you when we can."

Forty

Sylvia had called Ephraim's shop early Monday morning and left a message for Trevor to pick her up today, Tuesday, as soon as his morning chores were done. That would put her back on the farm in time to have lunch at the Blanks' table. If Aaron was still on the farm, she imagined they'd set aside farm work for the afternoon, take a long walk, and talk until time to milk the cows that evening. If he'd already moved to Owl's Perch, she'd go there.

Either way, she intended to talk to him today, to apologize and pledge to help him make a success out of the appliance store—if he'd have her. She didn't have any skills to offer him that would be useful off the farm, but she'd do her best to learn.

Mamm sat in the rocker next to her, shelling peas. Her Mamm found shelling peas as relaxing as Sylvia did taking baths. All her sisters were nearby, on the porch or in the yard, waiting to tell her good-bye. Beckie and Elam sat on the steps, holding hands while watching their twins play. The three of them hadn't handled a lot of things right, but healing had begun—thanks to Aaron.

She couldn't wait to tell him.

Daed came out of the house with a glass of water. He motioned for Lilly to get up. When she did, he took her place next to Sylvia.

Daed put his arm on the back of the swing and laid his fingers on her shoulder. "Girls," he said, and all her sisters immediately turned to look at him. "Go play or something. I want to talk to Sylvia."

They quickly dispersed. Beckie and Elam went for a stroll toward Mamm's vegetable garden, each one holding a twin's hand.

Her Daed reached into his pocket and pulled out two folded checks. "I shouldn't have kept your wages this long. You know it's typical for parents to keep the largest portion of earnings throughout their child's teen years. I had no right to keep holding the money from you this long, but I was afraid you'd take it and move off. Since you're determined to leave either way…" He passed her one check.

Sylvia unfolded it and about jumped out of her skin. "Thirty-five thousand dollars?"

"It only amounts to a little over two hundred dollars a month for all those years you worked this place seven days a week, from the time you graduated from the eighth grade until six months ago."

"Ya, but during that time you gave me some spending money each month."

"I'm glad you're pleased."

Her Daed didn't like to talk finances with a woman, so she'd wait and ask Aaron if she owed taxes on it.

Daed passed her the second folded check. "It's also time Elam and Beckie paid a little rent on that house you inherited. Not much, mind you, but say a hundred and fifty dollars a month?"

"That sounds great." She opened the check. It was signed by Elam and was for…five thousand dollars. She almost choked. "Back rent?"

"Ya."

"Wow. I should've come home sooner."

Her Mamm stopped shelling peas. "I wish you had. He held his ground, not allowing us to write or visit you so you'd miss us and want to come home, and all the while he's been a grizzly bear to live with."

"Susie Mae, do you have to tell everything you know?" Daed asked Mamm.

"It's true," she said.

"I didn't say it wasn't." Daed rubbed the back of Sylvia's neck, silently letting her know that he loved her. "Later on we'll figure out something about your portion of the farm. Rent it from you. Pay dividends. Buy it. Something."

Too excited to contain herself, Sylvia wrapped her arms around him. "Denki."

Her father held her. She knew he didn't want to let her choose her own path, yet he'd given her the funds to do just that. She rose and embraced her Mamm before returning to the porch swing. She rubbed the checks between her fingers. This money would keep Aaron from owing so much on the appliance store. Then he'd have an easier time meeting the monthly bills. That always made life more pleasant.

Or he might want to use it to pay off the extra loans on his parents' farm so it'd be easier to sell.

She couldn't wait to see him, but she had so much she needed to tell him that she wasn't sure what to say first or how to say it.

Gratefulness and relief filled her. Aaron had been right—she'd asked God to forgive her, and He had.

Today, as she reaped a harvest of grace, she felt forgiven. While sitting on the porch swing, gently swaying back and forth with her Daed beside her, waiting to return to Aaron and make things right, her heart cried *thank you* to God time and again. She was forgiven.

Trevor pulled into the driveway.

"My ride's here," Sylvia called out.

A stampede of young women and fast-growing girls hurried to the front yard.

Trevor jumped out and took her overnight bag. "Morning." He barely glanced at her before putting her suitcase in the trunk.

The next few minutes were a blur of hugs, farewells, and promises to write and visit. Her Daed held her for nearly a minute before opening the car door and saying good-bye.

She waved out the window to her family until she could no longer see them. Then she turned toward Trevor. "So what's going on at the farm?"

He grimaced and fidgeted with the steering wheel.

"What's wrong? Did we lose Charlotte or her calf?"

He shook his head. "Mom and calf are fine. It took me awhile to finish the milking and feed the calves, that's all."

"You did all that by yourself?"

"Yeah. Michael hurt his back, and…Aaron wasn't available."

A nervous chill ran through her. "What does *not available* mean?"

"Can't say exactly." Trevor shook his head.

Disquiet ruffled her insides. "Trevor, don't do this. Is something wrong?"

"I'm under orders to keep my mouth shut, but Michael will tell you everything you need to know."

Nausea rolled through her. She'd been unfair to Aaron and then walked off. Had he left the farm for good and Michael didn't want Trevor telling her? Was it possible Aaron had started drinking again? There'd certainly been enough stress on him lately to tempt him. They rode in silence, but Trevor seemed anxious. He pulled into the driveway.

"Go on up to the main house," she said.

"Let's drop your stuff off first." He turned onto the small lane that went to her cabin. She waited in the car while he stopped, got out her suitcase, and set it on the porch.

A stranger came around the corner of her house, spotted her, and retreated. She got out of the car and called to him. "Excuse me."

The man didn't return, but she heard a noise inside her cabin. She hurried up the steps and ran in. There were muddy shoe prints everywhere.

"Hello?" She followed the sound of dripping water and walked to her bathroom. New tile. New cabinets. New sink. Same beautiful old tub.

She ran her hand along the teal and beige tile. "Trevor?" She turned toward the hallway. "Tre—"

She gasped. Aaron stood there, so tall and strong.

"Aaron!" She ran to him and wrapped her arms around his neck. "I'm so, so sorry."

He held her. "Me too."

"I was so scared. Trevor wouldn't tell me anything."

"I wanted to surprise you. Do you like it?"

"Yes, of course." She took a deep breath before letting him go. "I have something for you." She pulled the folded checks out of her hidden apron pocket and placed them in the palm of his hand. "This is to go toward your purchase of the appliance store."

He opened them. "Where… But…"

"It's back pay and back rent. My Daed wanted me to stay, but I told him I had to go home, and that home is wherever you are."

Aaron's eyes grew large. "I…I wasn't expecting…" He put his arms around her. "I got my money back from Leo, all but a thousand dollars, and he's put the store up for sale again."

"What? Why?"

"Because I realized that this farm means too much to me to give it up and walk away. It's home."

"But…"

"So much happened while you were gone. Daed saved my life."

"He did? How?"

"It's quite a story. I'll tell you all about it later. But after he rescued me, we talked. He opened up and apologized, and I could feel how deep his sorrow ran. Like mine did after I got sober."

"I'm so glad." Tears stung her eyes. "But it doesn't mean we have to stay here. I don't care where we live, as long as we're together."

"You really missed me." He cradled her face, looking a little baffled by that realization.

"I did."

"Daed was afraid that once you got to Path Valley, you'd have to stay there. I told him you'd be back, that nobody could keep you from this farm."

"Nothing and nobody could keep me from *you*."

His hands were warm on the sides of her neck as his thumbs caressed her face. "I want to stay here. Even before your money, we had enough to revamp and start fresh. If you want to add yours, we can—"

She placed her fingers over his lips, stopping him from saying anything else. "Forget the farm, Aaron. Be here with me, just us and nothing else."

He drew her close. "Sylvi, will you marry me?"

She leaned in, her lips inches from his. "You know I will."

Epilogue

At the edge of the yard, Cara paused under a canopy of golden leaves, soaking in the remnants of her wedding. Her day had begun at sunrise. Now stars twinkled. The cool October air smelled delicious and earthy. Conversations and laughter carried on the breeze as the last of the wedding guests departed in their horse-drawn carriages, leaving only family and the closest of friends.

Nine hours ago, under crystal blue skies, Ephraim had walked her down the aisle between rows of borrowed chairs set up in his Daed's backyard. Before the bishop they vowed their lives to each other. Ephraim said it was the first outdoor Amish wedding he'd ever heard of, but the church leaders allowed it, and it couldn't have been a more gorgeous day.

During the feast afterward, they sat at the corner of the bride-and-groom table with the singles of the community. By tradition she and Ephraim couldn't share a table with just their closest friends, but they had plans for tonight that would make up for that.

She prayed a silent thank-you for the blessing of friends who had become so important to her and Lori. In many ways they had saved her as much as Ephraim had. It was becoming apparent to her that the strength to live Plain came from God, a supportive family, and dedicated ministers. Some things were worth every sacrifice it took to have them—and for her, this life was one of them.

She and Ephraim would carry memories of this day into their future together. There were many Amish wedding traditions, revelations to her, that she'd always hold dear—like the groom walking the bride down the aisle and loved ones sharing a day of feasting and singing with them.

There were also Amish traditions she'd never get fully used to, like the bride and groom cleaning up after their own wedding. As the festivities wound down, Ephraim helped the men move furniture back in place and load a wagon with benches. She worked with a group of women, helping to wash and dry dishes. But Cara loved having and being part of a safety net. She had people who'd always be there, no matter what. And they had her.

Ephraim's parents would head for bed as soon as their brood was asleep for the night. In a few minutes the newlyweds would go to Ephraim's house with their friends for a more intimate time of playing games, singing, and eating. When she'd learned that Ephraim and she couldn't have their closest friends at the wedding table, he came up with the idea of having a get-together after everyone else went home. He said that he'd braced himself for the possibility of not being able to marry her for another year or two. He had no qualms postponing their alone time for a few hours with good friends.

Ephraim came out the front door of his Daed's home, smiling. "There you are."

She'd seen him go in and out of that house many times in the last week. There'd been so much to do to prepare for their wedding that Lori and she had moved from Hope Crossing into Ephraim's place a week ago, and he'd been staying in the Mast home. His parents had welcomed her and treated Lori as if she had always been one of their grandchildren.

"Daed," Lori hollered.

Ephraim turned. Their daughter stood in the doorway of the Mast home, wearing her nightgown. Ephraim's stepmother, Becca, who'd been trying to get her children and Lori settled for the night, stood behind her.

He clapped his hands and opened his arms. That was all the encouragement Lori needed. She ran barefoot across the lawn.

Lori would spend the night with Ephraim's parents. Tomorrow, after they finished cleaning up from today's ceremony, she'd return with Deborah and Ada to Hope Crossing. Lori was enjoying being a niece to all of Ephraim's sisters, even the ones younger than she was.

She jumped into his arms. "Daed." Lori hugged him. "My Daed."

Cara suppressed laughter. Since the wedding ceremony that morning, her daughter had peppered nearly every sentence to Ephraim with *Daed*. Having spent most of her life without a father, Lori used the name as if she were applying salve to her heart.

"Will you tuck me in, Daed?"

"I will. But then you have to stay in bed and go to sleep. It's very late for little girls." He touched the end of her nose.

While still in Ephraim's arms, Lori reached out and hugged her mom. "Good night."

"Good night, Lorabean." Cara kissed her soft cheek. "You be good for *Mammi* Becca."

"Okay, Mom. Me and Daed's sisters are gonna play dolls tomorrow!"

Ephraim chuckled as he kissed Cara on the cheek. "I'll be back soon. Don't move."

"Would you bring my sweater when you come? I left it near the wood stove."

"Absolutely." He hurried toward the house, making Lori giggle with delight.

Cara waved at a carriage of folks leaving Mast property and heading home. Most of those who'd stayed this late had helped set up, cook, serve, and clean. When any of them had a family member marry, she and Ephraim would return the favor. The Amish cycle of service and gratitude had begun for her.

Her dad came across the yard toward her. He'd been extremely help-ful this week, doing whatever Ephraim or she needed to prepare for today. "Hey, girl, you look cold."

"Ephraim's bringing me a sweater as soon as he tucks Lori in."

"I'm taking the last few Hope Crossing guests home. If you don't need anything else, I'm going to stay there this time."

"You've made enough trips back and forth today." She hugged him. "Thanks for everything, Dad."

"You're more welcome than you can imagine." He squeezed her tight. "I'm proud of you."

"Today wouldn't have been the same without you."

"Thanks, Carabean."

She had never asked him why her mother felt the need to hide her whenever he was drunk. Was he mean, or had her mother wanted to keep her from seeing her father intoxicated? She didn't know. It didn't matter. He wasn't that man anymore, and she wasn't willing to embarrass or hurt him in any way.

"I'll see you at the cabinetry shop at ten, day after tomorrow," Trevor said, "to take you to that hotel you picked out."

"I sure am looking forward to spending a few honeymoon days at the beach."

As her dad left, Ephraim strode toward her, carrying her sweater. While walking, he waved to the people in the last buggy headed for home.

She wondered where their friends were. They had served two meals, plus rounds of snacks, for six hundred guests, so tomorrow she and her girlfriends had mounds of laundry to do. The men had to return heavy borrowed items, like serving tables and stacks of dishes, but now it was time to set all thoughts of work aside and go to Ephraim's.

He held up the sweater. "Here you go." His smile warmed her so much she almost didn't need a wrap.

She slipped her arms through the sleeves. The thick black sweater set off the dark purple of her wedding dress. She'd chosen to wear the color of royalty, for she truly felt like a daughter of the King.

The style of her dress was the same as everyday Amish clothes—plain and simple. For the first time in her life, she could have afforded a fashionable wedding dress with delicate fabrics and had a fancy hairstyle, but whether she was Amish or not, those things would never interest her. She was more of a no-frills woman, so that fit in well with her new lifestyle.

Ephraim kissed her forehead. "I can't believe we're finally husband and wife."

She snuggled into his embrace. "It was the best day ever, wasn't it?"

"I've never seen such a celebration." He ran his hand up and down her back. "And we're married," he whispered.

She could feel the intensity of his joy as he held her.

Cara tilted her head back, and Ephraim took her hint. When his lips met hers, he didn't hold back. As her mind rushed with thoughts of all she had to be thankful for, her heart swelled at the magnitude of her blessings.

Applause grabbed her attention. She pushed back from Ephraim and saw Lena, Grey, Sylvia, Aaron, Deborah, Jonathan, Ada, and Israel—all grinning.

Israel clapped the loudest. "Hmm. I guess I *am* ready for those lessons on how to give a kiss and make it count."

Ada gently elbowed him before easing her back against his chest. He wrapped his arms around her and kissed her cheek, then stepped forward. "We really appreciate the invitation to join you tonight," he said, "but if it's okay, we'll go visit Michael and Dora for a bit before calling it a night. Ada will stay with them tonight and be back tomorrow to help you."

"You sure?" Cara asked.

"Ya. It's Grey and Lena's first date night, and she doesn't need her Daed there. You know?"

"If that's what you want, we understand." Ephraim shook his hand, and Cara hugged him and Ada. They walked toward the barn to hitch their rig.

Cara slid her hand into Ephraim's and shifted her attention. "Where have you girls been?"

Lena glanced up at Grey, who stood directly behind her with his hands on her shoulders. "Oh, we had a little...rearranging to do."

Sylvia hid her face behind Aaron's shoulder, but she couldn't conceal her grin.

What had her friends been up to? She narrowed her eyes at Lena. Had the queen of pranks struck again?

Cara looped her arm through Ephraim's and headed for the house. The other three couples—Lena and Grey, Deborah and Jonathan, and Sylvia and Aaron—walked with them. Cara noticed that all their friends looked as if they were hiding something.

"Okay, spill it. What have you done?" Cara asked.

"Who...us?" Lena asked, feigning innocence.

Once in Ephraim's yard, Lena glanced up. Cara stopped short, following her eyes and studying the darkened shadows of the tree above her.

When she saw what they'd done, she burst into laughter. "How am I supposed to get all that laundry done now?"

"What's up?" Ephraim asked.

She pointed. "Our wringer washer!"

Grey nodded at Lena. "She did it."

"Uh, yeah. Like she could do that all by herself," Cara said. "And no excuse by you, Mr. Graber, is going to stop me from getting back at both of you at your wedding."

Grey chuckled. "By all means do your worst."

Aaron's laughter blended beautifully with Sylvia's giggle. "We want in on that action."

Cara knew that Aaron and Sylvia would have time to help her devise a plan. His creative ideas for transforming their farm, added to Sylvia's knowledge of milk production, had transformed an uphill battle into an enjoyable living. They'd reduced the size of their herd by half, rebuilt the milking stalls, rented the fields, and used the milk they produced to make A&S Yogurts, a product that would be fully organic within the year. They already had three health-food stores stocking the product.

Both of them would go through instruction classes next summer and join the faith before they could marry next fall. But they didn't mind the wait. They intended to enjoy the long engagement period by really getting to know each other.

Deborah and Jonathan would marry in January. Ada and Israel were going to marry a couple of weeks before Lena and Grey's ceremony in mid-February. But Lena and Grey wouldn't announce their plans to marry until after the first of the year.

Every couple was different. The things that had drawn each man and woman together were as varied as the colors of nature. All the couples had been through their own sets of trials and mishaps. But the ability to grow closer while navigating those heartaches had caused their love to become stronger. Love was so odd. It could fight the fiercest battle and cradle the most delicate creatures. It never failed to beckon or give hope to the hopeless, and she knew love would continue to do so, no matter what good or difficult things lay ahead. With Ephraim beside her, Cara opened her arms to embrace their future.

They all stood there, looking up at the dangling wringer washer, chuckling. One by one, under God's twinkling night sky, each man took his loved one in his arms and for a brief moment tuned out the world.

Ada's House Series

Main Characters in *The Harvest of Grace*

Sylvia Fisher—A young Amish woman who is the oldest of nine daughters. She loves the family dairy farm.

Beckie Fisher—Sylvia's closest sister.

Elam Smoker—A young Amish man interested in Sylvia.

Aaron Blank—Son of Michael and Dora. After his sister died, he went into rehab for alcoholism.

Michael Blank—Aaron's father.

Dora Blank—Michael's wife and Aaron's mother. Her daughter, Elsie, who was married to Grey Graber, died in a terrible accident.

Frani—Former drinking buddy of Aaron's.

Cara Atwater Moore—Englischer from the Bronx who lost her mother as a child, was abandoned by her father, and grew up in foster care. She married and had a daughter, Lori, but Cara's husband died when Lori was two. While fleeing a stalker, she discovered clues to her past in her mother's diary. That, combined with vague memories from her childhood, brought her to Dry Lake. She is now engaged to Ephraim.

Trevor Atwater—Cara's father, a widower. He was an alcoholic for most of Cara's childhood.

Ephraim Mast—Amish man who works as a cabinetmaker in Dry Lake with Grey Graber. He is Deborah's brother and is engaged to Cara.

Lori Moore—Cara's daughter. She calls Ephraim " 'From" and has a dog named Better Days.

Deborah Mast—Amish woman who is Ephraim's sister. She lives at Ada's House in Hope Crossing and was engaged to Ada's son, Mahlon, before he left his family, his home, and the faith. She is now in love with Jonathan.

Jonathan Stoltzfus—Amish blacksmith. He is in love with Deborah.

Lena Kauffman—Amish woman. She has a bluish purple birthmark on the right side of her cheek and going down her neck. She lost her teaching job in Dry Lake when she disobeyed unfair rulings made by the school board, and Michael Blank, head of the board, refused to stand up for her. She is in love with Grey.

Grey Graber—Amish widower. He's a skilled craftsman who loves his work at the cabinetry shop owned by Ephraim Mast. He was married to Elsie Blank for almost six years. Their son, Ivan, was born with a missing arm, and they had a stillborn son a year later. After Elsie's death, Grey fell in love with Lena.

Ada Stoltzfus—Amish widow in her forties. She is a friend and mentor to Deborah and Cara, who help her run Ada's House, a bakery and gift shop in Hope Crossing that allows tourists to participate in some traditional Amish events.

Glossary

all—all

begreiflich—easy

Bobbeli—infant

Daadi—grandfather

Daed—dad or father

denki—thank you

Englischer—a non-Amish person. Mennonite sects whose women wear the prayer Kapps are not considered Englischers and are often referred to as Plain Mennonites.

Gaule—horse

gegleed—dressed

gut—good

Kapp—a prayer covering or cap

kumm—come (singular)

kumm rei—come in

langsam—slow

letz—wrong

Mamm—mom or mother

Mammi—grandmother

Pennsylvania Dutch—Pennsylvania German. *Dutch* in this phrase has nothing to do with the Netherlands. The original word was *Deutsch,* which means "German." The Amish speak some High German (used in church services) and Pennsylvania German (Pennsylvania Dutch), and after a certain age, they are taught English.

Plain—refers to the Amish and certain sects of Mennonites.

Plain Mennonite—any Mennonites whose women wear the prayer Kapp and cape dresses and the men have a dress code.

rumschpringe—running around. The true purpose of the rumschpringe
   is threefold: give freedom for an Amish young person to find an
   Amish mate; to give extra freedoms during the young adult years so
   each person can decide whether to join the faith; to provide a bridge
   between childhood and adulthood.

schwarz—black

wunderbaar—wonderful

ya—yes

Pennsylvania Dutch phrases used
in *The Harvest of Grace*

Du hab eens Daadi un eens Grandpa.—You have one Amish grandfather
   and one Englischer grandfather.

Gott segen dich.—God bless you. [singular]

Gott segen eich.—God bless you. [plural]

Guder Marye.—Good morning.

Ich bin hungerich.—I'm hungry.

Ich kumm glei naus.—I'll come out soon.

Im Gott sei Lieb—in God's love

Saage es.—Say it.

Sell iss gut.—That is good.

---

* Glossary taken from Eugene S. Stine, *Pennsylvania German Dictionary* (Birdsboro, PA: Pennsylvania German Society, 1996), and the usage confirmed by an instructor of the Pennsylvania
Dutch language.

Acknowledgments

To my Old Order Amish friends who helped me so faithfully as I wrote about delicate events—My heart is yours.

To the Old Order Amish farmers who spent long hours helping me understand all the ins and outs and challenges of running your dairy farms without electricity while meeting government regulations—I admire the tenacity in you and your families. Thank you for sharing your stories about how the stream-bank fencing program affected your farms—the fair and unfair, the ultimatums, and the generous help the government provided.

To my expert in the Pennsylvania Dutch language—I struggle with the languages as Cara does in this novel, and you are even more patient than her teachers. Your expertise and your patience are both appreciated.

To WaterBrook Multnomah Publishing Group, from marketing to sales to production to editorial—With each book we produce, I'm even more honored to be one of your authors.

To Shannon Marchese, my editor—Only the two of us and God will ever know all the obstacles that kept falling across our path as I wrote this book. Because of how you faced every challenge, I respect you even more.

To Jessica Barnes, my editor on this project while Shannon was on leave—Oh my! You entered my life during the roughest of times and remained calm, helpful, and hard working. Without you this book would not be in readers' hands, and my nerves would be frazzled rather than healed. At the time I may not have let you know how truly and deeply grateful I am.

To Carol Bartley, my line editor—You do your job excellently, but more than that, you helped me believe in myself. In my most difficult times of writing, I reflect on that. Thank you.

To Kathy Ide—You are ever faithful when I need you. Thank you.

To Steve Laube, my agent, and Marci Burke, my good friend and critique partner—Both of you make me a better person and author. Thank you.

To my husband, sons, and daughters-in-law—Time with you makes life a beautiful patchwork quilt. I love and respect each of you with all my heart.

And to the newest member of our household, my brother Leston, who moved in with us when my dad passed—You are a challenge and a gift, as is every good thing on this earth. I love to laugh with you. I look forward to reading with you at night. I can't help but cry when you do—so stop that! ☺ I'm grateful to be your little sister. May your happiest days be ahead of you.

About the Author

CINDY WOODSMALL is a *New York Times* best-selling author whose connection with the Amish community has been featured on *ABC Nightline* and on the front page of the *Wall Street Journal*. She is the author of the Sisters of the Quilt series as well as *The Bridge of Peace, The Hope of Refuge, The Sound of Sleigh Bells,* and *The Christmas Singing.* Her ability to authentically capture the heart of her characters comes from her real-life connections with Amish Mennonite and Old Order Amish families. Cindy lives in Georgia with her husband, their three sons, and two amazing daughters-in-law.

To keep up with new releases, book signings, and other news, visit Cindy at www.cindywoodsmall.com.

Step into the first two books of the Ada's House trilogy

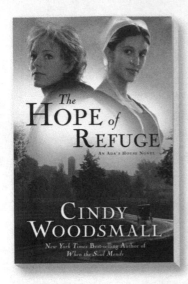

Two people from vastly different worlds. Can New Yorker Cara Moore and Amish man Ephraim Mast get past long-hidden secrets and find assurance in the midst of desperation?

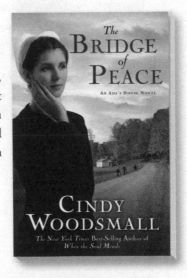

Lena and Grey have been life-long friends, but their relationship begins to crumble amidst unsettling deceptions, propelling each of them to finally face their own secrets. Can they find a way past their losses and discover the strength to build a new bridge?

Read an excerpt from these books and more on WaterBrookMultnomah.com!

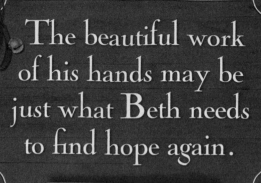

The beautiful work of his hands may be just what Beth needs to find hope again.

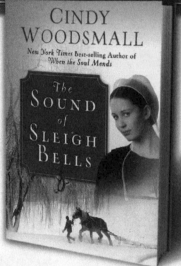

A beautiful carving and a well-intentioned aunt just might thaw two frozen, lonely hearts and give them a second chance at love—just in time for Christmas.

Read an excerpt from this book and more on WaterBrookMultnomah.com!

Can Hannah find refuge, redemption, and a fresh beginning after her world is shattered?

Also available in a 3-in-1 volume:

When Hannah Lapp, a simple 17-year-old Amish girl, finds her life shattered by one brutal act, she must face the rejection of family and friends and the questioning of her faith. Will she find her way back to the soul she fears may be lost forever?

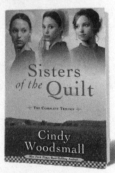

Read an excerpt from these books and more on WaterBrookMultnomah.com!

Two friends from different worlds— one **Old Order Amish**, one *Englischer* — share the truths that bring them together.

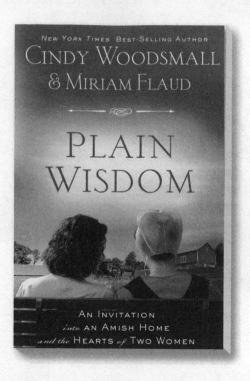

Best-selling author Cindy Woodsmall and Old Order Amish woman Miriam Flaud's book, *Plain Wisdom,* celebrates the common ground found in womanhood and the challenges of being wives and mothers. Cindy and Miriam reveal how God has brought both of them through difficult and enjoyable times as they each face life with grace and strength.

Read an excerpt from this book and more on
WaterBrookMultnomah.com!